BBC

DOCTOR WHO

THE DROSTEN'S CURSE

A.L. Kennedy

BBC

BOOKS

10 9 8 7 6 5 4 3 2 1

BBC Books, an imprint of Ebury Publishing
20 Vauxhall Bridge Road,
London SW1V 2SA

BBC Books is part of the Penguin Random House group of companies whose
addresses can be found at global.penguinrandomhouse.com

Penguin
Random House
UK

Doctor Who is a BBC Wales production for BBC One.
Executive Producers: Steven Moffat and Brian Minchin

First published by BBC Books in 2015
This edition published in 2016

www.eburypublishing.co.uk

A CIP catalogue record for this book is available from the British Library

ISBN 9781849908276

Editorial Director: Albert DePetrillo
Series Consultant: Justin Richards
Project Editor: Steve Tribe
Cover design: Two Associates © Woodland Books Ltd 2015
Production: Alex Goddard

Printed and bound by CPI Group (UK) Ltd, Croydon, CR0 4YY

Penguin Random House is committed to a sustainable future for our business,
our readers and our planet. This book is made from Forest Stewardship
Council® certified paper.

For Honor and Xavier

PAUL HARRIS WAS DYING. This wasn't something his afternoon's schedule was meant to include. Death, as far as Paul was concerned, was one of the many unpleasant things which only happened to other people. He'd never even attended a funeral – *all those miserable relatives.* He'd also avoided weddings – *all those smug relatives.* And he'd skipped every christening to which underlings in his firm had thought they should invite him – *all those sticky, noisy babies… all those sticky, noisy underlings…*

Mr Harris's death was particularly surprising to him as it involved being eaten alive by a golf bunker. At least, he could only assume that something *under* the bunker was actually what was eating him alive – now he'd sunk down past his knees into the thing – and he could only assume that it wasn't going to stop eating him because… it wasn't stopping.

First he'd been gripped around his ankles while he eyed a tricky shot for the thirteenth green. The process had involved an initial pressure, combined with a slight, but very disturbing, pain and then a type of numbness had set in. Next, he'd sunk into the sand by a few inches, before another – he tried not to think of the word *bite*, but couldn't help it – before another *bite* was taken with a little more gentle pain and then more numbness and another tug downwards. Paul liked to think of himself as powerful and unstoppable and there was huge power and a definitely unstoppable will at work here and he would certainly have admired them both had they not been ruining his very nice pair of lime green golfing trousers and his very nice legs inside them.

Paul was surprised to discover that he was completely unable to scream for assistance and there was no one about to even notice his rather unusual situation, never mind save him from it. His golfing partner, David Agnew, had unfortunately flounced off towards the clubhouse a short while ago. As Paul was jerked further into the sand, he reflected that Agnew had proved himself as bad a loser as he was a really irritating man. Still, it would have been helpful if Agnew had stuck around because then maybe he could have pulled Paul out of the bunker, or written down a few last requests, or got eaten too. Paul imagined that seeing David Agnew get eaten by a golf bunker would have been highly satisfying, because people like David Agnew were pretty much ideal golf bunker food, in Paul's opinion, although he was prepared to admit that he knew nothing about bunkers which ate people and what they might prefer. If he'd had any information on them, perhaps provided by his loyal secretary Glenda, then he might not be plunged to his waist in one right now.

The list of things that Mr Harris knew nothing about was extensive. He had never been at all curious about those aspects of the world which didn't benefit him directly.

Nevertheless, the most inquisitive human alive on Earth at that time still wouldn't have known Paul was being consumed by a creature so old and so mythical the universe had almost completely forgotten it ever was. The thing had passed beyond legend and was now simply a vague anxiety at the edge of reality's nightmares.

In a way, it was quite wonderful that such a being should still exist. Although, of course, it wasn't wonderful for Paul Harris, whose abilities to communicate – by signalling, crying out, or extending a subtle and sophisticated telepathic field, should he have been able to do so – had all been suppressed by his attacker. His attacker didn't like to be interrupted when it was feeding and fortunately evolution had allowed it to develop an ability to prevent its meals from attracting any kinds of aid. Unless, that was, the beast wanted dessert to arrive in one big arm-waving, or feeler-waving, or tentacle-waving, or slave excrescence-waving, or tendril-waving crowd of would-be rescuers, all panicky and delicious. In which case, screaming, pleading and pretty much anything else along those lines was permitted.

Evolution also meant that, although Paul was being injured horribly, he was feeling only mild distress. Eating a struggling meal was potentially dangerous and tiring, so the creature had developed many complex and fascinating mechanisms which meant that each bite it took of its prey released soothing analgesics and sedatives into – taking this afternoon as an example – Paul's ravaged circulatory and nervous systems.

By this point, Paul's arms were flopping gently on the bunker's surface and his torso was locked into the sand as far as his armpits. He wasn't a stupid man and he was fairly sure that as much of his body as he could still peer down at and see was about as much as was still available for board meetings and games of squash or, for that matter, golf (although he was definitely beginning to go off golf). It seemed strange to him that he couldn't seem to be too upset about any of this. He was, in fact, increasingly docile and happy in a way that reminded him of once being a quite pleasant child with many exciting and generous prospects ahead, every one of which he had ignored or wasted later.

As Paul's head was tugged down beneath the surface of the bunker, he could still feel the gentle summer breeze tickling at the palms of his hands which were raised and therefore still vaguely free. He experienced a brief regret that he hadn't kept up his piano lessons and that he'd gone on holiday to the Turks and Caicos Islands instead of attending his own grandmother's funeral. Paul then thought, 'Is that breathing? I seem to be able to hear breathing… A bit like a cow's or a horse's breathing… some very big animal. I wonder what it is.'

At which point, Mr Harris stopped wondering anything.

Anyone who had passed by the bunker at that exact moment would have seen two well-manicured hands apparently being sucked into the bunker and disappearing. They could then have watched the sand tremble and shiver until it presented a perfectly smooth and harmless surface again.

BRYONY MAILER WAS QUITE possibly the most inquisitive human alive on Earth at that time, which was 11.26 a.m. on 2 June 1978. She was a slim but wiry 24-year-old female human with a great sense of humour, huge reserves of ingenuity and a degree in European History. None of these things was helping her enjoy what she had once hoped was a temporary position as Junior Day Receptionist at the Fetch Brothers Golf Spa Hotel. There wasn't a Senior Day Receptionist, because that would have involved Mr Mangold, the hotel's manager, in paying Senior kind of rates. So Bryony was Junior and would stay that way for as long as she was here, stuck in perhaps the most tedious place on Earth. Lately, a couple of guests had even checked in and then simply given up on the place, leaving their luggage and running away. Their accommodation had been paid for in advance – it wasn't as if they were trying to dodge their bills – and she could only assume the sheer boredom of the Fetch had driven them out. And the wallpaper in the bedrooms was quite offensive – she didn't think she'd want to sleep inside it, either.

When Bryony wasn't folding away other people's abandoned pyjamas and storing their unwanted spongebags (in the unlikely event of their coming back for them), she was dealing with the health and beauty requirements of golfers' bored wives, coordinating the coaching and playing and post-game massage and bar lunch requirements of the golfers and generally fielding every bizarre request and complaint that an old hotel full of petulant people can generate on any given day. She didn't get a lot of down time.

But she'd been having a quiet spell lately. For as long as six minutes, she'd been able to ponder whether she'd have her tea with or without a biscuit and whether the biscuit would be a Mint Yo Yo or an Abbey Crunch. It wasn't so long ago that she'd been able to tease apart all the convolutions of French foreign policy under Cardinal Richelieu, but now even a choice between two biscuits was likely to give her a headache. And Mangold would probably have eaten them in the meantime, even though they were her biscuits…

And, now that she thought of it, she was getting a lot of headaches and that was probably Mangold's fault, too.

She decided to take the risk of leaving the slightly scuffed reception desk unattended and propped a small handwritten card next to the brass counter bell – PLEASE RING – ADVICE & ASSISTANCE OBTAINABLE IMMEDIATELY – before she slipped off through the door next to the scruffy room-key pigeonholes and along the narrow passageway that led to the Staff Office.

Bryony had never liked this passageway. It was too narrow and its wallpaper was dreadful – worse than in the bedrooms – a claustrophobic pattern of purple and red swirls which almost seemed to wriggle when you looked at them. And it was always either overly cold in here or – like today – much hotter than was pleasant. She tended to rush the journey.

As she rushed – it wasn't far and would take less than a minute – she wasn't aware that behind her the wallpaper not only wriggled, but swelled in two places, heaving and stretching until it seemed there were two figures caught behind it and fighting to get out. Had she turned and seen this happening, it would have made her very frightened and also slightly nauseous, but she kept on walking, hurrying, simply aware of an odd taste in her mouth, as if she'd been sucking pennies.

When Bryony reached the office doorway, she saw that both her packets of biscuits had disappeared and there was a little gathering of crumbs on the shelf where she'd left them.

She didn't see – because her back was turned and anyway why on earth should anyone be on the alert for such a thing? – that two figures had detached themselves stickily from the nasty wallpaper and were now padding along towards her. Each of them seemed unfinished, like rough models of small human beings made out of purple and red meat. Their outlines shifted and rippled horribly. Eyes and teeth emerged to the front of the two rudimentary heads, they showed white and shining and clever against the shifting masses of glistening flesh.

And there was no way out for Bryony. The Staff Office was a dead end in every sense, as she'd often told herself.

'Oh, bum.' Bryony sighed. This was going to be another awful day. And she had the very distinct feeling she was being watched. There was a tingling against her neck. She was filled with an impulse to turn round and also an idea that if she did she might not like what she discovered.

As they walked – now very close to Bryony – the figures kept altering, their outlines firming, features coming into focus and solidifying. Then four arms stretched out towards her and, as they lifted, were sheathed in fresh skin. Four hands became completely hand-like, with four thumbs and sixteen fingers and twenty fingernails, just as they reached out to clutch her.

As Bryony finally did begin to spin round, she felt herself

being held by both her wrists and heard the word, 'Boo!' being shouted by two very similar voices.

'Oh, for goodness' sake.' It was the Fetch twins, Honor and Xavier, looking up at her and giggling while they squeezed her wrists. 'You two nearly scared the life out of me.'

'That would be bad. Your life should be in you,' said Xavier, the boy twin. The Fetch twins weren't absolutely identical, as they liked to tell everyone. They were a boy and a girl, very alike, but not the same. 'We're very sorry.' Xavier didn't currently look sorry at all.

Neither did Honor. 'We didn't want to scare you… only sort of worry you a bit. To be exciting.' She smiled and looked very sweet. 'Excitement is nice, isn't it?'

Bryony forgave the little girl, as she always did. She always forgave both twins – they were just extremely… forgivable. Even though they did seem to turn up suddenly more often than not, as if they were creeping about and planning something only they understood. And it wasn't as if Bryony didn't need some excitement. She longed for it, in fact.

Xavier squeezed her hand between his, tugging. 'Grandmother says she would like you to come and visit her for tea.'

This was sort of good news – the twins' grandmother was the millionaire Julia Fetch, the reclusive widow who owned the hotel. If she had decided to like Bryony, that might make life much easier for the Permanently Junior Receptionist and maybe even mean Mangold didn't eat Bryony's biscuits. Then again, she really didn't want to work here for much longer. Possibly it would mean she got a good reference when she resigned, though…

The twins peered up at her, identically expectant and cute with their willowy limbs, perfect complexions and sun-bleached hair, Xavier in a blue and white striped T-shirt and blue shorts, Honor in a red and white striped T-shirt and red shorts. They were both barefoot, as usual. Bryony thought maybe she might mention to Mrs Fetch that running around with no shoes on wasn't terribly hygienic. Then again, maybe Mrs Fetch ran around in bare feet, too. No one ever saw her and she was incredibly wealthy – she could do whatever she liked. She could just not wear anything at all, ever, if she felt like it, or dress as a pirate. Of the two choices, Bryony was strongly in favour of the pirate option.

Honor squeezed Bryony's hand this time. 'Do say yes. We'd be ever so pleased and have cucumber sandwiches.' Both twins spoke like children out of an old-fashioned story book. 'Truly we would.' And maybe incredibly wealthy people talked like that all the time – Bryony had no idea, being what she might have called *incredibly not wealthy*, if it wouldn't have depressed her to do so.

Bryony nodded at the twins – while thinking *pleasepiratecostumepleasepiratecostume* – and both kids gave a cheer. 'Thank your grandmother very much. When I have a break I will come over.'

'This afternoon! This afternoon!' The twins skipped and chanted as they scampered away up the passage and out of sight.

'Weird little people.' Bryony shook her head and, in the absence of biscuits, pottered back out to the reception desk. There was no sign of the twins and the grandfather clock was, as usual, not ticking. As far as Bryony was concerned, life was dusty and hot and dull, dull, dull.

OUT ON THE GOLF course, now shimmering with heat under the June sun, a peculiar person struggled with his golf bag, which seemed to be much larger than was necessary. It was almost taller than him. But then, he was on the small side. Once again his putter fell to the grass and once again a fellow golfer spotted him flailing about just where he shouldn't be and yelled, 'Get out of the way, man! Fore, for heaven's sake! Fore!'

As he picked up his putter, only to watch several woods clatter onto the carefully manicured turf in a heap, the figure sighed and wondered, 'Four of what? I don't think I even have one of them… I don't think…' He was out of his depth, as he usually was, and felt distinctly hot and uncomfortable in his black woollen unsuitable suit. He peered in the direction of the Fetch Hotel and the Fetch Hotel front entrance and the Fetch Hotel reception desk and the area near to the reception desk and the precise spot – which he could only guess at longingly – where Bryony Mailer was standing at that very moment.

He sighed again, this time from the soles of his feet, right up to the ends of each hair on his head. It was horrible being in love. It was considerably more horrible being in love with someone too beautiful for you to even look at properly – unless you knew they were looking somewhere else and you wouldn't have to meet their eyes and blush and then want to burst into flames or evaporate or something. It was more horrible still when you understood completely that the person you loved clearly found you far less interesting than watching a pebble. It was most horrible when your love could never be, not in any way, not ever.

He sighed again until he felt completely hollowed out and didn't even flinch when a golf ball sliced past him, close enough for him to hear the way its tiny dimples disturbed the air.

Some of the balls had dimples and some of them didn't – Putta couldn't understand that, either…

'Fore, you *moron*! *Fore!*' An irate voice screamed away to his left.

He really would have to work out this four thing. He bent to gather up his clubs with a heavy and tragically romantic heart.

AS A GOLF BALL landed much further away from the twelfth green than its owner had intended, Bryony thumbed through her stack of pending reservation slips while deciding – yet again – that she hated golf, hated golfers, hated golfers' wives (did they have no lives of their own?) and that she really hated her ex-boyfriend Mick (a non-golfer) for having sapped her confidence, just when she'd been making postgraduate career decisions. A year ago, she'd thought working here would be relaxing and give her a taste of real life, and maybe she could write a book about… something… something to do with history… in her evenings off before becoming a stunningly attractive and popular young professor somewhere. Now she knew she was bored out of her mind and was never going to write anything if she didn't get away from the horrible Fetch premises and horrible Fetch guests and the horrible Mr Mangold. Bryony was equally certain that she had no idea what came next. Her lack of clarity about what came next was scary and why she hadn't left yet.

'Oh, I wouldn't worry terribly much about that, you know,' said a friendly, velvety kind of voice.

Bryony glanced up to see a very tall man studying her from the doorway. He grinned with rather more teeth than one person should have. He appeared to have been dressed by a committee, possibly a drunk committee: wing collar and something that might once have been a cravat, baggy oatmeal trousers, brown checked waistcoat, plum-coloured velvet jacket with bulging pockets, raddled shoes… an immense and disreputable scarf with a life of its own… 'These things quite often work themselves out in highly unpredictable ways. Luck has a lot to do with it. Although one can make one's own luck, I always think. At least I think I think that. Or else someone told me that. Probably someone lucky.' He made his way across the foyer towards her, half loping and half tiptoeing with a general air of being highly delighted to see everything around him including the dust on the broken grandfather clock. 'Ah, not a grandfather clock, you know – a *grandmother* clock. They're a touch smaller… Someone told me that, too. At some point.' Bryony thought she had never encountered anyone so remarkable in her life.

She was right.

As the man toped, or liptoed, up to Bryony's desk he continued amiably, 'Quite possibly you'll discover you're a creature of infinite resource. It's very warm for January, isn't it? Or then again I may have missed January and I'm definitely not in Chicago. Am I?'

Bryony heard herself say, 'Arbroath. Or a few miles outside Arbroath… And it's June.' Somehow the width of the stranger's grin was making her feel as if she had entered a different layer of reality – a previously secret and peculiar layer where locations and dates were no longer certain.

'Well, that's quite close. I degaussed the Mackenzie Trench circuit before I set off. Which sometimes works. But mostly not, now that I think about it.' And he smiled again, even more largely. 'Hello, I'm the Doctor.' He seemed somehow like her oldest friend, like a wonderful relative she'd heard a lot about but never met.

Bryony, while wondering how any human being could have that much hair – this kind of dense, lolloping head of wildly curly hair – fumbled through all the possible replies she could make to this Doctor person. Among them were, 'Who on earth are you really, though?' and 'How did you know what I was thinking?' and '*What?*' and 'Do you ever wash that scarf? Or can't you because it would object? Would it be like trying to wash a cat…?'

While she *urred* and *ahed* and didn't make any proper words at all, the Doctor nodded patiently, even slightly annoyingly, as if he were coaxing a dim child through a really easy sum. On the one hand he was clearly the type of person who should make anyone sensible very nervous, but on the other he filled her with the deepest sense of trust she'd ever experienced. Which took her right back to supposing she ought to be nervous.

Eventually, she managed, 'Do you have a reservation?' Which was a completely boring thing to say and made him look gently disappointed.

'A reservation? Well, no, I don't believe I do. When I travel I generally bring my own accommodation.' The Doctor's very large and very curious eyes lifted to ponder the ceiling while his monologue ambled along both gently and unpreventably. 'I might be due a holiday, of course. I always forget to take them. Usually someone reminds me, but there's no one to do that for me at the moment.'

Just for a second as she met the Doctor's eyes, Bryony experienced a stab of immense loneliness – almost unimaginable and inhuman isolation. This was followed by something much more pleasant, something very like the type of excitement she'd experienced as a child when she'd looked forward to holidays or birthday presents.

Bryony shook her head and wondered if she really should have searched about for overlooked biscuits, or rummaged in the second-from-the-left desk drawer for that dog-eared packet of Orangeade Spangles and eaten something, because she did feel a bit weird. But then – like so many humans – she let her mind simply dodge away from something too unusual to be comfortable. Instead, she decided to wonder if this Doctor person was just some weirdo who was camped in the scrub by the lake – they'd had that kind of problem before. He smelled a bit peculiar. Then again, it was a clean kind of smell: more like the way the air smelled right before a thunderstorm with a trace of added icing sugar than the scent of someone who had woken up in a tent.

The Doctor continued, while apparently trying not to laugh. 'I was lost in a virtual jungle for a while quite recently. Have you ever been lost in a virtual jungle? Takes it out of you. Perhaps I should have a holiday?' He eyed her name tag. 'Bryony Mailer, do you think I need a holiday? Should I stay here?' Then he looked straight at her the way an extremely bright boy might if he were expecting ice cream.

And Bryony Mailer thought – *This is it. This is what's next.*

Then she told the Doctor. 'Yes. I think you should stay. You should stay here.'

AT THE MOST SECLUDED edge of the Fetch Estate in a small, but dazzlingly well-equipped cottage, Mrs Julia Fetch rearranged her extensive collection of glass octopuses (or octopodes). She had them made in Venice by an increasingly elderly team of master glass blowers, lamp workers and glass artists. She softly ran her – she had to admit – increasingly elderly fingers across the rounded head of an *Octopus rubescens* and gently waved at the perfectly modelled tentacles of a red-spot night octopus, or *Octopus dierythraeus*. She smiled.

As the years had passed, she'd found that she had become slightly forgetful, perhaps even very forgetful – she could barely picture her long-ago husband's face – but she had perfect recall when it came to the names of octopus species. She had always been fond of octopodes (or octopuses) and she was using a tiny fraction of her monumental cash reserves to have every variety of octopus modelled in glass. There were over a hundred to reproduce and each exquisitely delicate sculpture took nearly a year of the craftsmen's work. It was very possible that she wouldn't quite manage to see the collection completed. She was also sole patron and very generous supporter of the Julia Fetch Foundation for the Care and Support of Octopuses (or Octopodes). These were really her only two remaining indulgences, apart from the cottage's fantastic kitchen – which she hardly used – and the marble-lined bathroom and generously proportioned bath in which she soaked her sometimes rather achy limbs, while wishing that she had more legs. Or more arms. Or both.

When she was younger, Mrs Fetch had enjoyed the usual toys and treats of the ultra-rich: buying sports cars and villas on sun-kissed coastlines, owning a London townhouse and a moderately sized castle (with village attached) quite near Folkestone, running stables full of racehorses and country estates all of which were seething with fat, juicy, slow-moving game birds and succulent deer. But she didn't really enjoy driving, and paying other people to drive her Bugattis and Duesenburgs and Alfa Romeos had seemed silly. Filling her villas (and the townhouse and the castle) with loud strangers hadn't been nearly as much fun as she'd expected, and filling them with friends was very difficult because having friends when you're vastly rich just gets quite *complicated*. Rattling around next to her swimmerless swimming pools or wandering alone across her dusty ballrooms had been depressing. She'd caught herself talking to the geckos in one place and half expecting them to answer. Her racehorses were beautiful, but had never seemed that fond of her – they tended to be slightly highly strung. And she had never been able to bring herself to kill anything on her estates. In fact, she'd been vegetarian for at least twenty years, if not forty, or sixty… Eventually, she'd given away all her homes apart from this cottage. They'd been turned into community centres and octopus research facilities. She'd sold her sports cars and horses and let her estates go back to nature and be overrun by un-shot-at animals and, by now, some quite rare plants, which nobody shot at either.

Or that was the past which she currently remembered.

She sometimes had the feeling that she had previously remembered other pasts, but she couldn't be sure. Being this old was slightly confusing. Then again – as the twins often told her – it was very reasonable to be confused when she knew so much and had been to so many places and done so many things, occasionally in diving gear (but never dressed as a pirate).

And as long as she had the twins – her beautiful, kind and charming Honor, her handsome, kind and charming Xavier – she knew that everything would be all right. That was something she didn't forget.

She never left her cottage these days. She didn't need to. A dedicated geostationary satellite poured a constant flow of information into her personal communications hub – located in what used to be the pantry – and she could spend all day, if she wanted, learning more about octopus camouflage techniques, or the cunning ways in which they could impersonate other sea creatures, or reading her Foundation's latest test results on octopus intelligence. From the hub, she could also keep an eye on the stock market and watch her money quietly making more money.

But she did feel the need for a little company now and then. She did think – perhaps regularly, perhaps only once a month, she wasn't entirely certain – that it would be nice to invite some pleasant people to take tea with her. Nothing grand, or fussy – just tea with small sandwiches and perhaps slices of fruit cake and maybe scones.

She did sometimes tell the twins about arranging to have tea and they did promise to go and find her suitable guests, but she couldn't – if she was honest – absolutely recall how often this happened, or if she had ever served anybody tea, or discussed the mating rituals of squid while buttering very thin toast and handing out napkins. Occasionally she dreamed that the inside of her mind was somehow becoming occupied by a being much cleverer than she was, something with dark tendrils, or tentacles reaching into her personality and softly wriggling about across her memories in a way that made them jumble and fade.

Still, it didn't matter. She was entirely happy and probably had forgotten her last tea party in the usual old lady type of way. Probably, if she concentrated, she could say how many cucumber sandwiches this or that visitor had eaten and whether there had been enough jam. And there was no reason to worry if she couldn't. As she stared out through her window at the well-groomed trees and glossy shrubs bordering her golf course, she nodded to herself and smiled again. She had a good life. And sixty-eight perfectly lovely Venetian glass octopodes. Or octopuses.

DAVID AGNEW WAS A man who purposely ate octopus whenever he could. He was currently sitting in the Fetch Hotel's Sweet Spot Bar and wishing he was, instead, lolling by the pool at his Greek island villa, tucking into some fresh octopus legs and shooting geckos with his air pistol. These were the kinds of things he enjoyed.

He was not enjoying his vodka and orange which was warmish and rather unpleasant and definitely hadn't involved fresh orange juice, even though he'd asked for it specifically and in his most commanding tone of voice. Some chance of proper service in a dump like this. Still, Fetch Brothers had a fabulous golf course and he could usually get round it in 86. Or 90. Definitely in 98. And soon his most commanding voice would really mean something around here.

Agnew considered complaining, but he couldn't be bothered because at present he felt extremely good about life. He'd showered after he left the course, changed into his new, rather dashing, safari suit and he wasn't due back at the office for another two hours. That gave him more than enough time for a spot of lunch. He snapped his fingers to summon the barman and ordered a prawn cocktail and a basket of scampi and chips. And a glass of Liebfraumilch.

While he waited for his bar meal, he glanced around at

the golfing prints, the photos of men in large caps and plus fours, the little shelf of donated trophies and the Challenge Cup. This year, he had a real chance of winning the Cup. There had been ten players who were better than him on paper, but seven of them weren't competing this time round.

Actually – he corrected himself – eight of them wouldn't be competing. Yes, he was sure of that. He was absolutely sure that Paul Harris wouldn't be trying for the Challenge Cup this year. Or any other year.

David Agnew tugged at his beige jacket to smooth it and grinned. The world was a very satisfactory place.

Then it became significantly less satisfactory as a grassy, shabby, scrawny, sweaty man, clattered into the bar with a golf bag he seemed quite unable to control. Knocking over a number of stools as he proceeded, he then sank to a halt at the table next to Agnew's and flopped the bag messily down beside him. Its ancient clubs emerged like a rusty threat and disfigured the carpet.

Agnew gave the newcomer his best withering stare and pointed to a large sign which read GOLF BAGS AND GOLF ATTIRE ARE NOT PERMITTED BEYOND THE CLUBHOUSE.

At this, the dreadful interloper flinched and said, 'Oh. Oh, dear… I… but I'm… well, I thought that as I was… I'm a resident… guest… that is… oh, dear… I am very…' He fumbled at the bag's shoulder strap, which had come adrift, and stood up rapidly in a way that produced a shower of tees, grass tufts and dried mud. Then he reached into his bag and pulled out – Agnew couldn't begin to guess why – its last remaining club, a battered putter, and waved it around as if he was conducting some type of interior orchestra.

'Careful! You nearly had my head off with that. What's wrong with you?'

The putter crashed down across Agnew's table while the ghastly little man mumbled, 'Wrong…? No, it's just me… me, you see… people always seem to find that me being me is wrong… I don't mean it to be…'

Agnew bellowed, 'Sit down!'

At this, the stranger squeaked, 'OK.'

Agnew announced, 'I have a headache and would like to finish my lunch in peace.' Which was a confusing thing to say as his lunch hadn't arrived yet, but he was too annoyed to make sense. Agnew frowned while the man peered at him.

'Well, I… Sorry for speaking… but I won't interrupt. That is… I'm Mr Ian Patterson.' The grubby man recited his name as if it was something he'd had to memorise recently. 'And I… being here without golfing was… it would have seemed… but I don't golf… and…' He shoved the fallen clubs back into his bag distractedly. 'They loaned me these… things… and I already had the… the putter thingy…' Then he started to thump at his clothing in a doomed effort to remove the layer of muddy dust under which he was now operating. This simply spread the dust further.

'Mr Patterson!'

'Ah!' Patterson ducked warily for an instant and stopped thumping. 'Yes?'

'Why don't I give you a golf lesson?' Agnew smiled like a crocodile approaching a fat gnu he'd caught out paddling by itself. 'Would you like that? Eighteen holes? I'm David Agnew. Allow me to be…' He clearly found it difficult to say the next word. '… Helpful.'

Before Patterson could even think about how unlikely this was, he found himself suddenly having his golf bag thrust into his confused arms and being propelled out of the bar while Agnew shouted to the barman, 'No lunch for me. Busy. Cancel it all. Back in fifteen minutes.'

This puzzled Patterson because even he knew fifteen minutes wouldn't give them enough time for a full round of golf, not that Patterson wanted a full round or really anything more to do with golf. It seemed a ridiculous game and – *oh, dear* – he was being badgered along towards the front entrance and – *oh, no* – here was Bryony, lovely Bryony, talking to a bizarre-looking guest and apparently getting on extremely well with him – *it was the curly hair, women loved curly hair* – Patterson's hair was as flat and lifeless as his hopes – and it was ginger – and…

'Good afternoon, Mr Agnew.' Bryony had lifted her head. Her extremely attractive head. And because of the whole attractiveness thing it was horribly impossible not to look at her, while she then said, 'Good afternoon, Mr Patterson.' And the whole looking at her thing meant that Patterson was completely, supernaturally, aware that *she* was looking at *him* in return. This caused a kind of searing pain to dart straight into his chest and then bang right out again through his back. It was such a real sensation that he worried about his jacket and whether it had been singed.

'Oh, I'm… sorry… covered in mud… and grass… and… trying some, er, golf…' And the last thing he saw of her as he was bundled down the steps and outside was a smile. It was a slightly confused, if not dismayed smile, but it had been for him.

She'd smiled at him.

That was wonderful.

AS THE GOLF-RELATED CHAOS receded, the Doctor continued talking to Bryony while also thinking a great many things at once. He was aware that the ability to do this was an indication of genius. He was a genius, after all, and what kind of genius would he be if he didn't know that?

Currently, he was wondering why the TARDIS had deposited him here. Even at her most random, the TARDIS always worked within her own kind of personal logic, so his arrival must have some kind of reason behind it. Unless it didn't. Why Arbroath now, as opposed to Chicago in a snowstorm several months ago when the Chicago Area Computer Hobbyists' Exchange was going to develop its MODEM work and create an inadvertent danger to all life on Earth? Which he'd just have to deal with later. Or rather, earlier… As his friend Robert Louis Stevenson had often told him, there did usually need to be an extremely pressing reason for someone to be in Arbroath, so what was it? And simultaneously the Doctor was finding it odd and worth considering that ever since he'd materialised his mouth had tasted of Maillindian Fever Beans, when he hadn't eaten any in years – dreadful things, just like chewing on old Earth pennies. That needed an explanation. *Metallic taste, metallic taste…* He searched his immense and extremely disorderly memory for dreadful, or marvellous, or significant events which having a metallic taste in his mouth could indicate were on the way. The words *Telepathic Clamp* flittered past for his consideration and he dismissed them. No one on Earth would have such a thing for hundreds of years. And there were very few creatures who could generate anything like one – each of them so staggeringly horrible that they would be bound to have already caused the kind of chaos that leaves definite traces: arm-waving, screaming, running about, the telling of wild stories… And meanwhile he looked at Bryony Mailer and thought what a splendid girl she was, really promising for a human being, and wondered why that very untidy fellow who'd just left hadn't mentioned being in love with her before he was pushed outside, because the chap clearly did adore her. The Doctor reflected, not for the first time, that it was a miracle human beings ever reproduced, given the way they seemed to make the whole process so *difficult*. When they weren't running about being scared and trying to kill each other, they were being *shy*. It was ridiculous.

At which point, what the Doctor could only understand as the most massive **THOUGHT** he had ever encountered battered into his consciousness and overloaded every one of his remarkably agile and adaptable neurons.

As he fell over, his mind had just enough room to reach out the single word *fascinating* and wave it about like a flag of surrender before everything went blank.

MOMENTS AFTER THE DOCTOR fell, Julia Fetch pottered across her cottage kitchen and set out a stack of doilies and side plates on the table, just in case they might be needed to slip under cakes later at tea. *You never knew when people might drop round*. Then she wondered if she actually had any cakes…

MEANWHILE – AND MUCH more helpfully – Bryony Mailer rushed round from behind the reception desk just in time to not catch the Doctor as he crumpled up into a multicoloured heap on the foyer floor. 'Oh goodness. Doctor? Doctor?' He looked quite serene, but was completely unconscious. 'Doctor whoever you are?' When she took his pulse it seemed very strong, which was good. It also had a kind of built-in echo which surely was much less good.

As Bryony knelt beside the large, horizontal, almost-guest and wondered if she should call an ambulance or just fetch a glass of water, she heard distinctive slithery footsteps approaching. Kevin Mangold, hotel manager and biscuit thief, had arrived to make an awkward situation worse. He always did.

'Miss Mailer, I hope you haven't knocked out one of our guests…?' Mangold snorted wetly and then waited for Bryony to appreciate what he obviously thought had been an impressive joke. She ignored him, so he stared through his dandruff-flecked glasses at the Doctor's highly personalised choice of clothes and then asked dubiously, '*Is* he a guest…?'

Bryony stood up, partly because she was several inches taller than Mangold and knew this annoyed him. 'He was going to be a guest. He was telling me a story about Charles Darwin and then he just turned very pale and collapsed.'

'Well, we can't have that.' Mangold tutted at Bryony as if having people collapse in the foyer and/or mention Darwin was some crazy new scheme of hers to frighten tourists. 'Not at all. Other guests won't like it… Perhaps if we dragged him out of the way. He could fit in the Office, or the linen cupboard…'

'We can't just put him in a cupboard. He might be ill. We need to call a… another doctor.'

'Another doctor? Have you already called a doctor?' Mangold was clearly remembering that the hotel's official physician, Dr Porteous, was over 70 and more likely to steal towels and bread rolls than be of any help in a medical emergency.

'No, no, the towels are safe… That is, I mean, *he's* a doctor.' Bryony pointed at the Doctor and saw his feet twitch as if he was a big dog dreaming of rabbits.

'Well, he can't be a very good doctor – look at him.'

Bryony found she was feeling protective towards the now faintly groaning stranger. 'I don't think that really follows.'

The Doctor flopped over onto his back, opened his eyes and declared, 'I told them the Dymaxion House would never catch on. Far too shiny.' Before passing out again.

Mangold swayed on his creaking shoes and sucked his teeth. 'Oh, I don't like the sound of that.' Bryony could have sworn a tiny shower of fresh dandruff rose and then fell as Mangold shook his head, like very depressing snow. 'You're Junior Day Receptionist. It's your responsibility to prevent outbreaks of this kind, Miss Mailer.'

Bryony was about to make a cutting remark about unfunny idiots, biscuits and hiding other people's packets of Spangles in desk drawers when the whining sound of the Fetch Resort's one golf cart interrupted her and Xavier ran in, holding a tartan rug and shouting, 'Someone is ill. Isn't it frightful? Someone is ill.'

A number of things then happened simultaneously: the rug was dropped over the Doctor's legs, Mangold sneaked backwards in case he was associated with anything troublesome while any member of the Fetch family was around, Honor ran in and took Bryony's hand and then the Doctor lurched up into a sitting position and sneezed, surprising everyone – apparently himself most of all. 'Now where was I?' He seemed remarkably unsurprised to be on the floor, surrounded by people and partially covered in Royal Stuart tartan. But there was a clear flicker of worry at the back of his eyes. And that made Bryony worry, too. She also asked herself, 'But how did the twins know that someone was ill?'

OUT ON THE GOLF course, David Agnew was marching his irritating companion along the path that snaked through the little stretches of woodland and scrub surrounding the fairways and greens. It was pleasant here and cool because of the shade from the trees and the small and picturesque stream that ran into the course's central lake. Agnew whistled as he marched and was in excellent spirits, but not because of his surroundings. He was, in fact, almost giggling because soon he would reach that especially deep and tricky bunker south of the thirteenth green and soon he would tell Mr Patterson to step down into it and practice using a sand wedge and soon after that Mr Patterson would be gone, gone, gone. The buffoon probably didn't even have a sand wedge, but Agnew didn't care – every time he left someone he hated in what he privately called Unlucky Bunker 13, they never came back. And he really, really hated this Patterson chap – the man was untidy, he didn't know how to behave and he was making a joke of everything Agnew believed should matter. And what Mr Agnew believed should matter was important. In fact, he'd recently become sure that what he thought was right should be the only thing that *was* right and should therefore govern everything worthwhile. Just lately, it had seemed clearer and clearer that if the world was run along the lines that he, and only he, could imagine for it, then it would be a much better and more orderly place.

It seemed to Mr Agnew that making two people disappear in one day would be perfectly reasonable and convenient. Then he could have his lunch in peace, or maybe a spa session first to unwind. Why not? Keeping the world as it should be was tiring and he truly couldn't see why he shouldn't have some time to pamper himself now and then.

ALSO OUT ON THE golf course was the Doctor, now striding along in the sunshine next to the golf cart as it trundled joltingly forwards. 'Reminds me of a dog I know.' He smiled down at Bryony who was riding in the cart with Xavier. 'How are you feeling?'

'How am *I* feeling?' Bryony snapped. She'd been really worried about the Doctor and didn't appreciate that her worry hadn't been appreciated. 'How am *I* feeling?'

The Doctor nodded encouragingly, 'Yes, that's what I just said. But you might not remember, you've had a nasty shock.'

Bryony was exasperated. She jumped out of the cart, 'Doctor, you were the one who fainted. I'm perfectly all right.'

Xavier patted her with sympathy. 'You looked awfully wobbly, though, old girl.'

And Honor, trotting along and holding the Doctor's hand, chipped in, 'Yes, seeing a fainted person must be a dreadful thing.'

Bryony heard herself growl out loud with frustration before beginning, 'You saw him being a fainted person, too. Why isn't everyone treating *you* like an invalid? And the Doctor *was* the fainted person. He should be riding on the cart. He should be *lying down*.'

The Doctor tried to calm her. 'But I *was* lying down. On the floor. That's what upset you.' Bryony slapped his arm and he suppressed a grin, because he was indeed teasing her. 'Oh, quite. Quite.' Annoying Bryony – and she liked being annoyed, the Doctor could tell – was distracting him slightly from the incredible pain in his head and neck and the tiny, unaccountable gap he kept running across when he checked his recent memories. Right at the back of today's record so far, there was a numb area. It was disturbing. There were very few things that could interfere with the Doctor's mind, even superficially, and the technologies powerful enough to intrude on him were all both dark and extremely unpleasant. He really wouldn't want to be around if any of them had been unleashed. Except he was around and it seemed highly likely that one of them had been unleashed. Or had unleashed itself… Telepathic and psychic energies were so unpredictable and so likely to colonise other available consciousnesses and then magnify… or even to generate rudimentary sentience in awkward places… Whatever it was, it was a whole lot worse than what now seemed the friendly and welcoming possibilities of a vast telepathic clamp, squeezing the free will out of every brain it afflicted…

Bryony turned to the Doctor and actually stamped her feet, which she hadn't done since she was Honor's age and which immediately made her feel foolish. 'I'm so tired of people talking down to me, just because I'm a woman! And I'm not a Junior Day Receptionist, I'm the Only Day Receptionist! And it's him you should be taking care of!' She waved her arms at the Doctor and then the twins. 'He's scared of something and trying to hide it and I don't think there are many things that scare him and I really…'

Bryony stopped and immediately regretted all of this so strongly that the Doctor was dimly aware of the precise trains of thought she was moving through. He understood that no one had ever wanted to hear Bryony discussing the role of women in the workplace and so even considering this now made her feel bullied and a bit stupid and as if she was weird and also she would rather be on the golf course with Mr Patterson just now because she thought he was sweet and not sexist and basically unlike almost every other Fetch Hotel golfer she'd met. Not that he really was a golfer… and…

Bryony, unaware she was thinking *really quite loudly*, was pondering the fact that her last sentence had made the Doctor look genuinely worried for a second or two. She hadn't been mistaken. He really was frightened. And the Doctor being frightened didn't seem like good news.

The Doctor looked at her, completely serious, and said very kindly and softly, 'Oh, I'm incredibly scared most of the time, you know. No one with even a basic knowledge of the universe wouldn't be – it's a completely terrifying place. And enormous. But it's also wonderful and lovely and more interesting than you could possibly imagine. Even than I could possibly imagine. It never lets me down. And I get to be alive in it all and to be scared and amazed and delighted and… I wouldn't be without it.' Then he adjusted his hat and grinned, playing the fool again. 'I've been without me and before me and after me, but I wouldn't be without the universe.'

Bryony wondered if she was absolutely happy she now knew someone who could casually consider being without the universe.

The Doctor turned to Honor. 'And where are we going?' He'd forgotten their destination again. All his thoughts seemed a bit sticky, or clumped, or hairy, like boiled sweets left in a jacket pocket – or a desk drawer.

Honor explained again. 'To see Grandmother and be in

her house and take tea and get better. Grandmother's teas make everyone better.'

Over in her cottage, Julia Fetch was carefully putting away her side plates and doilies, mildly under the impression that a very fine tea had just been enjoyed by a number of fascinating people, while the Doctor nodded and discovered this made his brain feel as if his Lateral Interpositus Nucleus had been prodded with a sonic probe, and the only time that had actually happened, he hadn't enjoyed it one bit. Something in there definitely wasn't as it should be. It was almost as if a new engram had been forced into his memories – a fake recollection. And the fake was there to make him believe there hadn't already been another alteration, it had been inserted to make him forget there was a gap. If he couldn't get control of the process, eventually it would all just heal over and then where would he be? A genius with a bit missing who couldn't recall there *was* a bit missing and maybe some added ends and odds which absolutely shouldn't be there – that would never do… Plus, he was starting to feel a little peculiar again. He put his hands in his pockets and whistled a fragment of the Song of the Arcanian System Exploration Corps, which was quite pretty and had lots of twiddly bits. Whistling twiddly bits often cheered him, although not so much today. He felt increasingly as if he wasn't walking on grass, but on green fur, annoyed green fur.

DAVID AGNEW WAS CHUCKLING and peering down at the tricky bunker south of the thirteenth green. At the bunker's deepest point, the pathetic figure of Ian Patterson hacked an ancient-looking sand wedge into its blinding white surface for something like the hundredth time. And for something like the hundredth time, his golf ball stayed exactly where it was while a great deal of hot sand went all over the place.

'You're doing incredibly well,' Agnew called, rubbing his hands together in anticipation. *Not long now.* 'I will have to nip off in a minute, but I think you should stay right there and enjoy yourself.' Agnew was waiting for the unmistakable sensation he got just before It started, this tingling in the soles of his feet and a feeling of immense sort of... Doom.

When the Doom got too bad he just ran. He'd never looked back. He was a man who didn't like to dwell on details – he preferred to just focus on results.

'I'm not sure about that, really.' Patterson swiped the head of his club wildly, producing another sand shower that reached as far as Agnew. 'I seem to be getting worse. Maybe if I took up swimming, or snooker...' He swung again and the sand wedge flew out of his hand, landing near Agnew's ankles.

Patterson was hot and miserable and wanted to lie under a tree with some lemonade and the memory of Bryony's smile. 'I'll just climb out…' He firmly believed that if at first you didn't succeed, you should maybe try once more, but then give up completely if you failed again.

'No!' Agnew handed back the club rather forcefully. 'You're really improving.' He smiled like someone who loathed everything he was smiling at and wanted to do it harm. 'Practice makes perfect if you want to be a top golfer.' He then adjusted his expression until it seemed only furious and painful. He didn't have a face designed for happiness.

Patterson ducked the new incoming smile by studying his sand-filled shoes. 'But I don't want to be a top golfer.' Terran shoes, he had decided, must be designed to pre-punish small social and criminal infractions. His were made of several inorganic materials, kept his feet uncomfortably hot and squeezed one of his toes. But they did provide a sizeable heel which increased his height and had the unusual effect of making him feel more confident – although not right now.

'Then you should practise until you do.'

Patterson sighed and wondered if he was getting sunstroke, because he was beginning to feel unsteady. Either that or the bunker was beginning to feel unsteady, which wasn't exactly likely. Up above him he heard Agnew giggle and then say, 'Wonderful. Oh, wonderful!'

'I beg your pardon? I haven't even hit it yet.'

Agnew was suddenly furious, 'Well, if you're not going to make an effort, I'm leaving!' Then he burst out laughing – which was very peculiar for someone who apparently intended to seem angry. 'Yes! Off I go!' And then Agnew was suddenly running – quite fast – away from the bunker and back along the path to the Fetch Hotel. 'It's a trip to the Spa for me. You've left me quite exhausted, Mr Patterson.'

Agnew guffawed weirdly. 'But don't you worry. The fun is on its way.' He yelled over his shoulder as he pelted into the cover of the trees: 'Good bye Mr Patterson. Absolutely good bye.'

Ian Patterson frowned. Then he felt unsteady again. Then he wiggled his sand wedge, set it down and reached into his golf bag for his putter. When he looked at the bag he could have sworn it moved slightly. Then, as he gingerly pulled out the putter, he had the distinct impression that something hot and wet had reached up and grabbed hold of his feet.

'JELLY BABY?' THE DOCTOR was feeling enormously hungry. He offered round the crumpled white paper sweet bag more out of habit than because he didn't currently want to eat every one of them at once, followed by a big roast dinner and a full Maori *hangi* all to himself. His headache had got worse and also felt as if it belonged to someone else, or maybe something else. Bryony didn't seem to want a jelly baby, but he tried encouraging her. 'Go on. Have a purple one – they taste of Zarnith.' It seemed that sharing a jelly baby might make him feel less lonely.

LONELY

The vast thought swiped in at him and, although it didn't knock him out this time, he did stumble and he was aware that Bryony was staring at him with concern. He told her, 'No need to worry. The world's my lobster. Honestly, I couldn't feel better.'

Like all good youngsters on Gallifrey, the Doctor had been brought up with a strong awareness of how little other species knew about, well… anything and how they usually shouldn't be told about, well… anything, because most of the information a Time Lord might be able to offer them would at least make them retire to the country and keep bees – should their planet have bees, or similar life forms – if not actually drive them irreversibly insane.

'Everything's absolutely fine. And by the way, do you like honey?'

Just for an instant the Doctor contemplated what would happen if he were to become irreversibly insane.

And then someone not very far away screamed horribly, which was a great relief, somehow. The Doctor knew exactly what to do when he heard horrible screaming – run towards it and help.

SO WHILE DAVID AGNEW slipped his safari suit into a locker at the Fetch Hotel Spa and wondered whether he should have a massage first or sit in the hydro-therapy pool, the Doctor was loping across well-groomed turf towards continuing sounds of horror and repeated dull thuds.

Bryony found that she, too, was running as if this was just the right thing to do and, although she was scared silly, she was also completely exhilarated and – despite his hugely long strides – almost keeping up with the Doctor.

'What are you doing? Grandmother's this way…' Xavier called.

But Bryony and the Doctor left the golf cart and the bemused twins behind, coming rapidly to the top of a gentle rise. From there they were able to see the thirteenth green quite far off with its pretty flag and manicured grass, along with a small flight of crows lifting away out of the trees and croaking in alarm. They could also see a deep bunker with Patterson at the bottom of it. He was flailing about in the pit like someone who had just found out a great deal of new and entirely unpleasant information about life and he was yelling. He was screaming. In his hand he had what was left of his putter, which was – as Bryony stared – both flaring and melting away with a cherry red glow. The club head had already gone and the metal shaft was disappearing.

As glowing droplets of what Bryony could only think of as *redness* fell into the sand, they landed with odd thumps and very clearly made it shudder. Each impact was producing thin trails of gently green vapour.

Like many humans when presented with a reality too strange to digest, she found herself saying something absurd, just to prove she was still there and could hear her own voice. So – as she continued to run forwards – she remarked, breathlessly, 'Well, that's unusual for this time of year.'

The Doctor half turned his head back towards her with a huge grin. 'Splendid. You really are. I knew you would be.'

By the time the Doctor had reached the edge of the bunker, he had already assessed the situation, in as far as he could. There was obviously something under the bunker's surface – something large and carnivorous, perhaps a sandmaster, which shouldn't be anywhere near this solar system, but never mind about that. Or else something worse… 'Take my hand.' There had, by now, been arm-waving, screaming and running about and the Doctor was sure that the telling of a wild story was just around the corner… 'My hand, take it!' The Doctor reached forward and held out his arm as the chap continued to fire – if you could call it firing – what seemed to be a very rudimentary fusion lance at the area around his own feet. 'Take my hand!' The man shouldn't have a fusion lance on twentieth-century Earth. No one should.

Patterson did as he was told as the last of what was indeed his fusion lance's fissile core sputtered and got actually much too hot to hold, although there was no way he was letting go of it while it was still any defence at all. 'Oh, thank you. Thank you.' He felt his free hand being grasped in remarkably strong fingers and found himself looking into precisely the type of reliable, experienced face he might have wanted a rescuer to have. 'Thank you.'

Just then he noticed Bryony arriving and shouted, 'No, keep back, darling!' And he was suddenly very angry that whoever his rescuer was had put the most wonderful human being on earth in danger by bringing her along. Although it was lovely to see her. Even though he was mortified that he'd called her 'darling'. And then Patterson felt an altogether different strong grip close back in around his ankles and this time there was a definite tug downwards.

Bryony watched, horrified, as Patterson's feet seemed to sink and jerk unnaturally backward and the rest of him fell forward towards the sand, then jerked to a halt, suspended lopsidedly by the one wrist the Doctor was gripping. Whatever device he'd been holding, dropped out of his grasp and he windmilled his free arm to try and catch at the Doctor with both hands. It was as if Patterson was drowning and clutching up towards his only hope. The Doctor himself was wrenched over the lip of the bunker when Patterson fell and was left hanging down into the pit, only his legs and waist still on the grass. The glowing, steaming, rippling sand waited below with a kind of dreadful appetite. Both men were clinging to each other desperately by this point, but it seemed certain that Patterson was very likely to drag the Doctor into whatever trouble he was facing, rather than the Doctor being able to haul him out.

So Bryony, without pausing for a second, raced down to grab the Doctor's ankles.

The Doctor managed, 'Just keep calm. Everything's perfectly all right.'

'No it's not!' chorused Bryony and Patterson.

'No… True…' The Doctor clung on with steely certainty to Patterson's hands while deciding that whatever was under the bunker might not be a sandmaster, it wasn't behaving like a sandmaster… and that metallic taste was very strong, along with a sense of true, primordial horror.

'Very true…' With relief, he felt Bryony working out exactly the most sensible thing to do and taking hold of his feet. She really was a wonderful girl. 'Everything is immensely dangerous, but I do feel we're managing terribly well under the circumstances.' And if he'd had the spare energy, he would have laughed. This was, after all, why one became a rogue Time Lord, wandering the universe… to be right on the spot when somebody needed rescuing from a glowing green death pit… a pit infested with something he was sure he should be able to remember…

Then the Doctor slipped a few inches nearer the position beyond which he would inevitably topple into the glowing green death pit himself. Which he guessed would be unpleasant. So he decided to stop raising everyone's morale and concentrate on keeping everyone alive by holding very tight and trusting Bryony.

Bryony wasn't that big or powerful, but she did know that her strongest muscles were in her legs. If she'd lain down and hoped her weight would act as an anchor on the Doctor, she would very probably have been pulled over into the bunker when the Doctor finally slipped forward past his tipping point. Instead, she lifted the Doctor's feet – it was a risk and he did find he was drawn even nearer the bunker as she did so, letting poor Patterson hang ever closer to the shining, oozy, hungry sand. But next she was able to crouch and then slowly stand, leaning back and letting her weight and her legs do the work of pulling. If she both tugged on his ankles and then let herself fall backwards, still gripping the Doctor, they might be OK. She concentrated all her will and strength into saving both her new friends.

Whatever was holding Patterson fast seemed utterly immoveable, but finally it did give way a bit, then a bit more and then, just when the Doctor gave a long and pained shout, it gave up entirely.

SAD

Another plunging, metallic word battered into the Doctor's mind.

Bryony landed suddenly on her back. The Doctor's legs were tangled in her own and then she was scrambling free as the Doctor was finally able to yank Patterson up and away from danger, Bryony hurrying to reach down and help with the last hard tug.

For a long space the three of them lay in a breathless heap, the turf beneath them shaking and sand – hot, steaming sand – raining down.

But gently, unmistakably, the turf calmed, settled, the sand stopped falling and all was peaceful.

The Doctor was the first to gather his senses, sit up and study his two companions. The girl was… an excellent girl… but the man was – of course – not a man, in the Earth sense… clearly not from round here. Not from anywhere near here… More like someone from Yinzill… In fact, exactly like someone from the planet Yinzill, which the Doctor should have noticed at once… It wasn't something a massive intellect should *just miss*…

He rubbed his face, found his hat – it had rolled to a safe distance and was calmly waiting for him – and dusted it to give himself something to do. This was all very bad.

BAD

The alien thought was slightly gentler this time and seemed to be leaving, somehow. The Doctor felt as if a large hand was being opened inside his skull and then withdrawn. His headache was back. He also wished that so much of rescuing activity didn't involve arm strain and tension in the lower back. Beings were always dangling off buildings, or cliffs, or into evil-minded pools, or bunkers and they always did need to be hauled back to somewhere less risky. There was a lot of hauling, generally.

HURT
BADHURT

After which everything was back to normal, expect for this renewed feeling that more bits and pieces had sort of been vanished away from his mind.

He didn't have any time to worry about this, because Bryony – human beings were wonderfully insane – then also sat up, stood up and went to lean over into the bunker and fetch out what was left of the lance. It looked like the blackened stump of a golf club handle. Although it surely wasn't.

As she bent and reached forward into the sand both the Doctor and Patterson yelled, 'No!'

But it was too late.

Or, at least, it would have been, if rummaging about a bit with her fingers, lifting up the lance and then turning round with a puzzled expression had still been dangerous activities to try. In fact, they were perfectly safe and meant Bryony could stare down into her hand, examine what she'd found and say to Patterson, 'It's very small.'

Patterson was dishevelled and defensive. 'It was quite big when I started.'

Bryony peered at it with distaste. 'Well, it's not big now. But it is ruined. Do you want it back?' She wagged it in Patterson's direction.

'Not… well, no, it won't work now. It's…' Patterson rubbed his sore wrists and stood up, blushing.

'I'll chuck it back, then.' And Bryony slung it back into the bunker, where it landed with a thump while another 'No!' rang out across the golf course. The Doctor and Patterson flinched.

But nothing happened. 'What?' Bryony turned to them and frowned at the Doctor. 'You were pulling him out of the bunker and onto the grass – obviously you think it's safe on the grass… We're all on the grass… I'm on the grass… So we're safe, right?'

'Well, I wouldn't say—'

'And how is it you know about these kinds of things, Doctor? People being dragged underground by a golf bunker kinds of things…?' She waited while the Doctor wondered why she was sounding cross. He'd saved the day, after all. Again. That was cause for thanks and congratulations and maybe that tea he'd been promised.

Bryony folded her arms as significantly as she could and frowned more. 'Do you want to explain what on earth is going on?' The Doctor opened his mouth, but seemed unable to let any words emerge – Bryony was a little bit unnerving when she was angry – and so she turned to Patterson. 'And who are you, Mr Patterson, and where are you from and what were you firing, or burning, or… what was that, exactly? And don't tell me it was a big sparkler, or an experimental… umbrella… or that you got struck by lightning, or something else unbelievable, because I'm not a complete idiot.' Patterson looked so bewildered at this and was so clearly on the verge of crying – Bryony could genuinely be quite fierce – that she softened a little and patted his arm. 'My dad always used to say that to me – "Bryony, you're not a complete idiot. I think we lost some of the bits."'

Usually people found this funny, even if it was a very old joke, but Patterson just swallowed hard and said, all in a rush, 'My broodfather hated me. He said I was a waste of perfectly good cloning equipment and I agree, I do, I really agree, but…' He stared from the bunker to Bryony and then to the Doctor and then took a deep breath, but before he could say anything, the twins appeared over the hill, Xavier driving the golf cart. They both waved tranquilly and shouted, 'Hello! Hello!'

Honor gambolled delightfully down the slope as if dishevelled strangers and steaming pits were all part of enjoying a normal and lovely summer's afternoon. 'We wondered if anyone would like a lift back in the golf cart again.' She didn't even glance at the plume of greenish vapour still hanging above the bunker. 'We're sorry there's only one cart, which really isn't big enough to fit five passengers. Grandmother did talk about having more, but she thinks that walking is good for people and should be encouraged and no sitting about unless you're incredibly old – Grandmother is incredibly old – or you can sit if you've had to look at somebody who's fainted, or had to be somebody who's fainted. Good afternoon, Mr Patterson.'

Patterson watched his hand being shaken solemnly by the little girl and then Honor led him up the hill as if she was the adult and he was the child.

The Doctor and Bryony followed on, Bryony noticing that she felt sore all over from the recent struggle. As they went, she asked, 'Doctor, do you get the impression those children are a little unusual?'

The Doctor laughed. It was marvellous that the one thing she chose to mention as unusual was the children. Everything else that had just happened had simply made her inquisitive and cross. *Magnificent.* He took off his hat and waved it at Xavier. 'I suppose twins are often slightly remarkable...' Xavier waved back. 'But yes...' He racked his brain, trying to recall where he'd read about adorable barefoot pairs of creatures. There was nothing like reading to prepare you for life, but if all the words were slipping and going dim... if everything you'd read was going to be taken away soon...

He felt a spasm of true panic.

Clearly an alien entity – or Patterson – was flooding this area with telepathic energy at immensely high levels, thousands of psychons, maybe tens of thousands… What could do that? And also lie in wait to devour other beings, just eat them up? Or rather, eat them down? He should know the answer to that. He almost knew that he *did* know, or *had* known a very good answer… And clearly the energy was already animating matter… Sand would be quite easy to form into shapes, limbs, silicon support structures, jaws… It didn't bear thinking about what might come next, but he definitely felt relieved that he *was* still thinking… even with gaps…

And the Doctor was a determined individual. He didn't give up easily, if at all. As long as he could think, there was hope. He looked up at the perfectly blue 1978 sky – not too radioactive, not too toxic, a gorgeous pearly dab of light when viewed from outer space – and he thumbed through recollections: the perfectly umber skies of Gallifrey, the first time he'd smelt a dew-laden Earth dawn in seventeenth-century France, swimming in the thick silky waters of Praxus Minor, avoiding the overly affectionate pseudo-sharks of Praxus Minor – and it seemed that his head was still stuffed with every kind of this and that. Maybe he'd just misplaced an occasional item, made filing errors due to telepathic shock.

Nothing to fret about.

The Doctor glanced down and noticed he was holding Bryony's hand. As if he needed to know someone was there to help him. It was extremely unlikely that a solitary Earth girl with almost no effective technology and not a clue about the space-time continuum, psychon dynamics or transchronic psychology would be of any help to him in any way. He didn't let go, though. He held on tighter than ever.

BACK AT THE FETCH Spa, David Agnew was disgruntled and tense. He hadn't enjoyed his massage. And when he'd shouted at Brian the masseur, two very strong elbows had been pressed very hard up and down his back in a way that probably wasn't strictly necessary.

He'd taken a shower – which wasn't the right temperature, somehow – and now, as a last resort – he didn't notice the pun – he was going to sit in the hydrotherapy pool. No matter what, a nice dip in the pool never failed to relax him. He attempted to feel content.

Agnew flip-flopped along the relentlessly calming corridor with its tranquilly scented incense burner, its photographs of placid lakes and its carefully positioned speakers softly playing the songs of whales who, if he could have understood them, were actually having a quite heated argument with each other about herring. He despised every simple-minded part of this imposed serenity, but told himself that the idiots and women who were usually in here must find it reassuring. He didn't need this kind of nonsense to help him relax – he just needed to focus on really, properly hating someone and then imagining them being devoured, bit by bit. After he had relaxed, he would run through his plans for the future – the future of everywhere and everything and everyone.

Emerging into the Hydro Room, Agnew came as close as he ever did to happy. He stepped out of his flip-flops and bath robe, revealing his strangely hairy feet and his checked polyester swimming trucks. Soft lights played on the bubbling surface of the large, warm pool – the room was currently green, the next shade would be blue, then red, then there would be a soft and flattering white light and then the coloured filters would cycle round all over again. A nice soak for a couple of cycles would be more than long enough to cheer him up. There was no one else around – no silly wives gossiping and flapping their hands, no morons boasting about their golf scores – there was only the wonder and the glory that was David Agnew, enjoying the presence of none other than David Agnew. Something told him – loud and clear – that he was the jewel at the heart of the universe.

IN HER DELUXE COTTAGE Julia Fetch stopped reading a thrilling article about the way an octopus tastes with its arms. She thought this would be inconvenient for humans, because then everything would taste of blouse. Which would be boring – even though her blouses were of a very fine quality and handmade by Markham & Lancet of Jermyn Street. She decided she was slightly peckish and probably that meant it was time for tea… Or had she taken tea already? It was so hard to tell.

OUT ON THE COURSE, Bryony was riding in the golf cart beside Patterson who was, as a result, practically writhing with joy and at the same time more depressed than he had ever been during a quite remarkably depressing life. She nudged him in the ribs, which meant he discovered a new bruise in one of the few places where he hadn't noticed he was sore, but was also enormously delighted. He stared down at his mangled shoes. They'd had little straps secured across their fronts for no clear purpose by tiny buckles. One of these was now flapping loose. The black plastic of both shoes – once weirdly shiny – was covered in vicious scrapes and something which looked suspiciously like greenish-purplish saliva. But that didn't matter. The being Bryony knew as Ian Patterson gave himself time to be very, very delighted indeed. This would probably be the last time she would want to be anywhere near him, but for now – *being delighted*.

She nudged him again. 'Don't thank me for saving your life, then.'

'But I did, I mean I have, I mean… Didn't I? I thought I thanked you both.' He gulped down a breath. 'I am grateful.' He said this with the tone and facial expression of a person who thought that saving him would always be a terribly bad idea. 'I just…' He took the plunge. 'I'm not called Ian

Patterson. I'm called Putta Pattershaun 5, because I'm the fifth Putta Pattershaun – we were a batch of ten – and I'm... all the others have *done* things, and *invented* things and... I was going to head off into the universe and *achieve*... Only then I met you and... I got distracted... not that meeting you hasn't been an achievement, it's been the best...' He made a noise like a ferret being held underwater and not liking it. 'No, that's not as important as me being from another planet. You should know that. I am. From another planet.' He waited for her to scream. Or hit him. Or call out whatever Earth force dealt with alien threats, possibly by dissecting them and freeze-drying their bits for snacking later.

'Yeah.' She shrugged. 'What I thought. OK.'

'OK!?'

'Yeah.' Bryony had worked this all out already – this or something very like this – because she *wasn't* a complete idiot. She *was* completely certain it was the coolest thing she'd ever heard of. She'd been eight years old when Valentina Tereshkova became the first woman to travel into space and that had seemed wonderful, but the rocket she used to do so had also seemed a bit clunky and somehow *unprofessional*. Likewise, when the Apollo programme had actually put people on the Moon, it had filled her with all kinds of hopes and an amount of embarrassment that the spaceships weren't... *more stylish*. When Bryony was a girl she could think of very few things more amazing than zipping about the solar system in a really well-designed spacecraft. Nevertheless, she was trying to look unimpressed now and managing well, even though she wanted to leap up and down and yell – *A space man, I've met a space man. I am sitting next to a space man. Who will have a spaceship. Maybe with elegant lines and fins and outlandish equipment... I know a space man. I fancy a space man. And I think he fancies me. Take that, Mangold.*

Take that, Cardinal Richelieu. She shrugged again, nonchalant. 'And…?' She wanted to seem like a sophisticated woman of the galaxy and also needed to appear stern, because she didn't like being lied to, or having things hidden from her by a potential boyfriend.

'And?!? I don't… that is…' The golf cart juddered slightly less than Putta, but only slightly.

Potential boyfriend? Where did that come from? Bryony tried not to look happy, or surprised, or whatever it was that she was starting to feel – she wasn't quite clear right now but, whatever the feeling was, it felt pleasant. 'Yes. And…?' Thinking of Patterson, or Putta or whoever he was as a boyfriend suddenly made Bryony realise she ought to consider him in more detail… He was cute. In a mangled way. And he seemed scared of her, which could be fun. And maybe the solution to having found Earth men so disappointing was to choose someone from well outside the neighbourhood. She realised that Putta was staring at her with a kind of adoring horror.

Putta waved his hands despairingly, 'And… you're an Earth person, a human being, and human beings are famous all over the… well, you would call it the Pisces-Cetus Supercluster Complex – famous for being…' He sighed and then blurted out, 'You kill everything you don't understand and then sometimes you eat it. You don't even like people from other continents on your own planet, you…' He faltered, while the Doctor chuckled audibly.

The Doctor was strolling easily next to the cart, covering the ground in that particularly light-footed, long-striding, tiptoeing way he had. 'They also have very promising features. And there's always evolution. They could improve endlessly. Almost endlessly.' The Doctor's large eyes shone benevolently. 'If the blacktip sharks and fruit flies don't get there first.'

But Putta wasn't paying any attention to the Doctor; he was meeting Bryony's eyes and blushing. 'I'm so sorry. I didn't intend to be rude about you.'

'Not just rude about me, rude about my entire species… that's a first.'

'Sorry.' Putta squirmed visibly.

'Then next time maybe mention that we do…' Bryony tried to think of anything human beings were good at. The 1970s hadn't been inspiring so far – starvation in Biafra, nuclear testing, terrorist attacks and hijackings, Nixon being Nixon – they'd cancelled the Apollo missions… At least the war in Vietnam was over, but things in Cambodia didn't look good… 'We do make a lovely shepherd's pie. For example. Sometimes. Some of us. By which I mean we kill things we don't understand and put them into pies… I don't mean we would make good pies by being put into them as a filling, although I suppose we could… by a superior alien race…' While Putta desperately tried not to look superior and absolutely managed, Bryony grinned, 'We are a bit disappointing… And shepherd's pie isn't even a pie – no pastry. And it doesn't contain any shepherds.' She nudged him on an especially tender bruise. 'You're from outer space. How great is that? That's just…' And she thought about kissing him, but then reconsidered and acted cool again.

'While I am glad that we're all friends…' The Doctor leaned in under the golf cart's gaily striped canopy as they progressed across the turf and fixed Putta with an icy look. 'Apart from the multiple treaties and byelaws you're transgressing… Explain yourself, young Putta. What are you doing here so far from Yinzill? It is Yinzill, isn't it? Your home world? Yinzill in the Ochre Period?'

Bryony interrupted. 'Never mind that – what happened to him?'

'Which is also a good question,' the Doctor admitted.

Bryony continued. 'And what happened to the bunker? I'm not a big fan of golf, but I do know bunkers aren't supposed to reach up and grab people's feet. Or Yinzillites' feet.'

Putta was, of course, aware that the proper word for a being from Yinzill was a *Yakt*, but thought it was sweet of her to make the effort and didn't like to correct her in case she punched him. She seemed to be a very physical kind of Earth person and was quite possibly stronger than he was.

'Well?' And she was glowering at him in expectation of an answer.

Putta tried to organise his information in a logical stream. 'Well, I… that is… my family… several of the other Puttas have done very well as… I mean…' He sort of knew this wasn't going to go well. 'I am a bountykiller.'

'*Wha-at!*?' The Doctor made the word sound much longer and more threatening than usual and suddenly looked completely furious. 'Barging round the universe, collecting trophies for ultra-millionaires? Making the shells of barber sylphs into finger bowls…!?'

'But I never—'

'You criticise human beings and you're throwing stun canisters into bandan nests!? *Of all the idiotic…!?*'

'I haven't… I like bandans… And sylphs… We only target predator species.'

The Doctor's whole frame was bristling with outrage and suddenly he didn't look at all like an amiable fool, more like a formidable enemy of injustice and wasteful harm. 'And who decides which species is a predator? You?! You think you have the right?!'

'There's a list…' Putta scrabbled in his inside pocket, then in each of his pockets, with increasing levels of despair. 'They give us a list.' He couldn't find the list. It was gone, along with his fusion lance. (His lance not-very-cunningly disguised as a golf club, given that he couldn't play golf – he'd somehow put his real name in the Form section of the formatting instructions of the synthesiser unit and ended up with a putter…) And he no longer had his Model G50 Threat Detector, which had started leaking psy fluid after he dropped it on a hard surface – which you weren't supposed to – so he'd had to throw it away before it dissolved his control panel. If psy fluid's psychons weren't taken up rapidly enough, by enough minds, or suitable devices, they could turn corrosive… Plus, it had given him (because his mind had provided an amount of take-up and got quite a big dose) this incredible feeling of soul-clenching and ultimate doom, it was appalling stuff, psy fluid…

The Doctor raged on. 'Is *she* a predator?!' He pointed at Bryony who couldn't help being slightly alarmed. She'd never seen him like this. 'Is everyone who eats shepherd's pie a predator?! Shouldn't they be!'

'I don't… I'm not sure… That is, I've never…'

'So many lives, so delicately balanced, so close to the abyss, so full of hope, and some greedy squad of imbeciles classifies them as a predator, as a resource, and you and your kind of destructive idiots come along and harvest them until they're gone.' The Doctor looked both furious and implacably sad.

He seemed so alone in his grief that Bryony touched his arm. 'I don't think he meant any harm.'

'His kind never mean any harm – they still do it!' The Doctor stopped himself, quietened. 'Very few species truly understand that actions have consequences. When you destroy something, that isn't an isolated act.' And for a second or so he looked like someone who had understood far too many consequences and who had been made very tired by that. Then he patted Bryony's shoulder. 'Our lives are connected. And other lives are connected to those lives and on and on. We are even connected… to Putta Pattershaun 5.' He glowered at Putta.

Putta responded with an apologetic babble. 'I thought it would be a good idea, I mean I don't like it, haven't liked it, haven't done it, not properly… I've never killed anything. I took aim at a Parthian mind wasp and I couldn't fire. And they're terrible. They can eat your whole personality and then lay their eggs in your face. But they have wonderful wings. There were colours in the wings that I'd never seen on any planet… I just couldn't…'

Bryony kept on with what she thought was a promising line of enquiry which would be much more use than additional shouting. 'Patter- Putter, whatever your name is. Never mind all that – what happened to you? Did you do something? Did you bring some alien thing with you that ended up in the bunker? A whatsit, sense wasp? Something else? Or do your people have a problem with sand? Does it usually eat you?'

'Which is what I would have asked. Roughly. What I would have asked if you hadn't kept interrupting,' nodded the Doctor. 'Except for the sand part.'

'Sand? No, we like sand,' Putta bleated miserably. 'Unless it gets into our shoes, or… elsewhere… Oh… I don't know. I thought… My detector, just before it broke, it showed this, this signal that couldn't even have been true, but I landed here to look for – no one has even heard of them, not for millennia, and I didn't expect to find… but then maybe the detector was broken already, giving a false reading before I dropped it… and I was left, anyway, with no more detector, no more signal, no more…' Bryony was glowering at him with such impatience that he gulped and steered himself round to the events of the afternoon. 'There was this man, this human man and I met him in the bar.' Bryony snorted with derision which would have made her seem slightly unattractive to anyone but Putta. He continued. 'The man definitely… he *lured* me into that sandpit. I'd never even seen him before.'

'Did you do something to him?' Bryony asked, with a hurtful level of suspicion.

'You are quite annoying, you know,' confided the Doctor. 'That could rub people up the wrong way. Not to mention your profession. Did you mention your profession – Bountykiller Putta?' He pronounced the last two words as if they were a disease.

'I didn't mention anything,' whined Putta. 'I was being as human as possible and that appears to involve golf and sandpits.'

'Bunkers,' corrected Bryony and then disliked herself for it.

'Bunkers. He was very angry all the time. I mean, so angry I could feel it on my skin somehow…' Putta wrung his hands.

'Can you usually feel other people's mental states?' the Doctor asked sharply. 'And did you have a strange taste in your mouth?'

Putta nodded and looked calmer, as if he now had the resident expert on his side. 'Yes, a funny taste and, no, I can't usually feel… well, my own feelings are a bit of a problem without anyone else's…' He caught sight of Bryony's frown and got back to the main issue. 'The man… I think he knew about the bunker and he got angrier and angrier as he walked me over there and then he made me play golf and got angrier still – only in a nasty, happy kind of way – and then the bunker got angry and then he left as soon as… once it started trying to eat me… he ran away.' He looked a bit sickly as he remembered. 'It grabbed my feet. If I hadn't already got out my fusion lance…' And then he didn't want to finish the sentence.

The Doctor tsked. 'Running around showing off advanced technology to a less developed and very... emotional species...' As if he'd never do such a thing himself. 'You ought to be ashamed.'

'Thank you for saving me.'

'Well, it's all part of a day's work, really, I—' The Doctor broke off when he saw Putta smiling carefully at Bryony and nodding.

Bryony wasn't currently that interested in gratitude. She thought she was on to something. 'If he laid the trap... If Mr Agnew laid the trap, he must know how it operates and what it is. It must be his trap.'

'Yes, you know, if you think about it, whoever laid the trap would understand what it is and be the one to use it,' the Doctor added. In case anyone had forgotten he was a genius. He was already hypothesising about how a telepathic bond would react if it were partially corporeal and suffered pain, because – for example – someone had repeatedly fired a fusion lance at it... if the mild psychic abilities of a sandmaster had been somehow magnified and tamed... and if its governing consciousness had run away and abandoned it while it was injured... A feedback loop in that kind of situation could be extremely bad news for everyone concerned.

Bryony burst in with, 'Then we have to find Agnew!' and looked pleased with herself. 'I mean, shouldn't we?'

Doctor nodded absently, murmuring to himself, 'My tracking skills are a bit rusty. I studied with the Miccosukee people for a while...' He began to stare significantly at the grass. 'It will take great skill...'

'Or we could look in the Spa,' suggested Putta.

'Don't be ridiculous.'

'He mentioned he was going back to the Spa.' Putta blinked. There was a pause.

The Doctor boomed, 'Why on earth didn't you say so?!'

'But you didn't ask.'

'Turn that thing round at once and back to the hotel!'

As Putta and Bryony swung the golf cart unsteadily round to follow the Doctor, the twins trotted swiftly into their path and stood.

Xavier told them, firmly, 'I don't think you should. Grandmother is expecting you.'

'Yes. And you shouldn't disappoint Grandmother.' Honor looked sad, but also very determined. 'She likes tea. A lot.'

The Doctor adopted his most persuasive voice, 'Oh, but we can come back. Yes, we can. Immediately. We have this one thing we must do together by ourselves in the Spa and then we'll be back and then absolutely tea with Grandmother will happen. I look forward to it, I do.' He wondered how a powerful effusion of psychons might affect the malleable minds of children. Probably quite badly.

The twins stared at him and suddenly didn't seem even slightly adorable. Their limbs stiffened and their faces hardened. It was possible to think that they might be dangerous in a fight – very swift and unforgiving.

Bryony found herself thinking they should just abandon the golf cart and run – it would be faster, even with Putta's very probably badly bruised ankles. She also suddenly felt certain the twins would turn out to be much faster than anyone else running and that their speed might not be a comforting or unthreatening thing.

'It isn't four o'clock yet, you know. And four o'clock is tea time,' the Doctor wheedled. He very carefully pretended to be someone who didn't feel scared in any way. 'We all promise we'll be back by four. If you wait for us. We'll follow the signs to the cottage, you won't need to show us the way. And then we'll have fun, which I always enjoy, there's nothing as much fun as fun, I find. Don't you find?' He wagged his hands and shrugged like someone who wasn't rapidly calculating and puzzling and trying to get back to the hotel *fast* and to work out the twins' real nature, while soothing them with unstoppable courtesy. Soothing with unstoppable courtesy often worked on most planets. It was one of the many reasons why the Doctor didn't carry a gun.

And then, as if the sun had come out – or as if they had finished their own calculations – the twins giggled and stood aside and Honor said, 'Yes, we'll see you later, then. That will be terribly nice. And fun.'

And Xavier patted Bryony on her arm and said, 'Good luck, old girl.'

This felt just a little bit creepy, so Bryony put her foot down and the cart zoomed – in as far as it could zoom – back towards the Spa with the Doctor loping alongside as though what he loved most in the whole universe was rushing towards dangerous situations without having a proper plan. Or any plan at all.

THE THREE ARRIVED AT the Fetch Hotel to see that the foyer was full of dissatisfied guests. Mr Mangold was just saying, 'I am doing my best, sir. Miss Mailer, my receptionist, has disappeared…' So he didn't call her Junior when she wasn't around, Bryony noted as she hurried past, shouting, 'Guest emergency! Can't stop!'

By the time they'd reached the Spa section, they had all realised that they certainly did look in need of relaxation and therapy. At the very least. Putta was covered in sand, grass, mud, vapour stains, fissile backwash and a tangible layer of anxiety. In places his suit looked as if something had recently tried to eat it, because something had. Bryony's own business suit had several small rips in it and was grass-stained, her tights were ruined, and her name badge was missing, along with her shoes, she now noticed – she'd taken them off when she helped wrestle Putta out of the pit. Or bunker. And her hair was alarming. The Doctor – he looked like the Doctor, which was always vaguely alarming to people like the Spa Manageress (who habitually patronised Bryony, because of her poor skincare, obvious split ends and Junior status).

'Can I help you?' There was a blatant sneer in the question.

The Doctor paced up to the Spa Welcome Desk like a jolly tiger in a maroon jacket. 'Indeed you can. How splendid that you're here. Just who we need.' He smiled in a way that made Byrony's gums tingle and made her wonder if his smiling was, in fact some kind of alien martial art. The Doctor continued: 'I was told you'd be entirely helpful by the people at the head office. They said to me – it won't matter if you turn up looking as if you've landed from outer space, you'll get a perfect welcome at the Fetch Brother's Spa.' He beamed again. 'Why look – you even have a Welcome Desk.'

'Head office?' The Manageress was wary, but deeply susceptible to flattery. Given that she was quite unpleasant to most people, she was very rarely flattered, despite her flawless complexion. 'We don't have a head office.'

'Oh, no. I meant *my* head office. The head office of the esteemed publication Elite Spas & Homes Away From Home.'

'I've never heard of it.'

'Oh, but you will.' And a last, extraordinary grin was unleashed.

The Manageress crumbled, her resistance transformed into a disturbing blend of fawning, flirtation and girlishness. She gladly showed the Doctor that day's register to prove how busy and efficient she was… David Agnew's signature was there. He'd definitely signed in…

The Manageress then insisted on giving each of them gift bags and free swimming costumes. It took all Bryony's powers of persuasion to get them into the Spa without having to accept a guided tour, free sauna and beating with twigs.

FAR ACROSS THE FETCH Estate, the golf cart had been parked neatly in its charging bay behind Julia Fetch's cottage. The twins were standing near it. Slowly, Honor pressed the palms of her hands against Xavier's and he pressed back.

Honor asked Xavier, 'Shall we go and speak to Grandmother?'

And Xavier told Honor, 'No. Let's not. Not yet. Let's do this instead.'

So they stood and pressed their hands together while the birds sang and little breezes pushed about amongst the rose bushes in Julia Fetch's garden.

THE DOCTOR AND HIS companions rendezvoused in the Tranquillity Lounge, which instantly became less tranquil. In fact, its two occupants – sisters Sylvia and Rosemary Hindle from High Wycombe – decided they might just head off somewhere else. Right away. As several firmly worded signs said they must when in the Therapy Areas, Putta and Bryony wore their new, slightly ill-fitting, swimming costumes, Fetch Spa-issue flip-flops and bathrobes. Putta was absolutely certain that he was never taking his bathrobe off, not even if it killed him. Bryony was never going to see him in swimming trunks. It was bad enough that his gingery-haired shins and monster-bitten ankles were so horribly visible.

The Doctor had managed to pass through the changing rooms without changing a bit – apart from having folded his hat into his jacket pocket and having donned a gift bag shower cap instead. His hair was fighting the shower cap. And winning.

'Now stay with me.' It was very hard to take him seriously in the cap. 'I mean it. No good will come from our splitting up and I can't be everywhere and…' His sentence trailed off and he seemed to become unfocused for a few breaths. But then he stalked off with immense energy, and they began their hunt for Agnew.

The woody heat of the sauna, the foggy depths of the Turkish baths, the bad-tempered massage rooms, even the towel cupboard were searched before they all – staying together, just as the Doctor had said they must – walked along the corridor to the Hydro Room.

As he pressed on, the Doctor felt that metallic taste in his mouth again and began to think that having a plan at this point might have been a good idea. There was something dreadfully uninviting about the warm, thick, damp air slowly oozing along from the pool. And wouldn't it maybe have been safer to split up, to let his companions wander off and not run the same risks as he was about to?

The Hydro Room lighting was on the red part of its cycle and the wide, round pool was bubbling and seething dramatically. Agnew was lolling back in it as if he was having the time of his life – eyes closed and a slight smile on his lips.

The Doctor understood at once that many things were terrifyingly wrong and he regretted absolutely having brought the others with him. He said, very quietly, 'Perhaps you two should go outside.' His head throbbed and his ears seemed filled with the roiling of the pool waters. His tongue and lips tasted coppery.

Putta stared at the red, restless liquid and at Agnew. And he was annoyed. Really as annoyed as he'd ever allowed himself to be. 'It's no use pretending to be asleep!' he shouted. 'You left me out there. With that thing! Now what is it?! Tell us what it is! Tell us what you are!'

The Doctor said, even more quietly, 'He can't tell us.'

'Of course he can!' Putta was enjoying being angry. Other people had always been angry with him and this time it was going to be his turn. Being furious was quite exhilarating and he realised now why it was so consistently popular across the universe. 'You! Wake up!' He leaned right over the edge of the pool and shouted with all his might across the water to Agnew. 'Wake up!'

Which was when the colour of the lights changed to a soft and flattering white, and yet the water and Agnew's face were still thickly red, and patches of damp on the floor were also red, and Bryony felt sick and then she *was* sick, and the Doctor seemed to be walking over to comfort her, but then he cried out, holding his head and dropping to the red-spattered tiles, kneeling and rocking, apparently in torment.

As Bryony rushed to him, she heard Putta call, 'Bryony! Bryony! Get out! Leave us! Bryony! Run!'

And when she looked up she saw the thin, funny, little man called Putta try to rush away from the pool, but what looked like ropes, like purple-red muscular ropes, were undulating and rushing out of the water and they caught at the hem of his red-stained bathrobe, snaked into its loose sleeves and wrapped around him, dragging him slithering and fighting back towards the water.

Bryony met his eyes and thought that he was a very brave man, or being, or whatever, and a good one and that it was a shame he'd never realise it. She thought he would have liked himself more if he had.

The Doctor yelled to her, 'It's a feedback loop – the pain drove it back here. Get out now! With no mind to control it, the creature will devour everything it can find! I should have known! Quickly! It doesn't know what else to do!'

And then a huge thought swept through him again.

BLOOD.

He'd led them all into the same trap that had just turned on Agnew, its creator.

'Run!'

Bryony wavered, as the Doctor convulsed and Putta battled the swift, repulsive arms swarming around him.

75

Clearly it would be sensible to run… She paused for a breath.

'Go!' Putta was fighting desperately to get out of the bathrobe that might very well kill him, as the pulsing tentacles slithered over his body, scraping his skin like gluey sand as they went. 'Please!'

But Bryony couldn't run.

'It was feeding on his rage!' The Doctor, was holding his head in both hands. 'I can feel it… this… fury… magnifying. It's so angry… so… scared…'

BLOOD.

'Then don't be furious! And don't be scared!' Bryony was yelling herself now. 'Relax!' Putta looked at her in utter bewilderment. 'Relax, Putta. Trust me. You can trust me can't you, you stupid space man!'

And she said this with such affection that Putta did relax. The arms immediately drew him right against the low wall that contained the pool, knocking the breath out of him, but then they too relaxed slightly. They seemed indecisive. The ends of a few tentacles twitched, shivered.

'Pat them!'

'What!?' Putta looked at her as if she was insane.

But the Doctor, still pale and wincing, nodded. 'Yes. Of course! Of course! The field is still operational. It will magnify whatever we feel.' He focused on thinking clearly, gently, willed the agony in his skull to retreat a little. 'If we can't dissipate it, we can change its orientation and bring it back under control. Well done, Bryony. Well done.' He trembled, frowned, but also managed to nod encouragingly. 'You're terribly good at this.'

'Then let's blooming well get on with it!' Bryony yelled again.

Putta just stared, locked with fear. He was in danger of quite literally terrifying himself to death. The Doctor knew that if Putta made the creature too frightened, in its wounded and sensitised state, it would defend itself – by killing Putta.

And he wasn't being soothed and anaesthetised first.

The Doctor tried to help. 'Imagine it's a big… like a giant…'

BBBBB…

He tried to imagine something huge but loveable with lots of arms and couldn't bring anything to mind apart from an immense and fluffy tarantula – which very few beings would find that adorable – so he just suggested, 'Tickle it. Go on, Putta. Tickle it.'

Bbbb…

Putta reached out tentatively – in as far as he could while the tentacles were tight round him – and patted and then did tickle the muscular bond fastening his other arm to his side. He was wrapped in an immense, clammy strength, but it was no longer contracting. It no longer felt quite as horrifying. He tickled some more. He patted the flesh he'd been trying to keep away from his throat.

'That's it.' Bryony nodded. 'It's working. At least, it's stopped.'

'Of course it's working!' The Doctor was still clearly in pain, but looked less grey. 'And we have to… we have to think calmly, we have to be friendly towards it. We have to like it. I think. If we…' He broke off for a few seconds as his headache peaked. 'Yes… We need to be very, very fond of it indeed. We need to love it.'

'Are you out of your mind!?'

'Just do it, Putta!' both Bryony and the Doctor bellowed. So he tried.

Aaabbb…

Bryony concentrated on attempting to find anything endearing about the heaving red and purple mass which had almost overwhelmed Putta. As she did so, the creature seemed to shudder and lose definition. Putta started to be able to gasp in complete breaths – much to his relief – and could move a little more.

As soon as he did move, the beast tightened around him again, but he tried not to panic, tried to let his limbs flop, relax, relax, relax, and to encourage the grating, sliding pressure to release again. It made his skin crawl. Which was because it was crawling over his skin. But that was fine. If it would just let him go that would be fine. Even if it simply didn't eat him, but kept a hold of him for the rest of his life and he just had to get used to wearing some kind of immense purplish slime and grit monster that would be fine… it would all be fine… he could be calm…

The Doctor filled his consciousness with the faces of all the companions he had enjoyed knowing – their faces and the times when they had helped him, the times when they had been amazed by the universe along with him. He thought about the universe: the light-producing microbes that danced on the walls of the Delling Caves, the Great Library, the Song Towers of Und, the unlikeliness of life existing anywhere in the first place and yet the way it blossomed and flourished and celebrated itself and was so beautiful.

A
A
a
a
b
c
d

And finally Putta found himself dumped onto the floor as the creature trapping him retreated across his skin. Its withdrawal was rapid, and immediately after it a dreadful gurgling and thrashing came from the jacuzzi behind him. Then what was left of the beast simply collapsed into sand, warm sand, warm wet clinging sand and a kind of rush of dissipating motion. The bloodstains slowly faded into the grains scattered all over the floor, dyeing them for a moment, before the colour disappeared and there was nothing left but... sand.

Putta looked up at the two beings he would most want to nearly be killed with – if he had to be nearly killed – as they came cautiously towards him. His bathrobe was several feet away, partly obscured by a sand drift – which meant that Bryony had seen him in his trunks. And being nearly crushed to death. And covered in slime. And sand. Which was also inside his swimming trunks. Oh, but things could be so much worse. They really could. Putta glanced flinchingly round at the pool – the creature had taken what was left of Agnew with it before... Putta didn't know what had happened... Did it lose its grip on that part of itself that was sand...? Did it absorb – horrible thought – Agnew before dying...? Or... Putta was too stunned and relieved and suddenly, deeply exhausted to think clearly.

The Doctor set out his arm to keep Bryony back from any remaining danger and advanced slowly, but with an increasingly enormous smile. 'Not so tricky, really once the problem was fully understood.' He kicked gently at the sand heaped around Putta. 'I had my suspicions, naturally.' And he frowned at the pool – even the blood had been removed from the water, by the hungry creature before it apparently imploded. Although it was far more sandy than would have been usual in an award-winning Elite Spa or a Home Away From Home.

Bryony, punched his arm. 'Your suspicions...'

'Naturally.' He winked. 'And we would undoubtedly all be dead without you. It was incredibly prescient of me to have chosen you. A sign of true genius.'

'I beg your pardon.' Bryony couldn't help smiling, too. '*You* chose *me*?'

'I just said that. Do keep up.' The Doctor grinned.

BACK AT JULIA FETCH'S cottage, the twins were still leaning against each other, palm to palm with arms outstretched.

Slowly their hands melted and melded and reformed, looking for a while like a reddish pink ball of dense fluid, caught spinning and writhing at the ends of their arms. Their enchanting faces blurred and their eyes blinked unnaturally open as their eyelids appeared to retract completely.

There seemed to be a vibration in the air around them and, had anyone been looking at them, it would have been difficult to see them clearly. Even the grass around their feet became almost liquid. Reality itself seemed willing to melt and pour away.

But then – slowly, delicately, the grass blades solidified, the air stopped shimmering and the twins' faces became suddenly very clear, peaceful, loveable and their hands became only the usual kinds of hands, with the usual kinds of fingers. Everything, everywhere seemed to be held in suspension – as if the universe was a sleeping cat, just about to stretch, but not yet – and if Julia had looked out of her window, she would have noticed that the area around the cottage seemed impossibly bright and perfectly formed.

And then Honor and Xavier – slightly as if they had been dreaming for a while – shook their heads and laughed, and the universe stretched and settled back into place, and they shouted together, 'Tea! Tea! It must be time for tea!' and scampered towards the cottage door.

THE DOCTOR HAD THOUGHT it best to lead his two companions out of the Spa through the fire exit. None of them remotely resembled individuals who had been through a sublimely tranquil and restorative experience of balanced wholeness. They looked if they been buried at sea. In a whale. And that might have alarmed Miss Pitcairn, the Spa Manageress. Who would eventually discover the scene of horror they were leaving behind. The Doctor found that leaving behind scenes of horror was usually wise, particularly if you might be likely to get an unfair amount of the blame for them.

Their unconventional route out – which hadn't passed the changing rooms – meant that Putta now had to cope with being outdoors in a sand- and slime-covered bathrobe (without flip-flops) in the presence of Bryony. Who had saved his life. Again. He was unsure about whether he wanted to burst into song, or make a break for his Type F378a Abrischooner, fire up the engines and never be seen again. At least he had discovered that it wasn't actually possible to die of shame. Which, in a day of hideous shocks, had still come as something of a surprise.

Bryony herself was sporting a marginally less grubby bathrobe. She was, Putta thought, looking quite graceful as they set off back towards the golf course. Trotting barefoot next to the Doctor, she peppered him with questions. Putta had never seen anyone trot barefoot more beautifully. Actually, he'd never seen anyone trot barefoot – but that didn't make her any less monumentally lovely.

Lovely and frustrated. 'But I don't understand—'

The Doctor interrupted. 'Naturally, you don't. You have no experience of what would happen if a completely reckless interplanetary vandal managed both to spill psy fluid on a planet where it didn't belong and accidentally introduce a sandmaster larva to a perfect environment to hyper-accelerate its developmental cycle. Sandmasters often co-exist with Parthian mind wasps – in the sense of spending part of their larval stage eating the wasps' brains from the inside out. *Beings who shall remain nameless should remember to decontaminate their hulls before they make planetfall… You…*' he growled at Putta as if he was only letting him remain nameless because he couldn't bear to pronounce his name and shot him a glance that made him huddle deeper into his oversized, but tattered robe. 'You, *Putta*, came much closer to wiping out every life form on Earth than anyone should on their first visit. Or on any visit. Do you intend to destroy *every* civilisation you encounter?' He continued to glare and then seemed to find further scolding impossible and lapsed back into explaining how cleverly he had worked things out, despite being subjected to a massive psychon dose.

'I had the largest available consciousness, you see… So it attacked me the most.'

'But where has it gone?! Where's the monster?' Bryony still wasn't satisfied and she didn't think this was because she hadn't got enough experience of whatever sandmasters were. She thought it was most likely because the Doctor was extremely bad at explaining.

He hadn't, for example, explained what planet he was from – even though it clearly wasn't Earth. And she didn't quite like to ask – somehow the idea of enquiring made her feel shy, or else nervous. *But it would have been useful,* she thought, *if he'd said, 'Hello, I'm the Doctor.' And then not forgotten to add, 'And I'm from some really strange other planet and quite possibly have an amazing spaceship somewhere hereabouts which you should take a look at and, by the way, I know how to deal with monsters – just about – so don't worry too much if one turns up.* That kind of information could save other people a good deal of stress. She looked over at him and thought, *He's used to monsters, though. He takes them for granted. He's almost happy to see them.* And something about that – about living a life which assumed there would always be monsters – made her feel chilly, even though it was a lovely day and the mature trees around the golf course looked magnificent and very normal and the birds were singing just as they had yesterday, before everything changed.

She tried to keep on chatting and suppressed the thought that – now that the major panic in the Spa was over – she felt slightly more like screaming than she had at the time. 'One minute, it's eating everyone it can get a hold of and the next it's a heap of muck. Which there will be complaints about. And… oh, Lord…' Bryony couldn't help remembering the body in the pool – Agnew's ghastly, bloodless face above the bubbling, crimson water… she felt clammy and bewildered, and the Doctor put his arm around her to keep her steady.

He gently distracted her with information, albeit not quite the information she wanted. 'The sandmaster's life cycle was advancing so rapidly that, while it was highly aggressive, it probably only had a few hours left before it would either join a mating stream – which it couldn't because we'd surely know if there was more than one around here – that would involve a positively huge table reserved for two with massive romantic candles and…' He was attempting to cheer her up with nonsense and checked her expression to see how he was doing before he went on. 'Or… well, beyond that instar, that developmental stage… well, they tend to either explode, or dissolve. We seemed to speed up its decomposition—'

'Explode! You didn't tell us that it might explode!'

'Would you have been happier if I had?'

'No, but—'

'Then I made a terribly wise decision by not mentioning it. And they don't *often* explode. Then again, they don't often come into contact with psy fluid and have their psychic abilities massively magnified so that they can control matter, interfere with minds…' The Doctor made a noise somewhere between a snarl and a sigh.

Putta winced, expecting to be shouted at again. But instead he felt the strong and heavy thump of the Doctor's free arm hugging his bruised shoulders. 'Putta. Let's go and have tea. Don't you think that would be a good idea? Tea, anyone?'

'Oh, well…' Putta gulped and felt mildly tearful. 'Um, tea. I think I've had that before. It was nice. It didn't try to kill me.'

And Bryony found herself making the decision unanimous. 'Tea.' Because tea might be what you should have after vanquishing an alien, emotionally sensitive carnivorous golf bunker monster. As far as she could tell.

'Yes. The cottage is this way, isn't it?' The Doctor released them both and paced languidly ahead across the grass, accompanied by his scarf.

But then he stopped, turned. 'By the way, Bryony. Thank you so much for saving my life.' And he looked at her, his eyes quickly serious, frighteningly intelligent, a quality in them that seemed to *know* her right down to her bare feet. 'I would have been completely done for without you.' Then he rubbed his face and looked more playful, seemed to be waiting for a compliment.

Bryony duly delivered one. 'Well, but you were the expert.'

'Yes, I was, wasn't I?' The Doctor nodded without a trace of modesty. 'I almost always am.' And he unleashed a startlingly huge smile.

'As long as the thing's gone…'

'Oh, I'm sure it is.' He footled in the grass with the toe of one battered shoe. 'Either that or I'm completely wrong and we're all still in horrible and increasing danger.' He chuckled and dodged from foot to foot, and once again Bryony had a feeling that the universe could be a cold and dark and terrible place if you weren't ready for it. She didn't feel ready at all. But then again – it did also seem more exciting and marvellous than anything she'd ever dreamed of.

'Doctor?'

'Yes. I do.'

'You do what?'

'I do travel in a thoroughly remarkable vessel. She's amazing in every way.' He winked. 'In case you were wondering… I borrowed her. Or she borrowed me. You might say we ran away together… Oh, it must be a good few hundred years ago, now…'

At which point Bryony realised that the Doctor's explanations were never going to be quite as helpful as she hoped. He winked at her.

'Well…' Bryony repressed a huge desire to just blurt out – *can I go and see it now, now, now?* She felt that she should give him the impression that earth people couldn't be impressed by just any passing space traveller.

The Doctor studied her carefully and seemed about to speak, but then turned and headed off again blithely, calling over his shoulder, 'You didn't do so badly either, Putta. There may be hope for you yet.' His long form loped over the grass as if he liked nothing better than walking across smallish, wettish, concretey, leafy and occasionally sandy planets full of promising people with tea and perhaps cake at the end of his journey. Tea and cake or horrible and increasing danger. Either one would be lovely.

AT ROUGHLY THAT SAME moment the Doctor was thinking tea would be lovely and also realising he was feeling a bit hungry, Mrs Agnes Findlater was pottering beside the Arbroath seafront, a few miles north west from the Fetch Brothers Golf Spa Hotel. She was heading along the West Links and away from the slowly declining old Miniature Railway station. A light summer breeze gently tousled the wave tops out to sea, and the afternoon light was sparking off the water in a way that did her heart good. These days, she was feeling her age a wee bitty and it was especially cheering to be outdoors and enjoying a nice day and a breath or two of salty air.

She was just remembering how much fun she used to have on what was then the fairly new tiny railway. While she'd been raising her children, she'd been able to take them to visit it in its huffing and steaming prime with queues and crowds gathering to climb aboard for trips up the little line. Tasty snacks had been on offer along with the sort of fun which seemed to have faded away at around about the same time gentlemen stopped wearing spats. Although she couldn't honestly say she'd ever seen that many gentlemen wearing spats during her life, there was something about them which suggested *fun*.

Agnes thought that today she would go as far as the

point where Elliot Water ran into the North Sea and then head home for a pancake and jam, maybe even two. She did seem to be feeling extremely peckish.

And this was when a number of unusual things happened.

Firstly, when Agnes – or Mrs Findlater, as she preferred to be known – glanced over at Mr Gillespie, who was walking his dog in the distance, she felt absolutely sure that he too was thinking about the model railway and long-ago summers.

Secondly, she was just as absolutely sure – while his dog leaped and barked about his ankles in some kind of alarm – that Mr Gillespie was also thinking about her thinking about the railway and about pancakes. There was this kind of terrible *echo* inside her head. It was making her feel seasick. She also had a terrible taste of pennies in her mouth.

Thirdly, the echo was getting worse and now seemed to additionally involve what were surely the very disorganised and slovenly thoughts of the two young men in overly tight jeans with ridiculous flares who were kicking about over there in the surf and – now that she looked more closely – falling over and shouting while holding their heads. Young people today simply didn't know how to behave.

Fourthly, Agnes observed – and she was an observant woman, as any of her neighbours would have stated with enthusiasm, had anyone asked – that the shoreline closest to where she was standing was… well, she didn't like to use this kind of word, but it was *writhing*. And while it was writhing it was also *thrusting* upwards and outwards with these really quite disgusting-looking growths, like living branches, or thick whips, or other things she didn't wish to consider. They were moving very quickly – and even hungrily – towards her.

Fifthly, Mrs Agnes Findlater of Heather View, North Port,

Arbroath, disappeared entirely in a swirl of sandy light, muscular goo and violent motion. And a brief glimmer from the metal clasp of an imitation crocodile skin handbag.

'It was as if the ground just swallowed her up,' Bobby Christie would say to a reporter for the *Dundee Courier and Advertiser* that evening. Bobby was one of the young men who had been harmlessly hanging about on the beach near Agnes and had seen some of the incident in the small spasms of clarity during which he wasn't experiencing the worst headache of his life and getting seawater in his eyes because of rolling about in the surf, helpless with pain. He regretted at once not adding 'man…' at the end of his statement and regretted this even more when his friend, Callum Smith, remembered to say both 'man…' and 'you know what I mean, yeah…?' Smith would therefore have made himself appear almost impossibly suave and sophisticated around the town for several weeks if his statement had ever appeared in the paper. Of course, it didn't and this meant that no one ever got to appreciate his attempts to sound like a soon-to-be bass player in a soon-to-be popular band with a soon-to-be catalogue of amazing progressive rock hits.

The sixth unusual thing involved the Northern Zone Regional War Room. This was a vast and beautifully air-conditioned, radiation- and blast-proof bunker, its entrance carefully camouflaged as an innocent-looking cottage near Creif. Inside the bunker, a number of members of the Civil Defence Corps experienced what they mainly described as *a weird feeling*. Their delicately calibrated instruments, ever-watchful for signs of nuclear attack and other dire perils, didn't pick up any trace of unusual activity, but nevertheless – they all *felt weird*. For several long and queasy minutes, being tucked away beneath three metres of tungsten-reinforced concrete, steel beams and nifty brickwork didn't feel like any kind of protection at all.

Seventhly, Mr Gillespie left his dog with his sister in Carnoustie at round 7 p.m. and then went quietly home, ate an entire loaf's worth of toasted cheese and then went to bed for a week. Mr Gillespie was generally agreed to be a sensible man.

'GOOD LORD, I AM really, one could say… just slightly…' The Doctor didn't look like a remotely sensible man. His long legs were stretched out ahead of him, lazily crossed and filling Julia Fetch's parlour rather more than seemed reasonable. He was still sandy and grassy here and there, and the knees of his trousers were heavily stained. His hair was responding to indoor air by being particularly active, as if it was trying to hide him from something, and he had to keep swiping it back from his face. And every time he waved his arms – and he didn't seem able to speak without a good deal of arm waving – it seemed inevitable that he would wallop one or other of the exquisite glass figurines that balanced on every available surface. As these were all models of octopuses (or octopodes) and therefore masses of ingeniously sculpted and fragile legs, both Bryony and Putta were flinching roughly every four seconds in expectation of terrible breakages. They were both more than slightly aware that they weren't looking quite their best.

Mrs Fetch hadn't been at all fazed by the appearance of a gangly, grinning man with wild hair and wilder eyes, a more than slightly tattered (and probably fired) receptionist and a slightly chewed (and wholly in love) ginger young fellow, both in bathrobes. She had simply led Bryony into a pristine guest room and left her to pick out – as it happened – a cashmere sweater and tweed suit, cut according to what was once called the New Look. Bryony was not very secretly pleased with how good she looked in this, even if the arrangements she'd had to make for underwear were slightly dated and complex and the only shoes she'd been able to get her feet into were a pair of galoshes which didn't quite complete the ensemble with the flair she'd hoped for.

She still took Putta's breath away when she emerged looking brushed and fresh and almost sand-free.

Putta himself was rather more eye-catching. He'd simply been supplied with an ancient, rather mothy pair of plus fours, left over by a long-gone acquaintance, some extensive socks, heavy golf shoes which were rather too large and a shirt, an Argyll tank top and good, stout tweed jacket with leather elbow patches.

Putta hadn't been at all sure – after Mrs Fetch left him alone in the kitchen to get changed – that his new outfit would impress Bryony and the fact that, once she'd reappeared, she snorted into her tea every time she glanced at him tended to make him think that trousers should probably always go all the way down your legs if you were going to look sensible in front of people you wanted to impress.

Just my luck, thought Bryony. *The one chance I get to meet my reclusive boss and all I do is prove that I know some very weird people. And end up borrowing her underpants and – for goodness' sake – the girdle that's supporting my stockings which I actually think are silk… Good lord, I can't even look at Putta – I'll start laughing and then not be able to stop. Then again, I'm hardly in much better shape. I suppose she'll assume I generally look as if I've been battling monsters all morning and wander about in a bathrobe.*

Bryony also pondered whether it had been an entirely happy coincidence that a thought-sensitive monster had ended up living in the grounds of a hotel owned by someone who was clearly obsessed with octopodes. Maybe that had made the thing become more like an octopus – even if it hadn't started out that way. Bryony was aware that she had no idea if the usual kinds of thought-sensitive monsters looked like octopodes. (Or octopuses – Mrs Fetch had explained that they could be called either thing and that both were correct. She was very nice, but seemed really firm on the point that anything to do with octopuses should be correct.) Bryony thought again of the tentacles snaking round Putta – of the body that had been in the pool – and found that she didn't want her nice ginger biscuit, or indeed her pleasant cup of tea, served in a cup and saucer that were so fine she was worried they might just crumple up while she held them.

The Doctor was being much less careful – of course – and was showing no curiosity about sea creatures. He was talking about food, reaching for food, asking for extra food, or cramming food gleefully into his mouth while still trying to discuss it. He was like a very tall toddler in a sweet shop. 'Mildly hungry….' He inhaled a small stack of elegantly crustless cucumber sandwiches and reached out for his sixth scone. 'Not exactly starving… Not far off, though.'

Out in the little garden, Honor and Xavier were playing catch between the rosebushes and managing to look like any number of greetings cards depicting delightful children having lots and lots of Summery fun. While Bryony watched, Xavier leaped up and snatched a Frisbee out of the air with remarkable agility and speed. Just then, both twins paused and span round to look in through the windows. Something about their warm smiles and slowly extending arms seemed impossible to resist.

'Ah, Doctor… Maybe we should give you a bit more room,' suggested Bryony.

'Yes.' Putta was on his feet before her. He seemed equally keen to get outside and enjoy himself with this strange Earth disk-throwing game. To be honest, the combination of Bryony looking and sounding like Bryony and the snug fit of her new suit (and even the rubber boot thingies she was wearing were terrific) all in close proximity to so many tiny ornaments that he could break if he got nervous or overexcited was making him feel hysterical – as was the tickling of the odd, heavy tweed of his plus fours. 'We should let you get on with eating everything else, Doctor.' He realised this sounded quite rude after he'd said it – and braced himself to endure a spot of shouting, or the usual kind of complaint about insensitivity and being a waste of breathable gasses that he'd always get from his broodfather or his brothers. But the Doctor just nodded his sugar-and-cream-daubed face and waved goodbye.

JULIA FETCH, QUIETLY DRESSED in immaculate tweeds and a cashmere cardigan, smiled benevolently at her guest. This was almost exactly the kind of tea she wanted to have every day and maybe she did. There were times when previous teas seemed so far away they might never have happened. On other days – or maybe just today – she was completely convinced that lovely gatherings of friends happened all the time. And sometimes they had just finished swimming and needed a change of togs – it was good to have chaps about the place in familiar clothes… tweeds, flannels, stout brogues, straw boaters for the summer and motoring caps for the winter… The Doctor was clearly delighted with all the treats she kept ready for guests every day – at least that seemed to be what she did – and now he was even chatting in just the way that people were supposed to over tea.

'Fetch…' The Doctor half-grinned and looked at her sideways while flapping his hat slightly. 'You have, if I might say, a slightly ominous last name.'

'Do I…?' Julia giggled in a way that she hadn't since she was a girl, or perhaps since she had flirted with those dashing young men who had once flown all her aircraft and driven all her cars: her Antoinette, her Curtiss and her Sopwiths, her Hudson Roadster, her De Dion Bouton, her

Benz Motorwagen… she had owned so many things in her life. And she had watched so many well-set-up young chaps dancing and going to regattas and being jolly and alive… 'I wasn't aware of that, Doctor. I suppose Doctor isn't that happy a name, either – one only sees a doctor usually when one is unwell…'

'Dear lady…' The Doctor smiled and swam his left hand suavely through the air, just missing a tiny glass *Amphioctopus marginatus*. He picked up an Eccles cake, studied it for a moment and then swallowed it in one. 'Oh, you look terribly well, though…' His voice was briefly a bit raisiny. He swallowed. 'But the word *fetch* – it always interests me. It used to be another word for *ghost*.'

'Heavens, how exciting.'

'Or the ghostly image of a person…' The Doctor gave Julia one of the fast, clever looks which tended to make people think – if they noticed them – that the Doctor might not be the dispensable idiot he liked to seem. 'And have you lived here long…?'

Julia Fetch frowned as if this question was somehow too slippery to grasp. It seemed to have layers that she didn't want to explore – and depths, too. There were definitely depths. While the Doctor darted another highly intelligent glance her way, she mumbled, 'Long…?'

'It is a difficult question, I'll admit,' burbled the Doctor. 'Long as my arm, long as your arm, long as a long piece of Betelgeusian twine… Hmmm…' His head was getting foggy again and that metallic taste was back. *Far away… a long, long… It was a strange word, wasn't…?* A long way away he seemed to think that having a metallic taste in his mouth was a very bad idea and he should stop it at once. The Doctor posted an entire éclair into his resilient but currently rather strained digestive system and then abruptly lost his appetite.

From that long, long, long way away, he could hear Julia Fetch's voice.

'Doctor?' she asked. 'My memory has become unreliable over the years, but I seem to have met you before somewhere. Have we taken tea together before?'

'Mmmm...?' He set down a buttered teacake on the arm of his chair and sighed. He had been – he thought – acting exactly as one should during a tea party and keeping everyone at their ease, but – in a distant way – he could tell that he was worried. He'd just eaten his own body weight in fat, sugar, starch and thinly sliced pieces of cucumber and yet he hadn't actually been hungry, not exactly. It was more that he had felt as if someone else was being hungry *using his body*. And his head... It was almost as if some tendril, some intelligent hand, were rootling about behind his left eye and rearranging things, shifting memories, scooping some possibly important items out and just making them disappear. Whatever he'd told Bryony earlier, he was sure that their troubles weren't over. Even if the creature that produced that massive psychon field had gone, the residual energy was bound to create some serious after-effects. Then again, he knew from very long experience that if you told Earth people they were in mysterious and most likely fatal danger they tended to break things, or scream a lot, or faint.

FAINT.

Once again, a large word, an impossibly loud word, squeezed its way into the Doctor's remarkably roomy consciousness and made it feel like a bedsit in Weymouth. For some reason he was recalling the exact proportions of a specific bedsit in Weymouth and the width of a stasis chamber on a Basic Type VI Interstellar Transport... It was as if his mind was being encouraged to distract him... 'Have we...?'

'Met.' Julia Fetch smiled peacefully, as is traditional in sweet old ladies who are taking tea. 'Before.' She blinked.

The Doctor peered across at her and thought that the air in the quaint little room seemed greenish, or foggy, or just *wrong*. And it hurt his eyes. 'Have we met before…? Well, you know, I do get about a bit.' Because the Doctor travelled in time as well as space he was very used to this kind of question and the various ways to answer it tactfully without going into how complicated life can be when you may – in the present – not have met someone before and yet may also – in the future – go back to the past and – in the past – meet that same someone in a manner that affects their future and, for example, the topics of conversation – in the present – which they might feel they'd already covered with you at an earlier date. 'Now, let me think…' The thing was, today, he didn't feel able to manage all those complications: the time streams, the sheer remembering of so many thousands and thousands of faces and names and customs and histories and… For a second he felt something flicking through those faces and names as if they were files, infotabs, neurolinks – as if he were a record-keeper for an absent master. One of many things the Doctor couldn't stand for was having a master.

SCREAM. FAINT.

He could see Julia's eyes observing him with concern.

'Doctor, you look rather unwell. Would you perhaps…?'

BREAK. SCREAM. FAINT.

The Doctor tried to shake his head and clear it, but that just seemed to make his frontal lobes clap together painfully inside his skull and so he nodded, carefully and murmured, 'I think… yes… It's this way, is it… Your bathroom…? With your taps…? And your water…? Yes. If I run my head under the tap for a moment.' His long form rose up and swayed along to Julia's enormous bathroom – the unsteady sweeps of his scarf missing every glass model as he left in a way that was almost miraculous.

She didn't watch him go, only sat recollecting what a wonderful tea party this was, how perfect in every way.

OUT IN THE SUN-KISSED and rose-scented garden, Putta was discovering that he was as bad at disk-throwing as he was at every other game he'd tried. The twins seemed almost to float over the lawn, lithe and graceful as young Peltain hawks. Bryony was also springing and laughing and catching like every other carefree, confident life form Putta had encountered on his travels. That was the thing about seeing the universe, rather than staying on your home planet – it gave you so many more opportunities to realise how clumsy and miserable and ugly you were in comparison to everyone else. And his new jacket was weighing him down... Putta watched the bare feet of his opponents scampering and dodging, employing skills he would never have, and suddenly tasted Maillindian Fever Beans and felt angrier than he ever had.

Bryony glanced across and he watched her smile curdle as she looked at him and noticed that she threw this Fizz B thing (was there a Fizz A?) over to him, as if she was skimming it towards a short-sighted child which had forgotten its glasses and was wearing thick mittens. She expected him to be pathetic and fumble and drop it.

He did.

And then, before he could stop himself, he had picked up the horrible piece of plastic and flung it back at her before fully realising that he had aimed it directly at her beautiful head – at her beautiful nose, to be precise. He watched her eyes register this fact and felt his heart break into a selection of jagged pieces and start scraping down the inside of his chest in despair.

THE DOCTOR HAD HIS own problems. He was now inside Julia Fetch's magnificent marble bathroom. The marble surfaces, the gold-plated taps, the marvellously soft Egyptian cotton towels were all of the finest quality and highly impressive. And if the Doctor had ever been that interested in luxury fixtures and fittings, the TARDIS would probably have provided them while he rattled across the universe. But he wasn't. So she hadn't. He'd now spent many lifetimes in adventures away from his ship, sleeping in caves, scuffling about on grubby floors with amazingly violent beings and scrambling up and down the dusty or muddy paths and scree slopes of the incredibly large number of planets which looked mostly like abandoned quarries. This meant that underfloor heating and Italian ceramics had rarely been available to him – while also never being a personal priority. He was mainly really pleased if there was sometimes a bit of soap available on loan near his location. Or clean water. Both being in the same place on the same day (or other convenient chronological unit) were usually a cause for celebration and elaborate thanks – if there was time for that kind of thing, what with all the scuffling and scrambling...

BREAK. SCREAM. FAINT.

The monstrous thoughts were back – punching into

his skull, like a fist the size of an office block. And it was impossible to recall a number of details, including the ways in which a dashingly handsome genius Time Lord might need to spruce himself up now and then, just to maintain standards.

The specially imported mango onyx marble of the walls had started to sway back and forth as if the room was breathing. The floor was also beginning to swash up and down like a thick liquid under the Doctor's abused shoes.

BREAK.

He staggered across towards the massive central bathtub, fell to his knees – because that felt more secure – and realised that his hip had thumped heavily against the side of the bath. In his hip pocket the Doctor almost always kept a bar of emergency Kin-Dahl Mint Cake. (It was amazing how many civilisations had developed a sucrose cake of similar type in a kind of parallel confectionary evolution.) Unmistakably, he felt the bar break.

Then his head was clamped by an incredible pain.

SCREAM.

He reached out blindly with what was very probably a shaking hand and tried turning on the cold tap so that he could splash water on to his face. He could halfway remember that sometimes this was a good idea.

The tap obligingly turned.

And turned.

And turned.

He couldn't feel any water.

He looked up – the effort of this making a sort of red blur run across his field of vision. There was the tap. No water was emerging from it… And yet… The tap itself was beginning to move, to flow…

The shining, tubular end of the cold tap was no longer frozen metal, drooping down to aim water into the bath. It

105

had reared up, horribly flexible and undulating, stretching and flaring – almost as if it were looking at him. And now the hot tap, too, had flexed into life and was snaking upwards, dancing with its fellow and making threatening little sallies towards the Doctor's horrified face.

For a moment, the end of one tap closed over his eye. It felt like a warm, soft, wet little mouth, testing, perhaps tasting, trying to understand him.

He batted it away, the motion making his neck tingle with pain and his head swirl.

Both taps now lunged towards him and he covered his eyes as fast as he could, while – he was pretty sure about this – he let out as loud a scream as he ever had.

FAINT.

But the taps weren't interested in his eyes any more. They sleeked past his sideburns, brushed through his unruly hair and found exactly what they were after.

The Doctor kept screaming as he felt the press of each tap swiftly burrowing into his ears, deeper and deeper, making his whole body shudder.

At which point, he did indeed faint, just as the Big Thought had predicted.

BACK IN THE GARDEN, Putta was so horrified that time seemed to have slowed and extended around him so that he had a considerable opportunity for anguished reflection. *The only time I throw something with any kind of speed and energy and it's going to really hurt my doomed love. At least my love for her is doomed. She shouldn't be doomed at all. Until I hurled a sharp-edged flying disk at her, there was nothing doomed about Bryony Mailer. I really am a waste of breathable gases…*

He would have gone on self-pityingly like this for a good while had he not been interrupted by a number of events. As it turned out, Bryony was a remarkably athletic woman and, although she was slowed by her shock as she watched the savage flick of Putta's wrist and the first threatening approach of the Frisbee, she was still able to flinch out of its way enough to receive no more than a glancing – but still painful – blow to her cheek.

Putta flinched almost as if he himself had been hit and had just enough time to feel very guilty and to hear Bryony yelp, 'Putta! What the–!' before he was gripped with immense force, as if he were being restrained in a maxsecure chair at some kind of HyperLocked facility.

When he managed to look away from Bryony, who was glowering at him and rubbing her zygomaticus major and zygomaticus minor muscles, he realised that Xavier and

Honor had caught his arms and shoulders powerfully with what looked like slender and graceful child-fingers. Now those same fingers had him in their grasp they seemed to be much closer to high-tensile arachnid webbing, or maybe steel…

He examined their perfectly calm faces, puzzled. They were still apparently two lovely young Terran humans, with willowy limbs and endearing features. But Putta saw in their eyes an absolutely blank darkness. It was as if he was gazing at two pairs of glistening rounded stones – stones filled only with night and the empty indifference of the universe – and expecting them to be sympathetic. And then he felt his feet being lifted off the ground.

'Wwhooo…?' Putta waggled his feet feebly as they left the grass and those two pairs of hands began to crush inwards around his arms more and more powerfully. He began to worry if his bones and muscles would survive this kind of treatment.

And, for the first time in his life, the being who was called Putta Pattershaun 5 turned to another being that he absolutely loved with all his massively underused heart and felt her frown at him with slight continuing annoyance but also real concern and – beyond that – genuine affection.

He liked someone and they liked him back.

Putta suspected this kind of information might have meant he ended up suspended in mid-air anyway. For a few seconds he felt like a tall, powerful and noble hunter of monsters, like a successful and agile hero, like the great and mighty Yakts of old who had strode across Yinzill like –

At which point he was dropped back to earth when he wasn't expecting it and his weak ankle went a bit wobbly on landing and so he fell over in a highly unheroic manner and ended up in a heap with his head in some kind of slightly prickly shrub.

He was aware of Bryony above him, making a small concerned noise while also giggling. He extracted his face from the herbaceous border and sat, blinking up at three completely friendly faces, all trying to seem helpful while being on the verge of laughing. Six hands reached out to him and hauled him upright with only the usual levels of strength. Six hands then brushed him free of small leaves and patted him, while saying things like…

'Goodness. That was a bit of tumble. Are you all right?' (Honor)

'My heavens, old chap. You need to be more careful. And perhaps we shouldn't have played such a rough game. Would you be better at cards, or perhaps chess…?' (Xavier)

And 'Oh, Putta… You do look an idiot. One minute you're trying to break my nose, the next you're leaping up and then throwing yourself into the flowerbed… Come and have some more tea and sit down before you actually break something – like your leg…'

And then – which was odd – Putta said, 'If I'd broken my leg I'd have screamed and then fainted.' At exactly the same time that Honor, Xavier and Bryony said, 'If you'd broken your leg, I'd have screamed and then fainted.'

For a long breath they all frowned and then laughed with each other.

But neither Putta nor Bryony laughed for quite as long as the twins or looked quite as carefree as they went indoors.

INSIDE THE COTTAGE, ALL seemed rather calmer than it had been before. The many, many tea things and many, many crumbs had been cleared away and, as Julia said contentedly, most of the stains would be removable. 'A little butter here and there is the sign of a really excellent tea gathering… You must come again. Perhaps tomorrow…'

The Doctor was nowhere to be seen, although his hat was lying on the floor beside his empty armchair. Bryony thought it seemed almost as remarkable without him under it as it did when it was keeping his hair in check.

Suddenly, Bryony had a strange feeling. It was the kind of prickle at the back of the neck which her early ancestors might have experienced when a both angry and stealthy mammoth was creeping up behind them to tread on precious and fragile things – things like their heads. 'Um… Is the Doctor about?'

Mrs Fetch nodded absently. 'Yes, dear. He just popped to the bathroom… a few moments ago… Perhaps longer… I was tidying. Gentlemen need so much more maintenance than ladies, don't they?'

Bryony wasn't quite sure what this meant, but she was pretty certain that the Doctor wasn't overly concerned with his personal appearance. She was just about to comment on this when she heard – along with everyone else – a loud cry. And then a much louder cry. It sounded like someone in horrible agony, like someone in despair.

As Bryony sprang forward to do something about this and Putta sprang backwards to prevent himself getting into trouble or being injured, the door at the end of the passageway battered open and the Doctor half staggered out. 'Ah,' he said. 'Ah…' His expression suggested that he had been to places no being should have to see and that he was very tired. 'Ah.'

Bryony held out her arms to him as he banged along the corridor and it became clear to everyone that he was completely drenched.

At which point he shook his head like an extremely tall dog, spattering Julia Fetch's carefully hand-printed wallpaper with daubs and splashes of water. Then he straightened and beamed at them – very much like a dog which has rolled in something terrible and wants to get a biscuit and tickled ears for being so clever. 'I feel much better now,' he announced. 'Remarkably refreshed, I'd say. At least I think I do…' He shook Julia Fetch's hand and then kissed it, a small torrent of water dripping from his sleeve as he did so. 'But there may be a slight problem with your plumbing. Although I do appreciate enthusiasm, even in bathroom fittings…' His shoulders seemed to flinch briefly and he motioned Putta and Bryony towards the door without meeting their eyes. 'Must head off now… places to do and things to meet…' He left heavy and dark wet footprints across the newly cleared carpet as he retrieved his hat and slapped it down on top of his soaked hair. 'Lovely tea, everyone. Charming and delightful. ' He gently shook Xavier's hand. 'Really the best I've had in centuries.' And then he shook Honor's hand. 'A pleasure to meet you.' After that he loped to the door, dripping as he progressed. 'Well, come on, then.' He span round, sending more trails and lumps of water in all directions and then was outside before Putta and Bryony could also say their goodbyes and hurry after him. 'We don't have all day, you know. We may have very much less than all day…'

Bryony left the cottage with Putta, refusing a generous offer of extra cucumber sandwiches for the journey back across the golf course. As she passed the delightfully perfect garden and walked out into the wonderful afternoon, she knew that all was not as it should be. She had that mammoth-creeping-up-behind-you-with-long-violent-tusks-and-big-bad-thoughts feeling, even more strongly than before. Something was definitely wrong.

AND AROUND ARBROATH THE afternoon was passing rather peculiarly for a number of people. In a restaurant on Ladyloan, staff found themselves amazed by the rapid appearance of dozens of famished visitors well after the lunch hour. Each of the customers demanded macaroni cheese and a pot of tea. It wasn't so much the order that was peculiar – macaroni cheese was always popular – it was more that the crowd of visitors all forked and spooned their meals in exactly the same rhythm, very rapidly until everything was gone. Then they sat in complete silence, motionless and looking puzzled.

Mr and Mrs Potter, up on a visit from Solihull, were walking round the local Woolworths quite contentedly until – as observers would confirm – Mrs Potter turned to her husband and started to throw handful after handful of pick 'n' mix sweets at him while shouting, 'Don't you dare think that about Sandra Billington!'

At this, Mr Potter had stared at her and then slowly begun laughing helplessly between bouts of shouting, 'You never did hide it! I always knew you hated my mother. And I hated her, too! She was a dreadful woman! And so are you! Good grief, I've married my mother!' He then started catching some of the missiles raining down on him and then jamming his mouth full of pineapple cubes, fizzy

113

cola bottles, white mice, strawberry bonbons and other treats.

And meanwhile, American tourists Martha and Paul Cluny, along with their son Paul Junior, were visiting Saint Vigeans and what Martha called 'the quaint little cottage museum' that housed a small but lovely collection of carved Pictish stones. The stones had been moved here from the Saint Vigeans church after Victorian renovations.

Their guide – who they hadn't strictly asked to guide them and who may only have been an overenthusiastic local, it was hard to be sure – told them about the legend that the village church of Saint Vigeans was held suspended over a vast underground lake. In the underground lake there was supposed to be a kelpie, or a demon, or something else unpleasant which might or might not have constructed the building out of sandstone while being enslaved.

The guide didn't clearly explain by whom the monster was enslaved and although this kind of missing detail didn't annoy his parents, it really did irritate Paul Junior. He was easily irritated. He was eleven and thoroughly tired of being called the same thing as his father. Or not even that – on some occasions he was just 'Junior'. It was humiliating. And he felt it indicated a lack of imagination on his parents' part. Paul, by contrast, had a great deal of imagination. When he was older he was going to have himself legally renamed – probably as Dirk, or Zandor. He didn't think that Akron Ohio (which is where he lived) had too many Dirks or Zandors.

The Cluny family were also told that, for a while, the congregation of Saint Vigeans would stay away from services for fear of the kelpie, or demon, or unpleasant thing's curse. What the curse might involve also wasn't made too clear.

This made Martha Cluny smile indulgently because she

already understood that her husband came historically from a strange and superstitious people and this just confirmed how weird his ancestors must have been and explained why he could never keep his den tidy and always injured himself doing simple chores. For some reason, her husband didn't – as was usual – find her smile endearing, or mistake it for an expression of affection. In fact, he got quite shirty with her and wandered off to study some of the carvings by himself, in great detail – because he knew this would annoy her, because she was still jet-lagged and didn't enjoy historical activities as much as he did.

While his parents went into a huff with each other, Paul stared at the back of the vast, impressive Drosten Stone. It was carved with the images of strange beasts: perhaps a bear, a dog, a wild boar: and an oddly caped figure holding a bow and arrow. There were also intricately winding knots carved there – as if someone had woven threads of stone together into patterns, or signs, or messages.

It made Paul feel dizzy, but also was oddly wonderful, to simply stare at the patterns and then into the patterns. As he stared, the carvings began to shimmer and then to ooze gently across the ancient, pitted surface. This didn't worry him – it made him feel very calm, in fact. It almost like dreaming in a very safe place with his eyes wide open – and his mind wide open, too.

Then gently, a tendril of stone dabbed against his right thumb, as if it was shy and trying to say hello – as if it liked him. This was when he realised that, somehow, he had placed his hand on to the stone. He hadn't noticed himself touch it and this was perhaps partly because the stone was as warm and familiar-feeling as his own hand.

He smiled and, across his thinking, strolled the exciting and inspiring sentence 'You are the jewel at the heart of the universe.' This made him feel spectacularly happy. Nobody called Junior would be anywhere near the heart of the universe – it would have to be Zandor from now on.

His hand softly, gradually, began to sink into the surface of the stone and, as he watched it do so, he thought this was exactly the right thing to be happening. For no reason he could identify, he was absolutely sure that if he was with the Drosten and the Drosten was with him, then everything would be wonderful for ever.

'Paul…' His mother's voice jabbed in from apparently very far away. 'Paul James Cluny, I am speaking to you.'

He began to think that setting his forehead against the stone would be the best idea yet and the sandstone rippled and glittered, right where he could tell it wanted him to lean.

And then, as generations of mothers have throughout human history, Paul James Cluny's mother did indeed yell. 'You stop that this minute!' And he felt a sharp tug at his shoulder.

'What…?'

'Don't you say *what* to me, young man. You say *I beg your pardon* if you know what's good for you. I swear, sometimes you are exactly like your father.' And she allowed a picture of hairy men running about in primitive clothing and not having invented civilised cookery to wander across her thinking.

Paul Jnr was slightly disorientated and seemed to have lost something very important. He even peered around him and down at the ground in case the something had fallen out of his pockets. He couldn't exactly recall what he'd been doing for the last few minutes, or when he had walked over to this part of the small museum – it wasn't exactly the kind of place you could get lost inside… He sighed and became a touch more like his usual self. He looked about, enjoying being unimpressed – this was just the kind of dump your no-use mom and dad would drag you to, because they hated you and didn't want you to have a really cool name.

As he was led off in mild disgrace, Paul Jnr began to enjoy something more like his customary resentments and daydreams for the future. But, just as the museum door was about to close behind him, he shivered. It was as if some monumentally large intelligence had flexed and turned in deep, deep water. It was as if the intelligence had swum up and looked right into him. He shivered again and – although he regretted this as soon as he did it – Paul James Cluny Junior took hold of his mother's hand.

THE DOCTOR WAS TALKING. He loved talking, adored it. When you were in real trouble, it was one of the better options. Many beings in the universe would opt for running away, which he felt wasn't an exciting or interesting enough choice for a bold and handsome time-travelling genius. Many more beings, on finding themselves in stressful circumstances, would try to kill other beings, or at least hit them, lock them up, or otherwise make them very miserable. In the long run – and time travellers know a great deal about the long run – the Doctor knew this kind of thing didn't really work. And as someone who had wide experience of all manner of futuristic and primitive weapons trying to kill him, not to mention being hit, locked up and bullied, he felt it wouldn't be all that possible for him to indulge in such things himself. So he talked. Just occasionally he ran away to think about what he needed to do before he ran back again. But mainly he talked.

Today he felt, in all of his bones, that running away and never coming back was his only option.

This was why he was talking so hard.

He had, since he left the cottage with his three companions, talked about the late designs of Leonardo da Vinci, the arrangements of streets in Cologne and the volcanic instability of the Yellowstone Caldera. He attempted to enjoy using words like *basaltic magma* and *rhyolitic magma*, which would normally entertain him no end.

It wasn't working, though. The Doctor was more frightened than he ever had been.

Worse than that – he couldn't locate the reason why. He knew the reason was out there, but he just couldn't find it. There were now whole areas of his memory that had apparently been made inaccessible. When he turned his concentration towards them, he felt as if he was trying to scale a very tall cliff made of highly polished marble. Or else as if he was being rocked to sleep.

At which point – preceded by a jolt of intense pain – another savage thought pounced into the Doctor's reeling head.

HELLO
YOU ARE THE DOCTOR
I AM I
HELLO DOCTOR
Whatever it was, it now knew his name.

BRYONY WASN'T ABSOLUTELY SURPRISED when the Doctor suddenly flopped to his knees. Although she didn't know him very well, she realised that it was odd and very noticeable if a man with such wide, striking and trustworthy eyes, a man who liked people so much, didn't meet your gaze even once as you walked along. It was probably also a bad sign if he talked nonsense at great speed, as if someone had a gun to his head and was ordering him to gabble. And it was also probably a really terrible sign if his scarf looked somehow *depressed*. Actually, his kneeling rapidly on to the turf at the edge of the eighth green was the only thing he'd done in ages that made a bit of sense.

'Doctor? Doctor, are you all right?'

'He's fallen over,' Putta told her, as if she might not have noticed.

'I can see that,' she snapped, regretting it slightly when Putta flinched. 'Doctor? Are you OK?'

'Oh, absolutely.' Those large, trustworthy eyes peered sadly up at her, plainly in pain. 'I take an interest in golf course grass varieties. It's a kind of hobby.' He ran his large fingers through the grass leaves, as if he were calming the fur of a large, uneasy animal. 'This is a mixture of creeping red fescue and velvet bentgrass.' It was clear that he was attempting to smile, but all that his face could manage was something half-formed and lonely. 'The peculiar thing is that I don't remember even knowing the rules of golf before now…I have the distinct impression that yesterday I was entirely baffled by what could possibly be appealing about repeatedly knocking away and then retrieving and then dropping into a hole and then retrieving a small white sphere across various reproductions of a common Scottish coastal habitat. I mean, it's not as dreadful a pastime as collecting bandan eggs…' He glowered at Putta and became himself again for an instant.

But then the Doctor subsided again, almost seeming to shrink as he continued, 'Not that one can't alter one's hobbies – no need to get in a rut, as they say. As someone must have said…'

When Bryony took the Doctor's hand, her consciousness was immediately filled beyond its capacity with a torrent of images and emotions: a Victorian policeman looking stunned by something near his feet, a magnificent sunset involving two suns, slender azure-leaved trees arching overhead while uniformed creatures with insect-like faces swung out of them on glistening ropes and then – for a breathless instant – a swirling tunnel of silver, blue, black, brown, this urgent rush of light and speed and… time… it was time, too… time was pouring and leaping up around her and she was falling into it…

'UMM, THAT IS… IF you're both going to fall over…'
Putta was now sitting on the grass between the woozy
Bryony and the groggy Doctor. 'It's not a very interesting
game. It makes about as much sense as golf…' Although
he was delighted to be able to gaze into Bryony's face with
devoted concern, he hadn't a clue how to help her – or, for
that matter, the Doctor. 'I mean… Please feel better…' His
knowledge that he was useless in a crisis of any kind – and
this did look very much like a crisis – meant he was feeling
sweaty and nauseous as a result. 'Get better… Please… I
have a Medipac in my, um…' He didn't like being on the golf
course – moving across it quickly was bad enough… sitting
on it reminded him of feeling alien teeth closing around his
ankles.

'Space ship… space man…' mumbled Bryony and half-
smiled at him.

This made Putta's heart – which was in any case
significantly larger than an average human being's – swell
with affection.

Bryony emerged a little more from her dream state and
started to look extremely concerned. 'He's a Time Lord. The
Doctor is a Time Lord.'

This was both disappointing and weird. Although she'd
said it with great assurance, Putta knew she was wrong and

couldn't even work out how an Earth woman had heard of such exalted and terrifying beings. Time Lord probably meant something else on Earth – possibly someone who made sure you didn't spend too long on golf courses. This came especially to mind because Putta could see a group of four pastel-clad golfers approaching them in what might be something of a bad mood. They were giving him – even from a distance – the impression that lying about on the tidily mown areas of the grass wasn't encouraged. 'Ah… I think we should get up now. That is, if either of you think that, too…'

'He's a Time Lord.' Bryony's voice was ringing with wonder, pure amazement. Then this faded and she simply looked puzzled and a bit mugged.

'Yes, you said that. Only he can't be. Time Lords don't wander about tedious little planets like this… I mean to say… lovely little planets like this… They don't wander about at all – they… well, they sit in judgement, or… um, think wise thoughts and wear robes… Look at him. He wouldn't even know how to put on a robe.'

'You start on the outside and work your way in,' the Doctor groaned. 'And much good all the robe-wearing and thinking does them – useless lot.' He sat up gingerly, holding his head. 'Yes, I am a Time Lord.'

'Argh!' Putta didn't know whether to bow, shake hands or cower and therefore managed to combine all three in a manoeuvre that made him look as if he had a rat in his jacket and would have preferred not to.

The Doctor blinked him and then turned to Bryony as his saner option. 'It just so happens that I am Time Lord who likes to get involved. How can you be wise, if you don't get involved. Is what I've always thought. And I think that's, as it happens, a particularly wise thought. Wouldn't anyone?'

Putta gulped. 'Is that a trick question?'

The Doctor patted Putta's arm inaccurately, while still fixing his attention on Bryony. 'The *important* question is… how do you know that I'm a Time Lord? I haven't told you and we can't really say that it was a lucky guess. I mean an infinite number of monkeys might eventually come up with a halfway decent… sonnet… But a late-twentieth-century ape-descendant coming up with a guess that lucky in one go…' His smile flickered on and off like a tired light bulb. 'Entirely remarkable, beyond imagining, really.'

Bryony looked up at the Doctor as if he was entirely remarkable, beyond imagining and a thing of wonder. This wasn't unreasonable – he was entirely remarkable, beyond imagining and a thing of wonder, but it annoyed Putta no end.

Putta heard himself almost shouting, 'She's clever. That's how she knew.'

'My dear Putta. I'm perfectly well aware that she's clever. She's extraordinary in many ways, but she can't have known I'm a Time Lord.'

Bryony interrupted, 'Yes, I can… do… you told me… I mean, you showed me… I mean… I saw… You've been to so many places… So many amazing places…'

The Doctor, looked immensely troubled, removed his hat and scrunched it between his hands. 'Well, we Time Lords do have the ability – mild ability – we're a bit telepathic… It's impolite to intrude into other beings' consciousnesses… But sometimes… but…' He growled to himself like a man trying to shake loose some kind of interior fog. 'I should know this! I should know about this! This is a phenomenon with characteristics I should be able to identify! Metallic taste, bare feet in contact with planetary surface, control of particulates, psychon energy, unshielded telepathic field… I do know this! I just can't find it!' he cried.

Putta glanced nervously at the approaching golfers.

He was able to pick out some of what they were saying by now – it included the phrases 'layabout hippies' and also 'Disgrace, absolute disgrace, the place is going to the dogs.' Putta guessed this didn't bode well.

And then Putta remembered… Oh, dear he remembered. There was this thing that he should have mentioned ages ago – it was exactly the kind of thing that he should have told someone – someone exactly like the Doctor, someone who was a Time Lord. It was the one absolutely important thing, a truly, life-and-death thing that he really ought not to have forgotten. And yet he had. 'Oh! Oh dear, I've remembered…' In fact, even while he was trying to say it out loud, he could feel the memory wriggling away from him again, swimming off like a finny pippereel in a pool. 'Ooohnoohnononono…'

Bryony sat up and turned to him while the Doctor asked, 'Putta, what's wrong? You can tell us.'

'Oh, I'm an idiot.'

The Doctor attempted another smile. 'Well, we needn't go into that now…. What's the matter?'

'It wasn't my fault. I just. I forgot to say why I came here. Really why I came here. Which I should have said. Only I thought… Or I didn't think. I couldn't. It's just that what I saw on the Model G50 Threat Detector… Which isn't the best piece of equipment… It's known for being unreliable, in fact, but it was all I could afford…'

'Keep to the point, Putta. Please,' sighed the Doctor, his face seeming more and more exhausted, his skin greyer and greyer.

'Well, I didn't come here for a sandmaster. There was no indication of a sandmaster, not even a larva… I scanned a lot and there was nothing like that – even a G50 would notice a sandmaster. But what there was… That's the thing about the G50 – it has all these weird settings and its archive is just basically a series of random, open-source infodumps…There are legends in there, about thirty per cent of the species identification catalogue entries are pure mythology…' Putta heard a groan from the Doctor which could have indicated distress, or deep irritation. And those golfers were waving their arms in a *clear off right now* kind of way… 'I'm no use at anything and I needed a really amazing… um… not necessarily bountykill… I don't think I could… I'm not absolutely cut out for bountykilling… But a sighting. And amazing discovery. That's it – a discovery. It would have made me famous. That is, when I saw what the G50 told me might be here on Sol 3… on Earth…'

'You there!' The tallest golfer, resplendent in his lemon yellow slacks, matching cap and powder pink shirt, was stamping ahead of his colleagues and had set his sights on Putta. 'What on earth are you dressed as? Are you some kind of joke!?' Putta was the only one sitting on the grass who looked close to being fully alert – but did also probably look as if he had dressed satirically in order to mock golfers everywhere. 'What you need, my lad, is a serious spell of National Service! They'll bring it back and you'll be sorry when they do!'

National Service on Yinzill was a punishment doled out, 10 STUs at a time – 10 STUs was about 6 Earth years – and involved clearing the National Forests of a toxic and violent invading plant species, nicknamed Spatch. The extra dose of panic that threatened Spatch-clearing provoked meant that Putta was finally able to blurt out, 'It was a Bah-Sokhar! Doctor, it was a Bah-Sokhar! The G50 gave me a reading for a Bah-Sokhar! A Soul-Eater!'

As soon as Putta heard himself pronounce the *Bah* of the almost-forgotten, unlikely, ridiculous and terrifying name *Bah-Sokhar* – a name from the bleak, dark past at the roots of the universe – he felt a horrible juddering in the grass beneath him. Before he could leap to his feet, the turf domed in two places just ahead of the Doctor and Bryony, split apart and then revealed the perfect, charming, flawless heads and then shoulders and bodies and legs and jaunty bare feet of the twins. Springing up from the earth as if it were water, here were Xavier and Honor, flawless, clean, terrible. Their eyes flickered like minute pools of clever emptiness.

'What on earth…? You can't…' The leading golfer stepped forward towards the twins with one arm outstretched. Then he stopped. He absolutely stopped. For a breath or two he looked something like a three-dimensional photograph of himself, snapped at an unfortunate and irate moment. Then his whole body seemed to tense, as if it were fighting some incredible force. It was dreadful to watch the quiet struggle and yet Putta couldn't turn away – it seemed wrong not to meet the man's eyes for an instant and at least care about him, while – this was terrible – he began to flatten, to collapse. The man's limbs, head, torso, all that he was, were being relentlessly crushed until he was absolutely as thin as a photograph. His expression at the end was one of utter, soundless horror.

Then the thin layer of matter the golfer had become folded and crumpled, smaller and smaller. For an instant he was reduced to a small dot in mid-air, like a full stop.

Then there was nothing.

Next Honor and Xavier span their heads round to look directly behind them – without turning their bodies – so that their loveable faces and winning smiles were aimed right at the remaining golfers. It made Putta feel cold all over. And, of course, each of the three men was then inexorably thinned away to the thickness of paper – before being wholly destroyed.

127

Putta turned away, sickened. Then he peered up at the backs of the twins' heads – blank shapes covered in soft, sun-bleached hair and set above their collar bones, exactly as they shouldn't be. While they were – as far as he could tell – focusing their attention elsewhere, Putta tried to stand.

But at this point the air thickened.

It thickened *a lot*.

A pair of lapwings directly above halted their progress across the sky, as did the clouds and a distant light aircraft.

While Putta wondered if he was going to be crushed now, everything which had been in motion halted. There was a vast silence.

And then.

'No!' the Doctor bellowed. 'No, you don't! Now I know your name! I may not keep knowing it for long, but right now I do!' His voice emerged between savagely gritted teeth. Slowly and with infinite effort, the Doctor fought upwards until he was standing. 'You don't! Not here! Not now! You don't come to this planet and do this. You don't come to any planet and do this.' Sweat was running down his face, while his chest heaved with what Putta knew must be the immense effort of breathing.

Putta tried to reach out and help somehow, but the air felt like needles being forced into his skin if he even pressed forward slightly. He was terribly afraid this was what it would feel like at the beginning of being flattened. With a pain that felt it was scalding the side of his head, Putta just managed to turn enough to see Bryony – Bryony with a look of such shock on her face and her hands holding each other close to her throat – Bryony who was brave and marvellous – Bryony who he loved with what he believed was going to be the last of all his – larger than the average Earthman's – heart.

As Putta wished he could cry, or yell, or do anything – he

saw the Doctor straighten his back so that he was standing very tall. The struggle of managing this clearly drained the Time Lord. The twins' heads whipped round to give him their full attention, their expressions savage, almost hungry, and their eyes glimmering with hard intentions.

Then, with what was plainly a monumental effort, the Doctor began to lift his hand and to smile, as if he were greeting an old friend.

And that was the last that Putta or Bryony saw of him.

For a moment he was standing in front of an unimaginable death and being like himself, like the Doctor – someone who always wanted to smile at the universe and give it the benefit of the doubt.

And then he was gone.

There was no thinning, no crushing, no small dot.

Just gone.

For a breath, Putta thought he saw something like the shape of an animal – a translucent shape with hooves, a long, strange head, horns and blazing eyes.

But it dissipated before he could even work out what it was.

The atmosphere returned to normal and both Putta and Bryony rushed forward towards the children – towards the children who clearly weren't children.

'No! What have you done! What have you done!' Bryony was yelling and crying, reckless with fury.

Putta saw the delightful little girl's head and the loveable boy's head shift to fix on her, tilting with a chilly curiosity as she lunged at them.

This wasn't going to end well.

THINGS THE DOCTOR DIDN'T KNOW
ABOUT THE BAH-SOKHAR

THE BAH-SOKHAR CAME INTO being at such an early stage of the universe's development that its true nature remained mysterious, even in the far-distant age when it was first identified. It was a creature capable of surviving in the depths of space, of withstanding the monumental forces which eventually created solar systems, sent comets speeding into flight, or ripped open the space-time continuum.

Early legends associate it most with a planet known on Earth as Kepler-22b and in some other places as Prax.

When the first generations of interplanetary explorers reached Prax they simply never returned. But, as the centuries passed, and the Lords of Carnage emerged – pillaging civilisations, melting asteroids, enslaving multitudes, murdering entire populations – rumours spread that some of their monstrous power was supplied by a secret weapon. Sagas were written, songs and poems were created to describe how dreadful the weapon was and each description was horrifying and completely different from every other description. The only thing which remained was the weapon's name – Bah-Sokhar.

This caused later readers and academics to believe that the Bah-Sokhar was an invention – a way for beings to express the fear they felt when they were faced by the size and wonder of the universe. Others assumed that tales of the Bah-Sokhar referred to some forgotten god.

According to one remaining text, thousands died in order to finally discover the secret of the weapon and bring it back to less powerful beings and allow them to control or imprison it. The Lords of Carnage – who may also have been mythical – were said to have destroyed themselves at around the same time the Legion of Seekers – possibly mythical – discovered the Bah-Sokhar's true nature. Other sources suggest they were destroyed in some dreadful star-threatening apocalypse.

The Bah-Sokhar was said to have been lost, or also to have been destroyed.

And yet its name echoed from system to system and age to age. There were – if someone wanted to look – always a few stories about the Bah-Sokhar in most cultures. These were sometimes used by more advanced civilisations to threaten less advanced ones. 'Obey us, or we will unleash the Bah-Sokhar.' There were no verifiable records of the Bah-Sokhar ever having been deployed.

Its threat slowly softened over the vast expanses of time. At some points, it was used by parents to frighten their offspring into behaving. 'Be quiet, or the Bah-Sokhar will get you. Go to sleep, or the Bah-Sokhar will make you go to sleep. Eat your Maillindian Fever Beans, or the Bah-Sokhar will make you.' And so on. It was also celebrated in a cycle of song-theatre. Although this period was brief, affected only four planets and ceased abruptly.

By the time Earth had reached 2 June 1978 in the Common Era, almost no beings had ever heard of the Bah-Sokhar and, if they had, it was a thing of legend – a lie that adults told to naughty children.

OTHER THINGS THE DOCTOR DIDN'T KNOW OR MAY HAVE FORGOTTEN ABOUT THE BAH-SOKHAR

THE BAH-SOKHAR IS A creature more terrible than any nightmare.

The Bah-Sokhar has lived too long to be surprised, or overwhelmed by anything.

The Bah-Sokhar is invincible.

The Bah-Sokhar produces a metallic taste in most sentient beings' mouthparts. It can generate pairs of defence-creatures which always seem to have bare feet in contact with the available planetary surface. It can control particulates. It produces unfathomable amounts of psychon energy, which in turn generate powerful and recklessly unshielded telepathic fields.

But the Bah-Sokhar also creates forgetfulness.

Even though the Doctor did know all the available information about the Bah-Sokhar – which wasn't much – he couldn't find it. The Bah-Sokhar prevented him without even fully waking from its immeasurably long rest.

If it had to, the Bah-Sokhar could destroy the body and the mind, even of a Time Lord, in order to keep its true secrets safe.

JULIA FETCH SAT IN her communications hub – which looked slightly like the cottage hobby corner of an older lady. A basket of half-finished knitting was in one corner, and a neat pile of gardening magazines and a tapestry kit were there too, along with a quaint Regency sewing box in brass and mahogany. She'd always liked the box, ever since she was a girl. Its silk-lined removable tray with so many little compartments still enchanted her, as did its full complement of original sewing equipment in silver and ivory. The equipment wasn't very practical – and she was very sorry that the ivory had come from elephants – but it made her nostalgic and that was always pleasant.

An old-fashioned telegraph machine produced tickertape, chattering away, while she skimmed through letters on octopus problem-solving abilities and a request for more office chairs from her new research centre on Hawaii. She also allowed herself to be nostalgic about the days when she had travelled more. That charming Doctor chap – he'd had the air of a traveller, a bold explorer like Ernest Shackleton of the South Pole expeditions, or the mountain climber Annie Smith Peck or Nellie Bly who travelled round the world in eighty days back in… when was it…? 1889… maybe 1889… There were so many people who were so interested in the world and so keen to discover how magnificent it was and often they needed a little money and might possibly call for tea with someone of immense wealth – like Julia Fetch.

It seemed that she really could remember pouring out carefully blended India tea to Shackleton and thinking what a formidable chin he had and giving Annie Smith Peck more cucumber sandwiches and deciding, when she saw Nellie Bly's dashingly neat haircut, that she would have one just the same. Perhaps the Doctor had needed money. His shoes were undoubtedly in an alarming condition. Perhaps she had given him some and he later would return with news about African languages she could learn, or Canadian berries that made good jam for scones, or else types of cake she hadn't yet served. The invention of good new cakes, Julia had found, sometimes took decades.

Then again, it did seem that the years went by remarkably quickly, or else that there'd been a remarkable number of years…. Either that, or she was turning into just the kind of woolly-headed old woman she'd found so funny and silly and frustrating when she was young and couldn't wait to leave her father's big, rattly old house in Cheyne Walk beside the Thames, and all his rules and regulations for proper ladylike behaviour.

Julia read descriptions of octopuses (or octopodes) unfastening containers to get at treats and climbing out of their tanks when no one was looking in order to have adventures (or, it had to be admitted, in order to eat less clever things in other nearby tanks) and of octopodes (or octopuses) who appeared able to appreciate different types of music and respond in a positive manner to Bach, the Brighouse and Rastrick Brass Band and something called the Electric Light Orchestra.

It might, in fact, be time for her to play something on her Gilbert Gramophone… perhaps some Duke Ellington or Bessie Smith. It still seemed thrilling to listen to jazz – it had such a joyful and marvellous swing to it and there were so many memories wound up in the lyrics and the tunes: nights of dancing and lovely young men safe home after some dreadful war or other. The chaps still had something terrible in at the backs of their eyes and she recalled that everyone had to dance a great deal in the 1920s, quite frankly, because of all the sadness that so very terribly many lovely young men hadn't managed to come home.

Meanwhile, the wallpaper gradually worked itself forward from the wall, as if there were two bodies trapped behind it. Then two forms – just blurry columns of papery, restless matter garnished with rosebuds and flowers – budded away from the wall entirely and balanced on her carpet, strange and seething with life.

She watched as the columns resolved themselves into slender arms, narrow shoulders, graceful legs, slim torsos, charming heads with glossy sun-kissed hair, delicate bare feet. And here were her grandchildren. Their faces were deadly serious.

But then Xavier and Honor broke into the lovely smiles she knew so well and loved so much, their beautiful eyes shining with tenderness and concern.

'Were you thinking of unhappy things, Grandmama?' asked Honor, her voice gentle and sweet.

Xavier took her hand and squeezed it as he always did. 'We can't have that, you know. Everything has to always make you as happy as happy can be.' He nodded, the light falling on the side of his face in a way that suggested the kind and honourable man he might one day become.

Julia shook her head and chuckled. 'I was only remembering.'

'But that's sad,' said Xavier, holding her hand more tightly. 'Why do something that makes you sad.'

'Well, I suppose there are kinds of sadness that are quite nice,' Julia pondered. 'It's good sometimes to think of wonderful times and people, even when they've gone.'

Honor frowned. 'We have to look after you and make sure that you're happy and safe and that everything is just exactly as it should be. We can't do that if you keep thinking.'

'I do have to think, my darlings.' Julia kissed each twin on each adorable forehead and felt so proud of them and so fond. She tried to remember when they had first showed her how special they were, the ways in which they were different from other grandchildren. It made her so glad that they trusted her in this way. 'And as long as I have you both, I will always really be very happy, even if I am a little bit sad.' She glanced out of the window into the well-maintained vegetable garden with its orderly rows of plants. 'Now then, why don't you scamper outside and bring me back something nice to go with your dinner. Perhaps some green beans, or some peas – whatever seems ready and best.'

And both of them did, indeed, patter delightedly off outside, laughing and attempting to play tag with each other – precisely like the good and adventurous and clever and wonderful children that Julia Fetch had read about in storybooks when she was herself a child.

As soon as they were out of sight, she forgot how they had appeared, forgot that that they were unusual in any way. More deeply in her mind was an area that forgot they had been the same age for as long as she had known them. She was unable to find the memory that would tell her how long it was that she had known them. And, deeper than all these clouds and absences and shadows, there was a space somewhere that failed to tell her she lacked all memory of their birth, or of their parents, or of ever having been a mother. If she had ever had a great love, a wonderful husband, a man she wished to share her life with, then her memories of such a man were locked far away, out of sight and out of mind.

BRYONY MAILER AND PUTTA Pattershaun 5 were
having an argument. Above them, the sky was perfectly
suitable for a summer afternoon with only a scatter of high
clouds. They could smell pine trees not too far away and the
sweet freshness of well-watered grass. They were walking
under the intermittent shade of trees near a burbling stream
and could see a merry breeze just tickling at the flag which
marked the second hole.

As far as Putta was concerned, he was having a lover's
tiff. In ways that he couldn't quite recall, he had courted and
won this remarkable woman striding along beside him and
waving her arms furiously while she yelled at full volume,
sometimes in his face and sometimes while growling at the
beautiful mature trees and beguiling landscape. He wasn't
too firm on the details of their courtship. Perhaps they were
a pair of lawyers who had met over a complicated case, and
having a good hearty discussion now and then brought
them closer together. Perhaps they were auctioneers and
enjoyed shouting. Perhaps… well, who they were was
generally pleasantly foggy and why shouldn't it be? Who
needed the pressure of knowing who they were all the time?
Putta was sure that if he really concentrated, he would
absolutely be able to come up with how they'd met and
what they did for a living and where they lived and why

they were on this golf course and whether they enjoyed golf – they didn't seem to have any golf bats or other equipment with them, so probably not – and why they were shouting. He knew he really liked this stuff he was wearing this… *tweed*. Tweed was a great word, he thought.

It was all just wonderful – that was the important thing. It was wonderful that they were here and wonderful that they were together and wonderful that they were screaming at each other and he couldn't have been happier without being someone else entirely.

Putta turned to his beloved and bellowed, 'What on earth are you talking about!?! That can't possibly be true! If it was true I would know about it, wouldn't I?!?' He then smiled and tried to take her hand as he was absolutely sure he usually did at round about this stage in every afternoon. Soon it would be evening. Evenings were so romantic, weren't they? And in the end they would get married and she would make a lovely wife and iron his socks, or ties, or gloves, or tweed, or whatever, and make meals he enjoyed while he went off and did whatever job it was he did… that would be established before he drove off to do it, or caught the bus, or… And Bryony – yes, that was her name – would be sweet and quiet and soothing and would rub his forehead with eau de cologne – whatever that was – when he was tired after a long day at the office, or the coalmine, or the lion-taming workshop, it would eventually be made clear which…

This all meant that Putta was more that slightly surprised when Bryony ripped her hand out of his grasp and shook him hard by his lapels while yelling at the highest volume she could produce, which was quite impressive.

BRYONY COULDN'T FOR THE life of her work out what was happening. Her head was spinning: literally spinning and also racing and swirling with information she couldn't manage to cope with. She also didn't really want to have to try.

She shook Putta again until his teeth clattered together. 'Putta! Putta! Come on! You can't have forgotten! The Doctor! You can't have forgotten the Doctor!'

'I don't need a doctor. I've never felt better in my life. You do have gorgeous eyes, you know.'

'No! *The Doctor!* He just…' A shudder of grief and loneliness swept over her. 'You were with me. You saw! It was horrible! It was so horrible!'

Putta grinned at her again like – she couldn't help observing – a complete moron. 'Well, if it was that horrible, why think of it? I'm obviously not.' He shrugged, in as far as he could while Bryony was still clutching his very resilient jacket. 'Where will we have dinner? It must be dinner time.'

'Those men – you can't have forgotten what happened to them! They were just crushed! They were destroyed! Something is here! Something terrible! And now the Doctor's gone we're the only ones left to stop it!'

'Of course, dear.' Putta tried gently easing himself away

from her. 'I'm sure you're right and I realise we do love shouting for some reason, but can't we stop for a bit?!'

'Why are you such an idiot!'

'Why can't we stop?!' Putta patted her arm and grinned. 'Really darling. I'm almost completely sure that we're enjoying some kind of shared holiday right now and that needn't involve shouting – not really. We've come from somewhere else to be in... in wherever this is... and we're having a marvellous time. Truly. I'm pretty much certain of that.' Putta met her eyes and appeared to be a sane and trustworthy and quietly handsome man – in a nervy and lopsided and scruffy, gingery way. 'Why upset yourself?'

And Bryony felt so tired and alone and weak while she looked at him. It was starting to seem almost sensible that she should give up and pretend she hadn't seen anything... Maybe that would be for the best. She did have such a stabbing headache, and maybe it really wasn't necessary to think about things if they were unpleasant and there was nothing you could do about them... Perhaps problems always ought to be left to sort themselves out...

Bryony's head drooped. 'Well, you could be right...' Something inky was rising in her mind. 'Maybe you're right...' There was this comfy, impenetrable cloud that was covering all the upsetting and spiky and frightening ideas Bryony had been having recently in a kind of marshmallow softness... 'Maybe...' The dark, blurry marshmallow felt comfortable, it felt pleasant. Her own thoughts and memories didn't.

Bryony looked across at Putta and felt herself becoming more and more convinced that she was on some kind of honeymoon and about to be fantastically happy. She was, in fact, beginning to be impatient to get married to this strange, skinny man with his charmingly ludicrous sawn-off trousers, oversized jacket and clumping big shoes. She thought that maybe her husband would stay at home after the marriage. This would leave her free to work as a world-renowned historian, giving lectures and receiving prizes in many glamorous ceremonies… Yes, that seemed likely. Really, it seemed to be a foregone conclusion. She could picture all the awards she was going to be given and all the fantastically impressive degrees she was going to earn and all the fantastically impressive award-receiving gowns she was going to own. Putta would cook and clean their home and do gardening in his spare time, she imagined, and she would come home after trips abroad with extra award statuettes and certificates for her achievements, which would be kept on display in a vast cabinet, probably in the dining room. And then she would be given a Nobel Prize for… Well, for something or other…

'WHY DON'T WE GO back to the hotel!?' howled Putta with the air of a man indulging a slightly quirky girlfriend who has decided to like loud conversations. 'I'm getting a little hoarse!' He chuckled. 'Ha-ha… That's what I would say if I wanted to buy a pony, wouldn't I? I'd say *I'm getting a little horse.*' Which was a remarkably silly remark to make and a very bad pun.

And at that point Putta suddenly and violently remembered the Doctor. The Doctor, that remarkable being – probably remarkable even for a Time Lord. The Doctor was exactly the kind of person who would say something silly right now – say something in his delighted and playful and deadly serious voice at just this point when everybody's mind was being manipulated by some exterior, powerful, seductive…

Hang on a minute…

I couldn't even really describe how I got here… I was doing something… No… Something terrible was happening… There was… The Doctor… Something terrible was happening to the Doctor…

And Putta – painfully, very painfully – remembered the Doctor's large and intelligent eyes, the gangly energy he had as he pelted towards dangers that scared Putta out of his wits. And then there was the way the Doctor had of making

Putta feel guilty about all the things he hadn't done very well in his life. And then again, the Doctor had also made Putta feel pretty sure that doing more impressive things later on could be possible. Sometimes, when the Doctor had grinned at him and slipped him a sideways clever look, Putta had believed that doing remarkable, brave and memorable things was going to be inevitable really soon.

And then Putta knew, all over again, how warm and alive and just *happy* standing next to the Doctor seemed to make you feel.

But the Doctor was gone. Putta had stood and watched and been scared and out of his wits as the Doctor had been disappeared – simply ripped out of existence.

'Oh!' Putta dropped to his knees. 'Oh, no!' He'd never had what other beings referred to as a family – a group of genetically related entities who liked him, or at least were willing to eat more food than was absolutely necessary with him on certain important festival dates and the anniversary of his first leaving the broodcapsule. Still, he imagined this was how losing a member of his family might feel. 'Oh!' Yet even as he felt terribly sad, his head started to throb as if someone had blasted it with a UB17 on the 5+ setting and he began finding it slightly hard to recall why he was upset.

'Bryony? What's happening?' Putta reached up from where he was still crouching, surrounded by a monumental headache. He tried to take her hand.

She seemed bewildered. 'I don't know… It's as if someone is taking a long, hot spoon and sort of scooping out my memories.' She slapped herself on the cheek. 'Ah – ow – that worked a bit.' She winced afterwards, but seemed encouraged. 'Yeah… Try it. Go on, Putta. Give yourself a good wallop on the face.'

'Um… I'm not that good at hitting people… I suppose I am good at being hit… But mainly I run away… But the

Doctor, Bryony – how could I have forgotten him? I miss him, Bryony. I miss him so much.'

Putta felt a thought being pushed into his brain from somewhere. It was the idea that the Doctor was perfectly fine and on holiday in Plymouth, wherever that was. Putta was even being given an image of the Doctor's face – the face that had encouraged him and taken the time to look friendly while he had stared up at it from the hungry bunker and wondered if he was going to not only die, but die in a horrible way – the face which had made him know that everything would probably be all right and that even terrible situations could somehow still be *enjoyable*. In the picture he was being given, the Doctor's face was nodding – a bit stiffly – and saying that Plymouth was lovely and he'd send them a postcard.

Putta realised he had to get rid of this lie before he started to believe it. And if slapping worked…

He swung his arm out wildly, hoping to hit his now strangely painless head.

He managed to miss entirely.

'Oh, for goodness' sake, Putta! Don't be so useless!' Bryony snapped at him. 'If you don't slap you then I'll have to slap you – it really does seem to… Oh, hang on, though.' Her face grew calmer, less alive. 'I think giving ourselves pain overcomes what it's doing to us, but it seems to adapt really quickly… And it gives us pain if we remember and takes it away if we can't… And it gives us horrible, fake bits of half-memory… And I don't like other people interfering with MY BRAIN.' She thumped her hand against a tree trunk and then yelped, alert once more. 'It might not be possible to keep ourselves in enough pain to resist it. And, then again, it seems to find it really easy to punish us whenever it likes… Carrot and stick… But mainly stick… whatever it is… Argh.' She grimaced as some spasm of hurt was inflicted as a penalty for trying to work out the identity of their tormentor. 'Oh, the Doctor would know what to do. I don't… I can't…'

'Me too…' nodded Putta, miserably. But as he allowed himself to be overtaken by gloom he noticed that his head cleared and felt less sensitive. He frowned and – as an experiment – he carefully thought how completely lousy he must look and how unlikely it was Bryony would ever think of him as anything other than an irritation and how pathetically easy it had been to convince him that he was going to marry her and they were in love. At once his heart felt leaden, but he also seemed to be freer and more himself. 'Being miserable seems to work as well, though.' And if there was one activity at which Putta excelled it was being miserable.

Gathering all his energy he conjured up the first – and last – time his broodfather met him and found him a disgrace to the family name and the reputation of the Yinzill Domestic Propagation Service. Putta scrolled through memories of being laughed at by his broodbrothers, mocked by his teachers, rejected by playmates, avoided by females and taunted by both streetyouths and Civil Security personnel. He listed all the sports he couldn't play and all the times he had injured himself trying to, all the abilities he didn't have, all the lonely nights he had spent – plus all the lonely mornings, afternoons and evenings – and all the times he had peered up at the night sky and wondered what the point of anything was and, more particularly, whether there was any point to Putta Pattershaun 5, because if there was it was really well hidden.

A thick wave of despair raced up and over him like the dirty swell from a cold and polluted ocean, crashing onto an ugly and useless beach. 'Oh-h.' His head was now savagely clear. But in immediate retaliation, it was also gripped by a new icy, clamping ache. 'Oww-www.' He found that –

kneeling as he was – he had folded himself over, bent double with his forehead touching the dusty path.

'Putta. Are you OK?'

'Not exactly.' As soon as the pain had forced him to stop thinking, in came those soothing tempting thoughts and mirages from outside. 'It feels like either my brain's going to burst, or I'm going to make myself depressed for ever. And this was the first time I was… you know… I mean, being here on Earth and at the hotel and… and…' He stopped himself before he said something absurd like – *and you, Bryony*. 'The atmosphere and everything was very… cheerful.'

'Cheerful!?' Bryony walloped her own leg. 'This place is appalling. And what's the nearest big city…? Arbroath. Not exactly as glamorous as Manhattan. Famous for smoke-damaged haddock… Lately my life has been making me feel the whole of human evolution was some kind of a nasty joke and…' She suppressed a look of glee. 'Oh, yes – feeling completely hopeless it quite effective. Aghgh!' And was clearly pummelled in the brain for it immediately.

Putta looked on, aghast, as what was obviously a horrible headache snapped in to overcome any avoidance of the implanted ideas. Bryony, grimaced across at him, 'Oh, Putta. I'm not sure we're going to win this one.'

'Well, then I'm really going to…' Putt had no confidence that he was really going to do anything much, but he had decided that if he managed to punch himself in the jaw and maybe knock himself out then maybe the alien intelligence might think he was dead and would leave him. Then he'd be OK when he woke up. He wasn't looking forward to this and, blushing to a temperature he suspected might be medically harmful, he again extended a hand towards Bryony and waited – unable to speak – until she did this time take hold of it, while narrowing her eyes at him and looking suspicious.

'Putta? What are you—?'

She didn't have a chance to complete her sentence, because Putta then flung up his arm and clenched fist in a reckless swipe which narrowly missed her right ear. His forward momentum and her backward flinch managed to combine enough energy to propel both of them – already tilting at an unsustainable angle – about two feet across the path on the side closest to the brook.

Unfortunately – or, in a way, fortunately – they only had one foot of path left before it cut away to become the sharply sloping bank which led down to the stream. And then there was the stream. Which is to say that, as they staggered and then toppled over, flawlessly obeying the usual laws of physics, they encountered one foot (measured horizontally) of level path and then one foot (measured horizontally) of thin air which allowed them to drop down four or five feet (measured vertically) of nettles, rocks, a few strands of bramble, more rocks, mud patches and then surprisingly cold water with more rocks and mud beneath.

It was just what they needed.

'YOU MANIAC!' BRYONY WAS first to scramble upright once they'd slithered to a halt in the water. She was cold, scratched, bruised, wet, shocked and – as a result – so overstimulated and present in the moment that she was completely free of any ideas that didn't seem to be her own. 'Oh, that feels better.' It really did feel great. Her irritation evaporated and she turned to see where Putta had landed.

Putta was wallowing about slightly further upstream and she called over to him, 'Well done. That did the trick.' Then she thought that was something the Doctor might have said and felt empty and worried. Still, their position had improved a little and the Doctor wouldn't have wanted them to give up. She hadn't been able to know him for very long, but she was sure he would never have been in favour of giving up, even in strange circumstances.

Putta kept on wallowing and looking like a dunked schoolboy. 'I've lost my shoe,' he bleated. 'They were too big... one of them's come off. I've lost it.'

'No, you haven't.'

'I have,' he wailed. 'These are the only Earth clothes I've got and they're not even mine – we've lost the Doctor, we won't know what to do without him and I'm going to get a foot injury and it's well known and written in all the manuals that foot injuries impair exploration ability and that shoe-loss eventually leads to death in 63.2 per cent of off-world expeditions.

Bryony couldn't help laughing – it was such a relief not to have those odd, bland, fake intrusions, banging about inside her skull. Plus, Putta did look very funny. The only thing more amusing than plus fours was wet plus fours. 'I don't know about all that. But your shoe's not lost – it's right here. Look… there it goes.'

Putta's shoe – sturdy as a tiny boat – was bobbing merrily past Bryony and continuing downstream.

'But… But don't just watch it go! I need that!' Putta struggled and flailed towards her through the knee-deep water. 'Ah!' And then stopped abruptly. 'See? Now I have a foot injury. It's the beginning of the end.'

'Oh, don't be so melodramatic. We'll catch it. I'll catch it.' She turned cautiously and began working her way along, through pools and over boulders, pursuing what actually was turning out to be a rather swift and agile escaped shoe. She could hear Putta groaning and splashing behind her.

Already Bryony could sense a mild bumping, as if some large hand was patting the base of her head. The force attempting to control her – whatever it might be – was closing in again. She focused on how chilly the water was and how the several bramble wounds on her shins and along her left arm were remarkably uncomfortable. She tried not to picture the glowing green horror of the carnivorous golf bunker and wonder whether this was the mental equivalent – something that would slowly eat up who she was.

The shoe wagged and swayed round a curve in the stream and she lost sight of it. The water was now flowing between high banks, overgrown with brush and little trees, and these completely obscured the course of the stream beyond. It must, at some time, have been a much more impressive river.

While she strode on, as best she could, she had no idea of what might be ahead. The banks kept the summer warmth and light at bay and here the air was dank. She couldn't leave the increasingly cold and deepening water, because the harsh slopes to either side were penning her in. The vegetation hanging above her looked both lush and threatening. She wondered if one ruined shoe was worth this effort. She wondered what she would find beyond the bend. She wondered where Putta had got to and yet couldn't quite manage to glance back and check. Bryony felt the external consciousness as it began oozing in again under her real experiences, her real self. Bryony could tell that something was trying to lift away all the facts and bits of information and jokes and habits that made her Bryony Mailer and no one else. It wanted them to drift away as if they were light, plastic, useless things. It wanted to act like a stream of living water, sweeping along – a stream that could become a torrent at any time, wiping her away.

I'm not having it, Bryony told herself. *I'm not allowing it. Nobody in here is going to do my thinking for me. That's my job.*

Still, despite her undoubted determination, she might not have been able to resist the inward rush and swell of flattering temptations and convincing new memories. She might not have been able to fight them as they shimmered and darted in at her. She might have lost the struggle.

Bryony Mailer might have been scooped up and washed away from herself, if it hadn't been for this other strange sensation, a kind of thrumming electrical tingle which started to prickle and dance along her arms. There was no reason for the sensation that she could figure out and there was nothing on her arms, but the tingling was definitely there and it was definitely, well… *good.*

Something about the air as she breathed it in and then let it back out also felt… *comforting.* The colour of the leaves overhead, the flickers of light on the stream – they weren't exactly brighter, but then again they seemed – Bryony couldn't quite get the right word – but very possibly they had been somehow *improved*.

While she wondered if these phenomena were a warning of some new assault, Bryony finally finished painstakingly rounding the jutting promontory and caught her first sight of the stream as flowed on, now lazing its way in wide shallows between a series of large rocks. A kingfisher – startling blue and fast – dashed across and away. She'd never seen one before.

But the bird wasn't what caught her attention. Over to the left, standing incongruously on a flat bank of yellowish sand, in a patch of sunlight close by the water's edge was a tall, dark blue box. It looked almost ten feet high, strangely substantial and utterly out of place – a blue box.

As she approached, a cloud of butterflies – with small wings in shades of brindled brown and red – rose up from around the box, hung for a moment in the remarkably golden light and drifted away, glimmering through the trees until they were gone.

A box.

A blue box.

It was a mildly battered, dusty, inexplicable blue box.

Bryony examined it and had the distinct impression that it was examining her in return. Something about it had an air of experience, as if it had been to places and done things, even as if it knew things.

She flinched for an instant, fearing this was the source of the mind control she and Putta had been suffering. But, no – there was something about the box that was reassuring. Bryony almost considered apologising for having doubted it.

Which is crazy. Then again – I'm not exactly having an uncrazy day.

She edged closer.

The nearer she got to the box, the easier it was to think her own thoughts.

A police box. Bizarre. Why here? It can't possibly belong here.

Then again, the box gave her the impression that it could belong wherever it liked. It was – Bryony almost wanted to think *it's dressed up as* – a police box. Here were the familiar rounded white letters placidly announcing POLICE PUBLIC CALL BOX. Here were the usual panelled sides and double door, the little notice on one of the doors with kind black printing which offered ADVICE & ASSISTANCE OBTAINABLE IMMEDIATELY.

'I've never bothered to read what the notices said when I've met other boxes… That is… I mean… This is all peculiar… and I am… talking to a box.'

Bryony wondered briefly if this was another kind of hallucination being foisted upon her.

'Sorry. No. Of course you're not. Of course you're not,' she told the box.

And she wanted to pat the thing – either to apologise or say hello, she wasn't clear. But it had to be done. That was clear. She advanced until she was standing on the smooth, calm sand. Gently, she reached out towards the high shape.

'Don't!' It was Putta. He'd caught up with her and was clattering and scrambling out of the water behind her. 'You don't know what it is. Alien vessels on alien planets have to be approached with extreme caution.'

Bryony was annoyed – this was her discovery – she was tempted to say this was her friend… 'It's not a vessel. It's a police box. And I'm not on an alien planet – you're the one who doesn't belong here.' She extended her fingers towards the looming, blue surface.

'No!' Putta tugged at his hair, even more nervous. Then he settled his breath a touch and asked, 'What's a police box?'

153

Bryony sighed and explained, 'It's a kind of mini office combined with a temporary cell – but mainly it's a call box. For calls.' Putta blinked at her like a badger considering a pianoforte. 'The police use them. And if you want help, anyone can pick up the phone – it's behind that little cupboard door there, I think, and you get put through to a police station. They're old-fashioned these days… But I think that's the idea of them. You use them to get help.' Even while she said this, Bryony was warmed by the possibility that she could do just that – something as amazingly simple as that. She very much wanted to be able to just open a little door in a big blue box that was nowhere it was meant to be and speak into a receiver and ask for ADVICE & ASSISTANCE. 'What I don't know is why it would be here – maybe it got washed down by a storm… Only it doesn't look at all like that…'

'There's something funny about it.'

'Well, yeah – it ought to be on a pavement somewhere. And the phone won't work, won't be connected…' And yet – there was still an atmosphere of helpfulness about the thing. Bryony made a decision and – despite a frankly undignified squeal of alarm from Putta, she took a firm hold of its door handle and gave a sharp tug.

Nothing happened.

She tugged again.

Nothing.

Bryony eyed the box again and it seemed rapidly less impressive, less fascinating, than it had.

'Well, it was worth a try…' Bryony paused, and this intense heaviness descended on her. Although she was a strong person and had been managing all of the day's surprises far better than most other Earth inhabitants would, she was tired, very tired, and slowly, inexorably, she could feel her hope leaving her. Even her dodgy boyfriend, even the tedium of her dead-end job, even the horror of today's casualties and the battering her consciousness was taking hadn't affected her underlying confidence that, somehow, things would work out and be OK. This was the moment when she allowed herself to consider that maybe nothing would work out, not ever.

And back came the alien consciousness – testing and prying and promising. Even though the calm it offered wasn't true, for the first time Bryony began to believe it was her best option.

Isn't life terrible? Isn't it all going to end in tears? Won't it be good to just give up and let something else run my mind, my life?

Clearly the consciousness had learned how to overcome misery. It had worked out how to use it to surf, ever faster and ever more hungrily, into their thoughts.

Bryony stared emptily into Putta's face and could tell from his expression that he was feeling probably even more awful that she did and yet was also no longer defended by his overwhelming despair.

Both of them, it seemed, were locked to the spot by gloom. And both of them were beginning not only to give up the fight, but to actively open themselves to the alien mind.

As they did so, the placid sand beneath their feet started to shift and stir. While neither of them could manage to pay any attention, the sand grains were shaped and coaxed into tendrils that rose around Bryony's ankles that began to grip firmly around her scratched shins. Putta's remaining shoe and long socks also disappeared into a sandy embrace.

And neither of them minded.

Bryony Mailer and Putta Pattershaun 5 were going to welcome the end of everything. To be honest, they were already convinced that it would be a great relief.

THE DOCTOR WAS NOT alone.

But that wasn't a problem.

The Doctor appeared to have been ripped out of one spatial location – at the very least – and propelled into another by a transmat process so effective and yet so primitive that it had left him feeling as if he'd been turned inside out and carelessly folded before being stored in some kind of existential sock drawer.

But this also wasn't a problem. That kind of thing happened every day. Or during a fairly high number of his days, anyway. And the Doctor chose to find this mainly fun.

The Doctor had materialised in mid-air and then dropped what he estimated was a comfy six inches until he hit something solid and load-bearing. Falling onto things was also usual and – now and again – fun.

That's the convenient thing about landing, he'd thought. *It's always there to stop you falling any further.*

Once he'd landed, he'd become aware that his bones were complaining and he was nauseous – which wasn't like him, he usually had an excellent appetite.

The condemned man ate a hearty breakfast – the first time anyone said that in this galaxy, they were saying it about me. And by supper time I wasn't condemned at all, I was having a bowl of delicious broth with the Supra Vizier of Mott. Lovely woman. Lovely heads.

156

Not a problem.

He felt positively over-stuffed and could also have done with a week of sleep in a hammock somewhere bracing – maybe Plymouth, for the sake of argument. *I don't think I've ever been there and I wouldn't want it to feel neglected.* And all his systems – nervous, circulatory, immune, autonomic, artronic – just every single one of his available systems were experiencing levels of distress that would have left many other wanderers in time and space lying on their faces and whimpering.

But even this wasn't a problem.

The problem is the…

Don't say It. Don't name It.

I'm getting tired.

Can't give it a name…

If I name It, I think It will win.

And that will probably – at least possibly – mean no more broth, no more Supra Viziers and no more me.

And where would the universe be without me?

Where would I be?

And since we're discussing where – and not that I want to be demanding… but where exactly I am now?

Having recovered from his short drop, the Doctor was sitting up with his legs laid languidly out ahead of him, crossed at the ankles, like a man who'd never heard of such a thing as a problem. He was leaning back at a relaxed angle with his hands shoved casually into his impossibly deep pockets.

If the problem doesn't have a name then It can't exist.

Maybe. I'm improvising. I would have to point out that improvising is something which I'm usually wonderful at… Perhaps less wonderful today.

His hat was tilted raffishly over his eyes and his scarf lay about him heavily, like something anaesthetised.

I would be perfectly safe if the problem didn't exist...

So the last thing that I should think of is the problem.

Maybe.

Don't think of It.

I should, in general, ignore the remarkable levels of danger on all sides...

He was also humming under his breath like a person completely at his ease.

The Doctor was used to all the weird surprises, odd transmat beams and, for that matter, harsh treatment that a universe – one didn't wish to be rude, but one did have to mention – a universe filled with some highly unpleasant characters could serve up.

That wasn't the problem.

Neither was his current location, even though it was – and again he didn't intend to pry – hard to define.

Quite literally hard to define.

That's a safe thing to think of – I'll think of that.

Where am I?

For a start, the Doctor couldn't quite say exactly what he was leaning against. The surface which was, at the moment, agreeing to support his back and shoulders was gently moving, like the belly of a massive beast. In fact, it was as if he were inside the belly of a beast.

But I couldn't possibly think of that.

That might be true.

And that mustn't be true, because that would mean that I have been swallowed and that would imply that I will be digested. A remarkable, handsome, charming and intelligent chap like myself being digested – well, that doesn't bear thinking about.

So I won't.

The Doctor concentrated on at least appearing to be relaxed, but there was sweat on his face and his breath was labouring. He forced himself to believe that he wasn't going to be digested – *breathe* – that there was more than enough air – *breathe* – that suited him in here.

And he kept on forcing himself not to think of the problem.

But It's here – the problem behind the problem. The big problem that makes all the other problems. I can tell that It's here and It could be named and then… Should I name It? Should I not? It seems shy… Is that a good thing? Does that indicate a weakness? Would naming upset It in a useful way? I wouldn't wish to annoy It? Or would I?

The Doctor closed his eyes for a moment and shook his head. Then he looked around as amiably and cheerfully as he could – as if he were inspecting a room in an apartment he might want to buy.

'No problems here. This is only a room. A warm, moist, unusual room…'

But he kept on puzzling, calculating, observing… The floor under his legs was just this blurry reddish blackish purplish surface which shifted up and down placidly, which was damp and vaguely slimy to the touch. It was warm. The whole place was humid, sticky. And the curved, pulsing walls / ceiling / floor had a habit of not exactly seeming to be there when the Doctor stared at them. When he'd tried to prod any of the surfaces with his fingers, sometimes they were resistant and sometimes he'd found most of his hand sinking into what felt like warm soup and looked like an organic jell with threads of silver running through it and sparkling now and then.

Which I can't say is a problem. It's peculiar, but then I love peculiar things. I could almost be said to seek them out. I'm marvellously unusual myself, although I often go unappreciated…

He heard a type of clicking and movement over to his right and made what he thought was an excellent effort to completely ignore it.

He could feel the tendons in his neck standing out with

the effort of being happy and interested in the good things of life – however short one's life turned out to be – and not remotely worried.

All round him – above, beside, behind, below – was this curious living substance, threaded with silver and unable to decide if it was a liquid or a solid, a colloid, or – this could happen – perhaps it would decide to be a gas. What would happen then? That could be terrifying, but it could also be fascinating…

There was no sign of a door, or any other way that he might have entered this space. There was no obvious way to leave.

I'm trapped. I'm trapped. I'm trapped.

But I might like that.

I could grow to like that. And then I might escape. I'm generally excellent at escaping. But that's mainly when there are guards to bamboozle and locks to unlock, doors that can be opened…

Still, at present I can enjoy being trapped. I can say I'm being held. Like a hug. I am being hugged.

I am not being digested.

I am not being tested.

I am not being tortured.

But then he couldn't help seeing the small problem – the thing he shouldn't give any of his attention. There the thing was – just a bit.

Problem.

There was a flicker of disturbingly swift motion, the shifting of a dreadfully thin leg, a predator's limb.

That wouldn't be my first choice for a companion…

'Ah, but you must understand…' The Doctor kept his voice steady while he talked to nothing that he wanted to look at right now… 'You're mistaking me for someone else entirely… Which is to say, the last time I met… something which resembled you, I was someone else entirely… Or not quite my current self…' His throat and mouth were dry. 'I tend to believe that you're someone else entirely, too… I think you're wearing a mask. I think you've been wearing a lot of masks…'

He didn't think he could keep this up for much longer. The smaller problem – he caught a glimpse of it as it ran up the wall – this minor problem behind which the big problem was hiding – he suspected that was now squatting on the ceiling, waiting directly above his head.

Something flicked off his hat.

And even though the something was a mask, a fiction, a temporary creation called up by something else – the thing was getting very real.

Because the Doctor had been subjected to a number of encounters with a number of nasty things since he'd arrived, and he'd been able to figure out at least a little of what was going on here in this room which wasn't a room in the place which wasn't a place…

When the Doctor had initially regained consciousness he had rolled over and seen something impossible. The smooth, weapons-grade surface, the raised reinforcement hemispheres, it had been instantly recognisable – this was Dalek construction, no other race built anything like it. He'd experienced the customary, irrepressible lurch of outrage and fear as he'd raised his eyes to see more, know what he must, start forming a plan. He had even been able to touch the unmistakable, slightly warm, slightly charged metal of a Dalek carapace.

But the first problem which had confronted him – once it was fully revealed – had been much worse than a Dalek.

And, of course, no one expects to end up saying something like 'much worse than a Dalek'. What's much worse than a Dalek…? Well, it's best not to mention…

Utterly alert at once, the Doctor had sprung to his

feet, hearts racing, and faced the living nightmare that was Davros. Somehow Davros was right there, alive, his wizened skull-like face sneering, his pink snaking tongue darting over those leathery, mummified lips. Davros, the creator of the Daleks, his wasted lower limbs coddled in the initial generation, basic Dalek transport module. The Doctor had even been able to smell that characteristic combination of stale air, not-quite-arrested bodily decay and malignant DNA that had haunted him when he was on Skaro, the Daleks' planet of origin. Skaro, torn apart by the hatred that spawned the Daleks, the universe's ultimate killing machines.

The Doctor had peered down at Davros, at that monstrous mind and tormented body. The Doctor had tried to stay certain that the Daleks had destroyed Davros as genetically unacceptable. Davros couldn't be here. Davros wasn't even behaving quite like Davros. He hadn't spoken. Not one word.

And I've rarely met a megalomaniac so fond of the sound of his own voice.

Davros had sneered, licked his lips over and over, hovered his one claw of a hand over the control stick of his module, licked again, hovered again, sneered again. It was as if the morally deformed scientist was caught in a bend of time.

It's like a transchronic loop, the Doctor had thought.

I can think of myself thinking that. I can think that I am remembering that from my recent past. I can build layers of thinking.

I can even think that an entity is gouging out my past and showing it to me like highly unpleasant movies – except these aren't just images, they are being given substance… I can think that.

I'm good at thinking. Geniuses are and I'm a genius. I'm several geniuses all together under one hat. Although my hat is currently over there…With those few pale fibres on it – like fragments of a web… Which it's best not to notice…

If I can only keep on thinking, I'll be all right. Thinking about other things, pleasant things, safe things, running off and thinking in strange places where It doesn't want me to… That's what I have to do.

And I always have had a talent for both running off and thinking in strange places. Einstein and Feynman and Leonardo and Zogg the Remarkable, they all complained about it.

But in the end I do always come up with a result, a solution to the problem…

Facing Davros, an engineer of terror, the Doctor had said pleasantly, 'And I can think of very few people I'd rather see caught in a transchronic loop, but it's not quite that either, is it?' He'd tapped Davros's carapace and his finger had penetrated it, sunk in. The hemispheres on its surface began to be more translucent, the less faith the Doctor had in them. 'No, this is… It's more like watching a recorded image, a repeating image.' Somehow his psychic energy, his artron energy, his belief, was being harnessed to create beings, to manipulate matter into complex living forms. While being rather horrifying, it was also a remarkable achievement.

And as soon as the Doctor had uncovered his nightmare's secret, the image of Davros had shivered, become a wavering shape and then been reabsorbed into the reddish blackish purplish surface confining the Doctor.

He'd sighed – shaken, but still in control.

He'd been permitted a moment to rest and to wonder why his mind's energy had been forced to summon up one of its own worst fears. That didn't bode well. Something was using his memories like an index file… and only accessing the fear-inducing data.

He'd focused on gathering his strength, because he had an idea he would need it.

And he'd been right. The Doctor usually was.

A Cyberman – solid, convincing, blank-eyed and slit-mouthed – had risen smoothly up from the not-quite-floor. The Doctor had managed not to flinch. This was absolutely a Cyberman. It had just the right air of obsession, and of a sick joke: as if someone had decided to make models of the living dead, cleanly metallic animated corpses, and then sent them marching across the universe to make more living dead until nothing had a heart, or a warm impulse, until all was cold and the Cyber Purpose had defeated itself and left them with nothing.

They were dreadful things, Cybermen.

So I'd be wise not to think of one too clearly. I will only remember how I get nightmares to go away… I give them no energy. I give them no belief.

The Cyberman had twitched a finger and given a slight nod. And again. And again. It hadn't been difficult for the Doctor to notice the tell-tale signs of repetition. This was another prefabricated creature, a fake.

Still, it had been difficult to lower his levels of fear. If something could make a convincing Cyberman, might not the fake Cyberman be just as bad as a real one? What was the difference between being killed by an imitation Cyberman and the genuine article? It wasn't going to be much fun finding out.

The Doctor had pressed himself to be as jovial as he ever had, to play the fool harder and faster than he'd thought he could. 'Ah, but no you don't. I really must insist that no you don't.' He had sat down, lounged, wagged one hand scoldingly. 'I really can't have just anyone barging in here, you know. Not that I know where here is – but I'm sure I only made a reservation for one…'

But perhaps having just anyone barge in was exactly what was going to happen. The Doctor had fumbled in his pocket, brought out a rumpled paper bag and offered it – 'Jelly baby?' – to the forbidding figure, the terror of so many planets. At once the Cyberman had seemed to lose solidity and melt away.

But it had taken longer for the Cyberman to fade than it had for Davros to leave the Doctor be. And the Cyberman had seemed more confidently constructed, more real. Whatever was conjuring up these things, it was a quick learner.

While he remembered all this, pondered it, the Doctor continued to bear something important in mind…

There's no problem, no problem overhead, no problem with a bulbous, unclean-looking body and long, sharp legs and longer, sharper mouth parts –

The Doctor's scalp tingled and crawled as he fought not to think of the thing overhead and made efforts to recall with absolute clarity how he had been confronted, not only with Davros and a Cyberman, but with a Sontaran warrior, then the hideous green parasitic worm that was a Wirrn larva, then an Auton – smooth-faced, implacable killer…

Each creation had been more real than the last, more able to move and function in a way that he found hard to ignore.

The Doctor banged his head back against the wet, hot surface behind him and announced to the general area, 'I do admire your abilities, you know. There are scientists all over the universe rattling their brains and breaking test tubes trying to get anywhere near your ability to form life out of… Well, what are you doing exactly…? Altering matter at a sub-atomic level and then knitting it up like a pullover into life. Or something quite like life. I'm impressed, really I am.'

Something hard and cold scraped gently through the Doctor's dense tumble of hair and touched his forehead for a moment before withdrawing. This made it tricky not to scream.

'But why won't you let me meet you – the real you? Why

the clever puppets? If you wanted to destroy me, I'm sure you could have. Are you running some kind of experiment? Because I love experiments and I must say I'm sure I'd be able to help you if you'd just let me know what you were trying to find out… Or… Is this a game…? I always enjoy a game. Do you know poker? Don't play it much myself, but I knew a man who did and he taught me a thing or two…'

There was no reply, and the Doctor couldn't avoid considering another possibility – that he was trapped here because It found him entertaining. Maybe he was going to be destroyed, but he was going to be destroyed in a slow, ornate way that It found amusing – by repeated attacks from everything he'd ever tried to fight against, everything that had ever troubled him. His memories were being ransacked and used against him. Eventually, he would be worn down, he would have no power to resist and this or that creation would draw out so much of his artron energy that it would become truly alive – before it drained him of all that he was.

That's why its other name is Soul-Eater.

'I do know what you really are, by the way… Who you are… I do remember what Putta said on the golf course. It seems that while I'm in here you can't manage to give me any of those nasty headaches, or make me forget things… So I must be very close… In the eye of the storm… Is that it? Have you let me into the eye of your storm…?'

And then, slowly descending from the ceiling, came a spider. It was sharply defined, intelligent and deadly. Its dark legs were covered in dense greyish fur that suggested underground places and lurking. It wasn't so terribly huge. Its cephalothorax was only about the size of perhaps a large orange, or a sizeable potato. Its abdomen was larger, beating faintly with a rapid pulse and straggled here and there with wiry, tawny fur.

The abdomen wasn't quite as big as a rugby ball.

Not quite that big.

The rearmost two of its fast, clever legs played out silk as it dropped while the others readied themselves.

The Doctor knew it would be a very bad idea to imagine the creature swinging forward and grabbing him, smothering his face and closing its limbs inescapably behind his skull.

He didn't think he'd like that at all.

And naturally I wouldn't enjoy having the thing leap on to my back and cling there, digging into my brain and controlling me, enslaving me the way it did the human settlers on Metebelis 3.

The Doctor swallowed audibly. He smiled the best smile he could manage under the circumstances. 'Cephalothorax is a wonderful word… Very useful for spiders. They don't have a separate head and thorax – which is why we use the term ce-pha-lo-tho-rax – the two parts are fused together in arachnids, just so…' He avoided actually touching the spider's cephalothorax in case he could feel it really clearly – all those hairs, all that poised energy. He didn't want it to seem any more substantial than it already did.

Plus, it was a monstrously large, dank, hairy, dangerous, brain-eating spider. Of course he didn't want to touch it.

The Doctor blinked and the spider's mouthparts fluttered, glistened. It had halted at his eye level and now span so that it could look at him. Then it span back – ready to grab him.

'I can tell you another marvellous word.' The Doctor took a deep breath. Saying Its name hadn't gone well the last time, but then again It had been so keen to be forgotten, hidden.. Surely that did indicate a weakness. 'Ahhmmm… Bah-Sokhar. Bah-Sokhar? You are a Bah-Sokhar, aren't you? Behind all the pretending and eating people – which really isn't any way to behave – and magic tricks… That's what you are, isn't it? Hello, Bah-Sokhar. I'm the Doctor.

Although I think you already know that – you seem to have been climbing around in my memories for a while… Shouldn't we meet properly now we've been introduced?'

The Doctor paused.

The Doctor waited.

The Doctor grinned his most friendly grin.

The spider flinched, then stretched its legs and swung forward on its silk. Any second now it was going to touch his face.

STANDING IN HER KITCHEN, Mrs Julia Fetch was preparing the lovely fresh vegetables her grandchildren had brought in for dinner. She was podding peas, collecting them in the old brown ceramic basin that had been in every family kitchen she had ever known. The children were helping, which was kind of them. Honor was washing spinach leaves under the tap and singing a little song to herself. Xavier was slicing broccoli very carefully because the knife was really sharp and he had been warned not to cut himself.

Julia glanced over when Xavier said, 'Oh. Oh, look.'

'What is it? Have you cut your finger?'

'No. He's fine.' Honor gave Xavier's answer. Each of the twins always seemed to know exactly what was happening to the other. Julia thought it was sweet. And it must mean they were never lonely.

Honor stepped across from the sink and peered at Xavier's hand. 'He's found something.'

'Yes.' Xavier raised his right hand and, dangling from it was a spider. 'I've found something.' He watched it spinning and flexing its tiny legs.

Julia didn't especially like spiders. 'Perhaps you could put it outside again where it lives…'

Honor shook her head happily. 'No, he's got a better idea.'

169

And Xavier lifted the spider higher. He angled his head, opened his mouth and then dropped the little arachnid in between his lips. Xavier swallowed the spider. 'There we are. Now I understand more about spiders.'

Honor clapped her hands delightedly – as if a puppy had just done a trick.

Julia wasn't quite sure this was the usual way to deal with such things, but if it pleased Honor and Xavier then it must be all right.

She went back to removing the peas from their pods. There were almost enough for the three of them. How marvellous. What a fine meal they were going to have with the pretty napkins and the shiny knives and forks and the thick white linen tablecloth that Papa had bought in Dublin… 'Well, don't get so full of spider that you won't want your dinner.'

Julia Fetch wondered what meat they were going to have for their meal. It seemed that she should have decided by now… Something tasty… Something fresh… Fresh meat would be best.

Bryony Mailer was – in a numb way – absolutely ecstatic.

Putta Pattershaun 5 was, if anything, even more numb and even more cheerful. Although they were both absolutely certain – as fingers and ropes of twisting sand raced up their bodies – that they would be dead within… let's say thirty seconds at the most, they were as content as they could be.

While sand slipped up her torso and contracted her breathing, Bryony sighed, 'Hmmm…' as if she was climbing into a lovely bath. Being dead seemed, just then, pretty much the same as a lovely bath, only longer-lasting.

And, meanwhile, Putta just about managed to giggle as ripples and curls of sand gathered under his chin – forming a sort of yellowish, undulating beard – and ribbons of sand snuggled round his throat and gently began to strangle him. He felt only one tiny regret as he began to pass out. He couldn't believe how stupid he'd been not to guess how magnificent getting murdered would be. If he'd realised, he'd have found a murderer and made a polite request years ago…

At which point Putta became unconscious and then Bryony joined him.

THIS MADE IT ALL the more surprising when they both woke up completely alive a short while later.

Bryony was awake first, her head tucked uncomfortably into an angle at the bottom of a short staircase. She had a stiff neck. Also, the rest of her was lying upside down on the short staircase and so her spine was in a fair amount of pain. She also knew – even before she half-tumbled and half-scrambled to her feet and sand seem to trickle out of most of her clothing – that her skin was covered in a thoroughly unpleasant gritty layer beneath everything she was wearing.

'Oh, for goodness' sake…'

She would have complained at greater length, but she was prevented by seeing (a) Putta lying on his side and looking safe – if sandy and still out for the count – and really quite cute in his 1930s golfing gear, and (b) the strange interior in which she found herself.

Bryony was in a largish room apparently decorated by a… actually, it was difficult to tell, but perhaps a Victorian scientist. The walls were panelled in something that resembled walnut, but which felt more like a cross between slick cloth and perhaps metal. There were inset circles set at regular intervals, a few of them decorated with warmly coloured designs showing nothing she could recognise. There was something that looked like an old-fashioned wireless cabinet, some fluted columns here and there, wooden furniture that managed to seem both old-fashioned and remarkably modern. And there were lots of brass hand rails. Loads of them. As if whoever the room belonged to expected to fall over a lot.

The only familiar thing was a hat stand. The sort of object you would see in an older aunt's hallway.

The hand rails and the woodwork, the brass, the hat stand, they started to suggest this was an older person's house.

Perhaps this was an older person's entrance hall.

It felt like an entrance, felt welcoming.

If felt – oddly – like home.

Even the strange sort of mantelpiece / sideboard thingy over on that wall seemed to be pleased she was there. It looked as if it ought to be a window, or show a picture – as if it wanted to do that.

And – right at the centre of the room – this waist-high wooden console thingy positively shone with something close to… pleasure. It had an air of importance and was festooned in hand rails. Bryony couldn't help exploring its snug little flip-down panels – each with a neat brass handle. Behind every panel was a different array of futuristic switches, press-buttons, dials and levers. And there were also a few jury-rigged controls which looked less futuristic and more as if someone had wired them together in a hurry and never got back to mend them or fix them properly.

As she explored, Bryony felt increasingly excited. 'Well, if a room could say – *pleased to meet you* – you kind of are, aren't you…?' It didn't seem that weird to be speaking to this room. 'Hello? Hello?' She was sure – even though she'd never seen any alien technology – that this was alien technology. And beautiful with it. She couldn't suppress a grin. 'Not that I'm really speaking to a room. It's the room's owner that I…'

At the word 'owner' the console looked very slightly annoyed. Not that a console *could* be annoyed… 'You are, though, aren't you? You're annoyed that I think you have an owner…' This made the console's many switches and polished surfaces glimmer with slightly richer tones. 'Well. I'm pleased to meet you, too.' Bryony stretched – apart from the incredible itching pretty much everywhere, she felt as if she'd had the best night's sleep of her life. 'How did I end up being here, though?'

With a shudder and a returning shortness of breath, Bryony remembered the sand: that horrible, unstoppable sand that had come swarming and clawing up over her and… She gripped one of the console's rails and immediately seemed steadier. 'I should be dead,' she whispered.

Just for an instant, Bryony wondered if being dead involved a lot of wood panelling. Certainly, without the soothing and calming influence of the Bah-Sokhar, Bryony was now shockingly aware of how close her death had come to her. It seemed that a chill bullet had just licked past her ear.

She also remembered – in a brief snap of colours and light – a pair of doors slamming back, wide open, and a sensation of being lifted, drawn inside them and taken care of.

'*You* should be dead…' This emerged in a sandy mumble from Putta as he wriggled back to life on the floor – the smooth, brown, not-made-of-wood-but-looks-like-it floor which thrummed comfortingly. 'I was practically asking to be dead. I was completely…' Putta rubbed his hair and produced minute showers of sand while looking up at Bryony, bemused. 'I couldn't wait to be the monster's breakfast. I can remember looking forward to it more than anything.' He tried sitting. Sand ran out of his jacket sleeves. 'Gets everywhere. Again.'

'Yes, doesn't it.'

'But it's not trying to kill us.'

'No. I think it's just back to being ordinary sand… And I feel… wonderful.'

Putta nodded, 'Now that you mention it – I'm a bit sore here and there and…' Yet more sand was shaken out of his plus fours and down over his socks. 'This really tickles. But other than that.' He looked suspicious. 'I feel really happy.' Putta managed to say this as if he was describing a disease. He peered around, 'What is this place?'

'No idea.'

'Well, how did we get here?'

'Even less idea… Or, at least, I don't have an idea that makes sense.'

'Does the idea you do have involve floating in a cloud of pearly-coloured light and… a kind of *whoosh*…'

Bryony nodded. 'It does.' She smiled. She was having another idea. 'Isn't this a beautiful room?'

'It's OK, I suppose,' sniffed Putta, pottering about and immediately banging his knee on the thing that looked like a wireless cabinet. 'Ah!'

'I think this is the entrance hall, foyer… kind of maybe… And if we open one of these doors…' Bryony decided that the door with an impressive light over it and the overcomplicated stubby staircase leading up to it – the door that seemed to be made of velvety darkness – looked most important. It also had a generous supply of brass rails. Therefore, she guessed, it must lead somewhere significant. She trotted up the steps, raised her hand and – it truly did seem – before she could even press against the door, it swung open.

Immediately, she was confronted by something she

didn't understand. 'Putta! Putta, this is…' She was looking out at the river she had recently waded along – the rocks, the trees, the sun a little lower in the sky than it had been the last time she saw it, just before she blacked out. Perhaps more importantly, just beyond the door was the angry sand – still writhing, peaking, dropping and frothing impotently. Bryony quickly withdrew the foot that had almost crossed the threshold back into disaster. 'Oh, my god!'

Putta peered over her shoulder and, at once, tried to pull her away, 'Bryony! Come back! I can't lose you! It can take me!'

Simultaneous waves of pride and embarrassment prevented him from saying anything else before Bryony could tell him, 'No, no. It's OK, somehow. The sand can't get in. It doesn't seem to be able to even see us, never mind taking anyone.' She studied him for a moment. *Take me…* What are you like…? Being all heroic.' She patted his arm.

'Well, keep back, anyway.'

Bryony instead leaned her head as far as she could out of the doorway and checked carefully to either side. Then she checked again. The sand seethed beneath her angrily, but with no real focus. 'Well… I don't know how this is or why this is, but we're inside that box.'

'What box?'

'The blue box. The police box – blue with a little light on top – the box that we were outside of before we started to…' She avoided saying the words *die horribly at the mercy of angry sand*.

'But that's not…' Putta squeezed gingerly forward until he was next to her in the doorway and then also peeked out to left and right. 'Oh, dear… Oh, dear…' And then he half-fell and half-staggered back down the steps and was sick. 'Oh, dear.'

Bryony closed the doors again gently and walked to

him while he heaved and coughed and then was sick –
fortunately into one of the now extremely numerous piles
of sand. 'What's wrong with you?'

'Spatial dissonance.'

'Come again.'

'What?'

'I mean I don't know what you mean.'

'Oh… *Ughghch*… It's just if a ship has a compression field
– and this has the – *oaagh* – broodmother of all compression
fields – then it always makes me – *hoooo*. Sick. Transmats
make me queasy. Most portals. Just plain motion sickness
isn't great…'

'Wonderful!' grumbled Bryony.

'No, it's not,' heaved Putta – Yinzill wasn't famous for its
grasp of irony… 'I'm supposed to be travelling the universe
looking for adventure. I spend most of my time feeling
dreadful and losing my meals. I'm basically malnourished
apart from…'

But then Putta stopped talking, because Bryony was
clearly paying no attention to him and was simply rushing
from the big throne-like chair, to the wall panels, to the
console… to basically everything else in the room…
touching each item, giggling, spinning round and punching
the air. 'I knew it! I knew this was a spaceship! I mean, I
guessed fairly quickly. Oh, it's beautiful.'

Putta mopped his brow with a corner of his shirt. 'It's
not that great when you're used to them… I've seen better,'
he mumbled, struggling to stand upright and join Bryony.
'Ow!' Then he seemed to trip over nothing in particular on
the floor and jar one of his ankles. 'I don't think it likes me.'

Bryony eyed the one other, less-impressive door in the
room. It seemed highly conventional and sported a nice
doorknob and a pleasing round panel with a red design.
'The rest of it must be through here. It's amazing! I mean,

huge! When you say compression field, I suppose you mean whatever's keeping all this inside a much smaller—'

But as she reached out and turned the doorknob, she was interrupted by a voice both she and Putta knew – a voice they had thought they would never hear again.

'Hello.' It was the Doctor.

They span round to find the source of the sound and watched as the space above what Bryony had been thinking of as *the mantelpiece* opened to display a type of viewing screen. (Bryony only had an unreliable 13-inch black and white television, so even this simple technology impressed her.)

And here was the Doctor's face – his slightly wild eyes, the grin with which he had irritated so many pompous and violent beings in so many turbulent times and places. He appeared to be sitting in his generous shirt sleeves and waistcoat – the image stopped halfway down the waistcoat – somewhere with very white walls which were set with circular indentations at regular intervals. 'Yes, hello.' He reached forward and adjusted what had to be some kind of camera recording him. 'Hmm…' He sat back, happier with image. And Bryony found it crossed her mind that the ship was now, somehow, *paying attention*. It seemed to miss the Doctor, too.

The Doctor sat back again and started to talk with his usual strangely irresponsible brand of authority. 'I must congratulate you on being able get inside the TARDIS. The Type 40 has a double-curtain, trimonic lock – which I suppose you must know – and there are very few civilisations advanced enough to produce technology that could open one of them… Are you a Time Lord…?' He pondered the screen intently. 'It's terribly rude, you know, to come barging into another Time Lord's TARDIS… Anyway, whoever you are, I do hope you're using all that knowhow in wonderful and interesting ways. Although, since you're creeping about like burglars, perhaps you're up to no good. I wouldn't want to speak ill of a stranger, but maybe that's the case.' He swept his hair back out of his eyes and continued, peering in at Bryony and Putta with so much focus that they felt he was, somehow, able to observe them. Which made both of them wish heartily that he still could. 'So right now you're probably wondering what kind of death-dealing defences the old girl will launch at you – force fields and omni-clamps, electron excitation beams, vaporisation nets… Well, I'm afraid I really couldn't approve of anything like that. Which means there aren't any defences to speak of… Although I would be a little careful if you decide to go wandering around any more than you already have. I would mind your step and be polite.' A huge grin loitered just under what was a stern expression. 'But if you're a friend – then you won't be in any danger. Or not much danger. I mean one never can tell really, can one…? And I can hardly be responsible for any damages to limbs and property and so forth – I mean, I haven't invited you, have I? I'm not even there.' Again there was a sense that he was studying their weaknesses and strengths. 'Equally, I do apologise that I can't be here to greet you in person. And I do hope that's not because I'm dead – it's so inconvenient when that happens. If I am still alive, I'm sure I'll be along directly. And if I'm not… well, I may be a little delayed.' At which, he reached down out of sight and his hand then emerged bearing his hat, which he slapped on to his head. 'Do take care of her. She takes very good care of me.' And then he leaned forward, obviously reaching for an off switch which he threw. The screen blinked out for an instant, after which it showed the river outside and the churning sand, all the details of the landscape around what they now knew was the TARDIS.

Bryony felt a wave of loss wash over her again.

And Putta doubled over. 'Ohnononononono…'

'I know. I miss him as well. But he wouldn't want us to–'

'No! You don't understand! We're in a TARDIS. We're in a Time Lord's TARDIS.' He squeezed his head in his hands. 'Nonononono. Nobody survives that. No one. I can't even begin… There aren't even any stories about what happens if you do what we're doing – there's just this… *silence*.' And then he folded himself into a knot of limbs, crouched on an area of the floor which had remained clear of both sand and vomit. 'We're dead.' He started to rock back and forth. 'And he's dead and he could have saved us. The Doctor could have saved us. But now it will all be…' He shuddered instead of finishing the sentence.

'Oh, do stop panicking,' Bryony snapped. 'Really. I mean, are you going to be a hero or a complete coward? Trying to be both is ridiculous.' She was attempting to sound sympathetic, but she had also worked out that they were going to need their wits about them and collapsing in a heap was something they could do later when they weren't trapped in a box that could think – and which might be dangerous – and when a terrible monster wasn't running amok just outside Arbroath and the only person who might be able to deal with it hadn't been… The thought of the Doctor simply being disappeared by some alien force was heartbreaking. She hoped that he'd felt no pain, that maybe at least he'd been lulled into a state of acceptance as she and Putta had been. She sighed. This was going to be hard if she had to deal with a spaceman having hysterics on top of everything else. 'Just… make up your mind.'

'Can't make up my mind,' gibbered Putta. 'He's a Time Lord!'

'So what? What's a Time Lord going to do – turn you into a frog?'

'Do you think?' Putta's ashen face glanced up at her. 'Could they do that? What's a frog?'

'Well, I wouldn't have thought…You're the spaceman. I was asking you…A frog's an amphibian.' Bryony decided a spot of action was called for. 'Look. I don't know about you, but I'm hungry and I need a bath and I'm tired and so I'm going to see if this place has a kitchen, or somewhere I can wash, or a bed. We obviously can't leave. So why not explore…? We can prepare – maybe there's equipment, weapons… maybe there's another exit…'

She didn't give Putta any time to howl, 'Why not? I'll tell you why not! Because we'll be punished for trespassing…!' before striding to the other available door, opening it and walking through, then hearing it close snugly behind her and muffle Putta's final, 'In a million ghastly ways!'

BRYONY FOUND HERSELF IN a slim line corridor. The blank walls, floor and ceiling were so perfectly white that their effect was slightly disorientating – as if she were walking along on nothing.

Apparently in response, the passageway mellowed to a deeper shade of cream and the lighting dropped to something that would suit a seedy nightclub with an interest in concealing nasty stains. 'Steady. I mean, thanks. But I do need to see where I'm going. Still, thank you, TARDIS.' The light levels rose again, but maintained a slightly orange glow which seemed more welcoming and gentle. Large circular indentations appeared in the walls, which made all the perfect whiteness less disorientating.

As she progressed, a doorway became apparent to her left, very much as if the wall had decided to provide one. Beyond it was a large kitchen of the sort a sizeable hotel might require – a sizeable hotel carved out of not-really-walnut. There were long work surfaces, banks of what seemed to be ovens and several square plaques of some goldenish marble-like material which Bryony guessed might act as stove tops. Brass hand rails were much in evidence. As were the kind of copper pans that no one used any more.

Not that it looked as if anyone had been using these –

they seemed brand new, hanging from their racks. Ranks of cupboards – some refrigerated and some heated – offered up their contents for Bryony's inspection: boxes, bags, bottles, cans, cartons, sacks, barrels, crates, jars – even some amphorae set into neat little metal stands – containing who knew what. Some of the containers were labelled, usually with what appeared to be outlandish script, or unfamiliar symbols – but when she looked directly at them, the jumbles of meaningless shapes resolved themselves into readable – if still pretty meaningless – words and phrases. Bryony read out, 'Pinebreath... Toxic unless fried... Ophoron... Maxxt... Powdered Maxxt... Rehydrated Maxxt...' Fortunately, over in the furthest corner, she spotted what was clearly the part of the kitchen the Doctor actually used. The work surface here was smeared with jam – among other less recognisable things – and there were toast crumbs, a toaster, half a loaf of slightly stale bread, a jar of carefully labelled homemade 'rhubarb and vanilla' jam – its lid missing – and a butter dish with enough smears and globs of butter left in it for Bryony to use it in the construction of an improvised jam sandwich. She couldn't find any cutlery – and was too hungry to make an exhaustive search – and so she had to use her fingers for buttering and jam application. And she'd had to tear lumps off the bread. Still – it was the best jam sandwich she'd ever met. It was so delicious, in fact, that she immediately made another.

As she noticed the tell-tale crunch of sand – ironically – in her second sandwich, she was already considering where she'd get a really good scrub down with some nice hot water and then a nap, when she heard a noise behind her.

More accurately, it came both from behind her and above.

THERE WAS ONLY ONE thing for it. Before the spider could close on the Doctor's face, he set his forefinger on the area where its eight legs joined its abdomen. The strength of the exoskeleton was plain, as was the power of the muscles within. This seemed absolutely like a real, genuine, enormous, giant, brain-dominating arachnid.

The Doctor swallowed with something close to a gulp.

Mustn't believe in it, but I do have to… engage with it.

His touch had made the spider's limbs jerk slightly in an ugly way, but for now it was still. He – *gently, calmly, gently* – rubbed his finger across the roots of its legs and then – *slowly, delicately, carefully* – he rubbed again. It felt like a vaguely oily machine – which wasn't as bad as he'd expected.

'I've never tickled a spider before…' he explained as amiably as he could while his scalp tingled with unease. 'I suspect you've never been tickled before, either…' He withdrew his fingertip, crooked his finger and then used his knuckle to stroke along the spider's fat, dangling abdomen. The harsh hairs bristled unpleasantly under his touch, but he kept on. He tried to imagine the thing was a dog – just a Labrador with a few too many legs. And threatening, glistening mouth parts.

'I could try to fight you off. That would be a reasonable response. As you're so well-finished and ready to do something thoroughly dreadful to me, I could grab hold of you before you get me and we could roll about on the floor and then I might tie you up with my scarf – which would upset you – or maybe I'd have to punch you. I've thrown a few punches before now...'

As he spoke, the Doctor stroked and soothed the pulsating curve of the arachnid's body. Its legs seemed to droop slightly, almost as if it were enjoying what was happening to it.

'But I have no intention of doing anything like that. A ready smile and a firm handshake – that's me. I wouldn't hurt a fly.' The spider's legs tensed again. 'I do beg your pardon. Poor choice of phrase.' He reached out with his other hand and began tickling the spider's leg roots and stroking its abdomen, both at once.

And gradually, gradually, the spider let itself down on its silk until it was standing – its eight legs braced horrifyingly to either side of his own, its body above his knees – as if it might leap now, as if it might pounce.

The Time Lord looked at the spider.

The spider looked at the Time Lord – its many eyes blackly reflective and unreadable.

Then – remarkably – it settled lower, rested its weight across his shins and angled its cephalothorax upwards enquiringly.

With infinite caution – the spider's obvious fangs were only inches away from his legs – the Doctor reached out once more. 'I can't tickle you between the ears, but how about behind the eyes...' The spider wriggled, apparently happily under his attentions and eased higher, so that it was resting partly on his thighs. He could smell the dank, cave-haunting, musty reek of its fur. This was almost too much for the Doctor, but he kept his nerve. 'Yes, there you are. Good spider. Yes, you are. I can't complain at all about you – all you're doing is being yourself. If I happen to find yourself rather difficult, that isn't your fault. I mean, usually I would steer clear of you… If we were both at the same birthday party, perhaps I might stay in the kitchen… unless you were in the kitchen… you'd more probably be in the bathroom wouldn't you… in the bath…?'

The Doctor was running out of spider-related small talk. (He never actually could see the point of small talk on any occasion – why offer a stranger you might never meet again all the most boring things you could possibly tell them?) But before he could guess what the weather was like outside and mention it – finally – the animal's shape began to waver a touch, and then a little more. The Doctor's hand began to pass through its substance where he was patting its back, as the spider became insubstantial. 'That's better. Much better.' And with a liquid rush the whole creation dissipated. After flinching slightly, the Doctor was alone.

'Or rather I'm not alone, am I? I'm with you. Bah-Sokhar.' The surfaces around the Doctor heaved more strongly and he wondered if – now the game was over – he was going to be digested after all, just dissolved alive in gastric juices. 'You're only being yourself, too. I do recognise that. And, quite frankly, nobody even really knows what yourself is. I mean, I've read the sagas and the histories and so forth… I may have skimmed here and there on the detail, but it was mainly guesswork…. because you're *so long ago*… Who's to say what you're actually like? Although you do have a bit of a bad reputation, you know.'

Suddenly, the wall facing the Doctor stretched and convulsed, then – fully formed – the figure of a small old lady emerged from the reddish blackish purplish surface and stood, dressed in a heather and olive plaid skirt, lamb's wool cardigan and anorak. Hooked over her arm was an imitation alligator skin handbag.

The Doctor suppressed any hints of fury, tried not to wonder who this woman might have been and casually murmured, 'I see we've moved on from people I've met to people you've… met.'

The old woman spoke with a strangely echoing voice that didn't suit her – it sounded like the cold, deep spaces between stars. 'This is the form of Mrs Agnes Findlater. I know more about her now. My own form is no form. I am noform, or I am eggform when I am I. This form is better for you to speak with. You woke me.' Her lips didn't move and the Doctor understood that the Bah-Sokhar's words were being placed directly into his mind.

'I did nothing of the sort.'

'Yes. The men who hit the ground with sticks, they wake me first. They get so angry and this… In the long ago, I would do what the hatethinks would ask of me and I would be fed. I am very hungry – even when I am only a little awake. The stick men hate. I wake a little for them. I wake because one of them wants me. I serve the hate stick man. Then I am hurt and I consume him. I know more about him now. But he is gone. I am lonely. I cannot serve. I need a mind to serve if I am awake all the way awake. You have big mind.'

'Thank you, yes, I know.' The Doctor could hardly take this as a compliment, coming as it did from the universe's most legendary killer – something which made a habit of eating golfers, old ladies in anoraks and who knew who else.

'I shall serve you. I shall make you the jewel at the heart of the universe.'

The Doctor found this completely untempting. 'Don't be ludicrous. You think I haven't been offered ultimate power and thrones and… all that nonsense. It wouldn't suit me. I don't really think it suits anyone and I'd suggest you stop offering – that kind of thing will attract some very seedy characters.'

'I shall serve you.'

'I've seen what your service looks like,' the Doctor growled. 'And, while we're chatting, nobody on this planet would intentionally summon you. Nobody would know how. Nobody woke you. Nobody knew you were here…'

'Long ago when I came here there were no minds. Then little minds. I have dreamed and been part of me awake. Not all awake. I have been dreaming. Your mind wakes me. You keep being in my dreams. I feel you. You have the largest mind. So I wake. You taste different. You wake me all the way wide awake.'

'Well, I didn't intend to and, quite frankly I can't imagine how – even if I do have the mind of a universal genius – I would have been able to… Unless… Putta Pattershaun 5 and his psy fluid… Amplifying artron energy randomly… That boy is a liability.'

The old lady form nodded stiffly. 'Put-ta. I know more about him. And his friend who is from this planet. I know more about them both.'

The Doctor tried not to let the idea of Bryony and Putta being consumed overwhelm him, or make him lose his temper – the Bah-Sokhar was clearly highly sensitive to negative mental states. 'If you want to serve me, then serve me by not knowing more about people. Stop eating people.'

'Must feed,' the creature continued in its rumbling and deep, but strangely childlike voice. 'I wished to speak with you.'

'I noticed.' The Doctor winced as he remembered. 'And thank goodness you've worked out how to turn the volume down – you could have killed me.'

'I am…' The voice paused. 'This is regret for me. Same as you regret. When something is broken and over you say you sorry. I am sorry. I am sorry I am awake. I want to sleep. This is a quiet planet when I come here. Now here is covered in little minds. There is noise. I will make it hush and I will feed. Must feed before I sleep again. There is only me now left. Once bigger Bah-Sokhar. Once manymany Bah-Sokhar. I cannot hear any Bah-Sokhar who is now. Now I hear you. You are not loud, but you are enough. I will feed and then I will speak to you until forever while I dream. You will stay with me. I will sleep and you will stay here. I will keep you. I will keep you for all the time.'

'But that's… Look, I'm a reasonable chap and I do love a good chinwag and paying calls, but really you can't…'

'I go. I feed now. Hungry.'

'No, wait!'

It was too late, though. The imitation Mrs Agnes Findlater was reabsorbed into the fabric of the Bah-Sokhar, and the Doctor was left, deep inside its formless form, trapped as it intended him to be.

'WELL, OF COURSE, QUITE naturally, I agree that a person can't simply disappear…' Kevin Mangold was having the kind of conversation he always avoided. 'And yet you do seem to be saying that…' To be more accurate, he was having the kind of conversation that he always let Bryony manage. 'Did he… ah…'

Mangold felt his voice wither while he faced Jim Palmer, the occupant of room 18 – the one with the nice view over the lake for which there should really be a surcharge.

The guest was insisting on being ridiculous. 'He did exactly what I said. I was walking down from the top floor – he was in room 56 – and he was only a few feet behind me and then he wasn't.'

'He wasn't what?' Mangold could feel his allergies starting to prickle.

'He wasn't there.'

Mangold set his glasses straight to play for time, 'And have you looked in–'

'Yes, I looked in room 56. He's not in 56. His missus is in 56. He's not. He's not in the bar, he's not on the course, he's not in the restaurant, or the bloody leisure place.'

Mangold had what he felt was an inspiration as his imagination scrambled about like a mouse in a greasy bucket for something to make this whole problem go away.

'Oh, I know what's happened!' he blurted – immediately regretting it when Palmer eyed him with hope, or at least mildly suspicious optimism. Mangold felt sweat break out at the backs of his legs. 'How might I put this… Not to take the issue lightly, but… Mr Palmer, did your friend perhaps not like his wife…?'

'I beg your pardon?'

'It's not absolutely…' This suggestion hadn't gone down as well as he'd hoped. 'Not… Just… One does hear of husbands wandering off… That is…' He wasn't supposed to deal with the public; Bryony Mailer was meant to deal with the public.

Jim Palmer thundered, 'Julia is lovely woman and distraught at the moment! She's had a headache all morning and now she can't find the man she's been married to for twenty-six years! A man who is my best friend! Do you want me to go upstairs and tell her he's run away because he hates her?!'

Although Mangold knew this was a completely dreadful mistake almost as horrible as his initial mistake, he couldn't help mumbling, 'Not run away… not that… not necessarily… I was suggesting… He could have fancied a bit of a change…' It felt for a few breaths that the floor was sinking under his feet and he fervently wished that it was and would hurry up and swallow him.

It wasn't.

It didn't.

Jim Palmer – dumbstruck by rage – simply reached across with a swift and confident fist and made a slight rearrangement of Kevin Mangold's nose.

BACK IN THE TARDIS kitchen, Bryony heard a distinct thrumming sound and a voice which said, 'I suppose that I couldn't expect any better – evolution can only do so much and Earth is essentially inhabited by primates with a flair for interior design…'

'Doctor?' Bryony choked on her last mouthful of bread and span round. Then she span round again. But there was no monitor, no screen, there was no one to see. 'Doctor?'

'You're a splendid girl, but there are a few more pressing things than simply shovelling Robert Frost's best jam into your face. People think of him as a poet, I realise – but he had a gift for preserves. Can we get on now?'

'Doctor? You're answering me?' She couldn't suppress a rush of relief and excitement.

'Well, I'm not giving myself another frankly dreadful headache for the fun of it. This isn't easy, you know.'

'But I don't understand.'

There was no sign of the Doctor himself, but his voice was definitely very present. And annoyed.

'Don't just stand there gawping about like a stunned owl – I'm up here.'

And there, indeed, the Doctor was. In the high corner where the walls and ceiling met, Bryony could see the wavering and translucent outline of that familiar scarf, the disreputable shoes, the louche jacket – and the face she had longed to see.

'Why?'

'Bryony Mailer, of all questions you could ask…' The image became exasperated and bounced lightly against one wall. 'Why? Why what? Why am I bothering to use the Bah-Sokhar's psychic field to amplify my own telepathic abilities and even – which is *immensely tiring* – projecting an image of myself for you, so you'll know it's me and – you're in my kitchen. I just aimed for you – or what might be left of you… Remarkable… You're in the TARDIS kitchen. How on earth did you manage that?' The image managed a half-grin. 'And well done for still being alive, of course. I am very pleased about that.'

'Well, likewise. And I don't know how we managed that. I think… the sand was eating us and there was this blue box and we nearly died and then… we were inside. We're inside the box, your TRADIS.'

'No. You're inside the *TARDIS*.' The Doctor allowed himself a laugh and then obviously regretted the amount of energy that required. 'She's a sly old girl.' He looked much more serious. 'When you say *we*… You mean…?'

'Me and Putta.'

'And where is Putta?'

'Back in the hallway.'

'I don't have a hallway.'

'The place with the screen and the front door and—'

The Doctor tugged his hair in frustration. 'My dear girl, you left him *there*!'

'He was too scared to go anywhere else.'

'You left possibly the clumsiest being I have ever encountered in the nerve centre of a beautiful and delicate… If he touches anything… If he breaks anything… I'm assuming you triggered the defence message…?

Bryony was about to nod when a bell began tolling somewhere far away, deep inside the ship. The sound was melodious but also melancholy, it even suggested a note of warning. The kitchen light flickered for an instant and the air seemed to grow slightly colder.

The Doctor's image flailed in mid-air, then descended and tilted until it was standing upright, its see-through brogues only a couple of feet off the ground. 'What's that? Ah!' As soon as he'd asked the question, the Doctor grimaced with pain. 'The TARDIS is… when my mind is this open and this… enhanced… She's terribly unhappy. She's even… She's scared. I've never known her be afraid… I can hear a bell. Do you hear a bell? Tell me you can't hear a bell.'

'I can hear a bell.'

'A rather musical regular chiming…? Clear chimes? That kind of bell?'

'That's right. It's quite nice.'

'Of course it's not nice!' The Doctor's translucent arms thrashed in irritation. 'It's the cloister bell. That's not nice, that's… It's always bad news. Bad news on a planetary scale. I think the Bah-Sokhar was able to hide from the TARDIS, but now I've… now I've done just what I shouldn't and let her know it's there. I am sorry. And –' His face convulsed with pain. 'I'm being… the Bah-Sokhar doesn't want even my thoughts to escape, I…'

'Are you all right? What can I do?' Never mind the bell, Bryony understood that the Doctor being sorry was bad news – and him being in pain was even worse. 'And why are you sorry?'

The image shook its head. 'I don't have long.' It began to blink and blur. 'The TARDIS will begin defending herself… Be very careful.' There was another break in the transmission. '… to Putta's ship and find more psy fluid, any psy fluid….

194

contact you again. I need to… it may understand me, know me more, it may understand…' The Doctor grimaced again and his voice stopped coming through.

Then the Doctor's projection shattered and fluttered downwards in flakes and curls of light. After that it was gone. The air in the room seemed to dull, as if the TARDIS had wanted him to stay, had wanted to know what it should do.

The cloister bell continued to toll. Bryony thought it seemed more than a warning now – it was a threat.

IN HIS LOCAL FISH and chip shop, Barry McGee was having a fight. He wasn't a large man and had only ever been in one other fight – when Ross Mackie stole his banana from his lunchbox in Primary 4. The matter hadn't amounted to much and the banana had been returned, albeit in a sad condition and not worth eating.

This evening, Barry had simply felt more than averagely hungry and – having driven back from his job in a Dundee insurance office – he had decided that fish and chips would be a quick option.

As he parked the car, he'd noticed that the High Street was unusually deserted. There was no one at all about – apart from a young mother, jogging urgently down the street, pushing a pram. Every now and then, she would stop in her tracks and jam her hands over her ears. Then she'd jog-trot onwards at an increasing pace. This wasn't quite what he was used to from Arbroath on a Friday evening.

Neither was the almost deafening din coming from the houses he passed as he walked to the chip shop. Everyone had decided to crank up their radios and televisions to the maximum possible volume and a chaos of music and yelling was the result.

Barry had thought that the quicker he got hold of his dinner and went home the better.

In the shop there was no queue and, at first, no one serving. Barry waited for a while – pondering the possibilities of perhaps having chicken and chips, or even a white pudding supper… Then, when no one had appeared after five minutes, he yelled, fairly politely, 'Hey! I'm looking for a fish supper! Hello!'

At this, a hefty figure in a white smock appeared from the back of the shop, sweaty and already slightly tense – in the way that a man who has been repeatedly poked with a stick all day might be slightly tense. 'What do want!' he bellowed.' Following this up with, 'Oh, and you think this is a dead-end job, do you?'

As it happened, Barry did think that working in a small Arbroath fish and chip shop wasn't the height of career success.

'You think I'm here because I didn't do well at school, because I'm ignorant. And you think I'm some kind of monster!' screamed the man, flipping back the counter and advancing across the lino floor of the shop. He halted right in front of Barry and yelled down at him, 'It so happens I'm lovely! I love working with the public! It's what I live for!' Before kicking him hard on the shin.

After that, things got confusing and Barry realised – several kicks later – that he was rolling about on the lino and wondering if it was clean.

Barry's opponent screamed, 'There's nothing wrong with my lino! I mopped it myself this morning! And after lunchtime!' Rolling about, mainly on top of him, was the man who loved working with the public. Then Barry felt teeth being sunk into his right ear. This wasn't how he'd anticipated his evening would begin.

And the weirdest thing was that the man had known exactly what Barry was thinking without Barry ever having to say a word.

PUTTA HAD TRIED COILING himself into a ball. The fact that this wasn't physically possible seemed to prove, in a way, that when so many of his broodbrothers had told him he was completely spineless, they'd been exaggerating.

He'd tried tiptoeing around the console room, patting various bits of furniture as if he liked them and this hadn't made him feel any less at risk, but had seemed to stop anything else bumping him, or clattering his ankles when he wasn't looking. 'Ah-ah… I'm sort of… It's that…' His voice sounded completely pathetic and he was glad Bryony wasn't there to hear it. 'I do think you're very impressive.' He leaned on the console in what he hoped was an admiring way and, at once, a bell began to toll. It didn't sound like a comforting or encouraging bell. 'I didn't touch anything!'

When the bell didn't stop tolling, he decided to sit one of the large chairs available, but something about it didn't seem to appreciate his attention. He edged over to the doorway and looked out again – the sand was still there, still furious, still waiting for something it could swallow. The longer he stared at it, the more tempting it felt to just step off, walk out of the terrible Time Lord trap he'd somehow been scooped up into and meet the fate he deserved… He bent further and further forward, more and more of his weight supported by the one hand which still gripped the doorframe. The nearer the restless sand he came, the greater his certainty that he was worthless. He should just –

'Putta! Putta! Can you hear me?'

It was Bryony. And her voice – somewhat muffled by the insulating effects of the TARDIS wall she was yelling through – brought Yinzill's least successful bountykiller back to his senses. 'Yurg!?' Putta yanked himself back inside the TARDIS's doorway – one of the brass hand rails really helped – and staggered down the little staircase.

'Putta! Are you there?' Her voice was coming from beyond the other door. It wasn't loud, but it certainly sounded like her, rather than some piece of Time Lord technology designed to destroy him in some horrible, ingenious way.

Putta darted nervily across and spoke – as cautiously as he could – to the not-really-wood of the exit through which Bryony had left him. 'Yes? I'm me. Are you Bryony?'

'I can't hear you.'

He raised his voice. It was likely that the TARDIS could hear him, anyway, however softly he spoke. 'Are you Bryony? Are you all right? I felt a bit weird again…'

'I don't have time for all that. Can you open the door?'

Putta relaxed a touch. If it was insulting him, the voice probably did belong to Bryony and wasn't some kind of simulation, wasn't part of a Time Lord trick. Putta grabbed the doorknob.

He tried turning it to the right.

It wouldn't.

He tried turning it to the left.

No luck with that, either.

'Putta! It's just a doorknob – you turn it and then I can get out of here and we can do what the Doctor wants.'

Putta assumed, when she mentioned the Doctor, that the strain had made her begin to hallucinate. Or perhaps she was being influenced by all that Time Lord technology which was meant to be so powerful and strange and about which his elders and betters had always been so respectful in hushed and ill-informed, blustering ways. 'That's not possible… um, my dear. The Doctor is dead.'

'He's not dead. I've just seen him floating on the kitchen ceiling.'

Putta didn't find this indicated all was well with Bryony's mental state.

'And did you just call me *my dear*? If there was a doorknob, or a handle or anything I could work here, I'd come in there and…' There was a sharp series of thumps from the other side of the door. 'I counted back the number of paces there used to be between this door and the one that leads into the kitchen and I'm sure there were twelve – thirteen at the most. There isn't even a door any more. There's… It's like it's healed over.'

This was perfectly true. Where Bryony was standing, the corridor was as comfortably lit as it had been, but was now uninterrupted by even the tastefully futuristic circular indentations. It was smooth, flawless, creepy white. 'Please Putta. If you open the door from that side maybe it will work.'

'But I've tried. It won't budge. I can't even see where there's a little gap between the door and the doorframe – that's not there any more.'

'Oh.'

This sounded so downhearted from Bryony that Putta immediately felt he should focus and, if not take charge, then be a bit more… well, he wasn't sure what he'd be a bit more of, but he'd work on it. 'Not to worry.'

'Not to worry!?' Putta was glad this was muffled – he hated sarcasm. Bryony went on: 'Look, the Doctor is somewhere else – I don't know where – but he got a message through.

He needs you to get the psy fluid. He needs the psy fluid.'

'I threw it away.'

'Then get it back. Where did you throw it?'

'I can't get it back. I can't leave the… the TARDIS. You may have forgotten, but there's a large amount of sand outside and it wants to kill me.'

'Do you hear the bell?'

'Bell?' Putta was amazed by how much the Earth woman's mind wondered. 'Yes, I can hear the bell. What about the sand?'

'The bell only chimes when something serious is happening. And we know something serious is happening anyway – the sand and the bunker and…' Bryony avoided mentioning the jacuzzi. 'Putta, I can't help you. But if the Doctor says he needs the psy fluid then he must have a plan and you have to get it. Putta?'

'I can't.'

'Well, I believe that you can.' She slipped down the wall and leaned close to it, hoping that she could speak more clearly like this – hoping that she'd got the location of the door at least approximately right. 'I really do, Putta. You were amazing back there. You've been amazing pretty often… On average…'

'Really?'

'Really.' Bryony lost her patience – partly because she wanted to be the one going to fetch the psy fluid – and added, 'Either that, or you're an all-round failure and always have been on every planet you've touched and you'll probably starve to death out there spending your last hours being able to realise how completely pathetic you are!' Because she had to shout this in order to be audible, it probably sounded slightly harsher than she intended – not that she didn't intend to be harsh.

'Oh.' Putta blinked and felt confused and also horribly

wonderful. Confused, because Bryony seemed to think he was both amazing and a complete dead meat sack – and horribly wonderful because that meant she'd been thinking about him a lot and assessing his character. And it made him feel as if she cared and certain – fairly – that she wanted to make him feel functional. She wanted him to *be* functional. This was both horribly wonderful and wonderfully horrible, because it meant he genuinely would have to open the front door again and somehow leave the TARDIS, somehow cross the sand and survive, somehow retrieve the psy fluid… which he'd thrown into the lake at the centre of the golf course – he had no idea where exactly – and then somehow… Well, if he managed all that he'd end up… He'd end up having to save the day.

He was the one who had to save the day.

'Oh. No.'

OVER IN HER COTTAGE, Mrs Julia Fetch was sitting down to dinner with her much-loved grandchildren. The place settings were perfect, the vegetables were steaming and glistening in their lovely dishes, there were bright crystal glasses of elderflower cordial and, at the head of the table, was a large platter of… something.

Julia couldn't quite make up her mind what she fancied this evening and the large shape on the platter wasn't helping her to decide. Sometimes it looked a bit like a roast chicken – only she wasn't in the mood for roast chicken – there had been a while when she was fairly sure it was a rack of lamb – lamb would be too fatty, she thought – then a joint of beef, a roast goose, a joint of pork, then something that resembled very large bird – a cooked swan…? Julia seemed to have read somewhere that only the Queen was allowed to eat swans, so that would never do.

Just now the meat course looked tired. It rested on the platter, its surface rippling vaguely like water under a light breeze and roughly the colour of well-roasted flesh. Its form was approximately cubic and it currently didn't seem interested in making any efforts to look like cutlets, chops, or anything more usual.

Julia rather liked the cube. It would be neat for carving.

'How many slices would you like children?' She picked up the carving knife and the fork.

Honor and Xavier both said, in their most courteous voices, 'Three please.' And held out their plates.

Julia nodded. She had forgotten that the twins never actually ate anything. This was good – otherwise, she would have worried about how they were keeping up their strength.

BRYONY WAS SITTING ON the floor of the TARDIS passageway, listening to Putta apparently freaking out through the wall. Now and again there were heavy thumps, or wild shouts, most of which weren't easy to decipher through the wall, but one of which definitely sounded like 'You're ugly!'.

'Putta! Putta! You really do need to get that fluid. It's the only thing the Doctor asked us to do…' But it was no good – the thumps continued, interspersed with more yowling.

Around her the TARDIS was obviously doing what it thought it should in case of dire emergency. The entrance had been sealed – with Putta on the wrong side, or the right side, depending on how you looked at it – and Bryony was being taken care of, after a fashion.

'I suppose it's good that you like me…' The lights dimmed. 'No, really it is good. I am grateful. I just would prefer to be useful.' She took a deep breath, wondered if making her frustration obvious was wise and decided – to hell with – that she'd yell anyway, 'But you're not letting me *be* useful!'

The TARDIS ignored her beyond returning the lights to their previous level.

And meanwhile, the passageway was apparently keen to provide for her needs as she'd announced them in the console room. Bryony had wanted food and a bath, so while the kitchen remained the kitchen – generously supplied with the mysterious Maxxt – and was just where it had been earlier, two new doors had appeared where she was sure there hadn't been doors when she first walked along here. One door concealed an intimidatingly complicated bathroom with a massive tub and a number of large plants overhanging it, none of which she recognised, or felt she could entirely trust if she was undressed. The other new door opened onto a bedroom which had rather more plum-coloured velvet than she would have expected, draping about the place, and layers of Persian rugs underfoot. This wasn't the cutting-edge space stuff she'd been expecting and she had the strong suspicion that she was being distracted by all this potential comfort so that she wouldn't begin searching out the source of the cloister bell and at least trying to do something about that.

There were, naturally, lots of brass hand rails in both rooms – not to mention the brass taps, the brass towel rail and the brass bedstead. When she flipped down the top of a little not-walnut bureau in the bedroom, Bryony discovered a wealth of futuristic odds and ends tucked into cubby holes, a plethora of dials and switches, several balls of twine, a small model of something like a leopard, a tin of hard sweets and a yo-yo. The bedroom seemed dusty. It clearly reflected the Doctor's taste, but either he didn't use it, or else he didn't sleep much. The bed – under its layer of dust – was freshly made and inviting. 'Perhaps you're a spare. Or you got mislaid.' It didn't feel as if these elements, these rooms, were being built from scratch – it was more as if they were being shuffled about to accommodate her by an increasingly nervous vessel accustomed to pleasing a semi-madman from another planet who favoured Earth's Victorian period, who never tidied up and who thought, in as far as he considered such matters at all, that the ideal guest bedroom would look like an opium den.

When Bryony paced back out of the bedroom she could have sworn that the passageway was smaller, that the area of the TARDIS she was being allowed was contracting.

AS BRYONY PUZZLED OVER the TARDIS's dimensions – a popular pastime with new visitors – Putta had a plan. For the first time in his life, he actually had a plan. Not only that – he was carrying it out.

His thinking was as follows…

I have to get out of the TARDIS. I can't get out of the TARDIS. Therefore I am a failure.

No. I have to get out of the TARDIS. Therefore I must get out of the TARDIS.

I will find a way.

How do I usually leave places?

I reverse what I did to get in there.

How did I get into the TARDIS?

Ummm…

Well, I was being eaten alive…

That doesn't help much. I am not currently being eaten alive and that hasn't meant that I have left the TARDIS. If I leave the TARDIS, I will, in fact, start being eaten alive and either I will get scooped back up in here again, or else I will be absolutely eaten, because the TARDIS knows me better than it did when it rescued me and it clearly doesn't like me, because it jabs me with things, or knocks me with bits of itself whenever it –

Ah.

Back a bit…

The TARDIS doesn't like me very much…

OK.

I'm on to something here.

I don't know what, though…

No, no, no – this is fine, this is planning, this is…

Right.

The TARDIS dislikes me, but not that much. So I'm still in here.
I'm not out there.

So…

Oh, dear.

I have to get the TARDIS to really dislike me. I mean hate me. I
mean loathe the sight of me. I mean, the TARDIS has to be sick of
the sight of me.

Oh, dear. Oh, dear.

Which wasn't perhaps the way that Napoleon would
have made a plan, or Genghis Khan, or Thraxtic, but it was
a kind of plan and nobody could deny it.

So what Bryony assumed was Putta freaking out, was
actually Putta stamping about in the console room, kicking
out with his one remaining shoe at the walls – which erased
the scuff marks as soon as he made them – and slapping the
little console panels up and down in a way that he hoped
was sore.

This produced a definite sense of smugness that
permeated the room. The TARDIS wasn't annoyed – it
was more amused by his antics in the way that a passer-by
would be if it saw a squirrel misjudging a jump and falling
out of a tree and then bouncing about being angry in an
impotent way to make up.

Putta was a mild-mannered sort of person, but this did
rile him.

And the riling helped.

He loosed off a volley of kicks to the console base,
flicked a number of switches that he should have left well

alone and began the shouting. He insulted the décor, he insulted the air purification levels, he said he thought the compression field was a cheap trick designed only to fool ape descendants and actual apes, he said that Gallifrey – the Time Lords' home planet – was a dump full of pompous bullies and then he poked the viewing screen.

The smugness receded and was replaced by a certain chill.

Putta was in his limping stride now – his filthy tweeds, torn shirt and unravelling tank top flapping about him as he slapped chairs, shook the hat stand, tried to break of one of its ornamented finials and said that Time Lords were an overrated bunch of pompous charlatans and that went for Time Ladies, too, only double.

The TARDIS closed the viewing screen up and was perhaps having a think about things. The air became slightly charged.

And then Putta kicked and banged his way up the steps that led to the front door, opened it and sat with his back to the seething sand before starting to do what he knew he must – saying bad things about the Doctor.

'He pretends he's all fun and crazy ideas and that genius act is pretty good, but where is he now? Nowhere. He's useless. I've met biscuits with more sense. And I bet… I bet he does this kind of stuff all the time – running about all over the universe, rattling up and down timelines and getting other people into trouble. Just to entertain himself. He *makes* trouble.'

The colour of the walls began to cloud and a kind of wheezing joined the repetitive tolling of that bell.

'I think he hurts people. Messing about with things he doesn't understand and interfering. Then he'll be off, won't he? He doesn't clear up the mess afterwards, does he. He's just off having more fun.'

It was getting harder to say any of this, partly because it made Putta feel terrible and partly because the air was getting hot and dusty – sandy, even – and that wheezing was becoming louder.

Putta drove on. He felt sick with fear and self-loathing, but he kept talking. 'The Doctor's not a good man. He doesn't have a good heart. He doesn't care at all. When you look in his eyes, you can see. There are graveyards all over time and space full of people who trusted him. He doesn't love anything. He can't. He wouldn't know how.'

Which is what did it.

Yes.

As he was lifted bodily into the air by a stinging force, a burning light, a kind of tangible fury, Putta thought, *Yes. All those years I spent annoying almost everything I've met have finally made sense. They were all just practice for this – for starting to save the day.*

Yes.

He'd needed the TARDIS to be too disgusted with him to keep him indoors for a moment longer. The way to make it hate him would be to pretend that he hated the Doctor. Then with the hungry sand right outside the door and no one to operate its more sophisticated systems, the TARDIS's only alternative would be to use roughly calibrated plasma energy to fling him as far away over its threshold as it could – to get him out and also away from the sand.

Wonderful plan.

Absolutely the best ever.

Ah…

Putta hadn't quite considered how painful it would be when he landed after being flung, however. Being propelled to the other side of the riverbank in one long, low swoop, Putta had time to enjoy his flight before landing on the steep slope which formed the riverbank opposite the one where the TARDIS sat. This slope was covered mainly in nettles, the nettles being interrupted in places by brambles.

Ah…

Putta rolled back down towards the river, but saved himself by impacting with his chest against a broad tree trunk.

He came to rest with extensive bruising, a cut over one eye and a sense of elation. And he'd lost his other shoe.

'I was right,' he whispered to himself. 'I was right.' Before deciding that hauling himself up the slope would be safer than going anywhere near the river.

It took him some time to claw and drag and yank his complaining body all the way up to the top of the bank and emerge in the brush under trees between the seventh and seventeenth holes. As he stood, breathless, sweaty, scratched and exhausted he felt taller than he'd ever been. Even in his stockinged feet. He might have looked, perhaps, like an old-time golf professional who'd fallen down a well, but he felt like a hero – the hero the Doctor would have wanted him to be. Now he just had to cross the seventh green and reach the Big Lake.

'You! You there! What are you doing there!'

A late party of four golfers was finishing their round and usually Putta would have kept out of their way. (He was beginning to think that golf's main emphasis was on its team elements – one team waving angrily and the other solitary player running and dodging across different lengths of grass while some unimportant stuff with a ball and some sticks happened.)

Even after a golf ball sang rather closer than it should have past Putta's head, he would still normally have chosen to slip self-effacingly round to the lake, wait until dark and then search for the phial of psy fluid he'd thrown there. Putta really didn't like annoying people / beings / creatures

212

/ mythical mind-controlled assassins / octopus monsters –
even though it seemed that he almost always did.

'Do get out of the way, moron!' a round-headed man
shouted while his partner chuckled and two other golfers
in dark blue sweaters and slacks looked at the grass as if it
were highly interesting, or as if something was happening
which they wanted to know nothing about.

Putta stood where he was.

Where he was – according to the customary rules of golf
– was in the way.

But this time Putta wasn't going to move. He was going
to play this game a different way – his way.

Yes, he might even go as far as to say this was his way of
playing golf…

'I said!' the man with the head like a boiled pudding
shouted again. 'I said! Clear off!'

But Putta didn't feel like clearing off.

There was one more shout. 'Don't say I didn't warn you!'
And Putta was dimly aware that two of the golfers were
moving away from their rounded companion and another
was tugging at his sleeve. 'Get off me!' was audible and then,
'I'll show him.'

In the evening light, Putta could see the angriest golfer,
perhaps, in the world addressing his ball, readying his
club… and then – the swoop as the ball was struck. It was
aimed straight at Putta.

And Putta – as if he always did this kind of thing – reached
up into the air and caught the ball as it reached him. It was
one of the undimpled, heavy golf balls that he didn't like.

Then he put it in his deep, tweed pocket and walked off
towards the lake.

Behind him, he thought he could hear at least one pair of
hands applauding.

Putta's right palm – where the golf ball had hit it – was in absolute agony, but Putta didn't mind. He'd done the sort of thing a hero would do.

He heard feet hurrying behind him over the grass and, looking round, saw the golfer who'd aimed for him rushing up with a strange expression on his face – a blend of confusion, admiration and embarrassment. 'If you wouldn't mind… Could I have my ball back?

Putta didn't answer.

The man winced. 'Please'.

And Putta handed over the smooth white sphere before walking on under the wide evening sky, reaching the lake and then continuing to walk.

I can do this. Heroes walk into lakes.

It'll look really cool.

Like catching a golf ball.

Ow…

THERE WAS NOTHING ELSE for it – she might as well settle down to wait and make herself comfortable while she did so. Bryony wasn't being allowed to move beyond the increasingly truncated section of corridor the TARDIS had assigned to her. 'I'm finding this sexist! It's annoying!'

It wasn't just annoying – the by now rather rapidly shrinking dimensions of the space around her were a cause for concern. The ceiling was definitely lower by about a foot. At this rate of contraction, it would only take a few hours and there wouldn't be room for fun activities like standing up. Beyond that, crawling and even lying down while breathing would get increasingly impossible. Bryony didn't think that the TARDIS would intentionally damage her, but if the thing got overly panicked maybe it locked into certain paths of action and couldn't get out of them. Maybe the TARDIS needed the Doctor as much as Bryony and Putta did.

Thinking of Putta, Bryony had been additionally worried by a final, very loud yelp from through in the console room. This was followed by a loud bang and then complete silence. Something had clearly happened – probably to Putta – or with him or around him. She tried to assume it was something good…

'TARDIS…? TARDIS, can't you let me help you? Is it

215

your compression field? Are you feeling poorly? Or tense?'
Bryony knew that the last thing you want to do when
someone is feeling tense was ask them about it, but what
else could she do? 'Maybe if you let me turn that bell off –
it seems to be making you… well… tenser. It's blooming
well making me tenser. It's doing my head in.' The corridor
narrowed by an inch in response. Bryony sighed. Then she
shouted pointlessly through the wall to Putta. 'Putta!?' He
hadn't answered or made any other sound since the yelp
and the bang…

And he didn't answer now.

Finally, she decided that the most reasonable thing to
do under her circumstances would involve having a bath.
Perhaps if she was herself more relaxed, this would calm the
TARDIS. Perhaps she would prefer to look her best if she
was going to be inadvertently crushed to death by a weird
box / spaceship… She'd be better prepared for whatever
came next if she wasn't covered in sand and dressed in an
impractical and pretty well shredded retro suit. It was a
shame – the thing had fitted her much better than the one
she had to wear when she was a receptionist. She briefly
reflected that her job was probably long gone by now.
Mangold wouldn't be best pleased by her association with
a fainting madman, some loud rushing and the horror in
the Spa.

She trudged to the bedroom – now conveniently much
closer to the kitchen and the bathroom… this section
of the TARDIS was basically turning into a bedsit – and
rooted in its chest of drawers. The gently thrumming
piece of furniture offered up a muddle of socks, small
electrical parts, a fossilised slice of cake wrapped in a dirty
handkerchief and some complex diagrams which might
have charted outlandish wiring plans, or a vascular system
– it wasn't clear. There was also a clean-looking towel, three

long-armed white shirts which clearly belonged to the Doctor and would have to do, plus a pair of pink and white striped overalls, which clearly belonged to someone else.

'Pink bib-front overalls…? What kind of people does he have in here? Feminine lady plumbers? Admirers of Andy Pandy…?'

The idea of wearing pink made Bryony feel slightly ill, but they were roughly her size and would be fairly practical. Once again she tried not get stressed about the idea of wearing pink when she was… *I will not think about being crushed to death. No I won't.*

'OK, TARDIS. I'm having a bath now. That's what you seem to want, so that's what I'm doing. But afterwards we need to chat, or something. And we'll be very happy and feel… expansive… We'll feel like branching out…' Bryony wished she'd paid more attention when that stage hypnotist had visited Dundee… then again, she didn't think trying to get the TARDIS to eat an onion or think it was Elvis would really improve her situation. 'And could you at least give me a clue about what's happened to Putta?' The lights dimmed and there was a kind of stiff silence, to replace the pervious silence that slipped along underneath the thrumming and that irritating bell.

It was troubling…

THE DOCTOR WAS TALKING. He'd been talking since the fake Mrs Agnes Findlater disappeared – which could have been minutes ago, or could have been hours ago… He hoped it wasn't hours… He'd been sitting and talking, projecting his thought-self to Bryony and talking, trying to figure out what came next and talking.

'Yes, I hope it isn't hours. I would be highly worried about my friends if hours have gone by… Arbroath is a lot more interesting than one might generally expect with you around. And not interesting in pleasant and entertaining ways…'

The Doctor had once talked a torturer on an iron satellite of Betatron 6 into a state of near mental collapse, and Betatron 6 torturers are hardened to almost every kind of experience and not known for their listening skills. Even so, the Time Lord was tiring, the previous mental and physical assaults had left him drained, he really was concerned about Putta and Bryony – and his throat was getting dry. But he continued, trying to establish a connection with an entity which seemed not to be simply an assassin without a controller. There had been signs of sympathy and when their minds met, apart from the great pain this caused the Doctor, there had been those messages of fear and loneliness and pain. The Bah-Sokhar was evolving. It was so old and so malleable it could, as an individual, be subject to the same laws of change which governed whole species.

He wriggled his neck and shoulders and began pacing back and forth across the undulating, warm and slithering floor. 'And with the rate at which your powers are increasing I know it can't be days that have gone by. I strongly suspect that in only a few days' time the world could well be a much emptier and more unpleasant planet if you go on as you are. I don't intend to be critical, of course, but surely you must see that creatures are suffering… You are making them suffer… You are making them hurt and afraid and lonely. I know you understand those feelings…' The Doctor could see that, if he couldn't stimulate the creature's more forgiving side, once the Bah-Sokhar was completely awake, full-scale feeding would begin… and could well be massive. And whoever survived that cull might find themselves no more than a mind-puppet, a way of keeping meat fresh for the creature's next meal.

It seemed that the Bah-Sokhar was perhaps more terrible than the legends describing it.

Then again… and the Doctor did like to give things the benefit of the doubt… The creature had tried to communicate. It hadn't harmed the twins and had clearly been sharing its consciousness with them for some time, perhaps also with their grandmother. Yes, there was something about that lady – charming as she was – which smelled of far too much time. Humans in the twentieth century had a predictably fixed lifespan and the Doctor suspected she'd been around for far more than her usual share. He wouldn't be much of a Time Lord if he didn't know the signs.

And for a monster supposed to thrive on hate, the Bah-Sokhar had responded to affection… There must be a way to help it through towards a more sustainable way of existing, a less bloodthirsty life.

'You seem to have a soft spot for those twins, don't you? And for their grandmother. For Bryony Mailer, too – impressive girl she is – mush less hysterical than most humans would be under the same circumstances... if anything, rather overly relaxed.'

Then the Bah-Sokhar came at him again – not disguised as a nightmare, not in the form of a memory raised from the dead – this time it made him a kind of offer.

DOCTOR

YOU COULD

YOU COULD BE THE JEWEL AT THE HEART OF THE UNIVERSE

USE ME

DO GOOD

The pressure reaching into his mind was monumental, but the Bah-Sokhar had modified its communication so that it caused less pain and more a sense of power and elation. Not that he didn't also end up on the floor holding his ankles for a while.

'Too... too loud. Please... I admire your enthusiasm... but... As I mentioned, I have received similar offers over the years...' Through his thinking span a sudden torrent of images of smiling peoples, saved peoples... his coronation as emperor at the beginning of a long rule over huge swathes of the universe... 'Yes, and that is... splendid and how pleasant that you're showing me myself in purple robes – I do love a good robe... a hood, too, excellent... but I would have to—'

PLEASE

The Doctor felt as if a long heated spike had been rammed into his forehead, 'Oh!' He gasped for a while, getting his senses back into order. 'I do thank you for using the magic word. I do. Perhaps we could discuss this more quietly at a later date.'

And he rolled onto his back, sweat once again standing out on his face and tremors racking his arms and legs. This was all getting too much, even for him. He needed to get out of here and fast – if not actually, then at least virtually. 'Perhaps if you show me more of my coronation and some extra crowds of delighted children offering me flowers and little gifts.' The Bah-Sokhar duly obliged, making this interior cinema seem a touch more seductive, adding colour and depth, tuning it all to suit the Doctor's weaknesses.

The Doctor dragged up a laugh from somewhere around his socks. 'Oh! Splendid. Yes. You are good at this, aren't you?'

He could feel his muscles straining, his head spinning – and the tumult of temptations rolled on. The Bah-Sokhar knew him now – he knew what to offer better than all the petty tyrants and monomaniacs who had tried to buy him with crowns and riches. Nightmares he was used to, monsters he could resist, wealth and glory didn't interest him… but happy endings, visions of rich and fulfilled lives, of saving and aiding lives… visions of his own life finally reaching a point where he didn't have to leave just as the good bits happened and the dangers were done with… That was much harder to resist.

'Well, you are sly… I'll say that. And do you serve, actually? Are you a servant, in fact – as you claim? I wonder if that's quite right. You seem to control the ones you serve, as much as they control you…'

The Doctor shivered again as another series of images ripped through him – this time a bright aerial display of vast, glittering spacecraft – part of a force he could create and control, one which travelled between planets bringing assistance, food, plants, teachers, doctors… Doctors were supposed to make people better, they were made for that kind of work…

His hearts strained and ached.

EVENTUALLY BRYONY HAD FIGURED out how to fill the bath. This had involved six taps, and temperature control had been a serious issue. But she'd had to admit – once she'd removed what was left of her clothes and slipped into the quite warm water – that the TARDIS did have a point. She'd felt better as soon as she'd started to feel the heat coddling her tired body.

She also felt much more clearheaded already, after only a bit of soaking. And maybe a clear head was required. 'You seem to want that, don't you? And I haven't felt as if that thing out there has been able to rummage about in my head since you saved us. You're keeping it locked out, aren't you?' An unpleasant idea occurred to her. 'Are you shrinking because it's getting stronger? Is that the problem?' There was, of course, no reply. Bryony pondered the unpleasant layer of sandy / weird stuff that had started forming as soon as she stepped into the bath and that was still floating on the surface of the water like a highly unpleasant blanket. 'I'm happier without that all over me. So thanks. And thanks for keeping me… um… cosy…'

But it's not going to be wonderful if you end up keeping me cosy in here and defended but eventually the area being defended is the size of a… of a vol-au-vent… I won't fit. And I never have liked finger food.

Bryony was thinking of changing the water and having

maybe a good wash down under the alarming-looking shower arrangement when that familiar voice interrupted her once again.

'Ah, Bryony.' The Doctor still sounded irritated, but also weaker. 'I've been hanging about in the kitchen for ages waiting for you… like an abandoned birthday party balloon. Do you have the psy fluid yet?'

At his first *Ah*, Bryony said something which sounded very much like 'Whyark!' before ducking under the filthy surface of the water. This meant she didn't quite catch what the Doctor said after that and he had to repeat himself once she'd re-emerged.

'For goodness' sake, I don't have time for all that. Do you have the… ow… psy fluid?' The Doctor's image wavered in quality while Bryony spluttered and blinked up at it while it drifted across the ceiling.

'You can't…' She was concealed by a layer of gritty goo, but even so Bryony would have preferred to be wearing clothes while being nagged by a ghostly Time Lord. 'I'm in the bath!'

'Instead of… My dear girl, this isn't some kind of holiday villa – it's the TARDIS.' The image winced and frowned, flickered.

'Doctor, are you all right?'

'The Bah-Sokhar is blocking me…' He sighed. 'I'm somewhere inside its matrix… If…' He looked terribly tired. 'I don't think it's unreasonable… more… unguided… With the psy fluid, I could…' His face sharpened visibly. 'Where is Putta?'

'I don't know. I'm trapped in here – the TARDIS won't let me go – and she's…' Bryony thought that maybe worrying the Doctor about the way his spaceship was behaving might not be the best idea right now. 'The Bah-Sokhar is outside… It tried to eat us… And then it just stayed… I mean, maybe

Putta got past it, though…' There was another possibility that involved the cowardly but brave little man from Yinzill going outside and being caught in that sand… She tried to think that the TARDIS wouldn't have let that happen. 'He would try if he could. I told him you needed it. The psy fluid – I told him you needed it.'

Above her, the image of the Doctor was fading. But with a groan of distress he seemed to force out a few more psychons worth of effort so that he could tell her, 'Bryony, I have to talk to the Bah-Sokhar. I have to *really* talk to it… And it's not listening – it's scared, it doesn't trust me. It doesn't trust anyone. In a way, it's a parasite – it feeds on negative mental energy, serves it and enlarges it… But there are other energies there now – it's not quite the kind of monster it used to be. And, frankly, if I can't use its own power to change it, I wouldn't bet much on the ability of any other force on Earth or anywhere else to overwhelm it.' The image shrugged slightly and tried a grin. 'But… If I can really get through – if I can let it feel how I feel and… the TARDIS – she can increase the intensity of my thoughts, my emotional field, if I access her psychic core – but that's not supposed to happen – she's designed to defend against that – even to defend herself against me and I'm being blocked and shielded from her by the Bah-Sokhar – she may not even recognise me once I've worked my way in… if I can… You're with her, though – and she trusts you and likes you and she's used to humans… Plus, sometimes the small size of the human mind is really useful. You would act like a lens, concentrating the information that I can aim at the Bah-Sokhar. If Putta can boost the energy with that psy fluid and you can withstand it and I… if I do what I have to… Help me, Bryony. Help me reroute the TARDIS's psychic energy, help me find out what the Bah-Sokhar needs – it's been dealing with humans for a long time, it's used to your configuration. Just… I need your help. It will be horribly dangerous, of course. We could both die. Probably we will.'

'What do I have to do?'

'I knew you'd be terribly good at this.' The Doctor gave her the impression that he'd have ruffled her hair if he could. 'Well, I don't know about you, but I do some of my best thinking in the bath.' For a moment, he was the Doctor she remembered – the funny, wise, resourceful being from somewhere far away. He smiled and then winced. 'Empty out the water, make yourself as comfortable as you can in the tub – you'll know when it starts.'

'When what starts?'

'You'll know.'

'Can I get dressed?' Bryony had the impression that the Doctor didn't especially notice what people were or weren't wearing, but if she was going to die of being used as a focusing lens for some kind of force – before she got squashed to death – then she'd prefer to be fully dressed – even if that did involve a candy-striped pair of dungarees.

'What?' The Doctor's image frowned down at her as if she was mildly insane. 'Of course you can get dressed. Earth people… they're always going on about what they ought to wear – evening dress, suits of armour, Hazmat 15 Nanoprotective membranes. I can be on six different planets before breakfast – in fourteen different eras – am I obsessed about whether my shirt will match the wallpaper…? My dear girl, I need you to concentrate – literally. Humans… You were the same, even when you were living in caves – should it be this mammoth skin, should it be that mammoth skin… Just!' He stopped himself playing the fool, blinked, soften his expression, 'Bryony Mailer, humans shouldn't meld with immensely complex biomechanical vessels – or with Time Lords, or with… Are you scared?'

'Not really,' lied Bryony, while thinking that either the

water around her had turned chill, or that she was shivering at the thought of somehow facing this Bah-Sokhar – a creature that could make sand, or anything else, into a deadly weapon, a creature that could trap someone as resourceful as the Doctor.

'You're really not frightened?'

'I want to help.'

'Good.' His image smiled. 'I thought you would. Personally, I'm completely terrified – I'm so glad you're not.' He paused, tiny holes appearing in his representation. 'The next time you hear from me, it will already have started.'

'OK.' Which didn't sound like a big enough thing to say on such an occasion, but Bryony couldn't think of anything else.

'Be ready.'

'I will.'

'And thank you. And do remember that—'

But whatever she was supposed to remember shattered into pieces of light and colour and then disappeared.

The bathroom lights – including the unlikely Hollywood-style bulbs set in strips around the big mirror – all shaded over into red for a moment and then shifted back to a yellowish dimness. Bryony couldn't tell if this was because the TARDIS was concentrating, or sad, or just bewildered. The ceiling had crept another six inches closer and it was now possible to put out her hand and reach the towel rail with no trouble.

'Well, everything is going to be conveniently close to hand before I'm killed for a number of reasons…' Bryony had intended that as a joke to cheer herself, but it sounded only grim once she'd said it and she clambered out of the bath with heavy limbs.

Once she'd dried herself and slipped into the shirt and overalls, she turned back to try and clean the worst of the muck off the bath, but discovered that it was apparently self-cleaning, or dirt-digesting. 'Well, that's one less thing to worry about…'

She padded off in bare feet to the – much nearer – bedroom and took pillows, the quilt and the velvet cover from the bed. (She also borrowed the pair of lumpily thick bed socks tucked under one pillow – they were too big, but lent a sense of security to the proceedings, somehow.) Then she piled everything into the tub, climbed back in herself and tried to settle herself as if this wasn't all completely alarming and horrible.

But she was going to help the Doctor. She'd only really just met him – it had been this morning that he'd loped into the hallway at the hotel and apparently brought so many daydreams and nightmares with him. Still, she was absolutely sure that if the Doctor needed help then you provided it if there was any way you could. And when you needed help – one way or another – she knew he would help you back.

PUTTA WAS FEELING COLD, wet and ridiculous.

There's no way I'm going to be able to find the flask – I just lobbed it in any old direction – I wasn't paying attention. I've never liked the stuff and once the G50 stopped working I didn't need it any more… Come to think of it, the G50's in here somewhere. And it will have leaked the last little bit of its fluid into this lake thing… but it was only a bit. It's not as if the water will now be full of telepathic fish, or anything… I think… Self-aware pond beasts… Yaagh.

As he considered this unpleasant possibility, he naturally felt something drag and cling round his ankle. He knew it was just some kind of vegetation catching at him and he was simply alarming himself for no reason. In the same way, it's easy for beings from Yinzill to imagine that something horrible is walking behind them and then to see weird shapes in the shadows under cliffs where, in actuality, there aren't lurking heart raptors, or just the standard kind of raptors that eat all of you. Or in the way that it's easy for Earth beings to imagine that a shark may be in their swimming pool and for them to then notice that big, dark shape approaching them in a way that suggests it isn't just the fat teenager they saw earlier – the one who likes holding his breath underwater, a way that makes the Earth beings swim very fast in the other direction even though the pool is indoors and has no access to the sea, and human municipal bathing authorities rarely add huge carnivorous fish to their range of leisure facilities…

Putta waded onwards, the light sinking fast in the west – which he thought was the least interesting direction for sunsets – and the water rapidly rising above his waist. The weed was now impeding his progress quite significantly – perhaps helped by the fact that he was scuffing his feet along the bottom of the lake in an attempt to find the flask. He hadn't thought this part of the plan through – mostly because he hadn't thought he would survive the earlier sections of his plan and even make it as far as the lake.

The weed really was getting to be a problem. He'd probably have to shove his hands down into the water and pull some of it off…

Which was when he did lean forward, his head dipping close to the surface of the lake and saw – dimly, but unmistakeably – the faces of Honor and Xavier looking up at him from beneath the cold water, their eyes unblinking, their expressions almost blank, apart from a terrible determination.

They were drifting along on their backs: slim, pale shapes lazily kicking their feet and sculling occasionally with a free hand. They had no apparent need to breathe. And each of them was gripping one of Putta's ankles – Honor to his left and Xavier to his right.

Now that he knew they were there, they gripped harder and smiled up, their mouths wavering under the ripples into impossible forms.

Then hands burst out of the wavelets and dragged him under before he could scream.

INSIDE THE BAH-SOKHAR, THE Doctor was sitting with his back very straight and his legs folded into the Lombukso Position, as he'd been taught by the High Metallama of X45ZD.

Actually, the Doctor could meditate in any position, but at least this felt familiar and comfortable and was something he'd done before without having his consciousness ripped apart, or being reduced to a dead-eyed shell, or simply evaporated.

By contrast, the Doctor had never attempted to access the full psychon energy at the psychic core of the TARDIS. From everything he knew about trying that – which was a lot – being ripped apart from his shoes to his personality was the least he could expect as a result.

He also hadn't attempted to open his mind to the Bah-Sokhar, to let it all the way into his thinking. Which was equally unwise.

The Doctor had also not ever considered trying to do both those utterly reckless things while also making sure that a very level-headed female human didn't get harmed in the process and while relying on a nervy young fool from Yinzill to help him out with a boost from some psy fluid at a point no one could predict – if it happened at all – a flask which was lost somewhere, probably on a golf course.

'Well, here goes then…' he told himself encouragingly.

He didn't exactly feel encouraged.

The Doctor closed his eyes, both his hearts galloping in his chest, his blood banging in his ears, his hands shaking as they held each other firmly clasped, at the required three centons' distance above the crown of his head. He breathed in the recommended manner for the Lombukso Ultimate Meditation. The Doctor was guessing that beginning with this particular, almost impossible, procedure would be his best chance of calling to the depths of the TARDIS and to the heart of the Bah-Sokhar.

The Lombukso Ultimate Meditation was usually only attempted after months of fasting and preparation, in the ideal peaceful conditions provided by the insulated cells of the High Retreat on Asdrak Island and with medically qualified attendants at the ready. The universe was a huge, wild place, after all, and the Ultimate was intended to clear the practitioner's conscious identity, accelerate its artron energy, peel back their subconscious and then open their essence completely to exactly that hugeness and wildness of the universe.

No one was meant to carry out such a severe and generally fatal ritual when they were tired, scared, unprepared and relatively full of cucumber sandwiches and cake.

And you would have to be completely out of your mind to do this while you were actually inside the hugest and wildest consciousness in the huge, wild universe – the terrible Bah-Sokhar.

The Doctor breathed, focused, pictured himself racing and sliding and burrowing along a vast tunnel, a plunging blue and silver and earth-coloured tunnel. He saw the dark at its centre – the emptiness which is not empty, the space which is more than space, the start of anything and everything. He let himself fall into it.

And somewhere, distant but beautiful and like the scent of home, he could sense the presence of the TARDIS. He could understand her concern for him, her general flurry of alarm – and an undertow of joy that she was also aware of him in this new way. He just couldn't quite reach her and he couldn't tell her his plan. He was too afraid to speak clearly while the Bah-Sokhar might be listening.

And – crushing and burning, twisting who he was at the roots – here was the first touch of the Bah-Sokhar. It was pushing him away, it was fighting him, blocking him. There was fear here – and a vast anger. Loneliness, too, sustained at levels which would have killed a lesser being.

For an instant the Doctor could feel the Bah-Sokhar deciding that he was a threat, that he should be erased from reality.

But something distracted it, blurred its intentions.

And in that moment, the Doctor was able to think as loudly as he could towards the TARDIS – *Bryony is ready – the in-the-bath girl – she will be our bridge – she will care about you and be a light – I need you to let me in – override all safety protocols and allow me full access – I am in the dark – we will not like the dark, but there will be light – there will be the Bah-Sokhar, but there will be light and courage – let me in.*

And of course he told her. *Please.*

PUTTA WAS STRUGGLING FOR his life. The two young creatures – for they surely couldn't be Earth children – had fastened themselves around him like iron and were dragging him far out into the deep point of the lake. Although Yakts have a greater lung capacity than humans, his whole chest was aching and burning with a need to breathe. The water was freezing here and dark, and his clothes were weighing him down. It was hard to tell which direction led to the surface any more and Putta was losing hope. He decided that he would like his last thought to be of Bryony – the Earth woman he had completely failed, while also failing to save her whole planet from certain doom… and then the back of his head – and this meant the back of his head was being forced along the bottom of the lake – hit something which hurt a great deal and also moved slightly and clanked against what must be some kind of rock. It sounded like metal – a metal container – a partially empty metal container.

Putta's heart flipped like a particularly happy dolphin – he didn't know this, he was completely unfamiliar with dolphins – and he decided to hope that this partially empty metal container was the flask of psy fluid.

At the same time, he managed to twist and wriggle out of his ill-fitting jacket, leaving Honor holding it, rather than

233

his shoulders. This meant he was a little disorientated for a second, but then he reached out blindly with his numbed fingers and – *not there, not there, not there, it has to be here somewhere, my lungs are going to burst* – *THERE IT IS* – found what absolutely felt like the cylindrical flask he was after.

Putta clung to the phial while Xavier dragged savagely at his ankles. Putta knew he wasn't going to make it to the surface… he was beyond his last gasp… he had no idea what to do.

AS SHE LAY IN the bath, Bryony was suddenly aware of a cool, smooth sensation on her forehead. She opened her eyes – for some reason she'd thought that having her eyes closed might be the best idea for whatever was going to happen next – especially if it was going to involve concentrating. There was nothing visible, but she had the distinct impression that a female hand was pressed gently to her brow. It reminded her of a time when she'd broken her leg as a child and been in hospital and her mother had come into the little bay in the A&E department and done just the same – pressed a hand to her forehead and made little Bryony feel OK.

I suppose this is it, then.

And it was.

Almost at once it didn't matter whether Bryony kept her eyes open or not – she could only see a rush of blue and silver and then a massive dark. She panicked a little – it didn't seem to her that she was going to be able to breathe – but that pressure stroked again across her forehead and she inhaled and there was air. She was OK. The TARDIS was trying to comfort her.

Suddenly, like two high ocean breakers crashing down over her, Bryony felt sweeps of massive energy tearing through her. She couldn't believe that her atoms weren't actually being shaken apart. She wasn't sure they hadn't been. She felt enormous pain. But she held on. She held on. She stayed as steady as she could, while colours and lights spiralled round her and forms seemed to eddy past – almost recognisable, almost frightening.

Bryony knew that she was supposed to keep as calm as possible and comfort the TARDIS. Things might get very strange, but she had to think safe and happy and friendly and calm thoughts and make them as big as possible and send them to the TARDIS.

So – knocking away the stinging and lancing hurt running along her limbs – she imagined friends laughing and the way plums tasted if you'd just picked then off the tree and a walk she'd taken in 1972 with a guy she'd thought was really nice, but had been too shy to tell – and the first time she'd been at a pantomime and been so thrilled by it all – the lights and the flashes of smoke when the villain turned up and shouting, 'It's behind you!'

Of course that's when she felt the *taptaptap* at the back of her neck and knew – there was something else here with her now.

It was behind her.

IN ARBROATH'S WEST PORT, the pavement was lined with surprised people. Shouting across the road at each other were, among others, Jimmy Findlay, Susan Findlay, Hughie Paterson, Gus Palmer, Brian Waters, Amanda Walter, Melissa Brown, Paul Cluny, Martha Cluny, Paul Cluny Jnr, a man called Clive Hughes who had intended to deliver Chinese food to number 15, and twenty or so others.

None of them had intended to yell at each other.

None of them had intended to have splitting headaches.

None of them – apart from Clive Hughes – had intended to be anywhere near the West Port. Some of them hadn't even intended to be in Arbroath.

And yet they were yelling – yelling because their brains hurt, yelling because they felt bullied and scared, yelling because they felt they were being spied on, yelling because they understood horribly clearly all the lazy and dull and selfish and nasty and uninspiring and greedy thoughts that everyone else who was yelling were having right at that moment.

As far as each one of them was concerned, everyone else was a completely repulsive person and deserved to be yelled at for the rest of their life.

Or maybe they deserved something worse.

TRAPPED IN THE MURKY waters of the Fetch Lake, Putta felt his throat and chest burning. Both twins were clutching his limbs now with astonishing strength.

I can't… I can't…

He could feel himself beginning to lose his grip on the world.

There's got to be… The Doctor would think of something… Bryony would… I got this far.

And, with his last remnants of strength, Putta unscrewed the flask and let the psy fluid escape into the water. He let it do what it always did – enhance the psychic fields of all available entities in the vicinity and render them more known to each other, or suitably calibrated detection devices.

It had been all he could think of to do and – suddenly, massively – all he could think of increased. He even – for a very brief period – awoke the dormant telekinetic abilities he shared with sixty-seven per cent of Yakts. And this meant that, at his most despairing, he became stronger than he ever had been.

The twins were disorientated by his surge of energy and also perhaps by this burst of ambient psychons. Putta was just able to break free from them and strike out towards the surface of the lake.

Once his head broke through the water he gasped, spluttered and flailed in a very unheroic manner, but he still felt immensely glad to be alive.

Which was just before he felt entirely horrified. The Doctor had wanted the psy fluid. And Putta had just emptied it out into a lake.

That may not have been absolutely the right thing to do.

FAR BENEATH FETCH LAKE, inside an extensive complex of watery tunnels and caverns hollowed out by millennia of geological activity and the repeated movements of a vast pseudo-body, lay the monstrous and ever-more alert combination of psychic energy and dissociated atoms which was the Bah-Sokhar.

And beneath that lake and within that vast assembly of matter and inside an air pocket sustained by the Bah-Sokhar sat the Doctor, trapped and alone.

And yet – just like his mind – he was also free and everywhere.

Passing beyond the pain his own body was undoubtedly experiencing, the Doctor was drifting in the oldest and most versatile kind of virtual space – that created by an imagination. Except this was more than just the world of only one imagination, one consciousness. The Doctor had travelled out of his own mind (some beings had remarked before that he was quite often out of his mind) and now he was partly in Bryony's. The Doctor had rapidly passed through Bryony's memories – that tedious argument with a guest, that midnight row, that tense exam, that red tricycle, that unpleasant spoonful of mashed pear, that answering wriggle she gave in the womb as her mother laughed at something – and on into somewhere slower, more stable,

240

more luminous – her deep self. It felt like a cathedral, like an endless horizon, like a fireside. Bryony's consciousness was, naturally, far smaller than the Doctor's – that was why it would make such a good focusing area for psychic energies – but it was still not unimpressive.

As he observed Bryony's past, the Doctor fought the pain imposed on him by the Bah-Sokhar. He also fought its fear of him and of the unknown, fought its uncontrolled urges to destroy. He tried to surround himself with this beauty that was Bryony.

And finally into the mind cathedral – the safe, relatively small space – came the TARDIS's consciousness, flinching and darting like a nervous animal.

The Doctor could tell she was holding back, being as tentative as she could, but still the force of her presence – the new, deep level of contact – was literally breathtaking.

He struggled to let go of the rush of images, the thousands of planet falls, the gape and rush of the time vortex, the spinning panoramas of galaxies, star births, supernovas… the flux and glimmer and growth of the TARDIS from its densely secret biomechanical roots.

Please.

The Doctor very rarely begged, but he was begging now.

His muscles were twitching, almost convulsing – his jaw was locked, but he kept on.

Please.

It seemed almost impossible, though – even with the help of Bryony as a kind of meeting point – to somehow grasp the essence of the TARDIS and harness it, turn her energy towards the Bah-Sokhar.

Please. Please. Come on, old girl.

He could tell that the TARDIS was afraid. She knew – perhaps better than anything else in the universe – how terrible the Bah-Sokhar was. Her genetic material was so old, so scarred by long-ago apocalypses, so wise and aware of the evils in reality… He just couldn't get her to trust him, to believe that she might come closer to the beast and survive it – even render it safe. Quite frankly, he didn't entirely believe that himself.

Please.

And then – far above in Fetch Lake – Putta emptied out the psy fluid into the lake.

This was absolutely the right thing to do.

The effects of psy fluid work in inverse proportion to the psychic abilities of those exposed to it. This is hardly surprising as it was developed by a species – the Tlatha – who had minimal psychic abilities and who were at that time ruled over by the notoriously despotic Simpilin – who were quite advanced telepaths. The Tlatha used the psy fluid to overthrow their masters and become equally despotic after a few years' practice.

This design feature means the fluid works best with inanimate objects – like the G50 Threat Detector – which have almost no consciousness. It also works well with relatively underdeveloped entities like humans and Yakts. The Doctor, as a Time Lord, was hardly affected by it at all – he had lazily exercised but not unimpressive telepathic abilities and massive reserves of artron energy, even for a Time Lord. He was also extremely clever.

Being extremely clever – and knowing how psy fluid worked – he was able to realise that Bryony, with her tiny human psychic capacities, was essential to his plan. (He did have a plan, he wasn't just making things up as he went along. Or not much.) He knew she could do far more than open her mind to act as a safe virtual place in which to calm the nervous TARDIS and perhaps negotiate with the Bah-Sokhar. She could do more than keep the Doctor away from the nightmares the creature seemed to insist on creating inside the fleshy cell it had formed to trap him. Holding her nerve and concentrating as she never had, Bryony could even be more than the friend he needed in the Bah-Sokhar's great darkness. She could also respond immensely well to the psy fluid if it were released in her vicinity – or even if it acted on the Doctor and flooded his consciousness, which would then reach her through him. All she'd have to do would be to weather the sudden rush of artron energy from – possibly – two directions and stay determined and, indeed, brave.

Or else – even if she was as incredibly brave as the Doctor thought – the psy fluid's energy might simply burn up her personality – along with the now vulnerable TARDIS and the Doctor himself, and along with his ability to regenerate.

But he was hoping not.

He was hoping that things would work out well.

The Doctor always tended to hope that things would work out well – his life would have been unbearably stressful if he didn't. Plus, a long lifespan spent travelling in both time and space had given him a certain perspective on hideous situations involving almost certain death. So far, none of them had ended that badly.

In the event, Bryony was close enough to the lake to be affected directly by the psychon energy and, 58 milliseconds later (because of the delay caused by Time Lord and – mainly – human nerve impulses) to be hit by the psychon energy which had rushed through the Doctor.

AND THAT'S WHAT CAUSED the sensation of two waves breaking over – or rather, through – Bryony while she tried to comfort the TARDIS.

The waves felt a little as if she was having the thoughts and emotions of a whole crowd of people pushed into her head, as if the *livingness* of too many beings to count had all leaped at her and were speaking, feeling, moving, burning inside her skin.

Even in the strange virtual space she occupied with the help of the TARDIS – somewhere that both was and was not her own mind – she had that sense of her skin, her body. Her physical self was something far away and under immense strain. She couldn't help wondering if she would be able to return to it. For a gasp of what felt like breath – *somewhere I'm still breathing, then, that's good* – Bryony was afraid she would never really be herself again.

And then she felt the *taptaptap* at the back of her neck and knew that she wasn't alone.

'Splendid. I knew you were just the girl for the job.'

Bryony span herself – or her idea of herself round – and was confronted by a virtual Doctor. He seemed much more solid than the projection she'd seen inside the TARDIS and so, obviously, he was able to creep up behind people and scare them half out of their minds.

'Doctor! What on earth!? Are you out of your mind?'

'Of course. We're both really quite far out of our minds.' He let loose one of his huger grins and his big eyes fixed her with a look that was ninety per cent down-to-business and ten per cent but-my-business-is-so-much-fun-and-look-we're-not-dead. 'But not out of the woods – not yet, Bryony Mailer.' Those parts of the environment contributed by the TARDIS – the strands of light, that sensation of being lifted and enveloped in warmth – all grew more intense. They were clearly suffused with happiness. She was glad to have him home – even if the home was only virtual and his body was still in the flesh cell, lost deep in his meditation.

Back in the Bah-Sokhar, the Doctor's real body was shivering with effort and hurt, while his strained face made him look – for once – as if he truly was hundreds of years old. But his virtual self was his best self – the flamboyant, charming person Bryony had first met. So although she was also glad to see him and deeply relieved, her relief emerged as a kind of defensive fury. 'You… You big…' She couldn't think of an appropriate word for what he was and opted for 'Don't call me a girl.' Which sounded a bit limp. Bryony found out that she too was, somehow, solid when she whacked him on the arm and he felt it.

'Ow!' The Doctor shook his virtual and yet very realistic head. 'No time for that. But I'm glad – I think – that your psy-form is consolidated enough to be painful. We're doing well, we really are, and you're not to worry in any way if—'

Probably, the Doctor was about to say, 'If our shared virtual space is suddenly torn open by the head of a monstrous snake, its tongue composed of blue / white and mobile, searching flame, its skin dripping with some terrible, unclean, thickish liquid, its eyes clever and merciless, their empty black seeming to drain the life force from you when they settle on you.'

Because that is exactly what happened.

Bryony had assumed the worst was over, that her virtual self would maybe hug the Doctor's virtual self and then they'd possibly send the Bah-Sokhar some really deep and philosophical thoughts

Just thinking the Bah-Sokhar's name meant one of those huge snake eyes swivelled and began glaring into her. Her entire consciousness started filling with all her worst memories: the choke of water when she almost drowned once; the day she heard her grandmother had died; every night she'd spent crying and every reason she'd had for being sad… And then the fears yet to be realised started closing in – being ill, being old, being alone, being a failure, being dead… Being dead.

As these corrosive thoughts worked at her, Bryony could see that her left hand was fading, becoming insubstantial. Her right was still solid, but she knew that the complex of energy holding her essence in this imaginative dimension was being forced apart by the Bah-Sokhar.

Worse, she could feel the TARDIS flinching around her and then withdrawing. Bryony guessed that perhaps the real body of Bryony Mailer was by now being compressed by the retreating and panicked ship.

The Doctor's mind was now deeply embedded in Bryony's, and he reached out for her hand to comfort her. As he did so, the snake's tongue lashed out to the side and swiped him away into the dark.

Bryony could hear him call out in pain, but could no longer see him.

The snake's head glowed with rabid colour and shattered into a spray of light and disappeared.

She was now in a dark that defied imagination – a space of utter emptiness, without mercy, without cruelty, simply without any interest in the existence of life.

And this is when the Bah-Sokhar spoke inside Bryony's head. The psy fluid had allowed it to reach her with a fraction of its monstrous telepathic strength.

YOU ARE THE BRYONYMAILER CREATURE

Bryony answered aloud – although she had worked out this wasn't necessary, she felt that speaking was more familiar to her and would help. She didn't want to let the Bah-Sokhar have everything its own way. 'What have you done with my friend?'

HE IS NOT YOUR FRIEND I WAS YOUR FRIEND I REMEMBER NOW I AM AWAKE I MEET YOU A LOT A LOT A LOT

Bryony couldn't understand this. Meeting a giant snake wouldn't have slipped her mind.

Of course, the Bah-Sokhar understood this idea as she had it, just as easily as it understood her speech.

WE MEET WHEN I PLAY I LIKE PLAYING WITH THE GRANDMOTHER CREATURE I PLEASE THE GRANDMOTHER CREATURE WHEN I PLAY

Bryony was still bewildered. And she wanted to know if the Doctor was all right. Before she could ask again, the Bah-Sokhar shouted into her head, blisteringly large words.

HE IS WELL OK OK

When Bryony screamed, there was a dense silence in her head for a few seconds and then, slowly emerging from the blackness as if it were fog, came Xavier and Honor. They looked as entirely human and friendly and lovely as ever. And they also looked worried.

Honor said, 'I'm sorry. I didn't mean to shout. Shouting is terribly rude.'

Xavier agreed. 'Yes, awfully. And we like you. We don't want to hurt you. The Time Lord chap, though – he knows who we are.'

Honor looked sad. 'And he knows what we do. Some of

247

the things that we've done. And that always makes people cross with us. And we didn't want him to be cross with us.'

Bryony blinked, stammered, 'But you're…'

Perfectly together, the twins said, 'We were your friend and we would have given you anything. We still could. We could make you the jewel at the heart of the universe.'

This wasn't in any way the kind of conversation Bryony was used to, but she decided that the Doctor would have expected her to deal with it, so she was going to. 'You're the Bah-Sokhar. That's… You are, aren't you?' She was going to deal with it on her own.

The name seemed to depress the twins. They sighed and shrugged, slightly like two youngsters caught out in having made a mess, or broken something. Xavier glanced at Honor and she nodded. Then they both continued to open and close their mouths in unison, but the Bah-Sokhar's thinking emerged. Bryony could sense that it was trying hard to be understood – it was used to speaking like storybook children – speaking as itself was more difficult.

WE HAVE MANY NAMES BAH-SOKHAR IS BAD NAME FEAR NAME

WE ARE ONLY US

I AM ONLY I

I AM I

I AM WE

WE ARE I

I

IF I AND WE HAVE NO NAME THEN WE CAN LIVE HERE HIDING HIDING AND BE ASLEEP

WE PLAY WE LIKE TO PLAY

I SLEEP AND DREAM OF PLAYING

HALF-ASLEEP PLAYING IS GOOD

I WANT TO PLAY WITH THE TIME LORD BUT HE DOES NOT WANT

I MAKE IT SAFE HERE FOR PLAY AND FOR
WHOEVER IS OUR CONDUCTOR

I NEED A CONDUCTOR THE TIME LORD
SHOULD BE OUR CONDUCTOR HE HAS THE BEST
MIND BUT HE WILL NOT TELL US ANYTHING TO
DO WE DO NOT KNOW WHAT TO DO

YOU TELL US BRYONY MAILER

TELL US WHAT TO DO

YOU TELL US AND I WILL MAKE ALL SAFE FOR
YOU

I WILL REMOVE WHOEVER SHOULD NOT BE

TELL I WHAT YOU WANT

IN ARBROATH, A TENSE situation was rapidly getting worse. The crowd gathered along the West Port had grown and now lined the pavements on both sides of Keptie Street and Millgate Loan. There were hundreds of people – children in school uniform, housewives in slippers, traffic wardens, men in overalls who had clearly abandoned late work on farms, or about the city, tourists in bright holiday clothes, pensioners. They faced each other across the empty road and screamed hatred. In Common Brae, the High Street and Abbey Street, more and more people were stumbling and shuffling into place, their faces masks of fear and furious contempt. Some of them were crying while they yelled; some were holding their heads as if they were in agony.

A young policeman, surprised by the mayhem, made half a report on his walkie-talkie and then felt himself overwhelmed by a painful barrage of threats and gossip and memories and hopes and terror – by the wild thoughts of so many strangers, so many neighbours, so many people.

Suddenly he understood why everyone was shouting, why everyone wanted to harm everyone else. It was because they were terrible people. And he had to *get rid of them*.

The constable started looking around for something, anything that he could throw at any of the outraged figures around him.

He believed that perhaps destroying everyone he could see would make the horror and the invading agony stop. He wasn't sure he would manage to do that, but he knew that whole planet would be a better place if he tried.

All over Arbroath, the shouting and jeering went on.

Then somebody threw a stone.

A ripple of motion ran out along the packed figures as somehow they all became aware of that first stone and its flight. Then there was a pause, as if everyone in Arbroath was breathing in.

Then everyone – men, women and children – all started hunting desperately for objects they could throw. There was the sound of breaking glass.

MEANWHILE, PUTTA PATTERSHAUN 5 had dragged his weary body to the edge of Fetch Lake and was lying back, breathless and close to passing out. Today had been more than he could take in so many ways. He'd almost been murdered by sand – twice – a pair of what he'd thought were lovely Earth children had also tried to kill him, he'd had a number of wonderful – and terrifying – adventures with Bryony, he'd nearly drowned, he'd attempted to save the day and been something very close to a hero... before he'd gone and poured the psy fluid into the lake and ended up being his usual failed self.

This meant, he was sure, that somewhere not far away everything was going wrong and it was completely his fault.

Over in the shadows, there was a small copse of trees and bushes and something rustled through the undergrowth in a way he might normally have found alarming. Just now, he didn't care if it was a large carnivore. He was too tired.

Oddly, as soon as he thought of whatever was bustling about in the leaves, his mind was rapidly packed with a stream of images and impulses. He found that he felt determined, peckish, nervy and highly alert, all at once – and furry... He definitely felt furry. He also had the idea that he wanted to eat a kind of cold, slimy, small titbit which he believed was called *a slug* by English-speaking Earth people. (It was so inconvenient of Earthers to have so many languages – he'd only been able to learn four.) It was also called *eine nacktschnecke* and *posta* and *seilide*.

Putta was just wondering if the dietary habits of Earthers were even more depressing than he'd thought when a badger romped out of the bushes and barrelled into him.

'Hwwaagh!'

This was not what he'd come to expect of Earth animals. Up until now they had all mistaken him for a human being and kept well away, as anything would, knowing how strange and violent human beings could be.

'Ho, yur… now… steady…'

This badger, though seemed to have decided that Putta was somehow also a badger and a close friend badger, at that. It was pawing at him happily, nibbling his shirt cuffs – what was left of them – and rubbing its rough, hairy back against him while snuffling, grunting and making little sort of clucking noises. Meanwhile, Putta's head was filled with slightly maternal-feeling sensations and a desire to eat worms. Apparently, this badger had decided he was her rather large and scrawny badger child.

A rather more scampering train of thought scrabbled through Putta's head now, followed by a manic need to sit and shout while up a tree and / or bury things – it was hard to decide whether the burying or the shouting should happen and then again it was time for bed… only there should be more burying… As Putta thought these things, out from the evening gloom came three field voles and a squirrel.

'Oh, for goodness' sake,' Putta protested as numerous tiny paws began clambering across him, grooming his hair and tattered tank top.

Obviously the psy fluid was having a slightly unpredictable effect on the wildlife around the lake. Putta was suddenly quite glad he wasn't still in the water. He shuddered when he thought of the steely little fists of the twins and wondered if they were down there watching him – or if they would walk up out of the lake at any moment. The animals around him twitched in response to his fears, but didn't seem to be aware of any threats. So perhaps Honor and Xavier had gone elsewhere. That just left whatever happened to all the other lake-dwelling creatures who might now feel he was a close friend, relative or indeed partner. The squirrel was being especially friendly and Putta could hear that branches and leaves all about him were restless with curious animal life.

As the sun set and another badger dunted against his bruised ribs, Putta didn't know if he should try and get back to the TARDIS – which hated him. Or else, he could just maybe stay close to it, while avoiding the sand outside the vessel – which wanted to kill him. He thought he might be able to keep safe by sitting in a tree nearby. (The tree-sitting part of that inspiration may have been made under the influence of squirrel thinking.)

What would someone else do? Putta thought. *What idea would someone who was good at ideas have? I've already had one plan today – that's more plans than I've ever had before and it turned out terribly badly. I don't have the right mind for planning.*

And then Putta realised – if he was this good at being joined with the minds of animals – beings who were only concerned with feeding, foraging and, it had to be said, mating…. What if he tried reaching out to more helpful minds. What if he could do that?

This did, of course, constitute Putta's second plan of the day.

He lay down – because that seemed likely to help – and was immediately overrun by shrews, but he didn't notice because – as he opened his mind inexpertly and nervously to the world beyond him…

'Putta!'

An unmistakable sense of the Doctor's presence swept through him and then was gone.

Putta couldn't be sure, but it had felt as if the Doctor had been in trouble, as if he'd been, somehow thrown past Putta's consciousness by some huge, swiping blow.

If the Doctor was in trouble – and Putta couldn't quite work out why he wasn't dead – that was completely terrible news because the Time Lord seemed to be the only one who had any idea about what was happening at the Fetch Brothers Golf Spa Hotel – the only one who had any idea about how to deal with it…

Doctor? Doctor?

Putta couldn't pick up any trace of the Time Lord.

But he must be here. I mean, I heard him.

Putta concentrated harder.

DOCTOR?

There was still no response.

And the wider Putta opened his mind, the more it seemed to fill with the same terrible darkness he had seen in the twins' eyes. There was also a hint of fury, not far away – that and a taste of pure, lonely horror. Putta realised that as he looked for the Doctor, called for the Doctor, he might simply lose himself in what felt like a vast pit of bleak emotions.

But he couldn't stop. He had to find the Doctor. He had to risk it.

Putta clenched his fists, held his breath and – while the animals which were assembled round him froze, their small hearts racing with alarm – he sent out his consciousness as hard and fast as he could and hoped that the psy fluid's effects would push him on to reach the Doctor.

The dark crushed in, it seemed that his skull would crack into pieces and Putta was aware of a high, sad wailing – perhaps from him, perhaps from some other creature, perhaps from the ultimate blackness which rushed towards him.

And then.

'Well, it took you long enough.'

And Putta was slowly able to feel the idea of the Doctor – the Doctor's idea of the Doctor – all that warmth and mischievous intelligence. There was fear there, too – Putta hadn't realised before how scared the Doctor could be – but there was courage answering the fear and a huge sense of relief.

Doctor?

Putta couldn't see much beyond a wavering outline in his mind's eye, which could have been the Doctor or almost any other humanoid, but that unmistakeable, plush purr of a voice was clear. 'The Bah-Sokhar knocked me halfway into next week… which, believe me, young Putta, at the moment would not be a welcoming place. If we don't get tonight readjusted, then next week will be past saving.'

Putta shuddered and thought, *Bryony… She's…?*

'Yes, Putta – she's in the mindspace we've created, alone with the creature. I underestimated its strength which was stupid of me.' Putta could feel a quieter part of the Doctor whisper, 'And it was unforgiveable.' Meanwhile, the rest of the Doctor's consciousness continued urgently, 'While the psy fluid is still active I need you to stop wasting time playing with your animal friends and get me back to the TARDIS – you've drawn me in this far… I was rather drifting in the wrong direction and… being lost at the margins of a mindspace isn't fun at all – you can cease to exist as a mind at all – just end up a physical shell with nobody home… Much like you, you silly Yakt. Now pull yourself together and help me get back to the TARDS.'

Putta's mind flinched. What little was left of his self-confidence crumpled.

The TARDIS doesn't exactly like me, Doctor.

The voice purred in, completely reassuring and even effusive. 'Oh, come along now, Putta. I do thank you, you know. You saved me from eternal drifting in a virtual darkness, or being lost in the Bah-Sokhar's consciousness.. I mean it's not clear where we might still – not to worry about this – end up. But you can do it, Putta. I know you can. You can save the day.' Putta felt the idea of a smile soaking through him. 'The TARDIS can be a prickly old girl, but she knows a friend when she sees one… Trust me. I'm not going to make it back in there without you, you know. So do stop fussing and generating negative emotions – it's such a waste of time. Our minds are joined, Putta – you know perfectly well that I'm as scared as you are – if not more so. I am a genius, after all – I have a lot more thinking space than you do that I can be afraid with. But I'm deciding that my fear isn't useful and I'm walking round it. I am imagining it is a very small wall and I'm walking round it.'

Putta received an image of a ludicrously small wall made of crumbly, cakey brick which wouldn't worry anyone. It was slightly comforting.

So Putta calmed himself as best he could and imagined sort of turning and reaching out to the Doctor. He imagined shaking hands. Which was OK. He imagined smiling. Which was fine. He imagined perhaps stepping to one side and then the other as if they were kind of dancing to the same tune. Which was fine, too. And then Putta imagined letting the Doctor take over his mental energy. Which felt a bit like volunteering to drown.

Whoo-hoo-wughghgh…

Putta didn't like drowning, and it seemed he'd been doing it a lot lately.

'It's all right, Putta. It's all right. Breathe. Think of breathing. That's all. Breathe.'

And so Putta pictured himself breathing and being alive and not choking on horror and pressing dark and then he felt something like being gripped by helpful hands, being pulled along by a lifeguard across risky waves, being safe. He felt safe.

Uagh- ughuguhugh…

Then Putta panicked again

'There's nothing to be afraid of. My dear Putta – everything is going to turn out very well.'

As Putta had access to the Doctor's thinking, he was fully aware that the Doctor was very much less certain than he sounded about whether anything was going to turn out well – but the idea of them both being brave anyway and going on anyway and rescuing Bryony anyway meant that he relaxed and set all his remaining focus and affection and purpose and – even – love into aiming his virtual self where the Doctor was aiming the virtual Doctor – right towards a dim, but lovely bluish light, far away in the mindspace's thick night.

The more Putta thought of the light, the closer it got, and the further he moved from his body where it lay on the wet lakeshore with a number of puzzled animals fussing at it or nuzzling against it. He could no longer feel them.

Putta was heading for the TARDIS.

Fast, fast and faster – here it came.

'Come on, Putta – nearly there.'

SITTING GLOOMILY BEHIND THE reception desk of the Fetch Brothers Hotel was the hunched Kevin Mangold. He stared at the non-working clock. The whole place was going to rack and ruin as far as he was concerned. He'd just broken up a fight in the bar and there was a strange atmosphere in the whole place. This was undoubtedly the fault of that Bryony Mailer excuse for a receptionist, who was going to find herself out of a job – just as soon as *he* could find *her*. It was typical that she'd disappeared. She was always doing that. She'd probably started this ridiculous fashion for doing that.

For a moment, Mangold recalled the inconvenient facts that Bryony only ever disappeared when she was off duty and that she did a lot of unpaid overtime – but he forced those thoughts away and then went on being angry with her.

And Miss Pitcairn said Bryony was waltzing around with that Doctor person and one of the guests in the Spa. They left the jacuzzi room full of dirty sand. What on earth would cause that, I can't think – hippy rock and roll carrying on, that's what would cause it. I always knew she was trouble. Her attitude was all wrong. Not like Miss Pitcairn. Lovely hair, Miss Pitcairn has…

While he pondered the Spa manageress, Miss Pitcairn, in more detail, Mangold didn't notice the surface of the reception desk bubbling, then swelling. It was only when it started to actually swallow his hands – almost tenderly – that he looked down in horror.

He had just enough time to say, 'Wha—?'

BRYONY COULDN'T HELP IT. As soon as the Bah-Sokhar had mentioned people she might want to be rid of, the quick thought and image of Kevin Mangold had slipped out and away before she could catch it.

And even though he was a huge pain in the neck, she really didn't want him to stop existing or for anything dreadful to happen to him – anything like what had happened in the Spa…

'No, no, no,' she told the creature. 'I don't want you to hurt anyone.'

I HAVE BEGUN REMOVING THE MANGOLD PERSON

YOU HATE THE MANGOLD PERSON

'Stealing biscuits isn't a capital offence. Neither is being annoying. Stop it. Stop what you're doing. You can stop it, can't you? You're a big all-powerful thing.'

I MAKE HIM NOT BE

FOR YOU

'But I don't want you to make him not be, and I didn't ask you to.'

YOU ASK

I FEEL YOU ASK

YOU HATE AND I FEEL AND I REMOVE I FEED

Bryony tried – and this was, in a way, her most difficult

261

challenge yet – to extend courteous and warm thoughts towards Kevin Mangold. She tried to like him. She tried to think that if she couldn't like him, then maybe his mum liked him. Or maybe he was horrible because his mum didn't like him. Or just that on some days he didn't pinch her biscuits and left her alone and he had given her a job when she'd been feeling quite depressed and needed to get away from it all and – until the Doctor arrived – you couldn't really have said that the Fetch Hotel was anywhere other than away from it all.

YOU NEED HIM

'Yes. I need him. I need everyone. I need all the people to stay where they are.' Bryony reconsidered this. 'I mean I need them to be able to move about in their normal way, and to keep on being alive… OK?'

YOU NEED THE MANGOLD CREATURE

'Yes, yes I do. I have no idea why, but I certainly wouldn't to walk about knowing I was someone who had ordered him to be destroyed in some horrible… Are you sure the Doctor is all right?'

YOU NEED HIM

'Yes. Yes, I need him. And I need Putta Pattershaun 5, or Mr Patterson or whoever. I need them. In fact I need them here. I feel lonely without them.'

LONELY

I KNOW LONELY

Bryony was scorched through with the enormous truth of this.

DOCTOR COULD STAY WITH ME
DOCTOR LIVES LONG TIME
I CAN MAKE HIM LIVE LONGER
WE CAN PLAY SOMETIMES
WE CAN SLEEP SOMETIMES
BUT HE HATE ME

HE WANT ME GONE AWAY
MUST DEFEND AGAINST BEING GONE AWAY
WE DEFEND I AGAINST BEING GONE AWAY
Bryony digested the sense of this and worked out that the twins were not simply the Bah-Sokhar's way of playing and having kind of friends in the real world – they were also one of its lines of defence.

WHILE SHE WAS WORKING this out, over at the Fetch Hotel reception desk, Kevin Mangold looked down at his hands while his heart cantered about in his chest and he felt horribly sick... then he felt calmer and calmer and began to push his forearms down into the soft, gluey something that had replaced the usual cheap-wood-made-to-look-quite-like-mahogany. He was keen to cease existing.

Only then, while Bryony was wondering how to proceed with her talkative monster, his terror revived and became almost too much to bear – before the desk top spat out his hands and healed over as if nothing weird had ever happened.

Mangold blinked. He shook his head.

He decided that he was overstrained and should withdraw for a cup of tea in the Staff Office. He put out the sign that said guests should ring for IMMEDIATE ASSISTANCE – he'd always thought that was an unwise promise to make – and wondered if there would be any biscuits hidden away in the office. It was probably, now he considered it, nice of Bryony to leave them for him. He needed a biscuit. And he thought he would phone his mum later. First he would fire Bryony and then he would call his mum.

UNAWARE THAT SHE'D JUST succeeded in saving a life, Bryony was improvising – her experience as a receptionist had left her with a fair amount of experience in dealing with the unhappiness and anger of others. 'You were Honor and Xavier, then? They weren't children, not real children?' There was the unpleasant possibility, of course, that the Bah-Sokhar had maybe digested the real twins and then learned enough about them to impersonate them. Or perhaps they were puppets that it worked inside – horrible idea…

OUR GRANDMOTHER WANT CHILD
WE GIVE CHILD
WE GIVE TWO
TWO IS BETTER
GRANDMOTHER HAPPY
GRANDMOTHER WANT HUSBAND BABY GRANDCHILD
WE GIVE LAST IN LIST
LAST IS LAST
IS MOST IMPORTANT

This made a kind of sense, Bryony supposed – the other desires of Julia Fetch could be seen as steps along the way to grandchildren. 'Well, that was kind of you. That wasn't about making people not be.'

KIND
GRANDMOTHER LOVE US
KIND
GRANDMOTHER LOVE OCTOPODES
GRANDMOTHER LOVE OCTOPUSES
WE MAKE EXTRA BIG FOR HER

Bryony's mind chilled when it remembered the grasping arms that had nearly conquered her and Putta.

REGRET

'Yes, that's all very well, but you don't have to regret things like that if you don't do them in the first place.'

BRING DOCTOR HERE
WE BRING HIM AND BRING PUTTA CREATURE
THEN YOU ALL STAY HERE FOR ALWAYS
WE PLAY
WE SLEEP
WE PLAY

Before Bryony could object, she could feel the approach of the tumbling, flustered virtual Putta and the mind of the Doctor – much more wary and harder to read as he approached.

And then – it did her so much good to see them – there were the images of her two friends.

SEE
YOU HAPPY
YOU BE HAPPY IF THEY BE HERE
FOREVER HAPPY
I MAKE PLACE FOR YOU

Almost before the Bah-Sokhar had finished thinking this sentence, the forbidding darkness began to sprout trees, rose bushes, a neat lawn… To Bryony it looked very much like a version of the garden outside Julia Fetch's cottage. It was just a garden that seemed to go on for ever and to sway up and down, or flicker very slightly at the corner of her eye and on the horizon. Bryony, started, 'But even children don't want to play all the time... I mean they want to grow up and—'

Before she could finish the Doctor had unleashed a burst of fury – which was an achievement for someone rapidly being surrounded by a particularly attractive shrubbery. 'Bah-Sokhar! You cannot have her. I forbid it. You cannot keep any of us. I forbid it!'

As soon as he yelled this – or rather as soon as his mind yelled this – the shrubbery became more wiry, more and more like a cage formed or briars and locking around him.

I AM I
I AM WE
I DO WHAT WE WISH

'Doctor! No!'

Bryony looked on helplessly as Putta was also wrapped in briars. The sight of his face – so shocked and sad, his eyes meeting hers – rocked her heart. Back in the TARDIS, Bryony's body shuddered in the bath. The ceiling sank lower. It was only a foot or so away from the top edge of the bath now and still descending.

'Bah-Sokhar! Please!'

While her mind cried out, the garden the Bah-Sokhar had planted was shaken by what manifested as a strong gale – branches and leaves whipped back and forth. The sky which had been developing as umber overhead with two suns visible, faded as the Bah-Sokhar's attention obviously turned elsewhere.

YOU SAD

'Yes, I'm sad!' bellowed Bryony's consciousness. 'You bet I'm bloody sad. You've been doing horrible things to people I love all day, and you've been lying to me ever since I came here, and I'm angry!'

'No, no, no!' called the Doctor. 'Don't be angry. Keep

being sad. We know what it does when people are angry. I think sad is altogether the better path. And being fond of people… Try and be as fond as you can of Putta. He's completely besotted with you, I can tell you. I know all the details. I mean, you're splendid and everything, I quite agree, but the detail when you get up close to his thinking is positively obsessive—'

Putta – confined by unreal, but still painful thorns – couldn't stand this humiliation any longer, 'Yes, thank you Doctor. She doesn't love me. But I love her and I don't care if she doesn't love me. I don't care if I die here – or where my body is, or… this whole situation is very confusing and I don't like it – I don't like anything about it, except that I know she's all right. I know you're all right Bryony and you'll be all right… and if you're the last thing I see, then that will be all right. That will be…' His speech dwindled away in surprise as the briars withered back and then replaced themselves with dahlias. The Doctor was, likewise freed and left standing in a fantasy flowerbed, complete with butterflies.

YOU LOVE PUTTA CREATURE

As the creature said this to Bryony, Putta made a noise like a cat being surprised.

YOU LOVE DOCTOR

This produced a noise from Putta more like a cat being stepped on.

The Doctor smoothed his way out of the flowers and onto the lawn, getting into his stride in every sense. 'Yes, we're all terribly fond of each other in the usual ways. You can tell that. It's not as if we can lie to you… Bah-Sokhar, the people on this planet they also tend to love each other – at least some of the people love some others of the people at least some of the time. I mean, they aren't the sanest beings in the universe and certainly they can be full of hatred and fear, but why only listen to that. You made those children, you pleased their non-grandmother with them… I'm pretty sure you've been keeping her alive for longer than usual… You make things. You don't have to destroy. You can learn.'

Learn

Bryony

The Bah-Sokhar became quiet, perhaps because it was thinking.

DOCTOR YOU BIGGEST MIND

BUT YOU NOT TELL

BRYONY YOU TELL

DOES YOU WANT I SHOULD LEARN

DOES YOU WANT WE SHOULD LEARN

Bryony tried to answer the creature without getting too excited, but she couldn't avoid feeling optimistic. 'Yes. Yes, the Doctor's right. You could learn. We would help. We could. Probably. I don't think I'll be working here any more, but I could come to the lake or the park or something, I suppose and we could talk… I'm not sure if I could be like this very much – it's really strange for me, but I could talk to the twins – you must have learned through them…'

HUMANS ANGRY

HUMANS HATE THEIR CHILDREN

HUMANS ENVY GREEDY RAGE FEAR

Putta felt he could contribute. 'The whole universe knows that. And they eat things in pies.'

'You're not helping,' Bryony hissed across to him

'No, no… that's… I just… You hear about humans and they're supposed to be completely… monsters… well, not monsters… well, yes, mainly monsters… but then you meet them and they're… that is… You know Bryony. They can be like her. They're not all bad.'

'Thanks for the ringing vote of confidence,' muttered Bryony. But she was virtually smiling a virtual smile.

Putta smiled back. 'Well, I can't exactly lie, can I?'

The Doctor decided things needed to move along. 'Yes, well, young love is attractive and so forth – although what your children would be like... you're two completely different species you know – that takes considerable planning... It's not as simple as her being from... Ipswich and him being from... Arbroath...' He rubbed his face just as he would if it had been his face and he had been tired and at the end of a taxing day. 'Bah-Sokhar, we will assist you. I will assist you. It would be possible for you to change. You already have, for goodness' sake.'

I CHANGE
WE CHANGE
I AM I
WE ARE WE
WE BE CHANGE
I BE CHANGE

And this all seemed entirely positive as a development and Bryony was full of hope about it and had time to feel thrilled that she was in a virtual world with three different alien beings and kind of helping in a significant way to save all life on Earth, which wasn't bad, considering she'd had nothing to look forward to for today beyond a film she'd seen before on telly and thinking about a man who clearly either didn't fancy her, or who would never be able to tell her he fancied her.

Putta was, likewise, allowing his consciousness to thrum with what could be the inrushing of a lifetime's suppressed optimism. He had been part of saving the day. It was all going to get better from here.

And the Doctor... the Doctor was cautious, but he could feel that the Bah-Sokhar wasn't lying. The universe's greatest and most feared assassin being had – over centuries in a quiet and lonely corner of the universe – slowly changed, altered its patterns of behaviour. The possibilities for good were almost endless.

Only then the garden disappeared in flash of utter blackness.

A force like the howling of wolves and broken children, like the end of many worlds, clawed through Putta, Bryony and the Doctor and they found themselves flung agonisingly out of the mindspace and into a bitter reality.

BRYONY AWOKE SCREAMING, BACK in her exhausted body, every muscle aching and her consciousness feeling torn. When she opened her eyes, she could see that the bathroom ceiling was only a hand's breadth away from the rim of the bath. She struggled – still groggy – to scramble out of her confinement, but she was too late. There wasn't enough of a gap for her to fit through. She was trapped in a kind of coffin as – outside in the TARDIS – the lights went out.

ARBROATH WAS STILL DENSELY packed with people, but now they were divided into individuals and what looked like pursuing packs – or else groups of fairly similar sizes were confronting each other across roadways and little parks. Cars – apparently abandoned at the roadside with their doors wide open – were dented, their wing mirrors missing and their windscreens were smashed. Jagged holes were visible in shop fronts and house windows through which curtains fluttered mournfully. Here and there street signs were bent. Small fires blazed in the hot summer night and were left unattended. Broken glass would have crunched underfoot had anyone been moving. But nobody was moving.

Faces contorted in pain, fear and hatred were fixed. Hands raised to strike were arrested, kicking feet, punches, attempts to deflect blows, desperate flights and desperate pursuits were all held motionless.

And then the faces cleared, smoothed and became mainly numb. What had been a chaos of fury turned into a dream of life's return to business as usual. Handkerchiefs were dabbed at cuts and grazes, children were dusted down, scattered shopping was gathered off pavements and put back into bags by dull-eyed and completely silent individuals. No one cried, no one complained, no one wondered what had

273

happened to them, or their torn clothes, or their wrecked cars.

A small seaside town simply shrugged and went back to its life without complaint – as if all its passion had been emptied out in the course of a few minutes and none was left.

The young constable limped out from behind the dustbins which had been concealing him, set down the length of wood he had ripped from a fence and used to keep off attackers and surveyed the battered High Street – all but one of its streetlights beaten out of action. It was a shadowy and fearful place, slow-moving figures straggling along it and disappearing. He seemed to find nothing wrong.

Paul and Martha Cluny and their son, Paul Junior, returned to their hired car and seemed not to notice that its windscreen was missing, as was one of the passenger doors. They climbed back into it without any comment, fastened their seat belts and drove away.

Putta Pattershaun landed back in his own body with a snapping jolt which rattled his teeth and made his eyes sting. The pair of badgers which had kept it company while he wasn't quite using it sniffed at him, paused and then ambled back into the brush and undergrowth, their round forms blending greyly into the dark.

He felt more exhausted and sore than he had in his life – and was also bewildered.

Why had the Bah-Sokhar ejected them from its presence?

It was great that it hadn't eaten them or –

He would have continued his analysis of the situation had the Doctor not landed halfway across him, appearing from the empty air at a point about three feet above the ground – not far, but far enough to be painful for both of the parties concerned. They'd both been spat out in roughly the same direction, but at slightly different speeds.

'Hhafff!' exclaimed Putta. 'Doctor?'

'Of course. Who else would it be? And don't just loll about there as if we have all the time in the world – we don't have any time. We have to get back to the TARDIS – if the TARDIS was also expelled by the Bah-Sokhar and frightened, then Bryony's body may be in terrible danger.' The Doctor had clambered up from his awkward position across Putta's shins and was now standing and hauling him to his feet.

'What do you mean – Bryony's body?'

'She may not even be in it. The Bah-Sokhar may have taken a shine to her consciousness and decided to keep it.'

Putta realised he was running, stumbling and lurching fast over uneven ground both in the dark and in his socks, the Doctor pulling him along by one arm. 'Keep it? What does that…? Well, then we have to save it, I mean her, I mean both.'

'What do you think we're doing? Honestly, Putta – keep up.'

The Doctor plunged on and eventually brought them both to a sharp slope. It was another section of the densely overgrown rise Putta had climbed when he left the riverbank what seemed an age ago.

'There's no time, I'm afraid, for anything other than hoping that gravity will assist.'

'I don't like the sound of—'

But before Putta could suggest what he didn't like the sound of, the Doctor gave him a healthy shove in the small of his back and sent him tumbling, sliding, thumping and cracking down the incline, hitting tree trunks and rocks as he went, feeling when his shin was cut, when his skull was clouted, when his cheek was scraped, when something almost caught him in his eye, when a tangle of creeper tugged off one of his socks as it almost put a noose around his ankle.

While Putta rocketed downwards, he could hear the Doctor, also careering towards the river. The Doctor was talking – rather loudly, it had to be admitted – but not really in the manner of a being currently using himself as a toboggan.

'Concentrate! Putta, listen to the sound of my voice!

Follow me!' the Doctor called as the din of his progress downhill moved from being behind Putta, to roughly level with him and then further out ahead.

The Doctor cried out after heavy splash which indicated that he had reached the water. 'Come on! Follow me! I can't hear her!' His words were full of anguish. 'I can't hear her. I can't hear the TARDIS thinking. I've never known her be so still. I know she's there, but I can't hear a thing!' And the Doctor battered on up the course of the river. The moonlight through the trees was able to spark on the wet rocks and to show the Doctor's tall form thrashing forward like a man possessed.

Then Putta remembered. 'But the sand. We can't go back, the sand will get us! We can't go near your TARDIS! We can't! Doctor, we have to stay away from the sand! Wait! Doctor!'

But the Doctor loped and slithered and struggled on regardless, getting further and further away.

IN HER LOVELY BATHROOM, Julia Fetch had already run the bath she would always take before slipping into bed, enjoying the cool smoothness of her linen sheets and falling asleep. She had been told, or had read somewhere, that people were meant to sleep less as they aged, but she found that she was sleeping more and more – sometimes she would even sleep right through an entire day.

She had sprinkled lavender bath salts into the water and was looking forward to a calming dip.

When she pottered over to turn off her taps she glanced down at the water and saw, furling and unfurling its delicate and clever limbs, a red-spot night octopus, or *octopus dierythreaus*, her very favourite octopus. It was a perfectly beautiful specimen – just like a living version of the glass model in her living room.

I can't think it's enjoying water this hot, she thought. *And I don't suppose it normally swims in lavender bath salts.*

She slipped her hands into the water, thinking she might scoop the red spot octopus out and keep it in more suitable water until she could rehome it, perhaps, in one of her ocean reserves. Or maybe in its own bath – it really did prefer hot, lavender-flavoured water… But then the little animal did a remarkable thing – it reached towards her and, well… it felt very much as if it was hugging her hand,

278

stroking her fingers with a sort of affection and kissing her knuckles with its mouthparts. The sensation was strange, but not unpleasant.

'Well, I never.'

The octopus withdrew, but watched her with its big clever eyes and continued to dab at her hand and wind the very ends of its tentacles around her fingers, like an attentive friend.

'You're a charming fellow, aren't you?'

She knew that octopodes were highly intelligent and communicative, but she had never encountered one which really seemed fond of her. It was so wonderful that finally such a thing had happened.

Somewhere in her mind she remembered that she had always wanted a moment like this – a time when she had been at one with nature and with the octopuses she was so anxious to preserve. And she had always wanted a time when she felt that something else alive cared for her and wanted to show that.

For a number of reasons, she went and sat on the bathroom chair, hugged her dressing gown tight around herself and cried. The octopus watched her fondly, bobbing and undulating in the steamy water.

Then Mrs Julia Fetch set her head in her hands for an instant to catch her breath. She wasn't sad, exactly – it was more that she was complete now in a funny kind of way.

When she looked up again, the octopus was gone.

This didn't disturb her. She felt very grateful, in fact. She felt she had been loved.

PUTTA COULDN'T KEEP UP with the Doctor's long-legged progress and lost sight of him round the curve of the river's course. Hobbling along in one sock, Putta finally came within sight of the TARDIS. Its weirdly reassuring shape was solid and neat in the moonlight. He supposed he should call it her… Her small, round light dimly glowing and flickering, as were the letters which spelled out POLICE PUBLIC CALL BOX. Putta was unfamiliar with how the TARDIS usually looked, but he was pretty sure that a functioning and healthy Time Lord vessel wouldn't have flickering lights. And in this he was mostly correct.

As he approached, slowing his progress and searching about, he could see nothing of the Doctor. Putta felt sick and desperate at once. The Doctor had disappeared. Again. He must have rushed out on to the fatal sand and been taken.

Putta snapped. This was too much. After all they'd been through and all that the Doctor had done, it wasn't fair that he should have been killed.

Then Putta Pattershaun 5, the small ginger male from Yinzill, completely lost his temper and rushed – boulders, mud, water and moss permitting – towards that border of sand between the river and the TARDIS. He no longer cared if he was going to be killed. If he couldn't help the Doctor, then he was going to try and rescue Bryony, anyway. He was going to risk the sand, anyway. He was going to be a hero, anyway.

Putta half leaped and half fell onto the sand, wheezing and swinging his fists. 'I won't let you have her as well! I won't!' He dug his hands into the pebbly grit. 'And you give him back. I need the Doctor! We need the Doctor!' And then he thumped his scratched knuckles against the TARDIS's door. 'And you! You're not helping! You're the only one who knows him! You're supposed to be his friend! You're—!'

At which point the TARDIS opened her doors.

While the sand didn't even attempt to eat him.

Stepping cautiously over sand which appeared to be just perfectly normal muddyish, lumpy sand – Putta walked inside.

What he saw next meant that he spent quite a while standing with his mouth open and his hands halfway to doing something which they had both forgotten. He also made a small noise like a rabbit sneezing.

The Doctor – perfectly healthy, although slightly leafy, wet and mud-spattered – was emerging through the door at the far side of the console room. He was finding this tricky, because he was carrying Bryony in his arms. Bryony was dressed in – as far as Putta could see – a blanketty thing, a big shirt and something else that was stripy and pink. She was not absolutely enjoying being carried. 'Will you put me down.' She wriggled like a very large, tetchy, striped fish

'You've had a shock. I told you to go and lie down for a bit—'

'Lie down?! Lie down?! I've been trapped lying down in a bath for I can't imagine how long!'

'And I saved you. All the old girl needed was a bit of reassurance. I'm a very reassuring person. I would reassure you if you'd let me get a word in edgeways.'

'Let you get a word in! I've never known anyone talk as much as you! And I don't ever want to lie down again! And I'm fine!'

'But my dear girl, you did come quite close – not awfully close and it would have been a complete accident… but contemplating being crushed by a ceiling will have been worrying for you…'

'Not as worrying as having it nearly happen!'

'Which is why…' The Doctor sighed, finally gave up and set Bryony down, slightly before she would have managed to fall out of his arms in any case, because she was trying so determinedly to stand up. He pushed back his prodigious fringe and beamed at her. 'You are good at all this.'

'Good at it! My whole brain might have been fried! I could have been squashed flat by your spaceship!' The TARDIS's lights dimmed. 'Who's lovely, but still… I don't do well when I'm less than an inch thick. I don't think it would suit me! And is that it? Is everything safe now? We surely can't just leave something like that to do what it wants with sand whenever it meets someone in a bad mood. You think I could nip off and have a nap with all this going on!? What do you think I am, a… a…'

No one found out what Bryony thought the Doctor thought she was because this was when Putta made that rabbit sneezing noise and the arguing pair turned to him in surprise.

'Wh—?' said Putta. His heart was cartwheeling in his chest because there was everyone, absolutely all right and fine and there and grumpy and grinning and… things were all much better than he'd expected. Apart from maybe how sore his feet were, how sore everything was and how foolish he felt in these trousers now that Bryony was looking at him.

And that doom-laden bell was still chiming.

That seemed a bad sign.

'Putta!' the Doctor exclaimed – almost as if he was delighted that Putta had made it and appreciative of all the work and bravery he'd put in, even though he was a naturally cautious being. But then, as Putta was straightening his shoulders in what he thought might look like quiet pride, it turned out that the Doctor was more exclaiming because he needed someone to help him out with the console. 'Well, don't just stand there like a wet hen.' The Doctor began switching toggles and lifting panels, turning dials, padding round the console as if it were a musical instrument and he was a virtuoso. Now and then he would stroke a control surface, pat one of the little brass rails. 'Putta, I need you on the Zeus panel. It's that one. We need more information and if there's a mammoth telepathic clamp still in operation, it won't be hard to detect.'

The Doctor paused expectantly while Putta blinked and tried to remember how his legs worked and noticed that Bryony looked amazing whatever she was wearing – even if whatever she was wearing was... pretty dreadful. And oddly reminiscent of the uniform worn by female members of the security forces on Penal Planet ZZ5#7^.

'Never mind her. She's perfectly all right.' The Doctor waved Putta fully inside impatiently.

'You said that without rest and rehydration I could collapse completely and that my psychic reserves would be dangerously low for months,' grinned Bryony.

'Yes, but other than that – you're really terribly healthy. And it's not as if you'll pay any attention to what I advise...' His eyes flickered with immense joy. It was clear that there were few things the Doctor enjoyed more than being at the console alongside companions he could bicker with and order about. 'Bryony, I need you to watch the screen and at the first sign of a signal yell out – and hold down that lever. No, not that one! That one. With the infra-jade handle.

Mind you don't cut yourself on it – it's slightly cracked.' He fiddled with a dial. 'Ow! No, it's this one that's slightly cracked. I knew it was something… Running repairs… one never has time…'

And Putta watched as Bryony held down the lever, eyed the screen like a trainee eagle and looked as pleased as anyone who'd always dreamed of being on a spaceship would, if they actually were on a spaceship and – much more than that – actually were being allowed to operate one of its levers. The screen altered the image it showed from the dim exterior around the TARDIS to a more bland dark grey.

Putta shut the doors behind him, shuffled down the steps and took his place as indicated by the Doctor's absently waggling hand. He was glad to be with the two people he cared about most in the universe, but that didn't mean he wasn't annoyed about their ability to enjoy something which still might be a complete catastrophe quite so much.

As he thought this, Bryony and the Doctor turned towards him. The Doctor smiled indulgently and said, 'Well, if one can't be cheery during a catastrophe there's really no point being cheery at all, is there? I mean, catastrophes are highly unpleasant and just the thing you'd want to face while feeling at your best.'

At the same time, Bryony told him, 'Of course I'm enjoying it. I'm not dead. That's three times I've been not dead in… I suppose… twenty-four hours or so. I like being not dead. And… *this is a spaceship.*'

'I beg your pardon.' The Doctor looked quite stern. 'This is the TARDIS. She's not just a spaceship… You should know that – you've practically met her. She's… well…' It was even possible the Doctor was blushing slightly. 'She's herself. And we travel in time. Not just space.'

'Time?' Bryony forgot the screen.

'Time.'

'You mean *time*?' Bryony stared at the top of Doctor's head – his face no longer being visible as he bent over the console. 'Time as in time?'

The Doctor nodded and flipped another toggle, while the floor shivered a little. 'Yes, time. Of course I mean time – that's the word I always use when I mean time. I'm a Time Lord, I'm not going to get that wrong.' The view screen seemed to throb deep crimson. The colour faded again. 'Ah. Putta, depress the harmonisation coils and increase – that one, there – increase the arc of the zenoxtil.'

Putta, fumbled at the controls, trying to guess which one was the zenoxtil, but couldn't help asking, 'But what happened? Why are you both all right? Squashed? Why would Bryony have been squashed? *And are we safe!?*'

As Putta shouted this last, the Doctor tweaked another dial and the entire screen was immediately washed with purple and red light, a leering yellow glow at its centre.

'Oh, no. Oh no, no, no.' The Doctor cranked round a small brass handle on one the console's panels, his face growing pale. 'That is not good…' The handle seemed to adjust the magnification of the screen's image. The Doctor stared up at the screen, his face turning pale.

Putta asked, 'And why did you both know what I was thinking? The psy fluid would have worn off by now.'

The room turned a touch colder – but from the view screen came a lurid glow – as if lava were boiling out from a vast reserve of molten heat.

The little handle squeaked as it turned and slowly, slowly, the yellow and purple core shown on the screen began to shrink and a border of crimson was revealed around it, its colour shading out towards purple. There were scatters of white which chased about across the dimmer outer areas, like impulses firing along larger and smaller nerves.

'What? Hmm?' The Doctor's face was paler – and now tinged with the lurid illumination of the screen. Bryony, too was focused intently on the image.

The handle kept turning. 'It's immense… immense…' The Doctor shook his head, disbelieving. 'And we knew what you were thinking, Putta – and we still do – because we're practically on top of the universe's greatest source of artron energy – a huge creature which is, in itself, basically a monumental telepathic clamp – just matter loosely held in stasis by the force of thought. I've adjusted the screen to register only artron, rather than photon energy… And I've been decreasing the magnification until… What we're looking at is miles across. The creature is miles across.' The purple rim of the shape was shown to split eventually into sections – as more and more of an overview was shown, the sections were shown to be like legs, tendrils, tentacles around a roughly circular body. They shifted and flexed. The white impulses fired in and out from the core. The Doctor caught Putta with a glance. 'Imagine a dream so powerful that it can make itself real, grip matter and shape it as it likes. So powerful that it can decide to be a nightmare. That's the Bah-Sokhar.' He patted an instrument panel consolingly. 'No wonder she's gone quiet.'

'But we… But you… It let us go…' bleated Putta.

'Yes, Doctor.' Bryony frowned and Putta was aware that she was mulling over how much the twins had liked her and how they had been kind to their grandmother and how generally pleasant they had been as long as the Bah-Sokhar hadn't felt threatened. They were the Bah-Sokhar's way of playing and being affectionate, responding to love – all things which were unusual in an assassin monster, she would have assumed. Then again, when they did defend the Bah-Sokhar, they were merciless – as merciless as the creature itself.

The Doctor nodded – there wasn't a lot of privacy inside an increasingly powerful telepathic clamp. He was remarkably good at shielding his mind – but he still couldn't help hearing the torrent of worries about everything and yearning about Bryony which churned constantly across Putta's mind. It was slightly anxiety-provoking. The Doctor was equally aware of Bryony's excitement at being on an adventure, her confusion about the creature and her fondness for Putta. Those two really should sit down and have a chat at some point – preferably a point when they knew whether they had more than a few hours to live. The Doctor clawed through his dense mop of hair and blinked while Bryony pondered how on earth they would be able to keep the Bah-Sokhar in a good mood when it was constantly being interrupted by humans enraged by their own and other's poor putting. 'I know.' He answered the question she hadn't asked. 'It's all very well hoping that the creature doesn't get alarmed by this or that – that it keeps on learning how to give and receive affection and doesn't come across anyone with a negative mind-set, but on Earth… a planet covered with human beings… it's hardly likely. It will be picking up radio waves, television broadcasts, military communications… Good grief, if it's fully awake during a general election the whole solar system could be destroyed and its atoms repurposed to form more Bah-Sokhar. And it has so much potential…'

Putta and Bryony then shared the Doctor's memory of the strange sensation he had experienced – at once gentle and authoritative – when the Bah-Sokhar expelled him, not only from their shared mindspace, but from the space it had created within its body to imprison him. You can bet that being hurled out of a communal consciousness and simultaneously booted clear out of a monster's fleshy holding cell would ruin anyone's inner peace. Simply attempting the Lombukso Ultimate could kill you. Even subtle fluctuations in your surrounding temperature could lead to an artron surge that fried your brain. And the Doctor had been suddenly shocked out of the Lombukso Ultimate Meditation – and his inner peace – that was always fatal.

But the Bah-Sokhar had protected him, cushioned his mind against the energy surges and deficits, had taken care of him and deposited him near – in fact on top of – his friend. That must really mean it was a being that could be reached by positive emotion. Treating it with affection in the Spa had saved their lives... there must be a way... If only Shangri-La still existed, the Doctor could have sent it there...

But if the Bah-Sokhar couldn't be rendered safe, it would have to be destroyed. The last of its kind, a wonder of nature – there was no way the Doctor could harm it.

He needed a plan. His brain – remarkable though it was – felt as if someone had been massaging it with an egg whisk and all he wanted to do was sleep for a while... But he needed a plan. He was usually good at plans... Well, maybe not good exactly... but he was very good at improvising and serendipity and paying attention and...

The TARDIS continued to toll her cloister bell. Clearly she remained less than confident that all would be well.

ABOVE ARBROATH, THE MOON was high and clear and had a playful look – or maybe a sympathetic look, maybe it was that.

Arbroath was perhaps not at its best after a riotous day, but it was peaceful now. Its residents all slept deeply and without stirring or turning – as if they were saving their energy for what might come next.

And in those hundreds of sleeping minds, dreams sprang to the surface. Dreams of loss and being chased and swimming in vast oceans, dreams of landscapes that never were on earth, dreams of searching and loving, or of brave husbands and of beautiful children and of never being alone, of always having company and being safe inside forever – they all rolled through the city, from bedroom to bedroom and head to head.

In Montrose, a dream involving carnivorous trees was immensely widespread. Carnoustie dreamed of Spanish dogs, burning hats and a long journey across water. Broughty Ferry woke up briefly at around 2 a.m. with the taste of ice cream in its mouth. Dundee saw beasts with twining limbs and horns, talking bears and boars and horses and sleepers felt as if they were dancing inside fur – and also crouched like a hunter under a cloak, watching magical animals and waiting…

And above the Fetch Hotel and Spa, the moon was also shining and dreams were also being dreamed. The guests were dreaming peacefully and yet strangely: the Spencers, who were an older couple from Cardiff, were sharing room 45. They were also sharing a dream about David Cassidy which rightfully belonged to Karen Clough, a 14-year-old travelling with her parents from Newcastle – they were staying in room 21. Karen Clough was dreaming a little about David Cassidy, but mainly about emigrating to New Zealand and becoming a fish-eating bird – which was also the dream being enjoyed by Daniel Taylor of room 38 and the occupants of rooms 23, 27 and 43. Several guests also found that – the following morning – they had dreamed of green. Just this remarkably pleasant shade of green. It provoked a surge of happiness and a desire for fudge.

Over breakfast the following morning, far from feeling strange, all the guests trooped down to eat with jokes and smiles, little chats about the weather, handshakes and contented sighs.

Even Kevin Mangold felt incredibly well. The rash on his shins was fading and, after a frantic search for emergency staff, he'd had a cat nap and woken more utterly refreshed than he had ever known himself to be. Refreshed, in the mood for ice cream and with an oddly clinging memory of being a colourfully feathered dinosaur for a while and quite enjoying having a tail.

AND AT 9.18 A.M. on 3 June 1978, the world began to end.

The reason for this was as follows:

While the Doctor had stared at the pulsing shape of the Bah-Sokhar, deep in thought, Putta had felt able to sidle across and murmur to Bryony, 'Are you all right?'

'What do you mean by that?'

'I mean – are you all right?'

'Yes, but you also meant a whole load of other stuff about the shape of my mouth and showing me somewhere with a greenish sky and thinking you ought to take off your other sock and... and... It's just... it's – please stop liking me quite so loudly.'

Putta swallowed audibly and tried to pack away as much of his thinking as he could, while repeating, 'No but—'

Which Bryony interrupted: 'Yes!' And then she said more quietly, 'Yes. I'm OK. I am. It's all kind of wonderful... Not the horrible death parts, but the rest is... I would let you take me to a planet with a greenish sky any time you wanted.'

This produced such a torrent of thinking from Putta that Bryony flinched and the Doctor yelled, 'Will you two keep your hormones under control. It's like witnessing the Great Mating on Cyrus 12 – only I wouldn't be standing this close.

Really… telepathy is always so irritating… And *intrusive*.'

'Yes.' Bryony rubbed her temples. 'No wonder the Bah-Sokhar chucked us out – maybe we were being too loud. We were probably the equivalent of a migraine.'

'Nonsense,' huffed the Doctor, like a highly experienced expert in all life forms. 'The Bah-Sokhar incorporated me in a kind of cyst – it was going to keep me for ever and I'm very grateful that it changed its… Aah… It kept me in an insulated cyst…' The Doctor batted himself on the forehead. 'And I was complaining that *it* was too loud in *my* head… ' He strode back and forth, his arms wheeling. 'That's the trouble with the universe – it's full of species I've never met before, I have to guess… and the volume was affecting my thinking and I'm tired… You slow down after the first few hundred years… Handsome and so forth but… I'm tired.' He grinned, his eyes sparking and then glanced at the view screen without any trace of anxiety – or hardly any. 'I'm tired and so I need to sleep. To sleep, perchance to dream…' His grin dialled up a few notches until it was almost audible. 'Right you two. You've been through a lot – you need to sleep and so do I.' He flopped himself down on what was – as Bryony's and Putta's thinking agreed – the hard, distractingly thrumming floor of the console room. 'It's fine. Lovely floor the TARDIS floor. I've slept in here often – nearer the instrument panels.' And he snuggled his shoulders about a bit as if he was on a comfy mattress.

Bryony and Putta felt a small hint of the TARDIS's presence for the first time since the Bah-Sokhar expelled them. Their spines were warmed by a gentle brush of comfort, watchful and nervous. And the lights softened to an orangey-golden glow, suitable for sleeping.

So the two sat themselves down and then lay as the Doctor instructed – 'Heads together, and I think if we hold hands…' They did the best they could to settle themselves.

'And now we'll do some top quality sleeping. How else would we knock very quietly on the Bah-Sokhar's door and see how it's feeling? It's the easiest thing in the world – obvious really…'

The Doctor gave a mighty yawn and then Bryony and Putta were aware of him quickly falling still while his breathing settled. Like all beings used to arduous travel, risks and wonders, the Doctor could fall asleep pretty much at will.

And although they simultaneously thought it highly unlikely that they would get any sleep at all, Bryony and Putta did get the distinct impression that the tolling bell stopped tolling and found that the floor seemed to soften under them and warm and generally behave as if…

Neither of them knew *as if* what, because they went to sleep.

And in that sleep – they were still together but standing, hand-in-hand on a gently curved, opalescent surface which shimmered wonderfully. Overhead, a night sky hung beautifully clear and bright with marvellous constellations.

The Doctor whispered, 'This is… I recognise this… I've dreamed this with the TARDIS before. Even she sleeps sometimes, in a way.' Out of the distance came a shape which looked like a walking human as it approached, ambling slowly, even nervously. But when it was closer, they could see that it was, in fact a tall, glisteningly black horse. Its well-developed muscles ticked under its shining skin. Its hooves were huge, dark, perfect like oiled metal. And yet it didn't fully resemble an Earth horse. Its head was very long and solid, the bone above its eyes especially substantial. And its mane writhed thickly between its pricked-forward ears and along its powerful neck, knotting and flowing into patterns, weaving, winding and shivering. It was both terrible and magnificent.

They understood it was the Bah-Sokhar in another form, one more fundamental and familiar to its identity. It was telling them that it had the strength of a beast, but also its nervousness.

The Bah-Sokhar tossed its head and pawed with one massive hoof at the milk-and-rainbow-light surface supporting them.

Bryony thought how amazing it would be to touch this incredible creature.

At once it wagged that massive head and sidestepped, uneasy.

Bryony heard herself thinking, 'Sorrysorrysorry.'

The Bah-Sokhar stilled again. It swung its neck and – one by one – examined them with eyes which were not only black – they were also flecked with a moving fire, deep in their gaze.

All of them experienced Putta's fear as his consciousness was peered into. And then they shared his sensations of guilt and shame. There was something about the great horse that was to do with justice, some kind of dreadful working out of justice and punishment which chilled him, chilled them all. But he came to no harm.

Bryony was next, forcing herself to stand still in her dream while she listened to the loud, large breathing of the beast as it took one step closer, its big nostrils widening, puffing humid air on to her face. She smelled the smell of an animal, a wild thing. And the animal leaned forward and breathed her scent and let her understand that it found she was self-defeating and someone who made simple things complicated, someone who could be better and bigger, someone who should waste no more time, someone who should know when to let gifts in if they were offered. Very gently, it lowered its neck and paused. She almost didn't dare – but then she did, she passed the test and reached out, placed her hand equally gently on the giant horse's pelt – it was almost too hot to touch and yet also felt like velvet, like trust and agreement. Then the Bah-Sokhar swung away and faced the Doctor.

All at once, the horse-formed creature reared up, the dangerous curves of its wide hooves, flashing and threatening. The Doctor didn't move. The Doctor, in fact – as the others could feel – admired how truly extraordinary the Bah-Sokhar was in this display of ancient majesty. The Bah-Sokhar's mane lifted and flared like black flames, the red glow of its eyes woke fully and blazed. But the Doctor stood, appreciated, let it be. He even slipped one hand into his trouser pocket, tilted his head to the side and edged towards the start of a smile. The air grew hotter and hotter, became thick with that animal scent and a monumental rage that sung and prickled and clawed at them. The Doctor nodded, more thoughtful, but still calm as the sleepiest ocean on Earth or any other planet.

And then the horse quietened, panted, dropped its hooves, stood. It dropped its great skull. It was alone. It was more alone than any being in the universe. And it wanted to be at peace and fade away.

The Doctor gazed into one of its great eyes, now only dimly alight, and he nodded again. And he leaned his head forward and the Bah-Sokhar lowered its own head until the Doctor was resting his forehead against the beast's.

Each being in the dream breathed.

There could be peace between mankind and the Bah-Sokhar, between the universe and the Bah-Sokhar.

Then Paul Cluny Jnr walked out of the former fisherman's cottage which his parents were renting as a holiday home for the week. His mother was cooking breakfast and his father was trying to get the wireless aerial to work. They weren't thinking about Paul Junior. They weren't – being remarkably insensitive people in every way – aware of anything Paul Junior was thinking.

That didn't matter.

At 9.17 a.m. on 3 June 1978, Paul Cluny Junior thought, 'I wish to be the jewel at the heart of the universe.'

He paused while nothing in particular happened.

And then, at 9.18 a.m. – here came the end of the world.

IN THE NORTHERN ZONE Regional War Room that weird feeling was back. Personnel felt the hairs bristle on the backs of their necks and then found that their mouths tasted of metal. Then they got headaches and blurred vision. Several of them made it as far as the medic before their minds were filled completely and indelibly and triumphantly with one word.

ZANDOR

With perfect calm, their eyes like dark pebbles, the officers and men left their allotted tasks, set down their papers, left phone calls unfinished and marched peacefully up and out through the entrance of their bunker. They didn't bother to close the airtight, radiation-proof doors. As they climbed the stairs to leave in a winding snake of uniforms, some of them collected weapons. Beneath their feet, the concrete shuddered, as if it were restless, or furious, or in pain.

Waiting for them outside the cottages which cunningly disguised the entrance to the War Room complex were two lovely children – twins with sun-kissed hair and agile limbs, their faces warmed by pleasant smiles. Only their eyes were disturbing – like chill fragments of an endless night. As each man and woman passed, the girl and the boy would intone together, 'Ever so well done. Now you serve the mighty hatethinker Zandor. It will be lovely for you. All power to Zandor and his rage. Defend our border bravely while we feed and grow.'

Each of the uniformed figures nodded when they heard this and then headed off in pairs, either along the roads, or taking rough tracks, or even cutting across country. They marched with utter determination.

IN HER KITCHEN, MRS Julia Fetch had been taking a breakfast of porridge with brown sugar on top after an especially wonderful night's sleep. But now she felt peculiar.

Not to put too fine a point on it – she had too many legs. And now that she'd admitted it, she also might have to accept that her number of arms wasn't quite right, either. She had four of each. Four arms, four legs, a nasty tear in both of her nightgown's sleeves and a slight difficulty in arranging where she should put all her knees – there wasn't quite room in her nightie.

She knew that getting older had its troubles and difficulties, but she did feel that being expected to accept extra limbs with no warning at her age was unreasonable. Then again…

Julia reached out for more tea and poured it while buttering toast with remarkable speed and dexterity. This was quite fun. She stood up, munching her toast and trotted into her living room where she kept her lovely gramophone. She put on a 78 record of 'Ain't Nobody's Business If I Do' being sung by Bessie Smith. As the horns sloped in and then that gorgeous wailing voice opened up, Mrs Julia Fetch danced as she never had, shimmied slow and smooth, wagged her four hands up high, swayed her four feet sideways and sang along: 'Some day when you grow lonely your heart will break like mine and you'll want me only…'

She'd first danced to this in… oh, it would have to have been 1927… when everyone was still so happy and jolly after the terrible war, because they had to be happy and jolly – there were so few of the people they'd known left. And it had also been good to have the blues, to be sad in such a beautiful way when so many of the chaps had gone and Bernard among them.

She didn't remember Bernard often – she didn't seem able to.

So much had been lost.

And yet here she was – dancing better than she ever had and feeling so deliciously strong and lively. Really, she felt better than she had in years, decades.

Bessie Smith's melodious heartbreak sang on around her and she danced and danced – her bare feet sliding and stepping, clever and dainty and deep in the beat.

WHILE PAUL CLUNY JUNIOR settled into his new High Throne, constructed from the intricately carved stones in the museum and set on the alter at St Vigeans church, the Doctor and his companions knew that something had gone disastrously wrong.

One moment the Bah-Sokhar's horse form was peaceful and awe-inspiring – the next it had shuddered and reared, growing as it reared, its hooves shining balefully, its mane writhing, its muscles taut under skin that was rippling with red light.

'No! No!' The Doctor tried to calm it. 'Whoever is talking to you, there's no need to listen any more. Please!'

But the dream collapsed around Bryony, Putta and the Doctor and they all found themselves lying back on the TARDIS floor, the cloister bell tolling faster and louder than before. The last vision they saw was of a towering stallion, all aflame, its head fluxing between that of a horse, of a stag, of a wild boar and of a human face – the face of a petulant adolescent boy.

That same face was currently troubling the remaining undisappeared guests at the Fetch Hotel. Kevin Mangold had been forced by multiple disappearances to help out with serving breakfast – and a delayed breakfast at that – because only the chef and one housemaid had bothered to turn up for work. This had been the worst thing that had happened today – until the florid purple wallpaper had begun to swell and heave and had then, one might say, budded into multiple human forms.

Although they're not human are they, I mean they can't be, I mean I have no idea, I mean this isn't happening anyway because it can't be and I'm asleep and everything is…

There were a dozen new humans in the dining room now – all of them looking a bit too newly made to be entirely convincing and all of them reproducing the same lanky, slightly spotty, round-shouldered youth in sneakers, jeans and a yellow shirt. Mangold was extremely grateful that this couldn't really be possible, because the chap looked like exactly the sort of demanding foreign oik that he couldn't abide. (Mangold wasn't exactly made for the hospitality industry.)

As soon as he thought badly of them, all of the youths turned to him with identical expressions of amused contempt. They all spoke with identical, whining, adenoidal American accents. 'I, Zandor the Magnificent, have no care of what you might think of me.' Grammar obviously wasn't their strong point. 'I must feed.'

At this, the youths herded the terrified golfers and golfers' wives into one corner of the dining room and singled out one slender, kind-faced lady. They closed in on her while her husband tried to stand in their way. But the man was cuffed to the ground by one youth. Although it was scrawny, it clearly had immense strength.

Next, as the woman tried to smile and be dignified in what was an intolerable situation, one of the youths extended his hand towards her. She took this as a good sign and reached out in her turn, holding its hand. But as soon as she touched the youth's skin, she cried out and – quickly, quickly – it was clear that contact was emptying her, literally emptying her.

Mangold and the rest of the guests looked on and her husband yelled impotently where he was restrained, still on the floor. But nothing could stop the woman's horrible transformation.

First her forearm emptied and flattened, as if it had been no more than a skin container for water, or air. Very soon, the whole of her right arm was shrivelled and hanging. The process was obviously hugely painful, but the woman could only stare at the ruin of herself as her body failed. More hands were reached towards her and at each point they touched, her substance was removed, leaving only her skin.

Mangold tried to think that at least the ordeal would be over quickly, but that didn't make it any better. And it was quite plain that every human being in that room was going to face the same fate.

Once the skin was completely emptied, it fell to the floor and then vanished in a flare of reddish vapour.

The husband was now sitting up and sobbing, 'Take me, then. Take me.'

The youths' faces flicked their attention to him and they began to close in on him, their arms reaching out.

Mangold was not a brave man – he wasn't anything like a brave man – but he couldn't understand why no one in the room was moving, or shouting, or trying to stop this. When he looked at the other guests, their faces were placid, numbed. Only he and the husband seemed to be aware of what was going on, of the dreadful threat which faced them.

In fact, Mangold's levels of self-obsession, combined with his shockingly low levels of artron energy were partly shielding him from the fairly low-level field of influence the Bah-Sokhar was deploying. It was busy feeding at a number of locations and it couldn't be bothered targeting him more precisely because it was going to eat him eventually anyway and he was no threat. Sadly, this meant that he would be horribly upset and afraid before his brain melted, along with the rest of his interior.

ZANDOR, OR THE GRAND High Emperor Zandor as he had decided he should be called, was enjoying his reign. Stuff was happening to keep him safe and that was cool. He'd asked the Thing to take care of the local army and police guys because they would be the ones who were a threat at this stage of setting up all the Empire and domination, etc. The Thing had shown him pictures in his head of the secret bunker and the local commando barracks and the cop station house and so those had been dealt with. Everyone with a uniform was standing along the rim of a fairly regular border which ran roughly in a circle with a ten mile diameter, which was OK for now. In the end, it would be the world, but for now ten miles was safe.

Zandor knew to pace himself and not draw attention to himself yet. He had to get more of an idea about how all these crazy new powers he had worked and did whatever he asked. But you couldn't rely on Things. In the end, Zandor would take all the power and get rid of it.

He imagined having a footstool and watched as one blossomed upwards out of the church's stone floor. He propped his sneakers up on it and imagined a hot dog with mustard.

Zandor guessed that he'd have to crank up his wishes a

little, because they weren't that impressive yet, but he was definitely enjoying himself. Maybe in a couple of days he'd be able to reach over and destroy his old school and feed all his teachers to the Thing. And his high school would have to go. And that weird guy who always shouted at him when he pushed ahead in the line at the drugstore, because waiting in line wasn't a thing he'd ever enjoyed doing, so why should he do it…

The one wish he'd loved so far had involved putting both his parents in quite a small cage that now hung from the ceiling by a chain. They could stay up there for ever, for all he cared – which he didn't. He'd made something happen that sealed up their mouths, so they couldn't speak any more. He didn't much care how that was arranged – he only knew they had no mouths now. It was cool and funny. They wouldn't be able to eat, either – which he hadn't meant to happen, but he didn't much care now that it had. They could starve up there and be out of his hair and think they were lucky. A lot of much worse stuff was happening elsewhere – the Thing let him see bits of it in his head and it was freaky. It was making him laugh. It was like the best TV show ever.

BACK IN THE DINING room, things were grim. The husband had been speeded to his end and the rest of the guests were backed into a huddle next to the chilled breakfast display of cold meats, spreads and cheeses. Mangold couldn't help thinking this was unpleasantly appropriate as he edged along the far wall. The youths weren't paying any attention to him and he was glad about that.

He was sad, absolutely, that they *were* paying a lot of attention to members of the public who had chosen to stay at the Fetch Brothers Golf Spa Hotel and who were therefore technically in his care, but what could he do about that now? They were being devoured by a horde of... things... He couldn't defeat a horde. He'd never even met a horde – although some coach parties had come close...

It would be best if he saved himself.

And got help.

Naturally.

He really was planning to get help.

Leastways, he had convinced himself this was the case right up until he had eased himself round the doorway – keeping his eyes fixed on the ghastly huddle of feeding bodies and the occasional flashes of fear darting across faces amongst the trapped crowd as they flickered slightly out of the Bah-Sokhar's full control.

'And where are you going, Kev?' He felt a hand laid firmly on his shoulder and twitched round to find Bryony Mailer glowering at him. 'Running away?' She was dressed like a children's entertainer and her hair was frightful, but she had a commanding presence that he couldn't ignore.

'Not at all. Not in the least… And I must say that… that… In your absence the hotel has not been—'

A tall and hideously untidy fellow with an even more strange and even more convincing kind of authority – it was that Doctor chappie – strode out from behind an aspidistra wearing a bizarre hat. 'Well, I'm very glad you're not running away. Because we need you to tell us what's going on. You were coming out to tell us, in fact, weren't you?'

Because they were all, in fact, sharing a high-grade telepathic field, the Doctor, Bryony and – now emerging remarkably from the shadows, still wearing his abused shirt and plus fours – Putta were absolutely sure that Mangold had been aiming to leap in his car and drive to Aberdeen as fast as possible. But they also knew there was no point mentioning that and realised that the Doctor usually decided that giving people the benefit of the doubt often seemed to bounce them into managing more remarkable things than they'd ever imagined they could.

Mangold blushed and shook loose a small blizzard of stressed dandruff. 'I was… yes. They're in there. These beastie things are eating, well… sucking the guests down into… It would be better if you saw for yourself.'

The three could see for themselves – in a blurry way – but still they tentatively leaned their heads round the doorframe to watch as the silent feeding frenzy continued its horrible work.

Putta felt the Doctor's rage and pain race through him and leave behind unshakeable determination.

'Ah, well, we can't have that, though, can we. I'm afraid not. Not at all.' The Doctor said this loudly enough to be audible in the dining room and – as the others stared – he strolled out across the tartan carpet and in between the deserted tables. At the far end of the room, the youths stopped moving.

'Hello, I'm the Doctor. I would say you're my old friend the Bah-Sokhar, but that's not quite right, is it?' He sounded jovial, even playful, but Putta and Bryony could feel the echo of his two hearts pounding with hidden fear. 'I think there's someone else in there too now, isn't there?' And his hearts were also racing with excitement – something terrible was happening and he was born to walk up and smile and all the universe's terrible things. He had to and wanted to and loved to stroll along and talk to them, and tease them and defeat them utterly. One day he might die trying, but it might not be today. 'Who are you, if you wouldn't mind my asking?'

The Doctor waited placidly, while the youths stood straight and walked together and formed a double line of identical curiosity and hatred. Behind them, a few of the guests blinked back into horrified sense and looked on, breathless.

'No really…' The Doctor grinned. 'There's no need to be shy – you're among friends.'

A few more of the golfers coughed and flinched into full awareness.

At last, the youths spoke together. 'We are Zandor.' They tried it again, this time with conviction and a bit more flourish. 'We are Grand High Emperor Zandor the Mighty. We sit on the Drosten Throne. We are the jewel at the heart of the universe. We are—'

The Doctor nodded sagely while interrupting. 'Yes, yes, I supposed it might be something like that. Zandor… You wouldn't believe the number of Zandors I've met... And High and Mightys... well, there are a great number of them around. You fellows intent on ruling over everywhere – I'm assuming that's what you want – you never have quite enough imagination for the job, do you?' He offered the insult in a charming and polite tone so that it confused the youths, rather than annoying them. 'Not enough imagination to think of a good name and a really impressive title. Not enough imagination to make it fun..'

As he had asked them to with his mind, Putta and Bryony had sneaked over to the buffet while the Zandor forms were distracted and begun to lead everyone out through the door that led to the kitchens.

This was going well until Mangold decided to help and – his horror compelling him to keep his gaze fixed on the youths – then clattered blindly into a fully set table, knocking over teapots and rattling cutlery.

The Zandor forms glared round at him and began striding out to make him their next meal. He hadn't intended to provide a diversion while Bryony and Putta tried to usher the diners safely away, but as it seemed that he was and that he would be dead soon in a repulsive way, he decided to abandon his usual self-interest and do his best. This surprised him because it was hugely out of character and because it meant that for an instant he could clearly hear the Doctor thinking *well done* at him.

But the youths were swift, adaptable and coordinated. As some lunged for Mangold, others split off and rushed at Putta and Bryony and others turned to menace the guests.

The situation wasn't hopeful until the Doctor announced, 'Enough!' The Zandor forms flinched but didn't stop. 'I said enough! I'm not having any more death this morning. I forbid it. You there!' He yelled at a woman called Mary Fleming who had wanted to spend a long weekend at the hotel to recover from a bout of flu. 'Yes, you! Do you want to be eaten!?' The Time Lord's gaze scouted back and forth across the more and less aware humans. 'Well, do you? Because either you can stand there and let it all roll over you while we're consumed along with you, or you can decide to resist.'

The crowd muttered, but was foggy and doubtful

Wake up, thought the Doctor.

And this thought, amplified by the Bah-Sokhar's indiscriminate telepathic clamp, did finally snap the Fetch's latest visitors into complete awareness. As that same awareness was then assaulted by identical portions of doom and the sight of a partially emptied skin and its pathetically heaped clothes.... Well, a good deal of chaos broke loose.

There was running, there was screaming, there was crying – and above all, there was rage.

The Zandor forms tipped back their heads and seemed to sniff the air before apparently inhaling the strength that rage provided for them.

The youths grew taller, started smiling – a few of them dashed playfully about the room at impossible speeds – mocking their victims and jabbing out with taunting, threatening hands.

Bryony couldn't think what to do. She felt Putta hold her arm and began to assume that they might at least get eaten together. Survival didn't seem an option any more.

Then she felt, along with Putta, the Doctor thinking *Nonsense.*

And the Time Lord drew himself up to his full height and called out, 'Enough!' He pointed at one man who had lifted a heavy coffee pot over his head, 'Put that down!' The man looked confused – a Zandor form was patting at him, teasing, its black eyes filled with red glimmers.

'I said enough! All of you!' The Doctor span round, his

arms spread wide. 'I know you're scared. I know you've seen terrible things done. I know you want to hurt the creatures that have hurt you and that you hate them. But you can't!'

'You didn't see what they did!' shouted an older woman.

'I've seen more than that and I know they'll do more than that. You have to love them.'

The room was filled with scrambling, flailing arms and panic – underlying that was pure hatred, tangible hatred.

Bryony understood this couldn't go on, that it would kill them all and leave the world undefended. 'It's true!'

'It's rubbish!' yelled back a couple who were swiping at a particularly avid Zandor form with a breadboard. 'Why don't you help?'

'We are helping!' Putta yelped back. 'Can't you understand! He's the Doctor. If you trust him, he'll get us out of this. If you don't we're done for. Come on!'

Fortunately, this attracted the attention of a Zandor form who was dripping with milk from where a jug had been thrown at it and whose eyebrow was slightly cut, but healing visibly. The form rushed towards them and, arm-in-arm, they swung to face it.

'Now!' hissed Bryony, and together they did their absolute best to find something, anything wonderful about that blank, mockery of a face, about those hollow eyes, about those clawing hands.

'It is… it is…' Putta struggled. 'It is amazing. The way it does what it does – the way it changes shapes, the way it adapts and survives, the way it was magnificent.'

Bryony nodded. 'That horse… I loved that horse… It was wonderful… Anything that could be that horse is better than this… It was the most amazing thing I've ever seen… It was an honour…'

The Zandor form slowed, became uncertain.

Putta took up the slack. 'Yes. The true form of the Bah-

Sokhar is awe-inspiring. I will never forget it. I loved it. I love the Bah-Sokhar.'

The Zandor forms all slowed and swayed.

The Doctor laughed. 'See! See!' He waved his arms as if conducting a kind of emotional orchestra. 'That's it!'

Gradually, the guests also dropped their improvised weapons and began to frown out various expressions of – if not love – then warmth.

I have a grandson your age.

I love living. I love being alive.

I love this day, this moment. I never realised. I love still being able to see that table cloth and to hear this man's voice and to have the light come through that window the way it is, it is, it is…

One by one, the Zandor forms put their hands to their heads and started to emit a high scream.

'Keep going!' The Doctor's face was a vision of kindliness and beneficence, but his eyes were stern and intent. 'That's it!'

And then the Zandor forms fell in a liquid rush and soaked away into the carpet. They were gone.

A residual thrum of fondness swashed about for an instant and then subsided.

'Oh, well done!' The Doctor threw back his head and laughed, while clapping. Then the losses already sustained hit him and he grimaced. The struggle was by no means over.

There was absolute silence, beyond the dripping of spilled coffee from a table cloth.

Then a grey-head man asked, 'Who are you? You're a doctor, you said?'

Putta answered. 'He's *the* Doctor. He's… He's the best—'

Much though the Doctor appreciated praise, he cut this particular attempt short, 'That's as may be. We've no time to discuss how wonderful I am at the moment. Arbroath – at the very least Arbroath – is very probably being consumed right now and this Zandor character is who knows where—'

'He's at the Drosten Stone.'

'No, he said throne. Drosten throne.'

A pair of men in plaid trousers grumbled at each other.

'There isn't a Drosten throne – it's a stone. It's up at St Vigeans.'

'They said throne. I remembered. I thought it was the last thing I was going to hear.'

The Doctor shook his head at them. 'It said throne. Now, where's St Vigeans?'

A number of the guests, recovering their senses slightly, gave directions to St Vigeans.

'And this stone…?' The Doctor folded his arm round a young woman who was weeping and shaking. He listened keenly as the legend of the St Vigeans church – built by an underground demon – and the famous carved stones were described. As he did so, he ushered over Putta and Bryony and murmured to them, 'We have to get to St Vigeans. If Zandor isn't there, there may be traces of him that will lead us to him. I would imagine the stones were at one time some kind of throne for the Conductor of the Bah-Sokhar. And anyone with any sense would break that kind of thing into pieces if they could… If they'd survived an encounter with the awakened creature and a ruler filled with hatred.'

Bryony offered, 'Perhaps the Bah-Sokhar did that itself. Perhaps it doesn't want a Conductor.'

'Perhaps…'

'Hang on a minute.' One of the bickering pair, glowered at the Doctor. 'You're not going to abandon us? You said you were going to help. What about the Hippocratic Oath?'

'I helped Hippocrates write it, and a very good oath it is, too. But we have to go to St Vigeans.' A groan shuddered round the huddle of surviving humans. 'And you have work to do. You know how to defeat these things. And you like Arbroath…' The Doctor paused while there was no response. 'Well, you can't mind it that much – you came here. And it's being harmed. People are being harmed. Human beings are being harmed. And you, as human beings, can help them. You have to go into the town and just… be as affectionate as you can… on all sides. Every Zandor form you see… tell it how wonderful it is. Or – as Bryony worked out – it would be even better to tell it how wonderful the Bah-Sokhar is. Bit of an odd name, I'll admit. It's from the ancient Egyptian and probably isn't its original name at all… But it will do. Let's all say it together, shall we.'

The guests frowned at this, but did half-heartedly agree to recite the name until they got it right.

'Very important. Tell the forms that the Bah-Sokhar is great. You couldn't imagine anything more marvellous. You love it. You're fond of it. The Bah-Sokhar is trapped by the supply of hate its getting – the old Conductor and Demon bond has been activated, but I think we can break it. So…' He peered round at them like a primary school teacher trying to think well of a lumpy class. 'Off you go. Those of you who haven't got cars, the others will give you lifts. He'll arrange it.' The Doctor pointed out Mangold, who'd been skulking behind the cereal display table and who now jumped slightly. The Doctor eyed him coolly – 'I did notice you being brave earlier… so now you'll just have to keep on, you know. It will get to be a habit – helping others.'

Mangold thought about nodding but then couldn't. He didn't want to be a helpful person – it felt odd – a bit like jumping off a building and assuming he could fly… He attempted to convince himself this really was a terrible dream he was having and the sooner he woke up the better.

It didn't work.

IN ARBROATH, THINGS WEREN'T going well. Although everyone had passed a more or less wonderful and restful night, the town was now filled with the misery, exposure and sheer irritation provided by the huge telepathic clamp in which they were held. Husbands were aware of how much they annoyed their wives, wives were aware of how often they drove their husbands to distraction (and the details of partners' distractions were sometimes quite alarming), children were aware of how little adults actually knew about anything and how much of the time they spent bluffing frantically and trying to look expert… every secret anyone had kept was out and jumbling about with every other secret – resentments, petty rivalries and uncharitable assumptions were battering against every, by now, deeply weary consciousness. And this was actually the most pleasant thing that the morning had brought. On the darker side, blocks of houses were being methodically cleared by police or soldiers with dead faces and deader eyes. All the occupants would be marched away, their faces also becoming eerie blanks. No one ever came back.

Citizens found this disturbing and also found themselves unable to do anything about it. They sat in their homes, or wandered the streets, harassed by the minds of others and waiting to be taken away.

A SHORT WALK AWAY from the Fetch Hotel, Putta was no longer feeling proud of himself. 'But, but, but…' He'd imagined that choosing to travel to Earth in Type F378a Abrischooner, because it looked uncannily like a Morris Minor Traveller (and because it was going cheap), would count in his favour. It had been perfectly feasible to land it in a field and then simply run it along in Overground Mode and pop it quietly in a car park. In fact, this rare example of foresight made Bryony snort down her nose and think he was joking for a while – not it a good way.

'This… *This* is your spaceship…?'

The Doctor shook his head and bundled them into the cramped and – it had to be admitted – fairly metallic and alien-appearing interior. 'No time for that now.'

Bryony banged her elbow on a cheap and unpadded bulkhead flange and then eased herself into the flip-down additional third seat which had added 6000 Credits to the Abrischooner's price but wasn't credible as something anyone could occupy over an interstellar, or even interplanetary distance. 'Is this even roadworthy…?'

The Abrischooner was – to be honest – only built for a maximum of two, small beings who were really fond of each other and therefore wouldn't mind being crushed up together for fairly extended periods.

The Doctor managed to sit in the co-pilot's position by folding his knees almost level with his ears. 'Really. No time.' He turned – with difficulty – and gave her a teacherly glare and then a slight smirk. 'You will be impressed after take-off… These rather more primitive models have a certain… um… quality in their handling that you lose in—'

He couldn't finish his sentence as Putta had fired up the two Formalone #7 engines (not bad, really for the Credits) jerked into Atmospheric / Aerial Mode and begun… well, not flying exactly – more tumbling roughly horizontally along at an average of 50 feet above the ground. The Abrischooner steered like a biscuit tin, but could make the equivalent of 300 miles per hour in 48 seconds. Travelling in a 300-mile-an-hour biscuit tin made for a slightly startling passenger experience. It scared lumps out of Putta.

But it meant that the three – now even more bruised – adventurers could arrive very rapidly at St Vigeans village and land in the graveyard at the back of the church.

Any doubts that they were in the right place were dispelled when they saw the array of undulating, fabulous animals patrolling the church walls: the ten foot high boar, its flanks covered with shifting runes, a massive bear, patterns and tendrils winding and lashing about its great head, a red-eyed goat with steely hooves. There were other beasts they couldn't identify, pacing and snapping and shifting shapes. Wraiths of shadow also drifted about the grass and – Bryony was very sorry she noticed – the grass above some of the graves was heaving and swelling like blankets with uneasy sleepers beneath. The Bah-Sokhar's control of matter could have all kinds of nasty consequences in a place filled with the dead.

And – naturally – as soon as they climbed out of the Abrischooner, they all felt the impact of skull-crushing headaches.

But – as the pain pincered in – the Doctor saw in his mind's quiet eye a brief image of that mightier, lovelier horse form and felt again the press of its forehead against his own. He made sure, as he loped across the undulating graves, to press out the thought, *I know. I know. You want to be other than you are. I know. We're coming to help you.*

The three ran – it seemed they couldn't do anything other than run – towards the door. The Doctor added. *Please try not to kill us. We'd really appreciate it.*

As the Time Lord reached out for the door, he could feel artron energy pattering thickly against his skin, pressing him back. The air was throbbing with malevolence.

Bryony was heartily regretting any wish she'd ever made for excitement and adventure. She felt sick and small and knew it was almost certain that she would die soon and never do anything of the things she'd wanted. She reached out for Putta's hand and he took it – his face pale and sad.

Putta felt Bryony's touch and let it anchor him to reality, to some type of hope, as he backed along behind his friends, watching the deer, the boar and the horses stalk closer, their eyes on fire.

AT ABOUT THAT TIME in Arbroath, a number of golfers and their partners (in the marital sense) were disembarking from a number of cars. They'd come in from the west and had been waved in through a cordon, composed mainly of grim, stiffly moving commandos. As they'd passed by the cordon, Kevin Mangold briefly thought how absurd it was that he was here at all and how unlikely it was that he would ever pass out of the cordon again. He had the idea that geese felt like this on 24 December when they were ushered into an interesting new van and about to be taken on a trip.

Still – they were here now…

And it was terrible to see the small parties of men, women and children being herded off by uniformed figures. It was terrible to be in so much silence outside your head and for there to be so loud a din inside… And yet, the din was fading…

Even the largely numbed Kevin Mangold could hear minds blinking out on all sides, being extinguished.

The fewer thought-voices there were, the easier it was to hear that those last thoughts before shutdown, before the long for extinction took over, were flickers of affection, memories of kindness, lunges of need and love – there was a terrible sense of all that would be lost, just before it was lost – removed for ever.

Even the largely numbed Kevin Mangold, couldn't stand it, had to stop it.

'Now then…' he began, peering round at the strange accumulation of plaid and pastel-shaded wool and grief which the assembled golf-lovers presented. He didn't feel like a leader. He had never acted like a leader. But the Doctor had given him a job to do and… that just sort of meant you had to do it.

'I know this is… This is horrible. This is terrible. Everything that's happening is terrible and I know I want to go to sleep until it stops.' As soon as he said this, his eyelids drooped violently and he could barely focus, but he kept on. 'We can make it stop, though. I think. I think what the Doctor said will work. We saw it did work.'

A recently bereaved husband started sobbing.

Even the largely numbed Kevin Mangold found this upsetting, but also inspiring. He wanted to do well for the Doctor and for these people that he didn't know. He might even want to do well for himself – do well in a way that wasn't about being important, or getting a pay rise, or filching other people's treats. 'We're sad. I know. And… look, we have to go and think loving thoughts and mean it and…' He dropped his head. 'You'll be better at this than me. Remember the people you loved. Remember what happened in the dining room. Remember you might be saving the world.'

He mumbled the last words a bit, but as the crowd of golfers heard him in their minds, too, and felt that he meant what he said, they did indeed begin – gingerly – walking into the side streets, taking strangers' arms, approaching puppet-like policemen and thinking at them loudly with affection.

Mangold watched them head off and then headed straight for a column of six postmen. They turned to him as one, stony eyes glistening. He felt his will draining from him, his arms turning heavy and clumsy, his mind draining peacefully into a grey blank.

He'd hoped he could hold out longer.

But he couldn't.

Mangold's face cleared, his headache went away, along with his memories and habits and his personality. He docilely stumped into line with the postmen, his head nodding.

He was no longer aware of other stumping bodies being added to the small herd of passive prisoners being drawn along by the Bah-Sokhar's psychic force and its human marionettes.

Mangold didn't notice as twenty or so young men – himself among them – were taken into a school yard and then left to stand while, up from the ground rose a legion of twins with grasping hands and icy eyes.

THERE WAS A KIND of blaring reddish light and something like an impact wave impregnated with loathing and distrust crashed in around the Doctor, Bryony and Putta. They were propelled into the church and fell – as was required – on to their knees at the feet of Zandor where he sat enthroned.

Bryony found she was gazing up at the slightly spotty face of a peevish adolescent. It wasn't possible that so much terror and wrong could be emanating from such an unimpressive person. And yet, when she saw the dark charge of selfishness in the young man's expression, saw the howling insecurity and the true, naked cruelty of his spirit, now allowed full reign she understood that whoever this had been, he was fast becoming a very real dictator. He was transforming himself into Zandor. The very fact that he was unimpressive and absurd was firing his desire for power almost as much as the vast psychic reserves of the Bah-Sokhar.

Behind Zandor, the perfectly fused Pictish stones were fiercely beautiful and it was clear that he didn't notice this, or respect it. It was obvious that he didn't care, or even think, about the ornate intelligence that sent complex and wonderful patterns of carving across its high back and sculpted arms. It was wasted on him. Pretty much everything was wasted on him. That was why he found it so easy to destroy pretty much everything.

Putta, although he'd been the underdog all his life, couldn't bear being forced into this undignified position – crouching and cowering – and he attempted to stand. Zandor simply glanced at him and the air around Putta shaded with tendrils of additional energy which shook him, set him into absurd positions, made a fool of him. His arms wagged as if he was dancing, his legs kicked high. Then he was simply left suspended when Zandor ran out of ideas... and then he was crushed to the flagged floor and pressed into a position of utter supplication.

Bryony was sickened and furious. Clearly Zandor was more than capable of tormenting or killing any one of them, just for his entertainment.

'Stop it.' The Doctor didn't shout, he simply spoke with natural authority.

The former Paul Cluny Junior twitched, but then sneered back, 'My parents used to say that kind of thing to me. And look where they ended up.' He raised a finger, indicating the roof cages that contained his mother and father. He didn't bother raising his eyes to them. 'You kinda interest me, Doc. That's your name isn't it, Doc? I got told that, I think – by the Thing... Or maybe you kinda interest the Thing that works for me... But you're getting pretty boring, pretty quick.'

The Doctor had been thrown to his knees before numberless thrones and forced to bow down before all manner of power-crazed despots. He knew that any being can preserve their dignity and refuse to serve injustice from any position. This tended to show and this, in its turn, tended to really annoy the despots.

'Boring...' The Doctor managed to kneel slightly sideways as if he was relaxing at home on a nice rug. Everything about him seemed just naturally *insubordinate*.

He grinned in his very broadest and most dangerous way. 'Well, I've always been of the opinion that only really boring people manage to be bored, wouldn't you agree? I travel a lot and I've found that to be case and kneeling before a throne – of course, if you've never had people kneel before your throne I suppose it would be interesting, but my dear fellow it is rather a cliché, isn't it?'

Bryony listened and felt herself cheering inside, felt herself thinking – through her headache – *He's done this before, hasn't he? The Doctor has done this before and he sort of even likes doing this and he must always have won in the past because he's still here… he's still here…*

But the Doctor wasn't going to have it all his own way. His triumphantly gleeful blend of rambling, insulting and philosophising quickly drove Zandor to respond. It was intended to. As Bryony looked on from her crouch and Putta breathed uneasily – compressed into a hunched knot of limbs by Zandor's spite – the Doctor was lashed with a blow of psychic violence.

He cried out and doubled over, his skull ringing and his hearts labouring. It was more than obvious that the young man was an idiot, and a self-obsessed idiot with massive power. The Doctor was in too much pain to nod tiredly as he found this out. (Despots were so tedious – even the clever ones were still too stupid to realise that the way they behaved was unsustainable…) But – as he'd intended – he had tested Zandor the Boring's reflexes and found them hypersensitive, unthinking and therefore basically weak. If you could call a mad child-man with the universe's worst assassin beast at his command weak…

But that's the thing, isn't it? I don't believe you really are at his command, are you? The old spell, the old behaviour isn't what you want any more… Isn't that right?

The Doctor play-acted being a bit more in agony than he

actually was so that he could send out a thought in the Bah-Sokhar's direction.

'Stop speaking to the Thing!' screamed Zandor. 'It's my Thing! I own the Thing! I'm the boss of that Thing!'

This time the Doctor didn't have to fake his agony. He was hurt so badly by a burst of psychons that he couldn't breathe for a few seconds.

But then he lifted his head, his face wet with sweat and carried on where he'd left off, sounding as amiable and comfortable and utterly self-assured as he could, 'Oh, I'm not so sure about that… really? A young chap like you? A great big Thing like the Thing…? It's called the Bah-Sokhar, by the way – I don't suppose you bothered to ask its name, though.'

What was once Paul Cluny Jnr glared and then growled, 'OK. Now you really did get boring. Now you gotta die.'

And a rush of fire seized the Doctor. It sprang up from the stone floor beneath him and Bryony gasped at it closed over the Time Lord's bowed head.

THINGS WEREN'T GOING WELL in Arbroath, either. The golfers were doing their best and, indeed, had minor successes when they approached the personnel cleansing the streets and houses of its people, feeding the beast.

Although they had recently experienced how utterly infuriating the thoughts of others could be, they were also aware of how similar some of the obsessions, the little lies, the fears and pleasure of strangers could be. It wasn't as hard as they'd thought to reach out towards the minds of those automaton-faced policemen, the men and women of the Civil Defence Corps, the Commandos. There would be moments when expressions came back to life with a start or a groan. But then the psychic clamp would tighten.

The Fetch Hotel volunteers fared better with the twin forms when they emerged. Something about adopting that shape seemed to leave residual traces of the original twins' kindness and desire to help humans.

After a while, though, the twins' faces would morph into that of a smug, furious, skinny youth and the Bah-Sokhar's defence forms would advance, hands ready to touch and drain any perceived threats.

On the outskirts of the town, commandeered vehicles – some scarred by fire or with broken windows – were being parked up by postmen and then left. Then up from the ground, from the pavements, from the tarmac, two by two, came Paul Cluny Jnr forms who loaded themselves determinedly into the cars and vans. Soon they would drive off to other gatherings of humans: villages, towns cities. They would feed the Bah-Sokhar and it would grow out beneath them, faster and faster, more and more furious.

THE FLAMES HOOPED OVER the Doctor, but he popped one hand insolently out above the burning field of psychic projection – refusing to take it seriously. He waved.

High Emperor Zandor frowned. His lips pursed. The flames fell away.

The Doctor, panting and shaking, still managed to start his monologue up again, albeit with a cracked voice. 'I do beg your pardon. I suppose you wanted me to scream and beg for mercy.' Zandor's mouth flinched while the Doctor continued. 'Perhaps if you torture me with something else I might… It's just that I've been tortured by experts, you see – beings who really knew how to torture other beings… and of course, they were fully in control of their powers.' For an instant the Doctor's eyes sparked.

Zandor didn't notice. He was too busy screeching. 'I'm in control! I'm in control! I'm the Grand High Emperor!'

The Doctor nodded like someone who isn't remotely convinced, like someone patronising an ugly-minded, silly child.

'I'll show you!' Zandor clenched the stone arms of his throne, shut his eyes and then looked as if he was a toddler holding his breath until his got his own way.

The walls of the church shivered, shapes and symbols raced over the surface of the throne and the air thrummed.

Putta and Bryony thought their heads would burst with the sudden increase in pressure.

And then, magnificent and haughty, noble and terrible, here was the full horse form, the deep old identity that the Bah-Sokhar had chosen for itself. It stood, clapped one vast hoof against the stone beneath it and raised sparks.

The beast glared at the throne, perhaps recalling those centuries-ago days when some other Conductor had called on it to make the throne and then called on it not to murder or destroy, but to build and carve and shelter, make a place for a village to gather, make beauty for them to see. It had left stones which had fed a legend, stones which had eventually been used as part of a church, charged stones, precious stones which had finally been moved into a museum and then touched by an angry young man full of hatred.

If hate touched the Bah-Sokhar it still couldn't quite resist what that hate required – not yet.

Zandor paid no attention to the grandeur of the creature – he was caught up in his loathing of the Doctor. He screamed on, eyes still shut. 'It will do what I want! It will do whatever I want!' His cheeks flushed and his acne reddened. 'I can make it dance! I can! Dance! Dance, Thing!' Zandor opened his eyes and glared at the elegant and huge horse. It bridled, tossing its head and its horrifying, writhing mane. Its eyes glittered with unquenchable fire. 'Dance!'

It appeared to struggle, its muscles straining.

But then it did start to lift its mighty hooves in ridiculous capering moves, to trot back and forth, nodding like a toy.

The Doctor said softly, 'I really don't think this is very wise.'

'I'll do what I like! I'll always do what I like! Shut up!'

The horse paced, crossing its front hooves, performing the clumsy idea of dressage that Zandor was imagining, that Zandor was using to humiliate it.

As Bryony looked on, she felt sorry for the great creature – it might have done terrible things, but it didn't deserve this kind of master and who knew what even more terrible things it would do under his command. When she thought this – gentle, but very clear – she heard the Doctor's voice inside her head saying – *Yes. Now.*

And she understood.

She glanced very carefully over to the Time Lord where he was kneeling on the floor. His face was drawn and ashen, but his eyes shone – he'd tricked Paul Cluny Jnr exactly as he'd wanted to… and now he would never get to be Zandor, wouldn't be the Grand High Emperor of anywhere. Paul was too distracted to monitor or control their thoughts and so now they could use them freely, as the Doctor had intended. The Bah-Sokhar had grown and changed in its long years on Earth and, although it had once fed off hatred, it had grown to love… well, it had grown to love *love*. Very few beings in the universe don't love being loved in one way or another and as an immensely sensitive psychic being, the Bah-Sokahr could appreciate love on a massive scale. While the would-be Zandor tried to torment it in ugly ways Bryony and the Doctor and – as best he could – Putta all reached out with their minds and loved the Bah-Sokhar.

They loved its amazing abilities, they loved its capacity to change and evolve, they loved its care for Julia Fetch, they loved that it hadn't killed them, that it had trusted them with direct contact – they loved it in detail. And they loved it in general. After so many taxing and horrifying experiences, with heads that were scrambled with exhaustion, shock and fear – they simply loved it.

And the horse stopped dancing.

They didn't dare raise their heads for fear of alerting Paul, although he probably wouldn't have noticed – he was so shocked and furious that he was being refused. 'What are you doing, Thing!? You can't disobey me! I am the jewel at the heart of the universe! Did you hear me, you stupid piece of crap! I am—'

The horse form of the Bah-Sokhar stood, magnificent and shining, its eyes full of justice. And the creature thought.

NO

The power behind the denial knocked the Doctor, Putta and Bryony flat onto the floor. As they rolled in pain, they could hear Paul howling in agony and impotent rage.

Putta – his body his own once again – lifted his head and watched as the shapes and symbols on the throne raced and convulsed. The air thickened with darker and darker clouds shot through with darts of silver fire. The clouds became more defined and showed themselves as a boar, a bear, a goat, a calf, a fish… all the beasts of the Drosten Stone, walking back to be confined as carvings. As each one entered the stone, it seemed to pass through Paul, making his limbs shudder. He had stopped yelling, stopped saying anything. His eyes were dulling and his shoulders were hunching.

And then the stones themselves began to blink and shiver, to flicker in and out of their positions as parts of the throne.

Paul Cluny Junior raised his eyes briefly to the Doctor, and the Time Lord could see how afraid he was, how horrified he was to realise that his dreams had betrayed him and that the power he had never truly controlled had come for him now and would not be denied.

The horse form reared high. As it did so, the stones making up Zandor's throne separated and stood, hanging slightly above the floor, somehow waiting and watchful.

Paul tumbled to the floor without his throne to support him and, although he tried to stand, to scramble up and start running… he couldn't.

The Bah-Sokhar dropped its weight forward to stand again, its hooves striking up fire. It tossed its head, breathed, set its gaze upon its enemy.

Cluny moaned, kneeled, hunched and a shadow seemed to rise over him, like a kind of cape. His body began to fade and turn transparent. And then, with a cracking sound that rocked the great Drosten Stone, Cluny disappeared from his reality and – for a moment – the caped figure at the foot of the Drosten's carving – the caped figure kneeling humbly underneath the beasts – seemed to glow redly. It aimed a little carving of a bow and arrow at nothing, as if it were afraid even of shadows. The Time Lord, the Yakt and the human bore witness as – perhaps – what was left of Paul Cluny Jnr melded with the sandstone and – perhaps – met the fate of other weak and greedy-minded humans who had sought to be Conductors, who had tried to control the Bah-Sokhar.

After that the church was utterly silent.

THE DOCTOR COUGHED AND sat back on his heels. He hated this bit. Of course evil had to be overcome, but he never did enjoy seeing any life form getting what it deserved – the more appallingly a being behaved, the more appalling what it deserved would be. The Doctor preferred mercy, on the whole – and sometimes he arranged it. *After all – if everyone got what they deserved all the time, no one would be very comfortable… or possibly even still alive.*

He stood and moved over to help up Putta and he noted that Bryony – great girl – was on her feet and brushing herself down.

None of them felt like speaking. All of them had their eyes mostly fixed on the Bah-Sokhar's form. It was extraordinary and still impossible to consider without a thrill of terror, but it also seemed…

TIRED

The thought slipped carefully out to sound in their heads, but Putta, Bryony and the Doctor realised that most of the telepathic clamp was gone – their heads felt quiet and private and strangely small. And their headaches were gone.

The Doctor broke the silence, his voice very warm, but a little ragged after so much screaming. 'I should expect you are… I should expect you are very tired indeed.' He stepped delicately and respectfully forward to the mighty horse.

The Bah-Sokhar rested its forehead down carefully against the Doctor's in a kind of salute.

I WILL GO

'Perhaps it's for the best, yes.'

And the Doctor closed his eyes, a spasm of weariness and sadness rocking him. Sometimes happy endings weren't that happy.

THE DEFEAT OF ZANDOR did mean that peace returned to Arbroath in a strange, dizzying instant.

No one could quite recall what they'd been doing up until the point when they discovered that they were driving a van full of strangers, cowering in someone else's back garden with a number of other people, far away from their usual delivery route with no letters to deliver, hiding in an uncomfortably small kitchen cupboard, waving a golf club at a traffic warden and yelling, 'But I love you!'

The Bah-Sokhar had not only removed the twin child forms and Zandor forms in a breath, it had sent out a pulse of psychons which wiped the memories of all the humans who had been caught within its radius of influence.

Because humans only pretend to like the strange and remarkable and mainly avoid it like the plague, almost everyone shrugged off their embarrassing or humiliating or peculiar circumstances. What came to be known as Arbroath's Lost Weekend was explained away as the result of flu, mass hysteria, food poisoning, nuclear testing, the effects of fresh air following on the consumption of 'bad pints', or the influence of aliens. (Obviously, very few people believed the alien explanation.)

The Commandos marched back to their barracks and the Civil Defence Corps sloped away to their secret bunker, determined never to mention anything about the whole affair again. Senior officers felt that if it couldn't be summarised in writing on the appropriate forms, then it must not have happened and all other ranks agreed. Policemen, postmen, traffic wardens, milkmen and a number of other uniformed professionals went back to their jobs with an oddly forceful desire to be very courteous and helpful, as if they were making up for something. Amongst the general population, neighbours occasionally stopped and felt slightly closer than they might have done before, or smiled at strangers and seemed to find them familiar. People got very good at charades and the local poker players did very well when they tried to guess if their opponents were bluffing. And there were four marriages which might not otherwise have happened.

And there was no grief or mourning – not because wives and husbands forgot they'd been married, or friends couldn't recall missing friends. It was because no one was missing.

The Bah-Sokhar really did have remarkable powers and really had been learning as it dozed and dreamed and played. So as that pulse of psychons swept aside multiple engrams full of pain and fear and confusion and bereavement, the Bah-Sokhar didn't just reabsorb its defence forms – it also returned those it had fed upon.

This worked well and meant that a number of men and women with various medical conditions were pressed back into reality with their health problems cured. The Bah-Sokhar built bodies as close to perfection as accuracy and its abilities could allow.

There were glitches, however.

Almost everyone was returned to reality correctly, but only almost. Paul and Martha Cluny, whose son had become a carving, were supplied with a male teenage child,

337

who bore an occasional resemblance to David Agnew at that difficult age which offers a young man the choice of being fairly pleasant to most people, or doing business with wholesale ruthlessness and understanding value only as a commercial concept. In effect, the Bah-Sokhar gave Agnew a second chance. The fact that he didn't take that chance and grew up to become, once again, a dreadful bully, mediocre golfer and boardroom tyrant wasn't the creature's fault.

In the absence of an adult David Agnew, the Bah-Sokhar transferred his business holdings, authority and directorships elsewhere and so Mrs Agnes Findlater came back to life, walking along the seafront and in possession of a healthy stock portfolio, a number of thriving factories and a chain of extrusion moulding companies. She lived out the last of her years enjoying this immensely and behaving like someone who has suddenly realised that she was sometimes allowed to relax. Her employees were fond of her – even though she insisted on the adoption of a corporate cardigan with a hand-knitted logo.

When Kevin Mangold returned – bemused and irritable – to the Fetch Hotel, he discovered that it was dreadfully over-booked and dozens of guests were outraged that they had nowhere to spend the night, that their luggage had been placed in storage and that they seemed to have lost up to a year of their time.

Although Kevin had completely forgotten that he had once been quite heroic when faced with insurmountable odds, he did retain a few vestiges of the imagination and empathy which the threat of death at the hands of the Bah-Sokhar had summoned up in him. Sometimes he would dream that he had been taken away to be murdered by something horrible and would feel himself facing what was about to destroy him with a surprising level of dignity. And then the dream would evaporate and he would wake. Or else he would dream that he was waking and that his memories had been rearranged. And then he would really wake up. This phenomenon – along with the 'disappearances' and 'reappearances' and 'luggage events' all came to define was christened the Fetch Triangle. And it made Kevin Mangold very successful as a hotel manager once he scaled back the golfing side of operations and opened the place to investigative documentary makers, researchers and thrill-seekers.

Naturally, no real thrills were provided. The Fetch was peaceful now. And, from a point slightly after 4 p.m. on 6 June, the grandmother clock in the entrance hall started to run again and to keep proper time.

Almost everything was as it should be – or as near as reality ever gets to that.

IT WAS SLIGHTLY BEFORE 4 p.m. on 6 June 1978. The Doctor, Bryony and Putta were sitting in Mrs Julia Fetch's parlour again. They'd used the TARDIS to skip nearly two days – or had lost them by accident – and had landed near her cottage. During the journey, the Doctor had told Putta and Bryony about various planets, various times and – rather pointedly – various beings he had met who settled down together and did rather well as a result. He'd even, although he couldn't quite think why it was necessary, shown them where the wardrobe was – or possibly asked it to come across and meet them. Bryony and Putta had picked out items they found more suitable – and less embarrassing than the scuffed, shredded, water-stained, adventure-stained and generally bizarre remnants they'd been wearing.

It was Tuesday 6 June, the worst of the confusion in the town and the hotel had been smoothed away and the sun was shining merrily on the garden outside. There had been a small shower of rain and the remaining droplets sparkled on leaves and blossoms. It was all staggeringly beautiful.

After the TARDIS landed, they had ambled under the trees along little paths for a while and looked at sand that wasn't trying to destroy them and streams they didn't have to wade along and slopes they didn't have to fall down. Putta picked up a couple of golf balls that hadn't been hit towards him and didn't hurt his hand. It was lovely afternoon. If rather dull.

Although, obviously, the fact that Bryony was with Putta and that Putta was with Bryony wasn't as dull for them. They were both feeling silently hysterical.

The Doctor had eventually led them back here to Julia Fetch's perfect garden and her pretty cottage and her cosy parlour.

Putta sighed as he peered out at that perfect garden. He sighed once more as he squeezed Bryony's hand, which she didn't mind him holding. She also – apparently – didn't mind him in general. His second sigh was bigger than the first – it rose from his second pair of borrowed shoes – two-tone brogues – and ran up his shins inside his pair of borrowed flannel trousers. Under his borrowed shirt, his heart clenched and unclenched as if he was either very happy, or gravely ill. He wondered if he should burst into song – it seemed appropriate somehow.

Bryony – finally comfortable in snug jeans and what she felt was a killer T-shirt – felt Putta squeeze her hand and, indeed, heard him sigh and sigh again and thought – *last week I was in a dead-end job and desperate for adventure. This week I've been in two spaceships – not outside the planet – and one of them was only going up the road and the other just hopped over a few fields – and a couple of days… a couple of days… oh, good grief, I've travelled in time… And I really like a spaceman and he seems to like me…* Her thinking paused for breath and she was, not for the first time, very glad that no one else was aware of the tumult going on inside her head. *And I actually… I mean, I love him. I do. He's kind of great. Not wonderful, maybe. But my goodness he's promising. And he was a hero – he really was. And he has a spaceship. It's not a great spaceship… I've met better… The Abrischooner is – to be honest – only built for a maximum of*

*two, small beings who are really fond of each other and therefore
don't mind being crushed up together for fairly extended periods…*
This made her smile. It also made her remember the very
confusing and mildly embarrassing speech the Doctor had
given them both which seemed to deal with inter-species
relationships – or seemed to want to mention them – before
he gave up and reached out a bag of jelly babies and said,
'Well, anyway…' And then again, now her smile vanished,
how could someone from Yinzill get together with someone
from Earth. And why would someone who was so clearly
all heroic and adventurous want to marry someone who'd
only just started having adventures and who'd never even
left her own planet… *Marriage*… The idea of being tied to
anyone from any planet for maybe the whole of the rest of
her life left Bryony queasy and disturbed – and, given her
recent experiences, it surprised her that anything could still
do that.

The Doctor was also sighing, but not because he was
happy. He was waiting until – yes – now it would start… in
walked Julia Fetch with more tea things. He hadn't managed
to raise an appetite for what was already set out around him
on cake stands and side tables and trays.

Even though not one of her guests had much of an
appetite, Julia – with only the usual number of limbs today
– beamed at them, 'Ah… another tea. And it was only
yesterday we had the last one… or maybe the day before
yesterday… Or close to that…' She balanced an extra plate
of cucumber sandwiches on the mantelpiece. 'Now does
everyone have enough to be going on with?'

The Doctor swiped his hand through his hair and sighed
again. 'It's time, I think… I think it really is time…'

Julia remained her usual, dizzy, charming self and then
her face lost a touch of its brightness and it was her turn to
sigh. 'Oh, yes. You wanted me to find out where I'd seen you

before…' She looked a little worried. 'But must I? It's such a perfect day…'

'When is the last time you had a day that wasn't perfect?' asked the Doctor tenderly. 'And isn't that a little unusual?'

'I suppose you know best,' nodded Julia. 'You are a doctor, after all.'

'Then come with me.'

And the Doctor walked outside, the old lady holding his arm and trotting along through the garden and then up the grassy rise beyond. At the top of the small hill, Putta and Bryony could see the blue box shape of the TARDIS standing where it had landed, something expectant about it.

THE PARTY WAS WONDERFUL. It was something like 4 a.m. on 6 June 1914, and the last of the guests were out on the lawn and either dancing under the moon, or lying on the sweet grass by the lake.

Julia Fetch had never enjoyed herself so much – not since ever so long ago in the days when she was a child and had walked on the beach and found a small white sphere – heavy for its size and vaguely warm. She'd known there was something inside the sphere – or *someone*. And it had seemed right to slip it under her pillow and to let it be warmed by her dreams.

In those dreams, it had told her of how old it was and how lonely and how it would come and stay with her and play and how she should let it wake up again and grow. It had asked her what she should like and she had said that she would like to play lots and to be rich enough to do what she wanted and to meet a nice man when she was older and to have babies and grandbabies. But mainly to play.

The someone had told her – had spoken into her mind – that it would grant her all the wishes she needed and that she should grow up a little so that she could speak to grown-ups and then she could do what she liked. All she had to do was throw the sphere into a body of freshwater – like the lake near her cottage. And in the end it had told her that she would own the cottage and the land and the lake and everything.

So she had thrown the sphere into the lake and the *someone* had been kind to her for… oh… too many years to count. And now she did own the cottage and a big house on the land, as it promised her. Her early requests had involved so many silly things she didn't really need. She had other houses and other land – and she owned the lake, Fetch Lake – the lake where she'd found the sphere. It was the same lake she was dancing beside in this wonderful evening, with gramophone playing deliciously and this man in her arms being absolutely the right one and the best one and – finally – someone she could properly love and get along with and laugh beside.

The *someone's* promise about love had come true and here was Bernard, Bernard Slater, who worked in a chemist's shop and who she had met quite by chance and she would never forget him. She forgot a lot of things – although she had people to remember all she needed to for her so this didn't matter. But she would never forget Bernard. She would be with him for ever. She would remember to ask the *someone* to make them both last for ever…

She held Bernard Slater very tight and danced and danced.

But she was going to forget to ask the *someone* about any more wishes. She was going to be too happy and full of too many plans and too busy making sure that Bernard didn't feel bad about not having a lot of money and not being used to the strange life of someone who did. She was going to ask him questions about what she could do with her wealth to make it more useful. She'd given a great deal away, but the *someone* seemed to ensure that her investments always succeeded and that she was always defended by great heaps of pounds and shillings and pence. Bernard would mention that he loved the ocean – he wanted her to look after people, but also to take care of the ocean. And she would be sure that they could spend as much time as they needed learning all about marine creatures together and then do what was right…

But in August there would be an announcement of war.

And Bernard would volunteer early and everyone was quite jolly about it all and assumed it would be a small affair and over very quickly, so Julia wouldn't think to make any requests about the matter. She would trust what she read in the papers and not trouble the *someone*.

And Bernard would be killed at Charleroi.

After that Julia would make no requests, beyond asking that she should no longer be young, because being young attracted attention.

She wouldn't ask out loud for children to love and wouldn't ask out loud for the worst of her pain to be wiped away so that she didn't have to stand it. The Bah-Sokhar would give her that all by itself.

And for now she was dancing and aching with joy, thrumming with it. And Bernard was talking to her about how this was a wonderful place, how he loved the lake and the trees… and everything. They loved each other. They were being kind.

The music licked and swirled round them and the breeze smelled of honeysuckle.

From somewhere beyond the little line of trees she had heard a funny sound like the dragging of metal up a gravel path, or maybe a wheezing animal, or something… it didn't matter. And it had gone now. Maybe it was only in her mind. She heard a lot that was only in her mind.

Bernard leaned in and whispered to her, 'You are the most extraordinary woman I've met.'

And Julia opened her eyes and said, 'And you are

extraordinary, too.' And they span half a turn and she suddenly saw – this was strange enough to catch her attention – an old lady standing in the shadows beneath the branches over to her left. She had her hands held close to her face. She looked a pleasant person and her eyes were shining with emotion. Behind her was a tall man with unruly hair and a remarkable scarf. Their eyes met. He nodded and waved, as if he were wishing her well.

Then the two were gone and she thought nothing further about them.

As she'd said so often to herself already – *I'm in love. We're in love.*

WHILE THE DOCTOR MARCHED away with Mrs Fetch, Putta was stumbling through a number of sentences he thought he'd better get out of the way. 'It's… I mean… I could… Perhaps I could get a job in the hotel doing… something.'

Bryony studied him and blinked. 'And what something would you do…?'

Putta rubbed the back of his neck, which had started to feel weird. 'Ah… umm… not golf… it's… not cooking… those pies that aren't pies and don't have shepherds in them, I'd get confused…' His stomach clenched as he considered that Earth was yet another planet on which he couldn't do anything useful. 'I could…' This time when he sighed, the noise was escaping from a Yakt who was unable to think of anything that he could. Perhaps insisting that the being he loved most in the universe hung around with an unemployable alien wasn't going to be a good idea.

Bryony was about to tell Putta that, although Mrs Fetch had made sure Bryony had a new job as Senior Day Receptionist, she wanted nothing more than to climb aboard the Abrischooner and get space sick and go on… well, maybe not adventures, but expeditions would be nice…

Only then the twins walked in.

Both the Terran and the Yakt chilled at the sight of them.

Honor skipped for a few steps and then stopped. She swung one arm indecisively. And then then she raised both arms and advanced. So did Xavier. He smiled, too.

In response, Putta sprang out of his chair and stood, braced, his arms out, blocking any attempt to devour Bryony. This would have worked out well and looked highly impressive if Bryony hadn't done much the same.

This meant that Putta collided with Bryony and Bryony clattered into Putta, at just about the same time that they felt young, slim arms closing around them and gripping tight.

Putta whinnied with fear.

Bryony held what she thought was his forearm and also held her breath because somehow her mind and body expected that might make dying in an appalling way a bit better.

Then nothing happened.

No one liquefied, no one was absorbed, no one vanished. No one – in short – died in an appalling way. Or even a pleasant way, should someone have found a pleasant way to die.

Hugging took place. This was rather boring after all the tensions, tortures and running about, but it was also a huge relief. Xavier mainly hugged Bryony because he was nearer to her and Honor mainly hugged Putta because she was nearer to him and both adults made small 'Wh? Wh?' noises until they were released and could peer down, their hearts still beating far too fast, at a pair of apparently happy and ordinary Earth children.

'Hello,' said Xavier.

'Hello,' said Honor.

They were both wearing socks and sandals, the way that two perfectly normal Earth children might on a summer's day.

INSIDE THE TARDIS, MRS Fetch was nodding. She was both very happy and very sad. She was holding the Doctor's hand as he operated the console and steered his ship back to Tuesday afternoon, 6 June 1978 – something after 4 p.m. Tea time.

'So that's where I saw you… I *had* met you before, just that tiny bit… I remember now… I remember everything… And it's far too much to remember… I have lived a ridiculously long time, haven't I?'

The Doctor inclined his head and gave her a half grin. 'I should imagine you've been alive for something like 300 years. The Bah-Sokhar found you and was fond of you – he knew you were a good thing. So he kept you around.' The TARDIS wheezed in a minutely different tone and he patted the console. 'And you're a good thing, too.' He shrugged proudly at Mrs Fetch. 'She can be temperamental but I wouldn't have it any other way and we're used to each other…' Then he continued more firmly: 'You know it's going to leave now – the Bah-Sokhar.'

'Yes, I rather guessed it intended to. It gave me all these treats… The way it did when I was a girl… It put a little octopus that was fond of me into my bath… and gave me all those new limbs for a while… can you imagine…? I did enjoy that…' She studied the Doctor. 'I think you've been alive longer than me, Doctor.'

'Yes, well…' He wagged one large hand.

'You aren't tired of it?'

'Oh, not really, you now. Not at all on most days. Not a bit. The universe is… The universe. One couldn't be tired of that. And it keeps me very busy.'

'You remind me of it.'

'Of the universe?'

'No. Of the Bah-Sokhar.'

The Doctor frowned briefly. 'The Bah-Sokhar kills people.'

'But I don't think it ever meant to. I think it was always trying to help. Living so long and travelling so far and trying to help.' Julia patted his hand. 'It will go back to being an egg, won't it? It will tuck itself away and have a think… And some other little girl maybe will find the egg and—'

The Doctor stopped looking quite so melancholy and began to enjoy being interested in a new life form and its possible ways of surviving. 'Yes, some mind will attract it, some way of thinking that it likes the feel of… And it will start again.' He hadn't had to kill it. He always enjoyed not having to kill anything. 'The Bah-Sokhar will transdifferentiate – its mature cells will become entirely different mature cells. Not like the visions and puppets and disguises its chosen… but – yes, why not – most probably some small egg, or a seed capsule… I've been known to transdifferentiate myself, now and again… One does miss out on being a child by hopping from one adult incarnation to another, but… Well, one can be a child at any time, can't one?' He lifted the old lady's hand and kissed it, but when he raised his head again, he seemed very serious. He began with a stumble of letters. 'Ah… of…'

'You want to say that I will have to grow old and die once it isn't protecting me…?'

'I'm sorry. But yes. You will.' The Doctor never liked these bits – the bits at the ends of stories, the bits that were natural and unavoidable and terrible all the same.

He threw a switch and the TARDIS jolted into its chronic descent.

Mrs Fetch laughed softly. 'It's very lovely all this – as a last day – I got a trip in your TARDIS charabanc and I got to see…' She swallowed. 'Bernard was lovely, wasn't he? He was such a handsome, good man.'

'Yes. Yes, I'm absolutely sure that he was.' The Time Lord consulted a dial swiftly – *4.46 p.m. precisely. Or thereabouts.* He coughed and then looked straight at Mrs Julia Fetch, a woman who had never been married, but who had spent most of her very long life remembering the wonderful marriage she'd never had and enjoying the marvellous grandchildren that hadn't quite existed. He gave her his best and widest and wildest smile – the one filled with the Time Lord's enjoyment of every second of every minute of every day – even the bad ones – because they were there – they were all so *there*. 'And I'm absolutely sure that dancing with you that night was his happiest memory.'

Julia smiled back. 'Now I can remember the real Bernard, not the one the Bah-Sokhar gave me. I think that's better – at my time of life. Dreams are nice, but it's good to wake up.'

'The real Bernard was a remarkable and handsome man. I should know.' As the TARDIS stabilised its presence in 1978, The Doctor beamed. He'd never really seen the point of modesty – it was so inaccurate.

JUST AS MRS FETCH and the Doctor walked back towards the garden, out through the gate scampered Honor and Xavier, their arms waving and their voices mingling pleasantly.

'You're back! Great!'

'Where have you been?'

'There's cake!'

'You look tired, do you want a seat? Do you want cake?'

'Granny! Granny! Granny! And you're with the Doctor – we missed him!'

And the capering, delighted children patted and tickled and yelled at the adults before running off again. They were almost inside the cottage when they stopped dead.

The Doctor steeled himself for some new strangeness, perhaps an attack – for the last shred of resistance as the Bah-Sokhar faced a kind of death, certainly the death of its current form. He put his arm round Mrs Fetch and prepared for the next threat.

The twin's faces focused on the Doctor, their eyes were penetrating and strangely adult, even ancient.

They opened their mouths wide and said simultaneously, 'Thank you. This is the last of us. They are they. I am I. Goodbye. Love. Goodbye.'

And then the long-limbed and sparky and elegant pair of

kids were just kids again. They were thoroughly alert again and giggling and – yes – he could see the last of Bah-Sokhar's influence withdrawing from them like a very faint vapour, or a tint in the light. They both seemed to be completely unaware of the creature speaking through them for one last time, of it leaving them, of it having pushed them fully into the world as independent new beings – children, in fact.

And as the Bah-Sokhar's presence left Honor and Xavier, the Doctor felt Mrs Fetch stumble slightly and lean against him more heavily. 'It's no fun Doctor, being really old.' Then she giggled and turned to him. 'I don't think you'd be up to it.' Then she made an effort to stand straight, shake off assistance and walked into her home – what had been maybe her first home, long ago. She had a while left to live there and to be with the twins. The children would grow old, too now – she might even get to see them be a man and a woman with lives out in the world. She might last just long enough to enjoy that.

The Doctor called as she went, 'Send out Bryony and that fool Putta. We'll take a stroll while you get reacquainted with your family. I think I need a little air.'

Because she'd learned a thing or two in her centuries, this made Mrs Fetch give him a sharp look and say, 'Goodbye, then, Doctor, and thank you. For everything. Thank you so much.'

The Doctor didn't exactly blush under his hat, but he did get a bit mumbly when he said, 'I do hate goodbyes... They're just... too much like saying goodbye... And one never knows...' To distract himself, he asked her, 'Oh – not that it matters so very much – but what did that egg look like? The one that contained the original Bah-Sokhar.'

'It was round and white and smooth.' She made a circle with her thumb and forefinger. 'It was about that size.

A pretty thing. I put it under my pillow and then in the morning it had disappeared – but the Bah-Sokhar was there – in my mind… Yes, just a small white ball. That's what it looks like.' Julia Fetch laughed, laughed like a much younger woman, hugged her grandchildren to her and went inside.

Honor and Xavier hugged her back, happy. They were creatures born of love and need and the psychic manipulation of matter at a sub-atomic level – and although that wasn't quite the usual way to make human children it wasn't that far off it, either.

THE DOCTOR STROLLED LANKILY across the well-tended grass. Up ahead the TARDIS was looking very elegant, he thought, in the afternoon light. He could feel that she was ready to be off, impatient, and he was a bit restless himself.

There were still a few things to deal with. Rather important things. He span to confront his new friends, 'Now. Putta.' The young Yakt flinched. 'No, no, no – it won't do. You can't save the day on numerous occasions, act selflessly and bravely and stop people dying and… stop at least one whole planet from being turned into a hell very literally on Earth and then eaten… you can't do all that and then just slip back into being timid and assuming you'll never amount to anything.' He slapped Putta loudly on the shoulder. 'Cheer up! You love her, she loves you and you really ought to get on with what's next.'

Both Bryony and Putta stared at him like stunned bandans.

'No, I'm not experiencing your thoughts… I've had quite enough of all that. A stunned bandan would be able to tell that. Now *please* stop being so complicated about everything – life is remarkably short when you really consider it fully – which you might not want to, that kind of thing can be worrying – and you have a lot to do. Other adventures to have – which you will manage splendidly – and… Putta, stop fiddling in your jacket pocket. What have got there?'

Putta held out his hand, the way a guilty schoolboy might and revealed a golf ball he'd picked up, because it was just like the one he'd caught with his bare hand when he was feeling much more heroic. He'd been considering keeping it for luck. 'It's my lucky charm. It's one of those bits of equipment for golf. You hit it at people and then shout and then they run… I'm getting the hang of the rules.'

The Doctor shook his head. 'Beings make their own luck, I told her that only the other—' And then he stopped short. 'Let me see that.'

'It's just a golf ball.' But Putta handed it over, all the same.

'This…' The Doctor fumbled in his pocket and brought out a complex-looking metal instrument, a little like a fat fountain pen with a touch of hairdryer thrown in. He aimed the device at the small white sphere while peering at it. 'This is not a golf ball. This is smooth. Golf balls have dimples to make them more aerodynamic in this atmosphere…' He turned the sphere round in his fingers, gingerly. 'You, Putta, may just have found something very wonderful and very dangerous – the egg of a dormant Bah-Sokhar. I think, if you don't mind, I'll keep it in the TARDIS for the sake of safety – you may find that improves your luck immensely.'

'Oh, would you like this one as well?' Putta rummaged in both his baggy tweed pockets. (He'd decided to like tweed jackets and had picked one from the TARDIS wardrobe. Or perhaps been nudged towards one while he considered a very unwise multi-coloured corduroy tail coat.) 'Here.' He brought out two more spheres. Both were smooth and slightly warm and gave you the feeling that they weren't exactly empty.

'But this is—!'

Before the Doctor could finish exclaiming what this was,

Bryony chipped in with, 'Well, they're nothing new. People have been complaining about them for ages. Players would pick them up instead of their own and they don't have dimples – or there'd be some mixed in with the practice balls on the driving range or… oh…'

The Doctor eyed her patiently.

'Oh, I see… Yes… They'd turn up when the boys would dredge up lost balls from the lake. They're all over the place.'

The Doctor nodded and it was hard to tell if he was terrified or furious. 'And they have no doubt sometimes gone home with visiting players and those players have no doubt come here from all over your golf-obsessed planet and so they have travelled to Canada, America, Australia, New Zealand, Singapore…'

'Germany… Belgium – we had some Spanish people in here yesterday and there was a couple from Barbados and… There are Bah-Sokhars all over the world waiting to wake up.'

The Doctor threw back his head and laughed and laughed.

The others watched.

'Oh, well, nobody knew how many eggs there would be, I suppose. Or how many there have been… Turtles, pestiadores, fingalls – plenty of creatures produce far more eggs than will ever survive into adulthood… The Bah-Sokhar needs such a very special range of circumstances – water, an oxygen atmosphere, and fairly complex life forms with appropriate thought patterns and, among them, the right mind that absolutely fits… Ten thousand dormant Bah-Sokhar eggs travelling through space might not be enough to ensure the creature's survival. But one landed here. And it only takes one…' He laughed again. 'And one amongst all these eggs isn't just an egg, one is the whole adult pressed into a new form and waiting to be released and start again.' He looked at them expectantly. 'So…'

He looked at them again – Bryony and Putta, two excellent and resourceful beings.

Although they could be a bit slow on the uptake sometimes.

He huffed out a breath of impatient air. 'So one of the spheres – probably not more than five or six miles from here – will be the Bah-Sokhar we met, the one that learned to deal gently with humans. The rest are either eggs from that Bah-Sokhar, which would know less than it does, or eggs from some previous Bah-Sokhar which fell to Earth here who knows when and from where. So…'

Putta flung both hands in the air and wagged them. 'I know, I know! Only one sphere is safe – all the others would need to learn again, or be worse than this one, so—'

Bryony cut in – as she often would throughout their lives – and finished his sentence. 'So we need to collect them.'

Putta grabbed her hand. 'We do! I mean we! That's us! That's what we'll do! We!' He had a light in his eyes that was impressive, but reckless.

'Yes!' Bryony agreed. The space travel could wait – might even be part of the deal… Maybe they should collect all the things and then take them into space.

The Doctor extended his long, heavy arms and flopped one down across Bryony's shoulders and one across Putta's. 'Excellent idea. You're just the pair I'd send off on a mission like this.' He could feel both of his friends tense mildly when he said the word *mission* – he'd known it would please them. He grinned and knocked his hat to a better angle with one hand, while stepping back and swiftly unlocking the TARDIS door. He reached inside and brought out a large bag that appeared to be made of canvas, but probably wasn't.

'Pop anything suspicious in here – it will damp down the psychon flow and it's impervious to artron energy.' He peered at Putta for a breath and then gave the bag to Bryony. Then he faced both of them like perhaps a driving instructor whose two best pupils are ready to take to the road. They both thought there was something softer and darker in his gaze, just for an instant.

And then he gave Putta a spare collecting bag and pointed them off to the stream. 'On you go now. There will be more there. Gather them up. Don't hold them for too long. I'll be here when you need me. Go on. I haven't got all afternoon.'

And Bryony Mailer strode away from the most remarkable man she would ever meet, beside her the second most remarkable man she would ever meet.

And Putta walked away from the most death-defying experience he had ever encountered and also – of course – began walking towards his next death-defying experiences.

Entirely by coincidence both of them then thought – *This is fantastic. We have no idea what's next and could die at any moment. Wonderful.*

The Doctor watched them go.

That is, they'd thought he was watching them and would be there when they got back until they heard that wild, strange wheezing and groaning and dragging noise which meant that arguably the finest Type 40 TARDIS in existence was taking flight, leaping up into space and time and on towards whatever came next.

When Putta and Bryony ran back to the place where the ship had rested, all they found was a square of flattened grass and a push of breeze and a sense that a large, strange heart had glanced at them and liked what it saw.

'Oh well, then.' Putta's shoulders slumped.

'I sort of thought he'd do that.' Bryony patted his arm.

'Oh you sort of thought that he'd sort of be thinking

that he'd do that did you – well, I sort of thought that you'd say that.' Putta tried a smile and liked it. 'I was going to…' He huffed in a little more air and wished passingly for a monster of some kind to appear and supply a distraction. 'I was going to, to… It's space law or something that the captain of a ship can join beings legally…' He waited while Bryony didn't say anything and mainly stared at the grass where it was squashed. 'I think you call it getting married on this planet… I didn't look up much of that vocabulary… I mean…' He stuttered to a halt and also stared at the grass.

And then he felt a kiss against his ear. Either that or very small perhaps flying monster was trying to climb into his brain… No… It was a kiss.

Bryony told him, 'We can find some other captain to do that. Or ask him if he turns up again.' She kissed him again. On the mouth.

A while later they started looking for the eggs of what was potentially one of the universe's worst scourges.

While they did so, they were mainly thinking about the kiss and therefore had to come back the following day to check over all that ground again.

It was OK. They had lots of time now. All the time they'd need.

THE
TIME TRIPS
COLLECTION

Cecilia Ahern, Jake Arnott, Trudi Canavan,
Jenny T. Colgan, Stella Duffy,
Nick Harkaway, Joanne Harris,
and A.L. Kennedy

ISBN 978 1 84990 771 2

Time Trips is a unique collection of *Doctor Who* adventures from
bestselling and award-winning writers.

Taking you from ancient Alexandria to nameless planets in the
far future, these tales are at turns funny, frightening, moving and
thought-provoking – short stories that are bigger on the inside.

CITY OF DEATH
Douglas Adams and James Goss

ISBN 978 1 84990 675 3

The Doctor takes Romana for a holiday in Paris – a city which, like a fine wine, has a bouquet all its own. Especially if you visit during one of the vintage years. But the TARDIS takes them to 1979, a table-wine year, a year whose vintage is soured by cracks – not in their wine glasses but in the very fabric of time itself.

Soon the Time Lords are embroiled in an audacious alien scheme which encompasses home-made time machines, the theft of the Mona Lisa, the resurrection of the much-feared Jagaroth race, and the beginning (and quite possibly the end) of all life on Earth.

Aided by British private detective Duggan, whose speciality is thumping people, the Doctor and Romana must thwart the machinations of the suave, mysterious Count Scarlioni – all twelve of him – if the human race has any chance of survival.

But then, the Doctor's holidays tend to turn out a bit like this.

Featuring the Fourth Doctor as played by Tom Baker, City of Death is a novel by James Goss based on the 1979 Doctor Who story written by Douglas Adams under the pen-name David Agnew. City of Death is one of the best-loved serials in the show's 50-year history and was watched by over 16 million viewers when first broadcast.

Also available from BBC Books:

BBC
DOCTOR WHO

Royal Blood
Una McCormack

ISBN 978 1 84990 992 1

The Grail is a story, a myth! It didn't exist on your world! It can't exist here!

The city-state of Varuz is failing. Duke Aurelian is the last of his line, his capital is crumbling, and the armies of his enemy, Duke Conrad, are poised beyond the mountains to invade. Aurelian is preparing to gamble everything on one last battle. So when a holy man, the Doctor, comes to Varuz from beyond the mountains, Aurelian asks for his blessing in the war.

But all is not what it seems in Varuz. The city-guard have lasers for swords, and the halls are lit by electric candlelight. Aurelian's beloved wife, Guena, and his most trusted knight, Bernhardt, seem to be plotting to overthrow their Duke, and Clara finds herself drawn into their intrigue…

Will the Doctor stop Aurelian from going to war? Will Clara's involvement in the plot against the Duke be discovered? Why is Conrad's ambassador so nervous? And who are the ancient and weary knights who arrive in Varuz claiming to be on a quest for the Holy Grail…?

An original novel featuring the Twelfth Doctor and Clara,
as played by Peter Capaldi and Jenna Coleman

Also available from BBC Books:

BBC

DOCTOR WHO

Big Bang Generation
Gary Russell

ISBN 978 1 84990 991 4

I'm an archaeologist, but probably not the one you were expecting.

Christmas 2015, Sydney, New South Wales, Australia

Imagine everyone's surprise when a time portal opens up in Sydney Cove. Imagine their shock as a massive pyramid now sits beside the Harbour Bridge, inconveniently blocking Port Jackson and glowing with energy. Imagine their fear as Cyrrus 'the mobster' Globb, Professor Horace Jaanson and an alien assassin called Kik arrive to claim the glowing pyramid. Finally imagine everyone's dismay when they are followed by a bunch of con artists out to spring their greatest grift yet.

This gang consists of Legs (the sexy comedian), Dog Boy (providing protection and firepower), Shortie (handling logistics), Da Trowel (in charge of excavation and history) and their leader, Doc (busy making sure the universe isn't destroyed in an explosion that makes the Big Bang look like a damp squib).

And when someone accidentally reawakens the Ancients of Time – which, Doc reckons, wasn't the wisest or best-judged of actions – things get a whole lot more complicated…

An original novel featuring the Twelfth Doctor, as played by Peter Capaldi

BBC

DOCTOR WHO

Deep Time
Trevor Baxendale

ISBN 978 1 84990 990 7

I do hope you're all ready to be terrified!

The Phaeron disappeared from the universe over a million years ago. They travelled among the stars using roads made from time and space, but left only relics behind. But what actually happened to the Phaeron? Some believe they were they eradicated by a superior force… Others claim they destroyed themselves.

Or were they in fact the victims of an even more hideous fate?

In the far future, humans discover the location of the last Phaeron road – and the Doctor and Clara join the mission to see where the road leads. Each member of the research team knows exactly what they're looking for – but only the Doctor knows exactly what they'll find.

Because only the Doctor knows the true secret of the Phaeron: a monstrous secret so terrible and powerful that it must be buried in the deepest grave imaginable…

*An original novel featuring the Twelfth Doctor and Clara,
as played by Peter Capaldi and Jenna Coleman*